Resu[illegible]
Men

Sooty Feathers
Book I

Resurrection Men

Sooty Feathers
Book I

David Craig

Elsewhen Press

Resurrection Men

First published in Great Britain by Elsewhen Press, 2018
An imprint of Alnpete Limited

 Amy Newfield's epitath is taken from *A Prayer in the prospect of Death*, by Robert Burns, first published in 1786 by John Wilson of Kilmarnock in *Poems, Chiefly in the Scottish Dialect.* Passages quoted in chapter twenty are from *The Tragical History of the Life and Death of Doctor Faustus* by Christopher Marlowe, first published in 1604 by Thomas Bushell of London.

Elsewhen Press, PO Box 757, Dartford, Kent DA2 7TQ
www.elsewhen.press

British Library Cataloguing in Publication Data.
A catalogue record for this book is available from the British Library.

ISBN 978-1-911409-26-7 Print edition
ISBN 978-1-911409-36-6 eBook edition

Printed and bound by CPI Group (UK) Ltd, Croydon, CR0 4YY

To Dana, with all my love

Prologue

The City of Glasgow
February 1893

It was long after dark when the circus came to the city. Gaudy caravans and travel-worn wagons journeyed through cobbled streets to the Glasgow Green, highlighted by gas streetlights. Circuses visiting Glasgow usually arrived in a parade of pomp and colourful eccentricity; this one slipped in like a thief in the night. Age and weather had faded the paintwork on the caravans, but birds, animals and flowers carved into the wooden frames signalled a Romani origin.

George Rannoch had expected their arrival, following them to the Glasgow Green. He watched as roustabouts and performers erected tents and set up stalls by lantern light. Most wore coats to ward off the late winter chill, but not all. Those like himself had no need.

After two centuries of suffered insult and the company of traitors, he felt something unfamiliar and took a moment to identify it; kinship. Marko, Lucia and Bresnik had spent those same years in rootless exile bending the circus to their will while awaiting his summons, and had travelled Europe to answer it. Three enemies had long awaited his revenge; three allies had come to help deliver it. He walked towards the circus.

His trespass drew attention and two heavy-set men left their work to intercept him. He took their measure and Unveiled, taking pleasure in the surprise and fear that crossed their faces. They let him pass.

A figure waited for him, silhouetted against the fire. "George Rannoch," Lucia greeted in rusty English. "It has been long time."

Chapter One

March 1893

The fog hung thick and stygian over Glasgow, smothering the streetlights. It wasn't a night for honest men, and it found Wilton Hunt swathed in darkness within the Southern Necropolis cemetery. He saw naught but fog-spawned wraiths and gravestone silhouettes, hearing only the steady rhythm of Tam Foley's digging.

"Why do you–" *crunch* "–think Miller wants her?" Foley asked as he dug deeper into the grave.

"Healthy sixteen-year olds don't habitually drop dead." In truth Hunt cared little why the medical professor wanted her or any other corpse they exhumed, and any lingering guilt he felt about their sepulchral desecrations was not enough to lose sleep over. Foley's opinion was that if the dead had any objections they were free to raise them. It had been funny last night in the Old Toll Bar over ale; less so now.

Foley grunted. He was making good progress, Hunt having dug the first few feet. The grave was fresh, less than a day old. "So long as he pays us."

Thus far Miller had been as good as his word, paying on delivery before ushering them back out into the night with an air of distaste. Accounting for the late hour, thick fog and cemetery wall, Hunt risked opening the lantern a little and held it over the gravestone:

Amy Margaret Newfield
Dearly Beloved Daughter and Sister
Born 29th August 1876
Departed 12th March 1893
Thou art good; and Goodness still
Delighteth to forgive

"Found it," said Foley. Iron struck wood in hollow agreement.

Hunt put down the lantern and lowered himself into the grave. They had widened it sufficiently to give a little standing room on either side of the coffin, making it easier to break open. Foley wrapped a vinegar-soaked cloth around his face and looked at him expectantly.

Busy securing a cloth-mask around his own face, a precaution in case of swift corruption, it took Hunt a moment to notice the attention. "What?"

Foley cocked his head, his voice muffled through the mask. "Is your head up your arse tonight? The tools."

"Damn." He hauled himself back out of the grave and collected two crowbars from the wheelbarrow before lowering himself carefully back down. The force of a heavy landing might save them time by breaking the coffin open, or it might warp the wood and nails, making their task harder. He handed one crowbar to Foley and jammed the other between the coffin and its lid, working the edge into the wood until it found a grip. Foley did the same at the other end, the coffin creaking beneath them.

Hunt looked at Foley. "Ready?" There was always an unpleasant anticipation at what might lurk beneath the lid.

"Aye." They stepped back in unison and forced the crowbars forward. It was hard work, the sturdy coffin made from elm. Had the Newfields been poorer, the coffin would have been cheap, flimsy pine.

The lid yielded, baring nails like fangs. Hunt peered into the coffin where the shadowed remains of Amy Newfield waited. "Ready?" he asked as Foley climbed out of the grave.

Foley leaned over. "Aye, are you?"

"This isn't my first corpse," Hunt reminded him. He hadn't been sick since their fourth exhumation.

"This afternoon's shit wasn't *my* first, but it still smelled." Foley squatted. "Hoist her up."

"You've the sweet words of a poet." Hunt put his revulsion aside and gripped the corpse's right arm. He lifted the body while Foley reached down and took hold of her left arm. They raised her together in defiance of weary limbs.

Once she was upright Hunt let go of the arm and took hold of her legs. He lifted, and her white funeral dress brushed against him in a soft, silken sigh. Foley dragged the body up onto the grass while Hunt replaced the coffin lid. Wordlessly, Foley reached down with a glove-clad hand to help him up out of the grave. Both men yielded to fatigue and sank to the ground.

There was a rustle of movement and Foley clapped him on the shoulder. "Let's move the body, fill in the grave, and get the hell out of here."

Hunt forced himself to his feet, arms aching as they dragged the corpse several feet from her grave. He put the lantern down and studied the dead girl's pale face and lank, dark hair. Her eyes had opened during the exhumation and now stared up sightlessly. That was a first; the restless ones usually just farted.

"Shame," Foley said as he moved the wheelbarrow next to the body. He pulled off his mask and shoved it into a pocket.

"Yes," said Hunt, following suit. The pair picked up their shovels and re-buried the empty coffin. He wondered how many other graves in the cemetery had been likewise emptied over the years.

"A job well done," Foley huffed between breaths. He mopped his sweat-soaked brow with a sleeve, smearing dirt over his face.

"Well done, indeed. Except we forgot to strip the body."

"Shit, so we did." Foley stared down at the dirt. "I'm not digging that up again." They habitually stripped the exhumed corpses and threw any clothing or burial shrouds back into the coffin before reburying it.

"No. We'll just have to take our chances." Under the law a corpse was not property and thus taking it was not legally theft. However, a corpse's clothing *was* considered property, enough to untie a sheriff's hands and let him drop the full weight of his displeasure on top of any body snatcher caught with so much as a burial shroud.

Enacted in response to the infamous Edinburgh Westport murders, the Anatomy Act had ensured a steady supply of medical cadavers, ending the body snatching epidemic from the early years of the century. The medical schools, however, did not have the luxury of picking and choosing their corpses. *Which is where we come in.*

They trudged to the wheelbarrow, Hunt lagging behind.

Foley stopped. "Where's the body?"

"She slipped off to answer nature's call," Hunt answered as he adjusted his boot. On their third exhumation Foley had rigged the corpse's arm to wave with a piece of string, causing Hunt to almost foul himself. He considered himself well-prepared for future tricks.

"I'm not kidding."

"And I'm in no mood for this," Hunt said, but the edge in Foley's voice gave him pause. "She's right there, where we…"

There was only crushed grass where the body had lain. The lantern still shone where he'd left it. They searched the area but found neither corpse nor explanation for its absence.

"Keep looking," Foley said. "We've just walked to the wrong bit."

Hunt knew differently, the hairs on his neck rising. "Let's get out of here."

"We can't leave without that body."

"It's gone, we should be gone too." A dread certainty told him they shouldn't linger. "Let's give the good professor the bad news." Hunt tugged off his gloves and dropped them into the wheelbarrow. Two bowler hats sat on the grass. He put his on and handed its shabby brother to Foley.

Foley put his hat on, muttering under his breath. He dropped the shovels and crowbars into the wheelbarrow and headed off.

Hunt took one last look around and followed after. He gripped his lantern, its bobbing light cutting through the fog. Foley was somewhere ahead, his tools rattling inside the wheelbarrow with an urgent tempo. He didn't bother waiting for Hunt to light the way; he'd trip if he wasn't careful–

Hunt's foot caught on a branch or toppled gravestone, and he fell. Light died as the lantern struck the ground and shadows closed in around him. He sprawled face-down, mired in inky darkness as the rattling faded in the distance.

He was alone. His clothing was damp with sweat, and a clammy chill left him shivering. He lay still, hardly daring to breath as instinct shrieked at him to move. A memory of the exhumed girl's cold, pale face came to mind. She was out there somewhere. He listened, but heard naught save his own ragged breaths and the *thump-thump-thump* of his pounding heart. Nothing else. No one else. Alone–

–Am I? His mind played through a macabre logic. The corpse had gone, but she hadn't *vanished.* Maybe she still lurked in the cemetery, cold death stalking him through a forest of gravestones.

He *could* hear something now – the rustle of grass, cloth brushing against cloth, closer, *closer!* His eyes were shut, and his limbs tensed, breath held tightly. Something was close, closer, above him, reaching down! A cold hand gripped his right wrist…

God! Oh God help me! Air exploded out of his lungs in a wordless scream. His legs bucked against the ground and he jerked his right arm back in a bid to break free.

"What're you playing at?"

He opened his eyes to see Foley backing off a step. "Fuck," he gasped, almost limp with relief. "I thought…"

"Thought what?"

"Nothing." He got to his feet, trembling.

"Then let's get out of here." Foley led them through the fog to where he'd left the wheelbarrow.

They reached the gatehouse and egressed onto Caledonia Road where Foley's wagon waited under a gaslight. Red-faced from the night's work, and his dark moustache slicked with sweat, Foley re-locked the padlock securing the gates. He'd bought the key from a corrupt town council official.

Hunt considered his friend. There were times when he regretted defying his parents, but less often since meeting Foley. Almost five years Hunt's senior, Foley had joined the army as an officer at the age of sixteen, serving in India and Africa, where he'd attained the rank of lieutenant. His older brother died of consumption when Foley was twenty-two, leaving him the sole heir. He'd bowed to familial pressure and resigned his commission to follow in the family's pharmaceutical trade. Influenza had taken both his parents two years ago, leaving him the owner of both the Foley Pharmacy and the tenement flat above.

Foley never spoke openly of it, but Hunt suspected that he found little satisfaction in his late father's trade, seeking it instead at the bottom of a bottle. If Hunt surrendered his interest in the natural sciences and took a role in his family's shipping company, he wondered if he too would turn to drink. *Not that temperance counts among my present virtues.*

Foley's horse, Wilfred, whinnied as they loaded the wheelbarrow onto the back of the wagon and prepared to leave.

Chapter Two

Foley's wagon rolled along Glasgow's deserted streets and left the Gorbals behind as it travelled north. The Victoria Bridge took them across the River Clyde into the fog-shrouded heart of the city. Foley guided the wagon into the prosperous West End and onwards to the Glasgow University's medical school on Gilmorehill. It was only twenty years since the university had relocated here from its original site on High Street. They passed through its gates and halted in the courtyard. The senior professor's residence was attached to the college building, a circumstance of convenience for its present incumbent, Angus Miller. Hunt walked alongside Foley to the front door, all too aware the professor expected a body.

He knocked on the door and waited, wondering at the circumstances that had conspired to land him in such a situation. Had it not been for his parental estrangement, he would not now be lodging in Foley's spare room stealing corpses for money.

The sound of a bolt being pulled back snapped him from his reverie. The door swung open and Miller's grey-haired housekeeper greeted them. She looked tired and resentful at the late hour imposition.

Hunt removed his hat and smiled. "Good evening, ma'am. Professor Miller is expecting us." Her silence spoke volumes as she allowed them in and led them to Miller's study.

"These young *gentlemen* are here to see you, sir." She sniffed.

The professor waited inside for them, a fringe of grey hair hanging from the back and sides of an otherwise bald head. He wore a black frock coat, one that barely contained his stout figure. Miller stood up from behind his desk. "Yes, yes,

Mrs Abbot. That will be all." He watched her leave. "Thank you, good night."

Hunt and Foley echoed Miller's sentiment, their courtesy earning them a tight-lipped glare as she shut the door behind her.

Miller's right hand rested on the college keys. "One of you should have stayed with the wagon. I'll unlock the mortuary and you two can carry the body in."

"Professor," Hunt said, "we encountered a problem." *How am I going to explain this?*

Miller pulled off his spectacles and rubbed his eyes. "What manner of problem? You dig up the body and then you bring it here. How can there be a problem?"

"The 'how' escapes us at present, Professor," Hunt admitted. "We exhumed Miss Newfield without incident, but her body disappeared while we were filling in the grave."

"Disappeared, what do you mean disappeared?" Miller's eyes darted between the pair.

"We mean disappeared," was Foley's unhelpful contribution. "As in, we couldn't bloody find her. Aye, we looked."

"She was dead." Miller paced up and down behind his desk, ringing his hands. "Dead and buried. And you two cretins managed to lose her?"

Hunt and Foley sat uninvited on the two chairs in front of the desk.

Miller eyed them. "Maybe you sold the cadaver to someone else, someone willing to pay more."

"There is no one else, Professor," Hunt said. The pair *had* looked discreetly for other medical professors willing to pay for supplementary corpses, but their circumspect enquiries yielded nothing, and they'd decided not to press their luck.

"This is a risky enough business without us selling each other out," Foley said.

Miller slumped down into his chair and put his spectacles back on. "Maybe she was buried alive. Wrongly diagnosed as dead by some quack trained at a lesser institution, perhaps?"

"She seemed dead to me," Foley said.

"Clearly not dead *enough*," Miller snapped, "or she'd be on your wagon and not off God knows where. You dug her up and she regained consciousness. Only just buried, breathing shallowly … aye, it's possible."

Hunt was unconvinced. Her limbs had been stiff, and he'd seen her marbled skin. "Professor, she was dead, I assure you."

Miller snorted. "Nonsense. She was buried while on the edge of death and by God's grace recovered. She had the good fortune to be dug up by you two and wandered off with her wits befuddled. I've no doubt she'll be found in the morning, and the newspapers can proclaim her a second Lazarus." His expression did not invite contradiction.

"If you say so," Foley muttered.

"I do say so." Miller opened a cabinet and pulled out three glasses. Foley's sudden interest in the cabinet told Hunt he was not alone in spotting its remaining contents; a bottle of Walker's Old Highland Blended Whisky and a half-full decanter. Miller removed the decanter and poured a measure of whisky into each glass.

Hunt took a sip. He had been fortunate enough to sample Walker's Old Highland in better times, and whatever came from that decanter was a poor substitute indeed. Evidently Miller was reluctant to waste his better whisky on them; more distinguished guests no doubt enjoyed a dram poured from the bottle. Foley emptied his glass in one smooth motion, and they enjoyed a companionable silence.

Miller rubbed his balding head. "I've got another collection for you, if you can be trusted not to lose it." He pulled a newspaper clipping out from the desk drawer and slid it over to them. An obituary was circled. "Gentlemen, Billy Nugent died recently, after having consumed a prodigious amount of gin. I've no doubt you've heard of him, fond as he was of making an exhibition of himself down the Saltmarket. I would appreciate making his posthumous acquaintance." He pointedly lifted two bank notes from the top of his desk and placed them back into a drawer; the money they were to have been paid for Amy Newfield's remains.

Noting that the funeral for the notorious but well-liked drunk was to take place on Friday, Hunt assured Miller that the job would be done.

Miller eyed him, barely mollified. "See that it is, or I'll be forced to make other arrangements."

"We'll deliver him." He ignored Miller's threat to look elsewhere for his resurrection men.

"Then I'll see you both after midnight on Saturday morning. Don't let me keep you."

Hunt took the hint. "We'll see ourselves out, Professor."

As they left, Miller called out, "Try not to lose this one, lads. I'll be waiting."

"Try not to lose your head up your arse, you arrogant prick," Foley muttered.

*

Hunt wrapped his arms around himself during the journey home, tasting damp in the air. They rode the wagon back into the heart of Glasgow and re-crossed the Victoria Bridge, continuing on into the South Side. Their last chore was to secure the horse and wagon in the stable. That done, they walked to the Paisley Road Toll where Foley's flat waited above his pharmacy.

They entered the common close and climbed the stairs, fatigue making each step a trial. Hunt unlocked the door and entered the hall, memory guiding him to the small table where Foley kept matches and a candle. Hunt lit the candle and carried it into the parlour to light an oil lamp on the mantelpiece. He missed the convenience of the gas lighting installed in his parents' townhouse, finding the candles and oil lamps in Foley's tenement a chore. He collapsed into an armchair and gratefully accepted a glass of whisky marginally better than the one Miller had served them. Foley poured himself one, downed it and poured another before sitting down.

Hunt sipped from his glass, feeling the liquid fire warm his belly. *What a bloody waste of time tonight has been.*

"Are we really going through this again on Friday?" Foley held his glass up to the candlelight and watched the whisky glow.

"We need the money." Hunt refrained from pointing out that Foley's pharmacy had suffered under his indifferent stewardship; he lacked his late father's dedication.

"How much money did we make tonight? Wait, I know – not a penny."

"How was I to know the body would walk? It's been nearly two thousand years since that last happened – I can't anticipate everything."

Foley smiled crookedly. "I thought old Miller would have a fit." He paused. "Do you think he's right, that she's out there alive?"

Hunt felt cold at the thought. "I'd swear she was dead." He left his doubts unspoken. "I'll visit the cemetery tomorrow and see what the day reveals."

"Good idea. And I'll see what the morning papers have to say." He poured another drink.

Hunt rose. "Till the morning." He retired to his bedroom and left a small candle on the bedside table. The light was poor but sufficient for him to undress and wash before embracing the warmth of his blankets. He watched the small flame dance on the wick, tears of wax sliding down the candle.

Foley's flat had been his home for the past ten months, Hunt having been commended there by Professor Charles Sirk, a customer of Foley's who knew he sought a lodger. Hunt had spent his first year of familial exile living in university accommodation to the diminishment of a small legacy inherited on his eighteenth birthday. A second year of such indulgence was beyond his means, so he'd looked for both a cheaper residence and a means of income.

Body snatching. Even after six months of such work he still found himself torn between wonder and shame at how far he'd go to maintain his independence. Delivering messages for Professor Miller had earned him a pittance until one afternoon he'd endured a diatribe about the quantity and quality of the medical cadavers. Hunt recognised Miller's need for corpses, and Miller recognised Hunt's need for coin. The autumn of 1892 saw an arrangement quietly reached between the pair, with Foley a willing third partner. Miller used obituaries and other sources to identify which of the newly deceased he wished to closer acquaint himself with, leaving the practicalities to Hunt and Foley.

Hunt listened for the creak of the parlour door but heard

nothing, suggesting Foley was still within drinking. He suspected he was taking laudanum as well lately, but put that concern aside for later consideration. He blew out the candle.

Chapter Three

Hunt awoke reluctantly, his arms and shoulders aching from the previous night's exertions. He stared up at the ceiling, the morning chill against his face a contrast to the warmth hoarded beneath his blankets. Another ten minutes? He was tempted, but threw the blankets aside with a muttered curse, then rolled out of bed.

He tugged open the curtains but saw little through the fogged-up window. He wiped condensation from the glass only to find it equally misty on the other side. A few blurry figures walked along the pavement, and a tram's bell rang out in the distance.

Hunt threw his nightshirt onto the bed and splashed water from the basin against his face. He washed his upper torso and dried himself with a towel, shivering as he did so. Dark grey trousers, a lighter grey waistcoat and a white cotton shirt hung from the wardrobe handle. His floppy maroon bow tie had fallen to the floor.

By half-eight he had porridge simmering on the coal-fired range and water on the boil for tea. Foley had yet to make an appearance, which came as no surprise. Mornings were an ever-increasing chore for the man.

Hunt finished his porridge and drank tea from a chipped mug. Footsteps thudded off the hallway floor and the kitchen door opened. Foley entered, unshaven and dishevelled.

"Morning," Hunt said. "There's porridge in the pan and tea in the pot."

Foley shuffled past the table. "Good of you," he muttered, his bloodshot eyes blinking against the daylight.

Hunt listened to the dispirited clattering of Foley hunting for utensils while he finished his tea. He pulled on his light-grey lounge coat and walked out into the hall, fetching his bowler hat from the hat stand. "I'm off," he called back. "Can you manage to open the shop?"

"Aye," was the indignant response. "Why wouldn't I?"

Hunt looked back at the half-closed kitchen door but held his tongue. He wondered just how much whisky – and laudanum? – Foley had consumed before going to bed. He left the flat and walked out of the common close onto the street.

Indecision stopped him. His pocket watch revealed that he was uncharacteristically early; he could either wait for the tram or walk to the Southern Necropolis and do some snooping first.

A brisk pace saw him reach Caledonia Road in good time, but as he faced the Southern Necropolis he felt less certain that he'd made the right choice. The cemetery looked different by light of day than it had the previous night, but remnants of fog still clung to the damp cobbles and drifted between the gravestones. He surveyed it, one hand resting on the perimeter wall. His intention had been to enter and visit Amy Newfield's grave in search of answers.

They could wait. He had lectures to attend.

Hunt stared out of the tram window and stifled a yawn as a team of horses pulled it along the city streets. The ride was as monotonous as ever. He normally dozed off during the journey, but not today, dwelling instead on last night's misadventure. He was unconvinced by Miller's theory that Amy Newfield had been buried alive and that they'd conveniently rescued her. She had been *dead*. He was sure of it.

Almost.

*

"Not bad, Mr Hunt, not bad. A trifle messy, perhaps."

Hunt felt oddly exposed. His mind had wandered as he'd sketched the orchid, lacking his usual focus. The professor, an emaciated scarecrow of a man, turned his attention onto the next student.

The rest of the class and those following passed by in a haze of fatigue and restless distraction, every attempt to concentrate thwarted.

Hunt left the university at two in the afternoon, grateful for no further lectures that day. The afternoon sun had vanquished the last of the morning mist, the warmth on his face emboldening him to finish his business at the Southern Necropolis. The streets were congested with trams and wagons, so he elected to walk.

He strolled along the River Clyde and watched the bustle of the river-craft. A small paddle-steamer slowly left its berth, one of its crewmen hurling profanities at jeering teamsters on the promenade. Dockworkers struggled and swore as they moved cargo from a lithe schooner onto a cluster of wagons. A plume of smoke marked a steam train hauling carriages out of the city, bound for parts unknown.

Incoherent cries rang back and forth as newspaper vendors made their pitches. A trio of children splashed around in the river to the ire of a small steamboat's captain. A tram passed by, heralded by the crack of hooves against cobbles and the squeal of wheels on embedded metal tracks. The Second City of the Empire conducted its daily business.

Hunt crossed the Victoria Bridge, its grey sandstone faced with granite. The river flowed under its five arches, sparkling with sunlight and caressed by a wind carrying the stench of industry. Once across the bridge he walked back to Caledonia Road where the Southern Necropolis waited.

Last night's fog was gone, and the sun had banished the morning haze. In its place lay grass and stone, peaceful and sun-warmed with branches swaying gently in the wind.

Hunt entered through the same gate as before, deftly avoiding night soil left by Foley's horse. The cemetery looked smaller in daylight than it had by night, giving him little difficulty in finding Amy Newfield's now-vacant grave. To his chagrin he couldn't quite quell his nerves as he neared the grave he had personally emptied half a day earlier.

He took his time examining the ground, satisfied they had exercised due diligence in filling in the grave. No one would have any reason to suspect it had been disturbed, not unless its former occupant returned home. If indeed she was able.

Hunt studied the grass for signs of dragging. Nothing. Perhaps Miller was correct, and their exhumation *had* saved a poor soul buried alive. He remembered the struggle to prise off the coffin lid and his first sight of Amy Newfield's dark-shrouded body. He remembered the struggle to haul her up, the rigor mortis of her limbs. She had been dead, he decided. Then wondered; digging up graves was hardly conducive to rational thinking, and it *had* been dark and foggy.

Clouds drifted across the spring sun and he shivered. He left the cemetery with his questions still unanswered and turned towards the Paisley Road Toll.

He didn't quite make it home. Just prior to Foley's pharmacy sat the Old Toll Bar. Inclined towards a drink despite his overindulgence after the Newfield job, he entered and perched on a stool at the bar. Eight large casks sat in the back gantry and sunlight filtered through etched glass windows. Several present within were regulars who traded nods with him. Miss Jenna the barmaid recognised him and placed a pint of ale on the bar with a flirtatious smile. He reciprocated the smile and added a small gratuity to the payment. He sipped ale and listened to the congested noises from the street outside.

Hunt was on his second pint when a hand fell on his left shoulder. Several patrons had come and gone, leaving a space to either side of him. Foley slumped down onto a stool.

He looked haggard, black stubble coating his jaw. "Busy day?" Hunt enquired.

"Aye," said Foley as he tried to catch the barmaid's eye. He succeeded and was soon supping contentedly from a pint. Sighing in satisfaction, he wiped the froth from his mouth with the back of his hand and placed a *Glasgow Herald* newspaper in front of Hunt. "Read," he said, pointing to a column on the front page.

Hunt read the column, bile pricking the back of his throat. A woman had been found dead on Caledonia Road near the Southern Necropolis, believed murdered. *Ah damn it, no.*

Foley drank from his pint while Hunt re-read the article with unhappy suspicion. The woman had not been identified and there was no mention as to how the murder had been committed, but there seemed little doubt foul play was involved. He kept his voice low. "Do you think it's Amy Newfield?"

Foley shrugged. "We dig up a supposed dead girl who buggers off, and a body is found in the morning. Aye, I think it's her."

Hunt conceded it was an unlikely coincidence. "So, she wandered off and died nearby?"

"Maybe," Foley said. "But it says here 'murdered'. If she'd just collapsed, it wouldn't say that."

"It also says," said Hunt, unwilling to identify the body so readily, "that the victim may have been a prostitute. Amy Newfield's funeral dress is unlikely attire from a prostitute's working wardrobe."

"True," allowed Foley, "but maybe that prostitute bit was dreamt up by the paper, or maybe her clothes were taken? That wasn't a cheap dress."

Hunt was unhappy at the thought. "A possibility."

They finished their pints in silence. Hunt was about to stand when Foley signalled to the barmaid. "Two whiskies, love."

The fumes made Hunt's eyes water as he raised the glass to his lips. "We should discover if the dead girl is Amy Newfield, for our own peace of mind if nothing else."

"Any ideas how? We can hardly visit her family and ask if their dead daughter's home and accepting visitors."

"That could prove awkward," Hunt said with wry understatement. "I'll visit Miller tomorrow. He's a doctor and might be able to learn about the victim." He grimaced. "So we can find out if the 'dead' girl we dug up ran off only to be murdered down the road from her grave."

Foley downed his whisky. "That sounds like a plan. One more for the road?"

Chapter Four

The wooden seat creaked in brittle protest as Hunt shifted restlessly. He suspected Miller was deliberately making him wait. A large grandfather clock marked each passing second with an audible tick and swing of the pendulum.

Upon awakening with a pounding headache and sour belly – Foley's "one for the road" had arrived courtesy of several glasses – he had been relieved at the prospect of an easy day without lectures. Until he remembered his plan to visit the professor.

The study door swung open and Miller poked his head out into the hall. "Come in."

Hunt obliged and shut the door behind him. Miller sat behind his paper-cluttered desk and motioned for him to sit.

The professor made a poor show of hiding his agitation, preferring to keep his associations with Hunt and Foley confined to the post-twilight hours. Hunt felt confident he could use Miller's discomfort to his advantage.

"What do you want?" Miller asked. "I'm giving a lecture in an hour, and I've not had my luncheon."

"Apologies, Professor, I won't delay your victuals any longer than necessary."

Miller leaned back, not bothering to hide his impatience.

"A woman was found dead yesterday morning, not far from the Southern Necropolis. The newspapers claim she was murdered."

"And what does that have to do with me?"

Hunt looked him in the eye. "Foley and I fear it may be Miss Newfield and would appreciate any enquiries you might make on our behalf."

"I'm a busy man, Mr Hunt. If you wish to spend your time looking into this foolishness, then by all means do so. But I'll thank you not to waste mine."

Hunt hardened his voice. "Professor, we dug up a body which disappeared, and a young woman was found murdered nearby hours later. Mr Foley and I would be grateful if you made enquiries with the doctor who examined the body and obtain a description. To confirm our suspicions or put our minds at ease."

Miller blinked at Hunt's tone, more accustomed to honey than vinegar. "Aye, well. Maybe I can look into it, if only to draw a line under this matter." A thought seemed to occur to him. "But I would require you and Foley to collect something for me next week in return."

"Something? Care to elucidate?"

"A murderer is being hanged on Monday and his corpse is to be brought here for study, at my expense. If you and your friend collect the body from the prison and bring it to the college, I would be more inclined to look into this matter."

It sounded a simple enough task. "Thank you, Professor. I'm most appreciative. We'll attend the prison and collect your hung man."

"Hanged man." Miller scribbled down the details and passed the paper over.

Hunt accepted the correction with a self-deprecating nod. "Hanged. Of course, sir."

Miller raised a cautioning hand. "We have a business agreement, Mr Hunt. Your exhumations could see us arrested and disgraced. It would end my career and shame your family. Don't come here again, not without proper reason."

Hunt stood. "Of course not, it won't happen again." *Unless necessary*. He walked to the door.

"Hunt."

He stopped and turned, wondering at Miller's insistence in getting in the last word.

The professor didn't look up, his attention occupied by the paper he was writing on. "Don't forget tomorrow's delivery or I may find it difficult to satisfy your curiosity. Good day to you."

Ah yes, our dearly departed drunk. Hunt nodded and left.

*

The bell above the door rang as he entered Foley's shop. Foley started at the sound but resumed his slouched posture against the counter on seeing Hunt. "Well, did Miller agree to help?"

"He did, reluctantly, so long as we pick something up for him on Monday morning." He dropped a newspaper onto the counter. "I hoped there would be more information today, perhaps even a name, but there's nothing. Odd that the papers have lost interest so quickly."

"We'll find out soon enough." Foley rubbed bloodshot eyes and reached for the newspaper.

Hunt nodded. "Remember, we've a body to recover tomorrow night."

"I know, I'm not daft."

Hunt left the shop and went upstairs to the flat.

He sat at the desk in his bedroom, pen poised over a sheet of paper. The desk had been gathering dust in Foley's bedroom until he'd rescued it on moving in. He scribbled a few lines on the paper but struggled to concentrate. The mail had contained a short letter from his mother advising that he was expected home for his twenty-third birthday on Saturday. He wasn't sure what annoyed him more; that it had been worded like a summons, or that he would probably obey it.

He'd last stayed overnight at the family home during his previous birthday, an ordeal he was reluctant to repeat. He had assumed his parents felt the same since they'd spent Christmas with his father's uncle. They'd met Hunt for lunch in December and managed to maintain civility long enough to exchange Yuletide gifts. All contact since then had been conducted via letter.

Hunt thought back to his childhood, to his earliest years spent in Glasgow before his father's career in mercantile law moved them to London. His mother was the daughter of the late Joshua Browning, founder of Glasgow's Browning Shipping Company. Ryan, the son and heir to the company, had died before Hunt's birth, leaving his mother as next in line on Joshua's passing. The family spoke well of Ryan, but some of the older employees described a young man given to intemperance and excess.

Hunt had been ten when his grandfather died, after which

the family moved back to Glasgow. His father, Lewis, had been expected to manage the company, but instead focused on his Law career while Hunt's mother, Edith, assumed her father's role. Hunt had been raised with the expectation that he would follow in the family business. His silence on the matter had been taken for assent.

His schooling had finished at the age of eighteen, followed by two years working for the company in minor positions before attending the University of Glasgow to study Law. His choice of study had met with parental approval. In hindsight, he knew he'd only chosen Law to delay making a decision regarding his future, having little enthusiasm for either shipping or Law.

His interests lay elsewhere. On the day he was to matriculate for his second year at university, he abandoned Law to study a range of Natural Sciences, including Zoology and Botany. His mother's reaction had been predictably voluble. There had been much shouting, interspersed with strategically employed tears, followed by more shouting. His father had been equally disappointed, albeit quieter in his disapproval.

In a last desperate attempt to sway Hunt from his path to certain destruction, he was told in no uncertain terms that he would be cut off from financial support. The termination of his part-time work with the company only strengthened his resolve, and he acrimoniously left home with a trunk filled with clothing and a few personal possessions. His visit home was unlikely to be dull.

*

The Reverend John Redfort watched with anticipation as a servant piled steaming vegetables onto his plate. His table was long and built from dark oak, the pride of his dining room. Satisfied that his guests had all been served, he raised his glass. "Ladies and gentlemen, may God grant you good health."

His guests raised their glasses in answer to the toast. "To your good health," they echoed. The port was expensive and met with appreciative murmurs.

Redfort motioned for everyone to begin. He attacked his plate with relish, carving up the beef which was pink and moist in the middle.

Archibald Stewart, a noted industrialist, caught his eye. “You set a fine table, Reverend. My compliments.”

“Thank you, Mr Stewart. My cook was a fortunate find.”

His butler, Hendry, approached his chair at the head of the table. “Reverend, there is a gentleman at the door asking to see you.”

Redfort looked up at Hendry, masking his annoyance. “I left instructions that we were not to be disturbed this evening. Tell whomever it is to return tomorrow.”

Hendry cleared his throat. “I’m sorry, but the visitor was insistent. He said to give you this.” He handed Redfort a small piece of paper with a black feather inked thereon.

His chest tightened. *Why tonight?* “Escort him to my study. I’ll be along presently.” He watched Hendry leave and took a long sip from his port, hands trembling slightly. It was unusual for the Council to send messengers to his home. For the emissary to insist on speaking with him, to *press the matter* while he had guests was troubling indeed. He stood and bestowed a smile upon his chattering guests. “Humblest apologies, a matter requires my attention. Pray excuse my absence.”

Redfort hovered in front of the closed study door and smoothed his jacket before entering. The man within, taller and stockier than himself, was familiar. Redfort had dealt with him several times previously, and familiarity caused him to speak bolder than intended. “My beef grows cold, Mr Fox. This had better be worth the inconvenience.”

Mark Fox looked unimpressed. “Cold beef is the least of your concerns. I bring word from the Council.”

Redfort clasped his hands together. “Very well, speak.”

The emissary obliged. “Some recent deaths have come to the Council’s attention.”

“You interrupt my evening for this?” he sneered. “Does the Council have so little else to occupy its time?”

Fox scowled, one hand tugging at his hair as if trying to pull it back towards his forehead. “Show proper respect, Reverend. Your usefulness to the society has been noted, but that does not give you leave to speak as you will. Two bodies bearing significant wounds have been found in the South Side of the city near the Southern Necropolis, the first yesterday morning, the second today."

Redfort rubbed his chin, choosing to ignore the rebuke. "Perhaps someone has slipped their leash and indulged themselves? It would not be the first time."

"Perhaps, but the Council wishes full enquiries made into this matter. We were able to suppress the discovery of the second body, but not the first. If it is, as you say, a rogue element not exercising proper discretion, then Regent Edwards will deal with the culprit personally. What is a concern is the possibility of outsiders being responsible, and as such Miss Guillam is taking a personal interest."

He felt a deep unease, not least at Margot Guillam's involvement; he knew what she was. Redfort's association with the Sooty Feather Society had benefited him greatly, but if a rival was muscling in then he risked being caught in the middle of a war older than civilisation.

"I'm sure I don't have to explain the consequences if we are exposed. It's in all of our interests that this matter is dealt with swiftly."

Redfort nodded. Fox's meaning was clear; if the society fell, so would he. He wondered how many other members had endured a similar meeting this evening. "Assure the Council that I will learn what I can." *Perhaps I can turn this situation to my advantage.* He escorted Fox from his study and summoned Hendry.

As his butler showed Fox out of the house, Redfort re-joined his guests with an undiminished appetite.

Chapter Five

Foley took care not to drink too quickly as he sipped from the wine glass, surprised by its rich flavour. An indifferent wine-drinker, he conceded this West End club's cellar stocked a finer selection than the cheap wine he was acquainted with.

"Good, yes?"

He put the glass down, irritated by Hunt's comfortable familiarity with the club. Foley himself felt out of place. His evening wear had seen better times; his father's old coat tails covered a tattered waistcoat and a formal white shirt borrowed from Hunt. His black woollen trousers – purchased during his leaner army days – now pinched at the waist. "Aye, it's not bad," he said with feigned indifference. His father's bow tie had required several attempts to get right.

Hunt carelessly lightened his own glass, the deep purple reddening in the candlelight. His unruly reddish-brown hair had been tamed with wax and parted down the left side, and his face was clean-shaven, a trend growing in popularity. Hunt wore a less formal dinner jacket instead of coat tails, and his attire was of a better quality than Foley's. A better quality but a looser fit; eighteen months away from the Hunt family's cook had taken its toll.

Foley leaned forward. "It's damned expensive here, Hunt. I hope to hell you've got enough money, because I've not."

Hunt answered with a wink. "Calm down, I'll take care of the bill. And try to relax, the steak here is the finest you will ever eat. Trust me on this."

A waiter in a black suit and over-starched white shirt arrived with their meals and assorted condiments. Foley surreptitiously watched Hunt and aped his preparation for the meal.

They began eating, and for once Hunt had not exaggerated; the meal was delicious. The steak was tender and juicy, and the vegetables well-cooked but not so the flavour was boiled out of them.

Foley leaned back afterwards, his hunger fully sated. He sipped brandy and savoured the warmth of it sliding into his belly. "That was grand. It was good of you to sign me in." Majestic mountains, untamed moorlands and raging seas were depicted on paintings that decorated the dark grey walls. "Why aren't you in here every week?"

"As you say, it isn't cheap. We'd have to sell every corpse from Greenock to Edinburgh to dine here regularly."

Damn me if it might not be worth it. Foley exhaled, cigar smoke drifting across the table. "And just how are you going to pay for tonight?" he pressed. He had a vision of being wrestled to the ground by outraged waiters as Hunt dashed out the door.

Hunt's smile took on a cruel edge. "I'll show you." He signalled the waiter his desire to settle up.

The waiter delivered the bill which Hunt made a show of reading. "Please charge this to the Hunt account." He handed over a coin as gratuity.

Foley stared. He knew Hunt was estranged from his wealthy family. "You're making your parents pay for it? The same parents who've all but disowned you?"

"The very same." Hunt smiled. "My family may be displeased with me, but it's not something they're keen to advertise. Scandal, you see? They'll pay without a quibble so long as I don't make a habit of it."

Foley shook his head, both impressed and appalled by his friend's gall.

Hunt glanced at his pocket watch and looked up, his face absent its previous mirth. "Time we were leaving".

Sitting content in a haze of brandy and cigar smoke, Foley had little enthusiasm for exchanging the comforts of the Albert Club for a cemetery. Their tools and work clothes waited in his wagon nearby. As his anxiety about the job returned, so did a familiar craving for laudanum. He'd foregone his habitual evening intake. Postponed it, anyway. Until the job was done.

*

Hunt wiped the sweat from his eyes and studied the corpse. Foley limped over, breathing heavily. They stared down at Billy Nugent's ravaged skin, the lantern-light doing it no favours. Hunt nudged an arm with his boot. Nothing happened. The corpse's limbs were stiff with rigor mortis, and it lay motionless on the sacking. If life had been hard on the man, death was proving no kinder.

"He *is* dead, aye?" Foley asked, wrinkling his nose. The rot had started early.

"Yes," Hunt said with as much confidence as he could muster. Amy Newfield had appeared dead, too.

"You're sure?"

"I'm damned sure." Nothing alive could produce such a stench.

They stripped the body and wrapped it up in sacking. Foley dropped Billy Nugent's clothes into the flimsy pauper's coffin – paid for by donations - and they filled in his now-vacant grave. Hunt found himself sneaking glances over at the wrapped-up corpse, but it showed no inclination to move.

Hunt and Foley lifted the corpse onto the barrow, and Foley wheeled it to the cemetery's exit. Once there they loaded their cargo onto the wagon bed and covered it with more sacking. Hunt joined Foley at the front of the wagon and they exchanged a look.

"That went well," said Foley as he took up the reins.

"Very well," Hunt replied. "The professor will be pleased."

"He should be, all the hard work we do for him."

The journey to Gilmorehill passed without incident.

Miller's housekeeper showed Hunt and Foley into the study with her usual thin-lipped disapproval. Miller was working behind his desk and looked up as they entered. "Well, gentlemen?"

Hunt and Foley exchanged grave looks. Foley cleared his throat and looked away as Hunt clasped his hands together like a penitent child. "It's like this, Professor–"

Miller clenched his fists. "You pair of bloody clowns haven't lost *another*…?"

Hunt smiled. "Not at all. The body's in the wagon."

Miller's face reddened. "Come," was all he said, stalking out of the office with a lit candle and leather bag.

Hunt and Foley retrieved the corpse from the wagon and carried it to the college. "Our little joke wasn't well received," Hunt observed.

"Not as well as I'd hoped," admitted Foley. "I don't think he'll be sharing his whisky with us tonight."

"That's one small mercy."

Foley grunted, evidently of the opinion that cheap whisky was better than none.

Miller waited by the side door until Hunt and Foley returned with the covered corpse. He led them inside, his candle giving enough light to navigate the halls. He unlocked the mortuary doors and they carried in the corpse. Miller usually helped them lift it onto the mortuary table, but on this occasion he stood coldly by and watched. Hunt was unconcerned; Miller's mood wouldn't last. They unrolled the sacking from the naked corpse.

The mortuary looked eerie in the candlelight and smelled rank with decay. There were two other tables within bearing covered cadavers. He suspected the one they'd brought was the foulest, but was disinclined to test it.

Miller looked down at his newest corpse with possessive pride, his irritation forgotten. "I thank you, gentlemen. This will do nicely, yes it will."

So glad you approve. "We're happy to be of service, Professor." Standing in a mortuary with the pungent corpse of a chronic drunk, Hunt found Miller's pleasure disquieting.

Foley cleared his throat meaningfully.

"Oh, of course." Miller straightened up, his expression faintly contemptuous. He pulled a sheet over the now-naked dead man. "Over here." His black bag was on the table next to the candle, its well-worn leather gleaming. He paid them exactly, with an expression of distaste.

Miller reached into the bag again and pulled out a crumpled document. He squinted at it in the candlelight with scant success before putting on his spectacles. "Gentlemen; as per our agreement I spoke with a colleague involved in the recent Caledonia Street murder investigation and obtained a description of the victim."

He paused, possibly expecting vocal approbation. When none was forthcoming, he continued with a slightly disgruntled air. "The dead woman is dissimilar in appearance to Amy Newfield. She had fair hair and was in her early twenties."

"So, she's too old and too blonde. How did she die?" Foley asked.

Miller squinted down at the parchment again. "It appears her throat was mutilated. The procurator fiscal's report mentions heavy blood-loss." He adjusted his spectacles and sounded mildly interested for the first time. "Curious."

"What's curious?" Hunt asked.

"The doctor hasn't given a cause for the mutilation. An odd omission."

Foley frowned. "A knife, no?"

"There are many types of knife, Mr Foley. Knives with serrated blades, smooth blades, sharp, blunt."

Hunt felt relief that the victim wasn't Amy Newfield. To be buried alive and exhumed by body snatchers, only to be murdered shortly thereafter seemed an unkind fate. It still left them with a mystery, however; what had happened to her? "Thank you, Professor. If there's nothing further, we'll be on our way."

"I've kept my side of the bargain, I expect you to keep yours on Monday morning," Miller reminded them.

"You can count on us, Professor," Hunt said as Miller escorted them outside.

Hunt turned to Foley once they were back at the wagon. "By the by, it's my birthday tomorrow and I'll be visiting my parents." He glanced at his pocket watch, noting that it was well after midnight. "Today, rather. I'll be back in a day or two."

"They've all but disowned you, but still expect an appearance on your birthday?"

Hunt smiled wryly at Foley's incredulous tone. "They doubtless hope that a second year of penury and exile has returned me to my senses, and what better time to see how matters lie?"

Foley gave Hunt an amused look. "Happy Birthday, I'll see you when you get back. I might even get you a cake."

"I'll look forward to that with *great* anticipation."

Chapter Six

It was a pleasant spring Saturday afternoon, warm in the sun but cool in the shade. Hunt climbed the front steps of the house he had grown up in, with no little trepidation; billing last night's dinner to his family's account was less amusing in hindsight. A townhouse built in the affluent West End, it looked just as he remembered. The front garden was small but bloomed with spring flowers such as daffodils, one of his mother's passions. It was immaculate as always, and the cause of many a childhood scolding. He blew out a breath. It was too fine a day for this. He banged the door knocker lest he change his mind and leave.

It was answered by Smith who stepped aside on seeing him. "Welcome home, Master Wilton. Happy Birthday."

Hunt crossed the threshold and left his small trunk by the door. "Thank you. It's good to see you, Smith." The butler was more stooped than the year before, but still possessed a frail dignity. "Where's my mother?"

"Mrs Hunt is in the drawing room, sir." Smith took Hunt's top hat – he'd left his bowler hat in the flat, knowing his mother would consider it too common for a respectable young gentleman.

The hall was gloomy with old oil paintings of dead relations standing sentinel on the dark green walls. Potpourri lingered in the air thanks to a clay bowl on the sideboard. Smith gave the drawing room door two discreet knocks and opened it. "Ma'am, Master Wilton is here."

"Thank you, Smith. Show him in." Mother's voice was laced with cool authority, suggesting an expectation of immediate deference to her wishes.

Smith bowed fractionally. "Yes, ma'am."

Hunt walked in and Smith withdrew, closing the door.

Unlike the hall, the drawing room was bright with sunlight bouncing off white walls. A pair of bookcases filled with well-used books stood near to the door. The books all belonged to his mother, limited editions of Sir Walter Scott's works being the pride of her collection. Lewis Hunt's legal books were in his study, and Wilton's penny dreadfuls certainly had no place in the drawing room.

Three small dark-wooded tables bearing vases of fresh daffodils culled from the garden sat neatly against adjacent walls, and a mature oak sideboard squatted to one side, offering fresh green apples from a bowl. A three-seat couch held dominance in the centre of the room, flanked by a pair of armchairs facing each other and separated by a wooden table inlaid with carved elephants.

Mrs Edith Susan Browning Hunt, wife of Mr Lewis Hunt and mother of Mr Wilton Michael Hunt, held court in the drawing room. She sat in the centre of the couch and carefully marked her place in the book with a slim, leather strap. Hunt spared the book a glance as it was set aside on the table. It was *Paradise Lost*, an old favourite of hers and one she often re-read. For no reason Hunt had ever discerned, his father regarded it with distaste.

He turned his attention back to his mother and found her regarding him in turn, her face composed into a mask of cool neutrality. "Hello, Mother. You're looking well." He dutifully bent over and bestowed a familial peck on her cheek. The pleasantries observed, he braced himself for an inquisition into his recent activities, and advice on how he *should* be spending his time. He remembered Reverend Mitchell warning him as a child that the devil found work for idle hands. Whether there was truth to the maxim, he couldn't say; his father had kept him well-occupied with chores.

"Thank you, Wilton. Happy Birthday." She studied him, her eyes missing little. "You're looking well, perhaps a little tired. I do hope you're not staying up all hours of the night. You're also on the thin side, you really must eat better." Aged in her mid-forties, her light-brown hair was speckled with grey. Long years and an unyielding nature had lined her sharp features.

"Study keeps me up late, but I'll try to eat better". He fantasised about confessing his recent ventures into body snatching. Her reaction would be memorable.

"And how are your studies progressing?" Her mask cracked slightly as her tone and tightening eyes betrayed disapproval.

He stiffened his back, in no mood to resume that old argument. "Very well," he said. "I'm participating in a Zoology field trip over Easter."

"I'm gratified to hear your time hasn't been *completely* wasted."

"No, not completely, you sour old cow," he refrained from saying. He forced a smile and *did* say, "My class will be staging a small exhibition of our findings in May, I'll be sure to send you and Father tickets."

Her lips tightened at his tone, but for once she chose to overlook it. "We will look forward to it," she said with scant sincerity. She gestured at the chair to her right. "Be seated, Wilton. Luncheon will be served shortly."

Interpreting the subject change to mean she was done with that topic for the time being, he took a calming breath and sat down. He'd held his own, all things considered. "How's Father? Is he home?"

Mother knew how to play the game, her face and tone showing no remembrance of the earlier tension. "Your father is well, dear. He's travelling up from London by train. We've reserved a table at the Viceroy Restaurant and will meet him there. Aunt Mary, Uncle Richard, Neil and Helen will be joining us."

Hunt assumed a look of pleased surprise, no stranger to the game himself. "That's very thoughtful of them. It's been too long since we've all been together." In truth, he was indifferent to the idea of dining with his aunt, uncle and cousins. They could be tiresome.

His packed dinner jacket was suitable (barely, in his mother's eyes) for dining at home or in a club, but less so for a restaurant like the Viceroy. Fortunately, he had left his tails in the wardrobe upstairs, and he could borrow one of Father's formal shirts.

He was ambivalent at the thought of meeting his father.

They got on, by and large, but Hunt never knew exactly where they stood. Father had certainly been attentive while he was growing up, but he sometimes got the feeling that Lewis Hunt didn't know quite what to make of his only child. Hunt's parents had been united in condemning his decision to abandon studying Law, not unexpected given Father's own status as a respected lawyer. Further reflection, however, led Hunt to suspect that his father's objections had been expressed out of expectation rather than genuine disapproval. He also believed that Father's influence was to thank – or blame – for Mother still maintaining contact.

Her regal tone refocused his attention back to the present. "How else have you been occupying yourself? Have you been courting any young ladies? I do hope you've not been spending your time in *low establishments* drinking."

"Well, I've been digging up and selling dead bodies," he didn't say. "No, Mother, no young ladies. My current circumstances don't permit me to entertain them in a manner of which you would approve. And no, I don't spend my time in low establishments." *Well, not all of it.* "I help Mr Foley run his pharmacy when I'm not at the university or studying."

"If…" his mother began, but pursed her lips.

Hunt knew well enough what she wanted to say; if he went back to studying Law he could return home with the less said about his little rebellion the better. He couldn't deny it; the thought of living in comfort and not having to rob graves appealed.

"Have you considered how this may affect your *other* inheritance?"

Ah. He had wondered where this was leading. "I confess I've given it little thought. I don't see how it is an issue. When Great-Uncle Thomas dies, Father will inherit his title and the estate, what little remains of it. I don't enter into the matter until Father's death, many years from now, God willing."

"And if your father precedes his uncle in death?"

It was an unlikely scenario. Thomas Hunt was old and in fragile health, whereas Lewis Hunt was middle-aged and vigorous. Still, illness and accidents did happen. Hunt's paternal grandfather, the youngest of three brothers, had died when Father was still a child. The eldest brother, Henry, had perished at sea with his wife and heir about thirty years ago. The middle brother, Thomas, became the 5th Baron of Ashwood, but as he had never married, his nephew Lewis stood as Heir Presumptive. Aged eighty-three and almost bedridden, there was small chance of Lord Ashwood marrying and breeding an heir, leaving little doubt that the title would pass to Hunt's father. And in time, to Hunt.

"Your great-uncle is displeased by your choice of study. He has hinted that should your father precede him in death, he would disown you from the inheritance," Mother revealed. "The 3rd Baron was a wastrel who fancied himself an artist and spent much of his time and money hosting those with similar interests. He also had a fondness for cards."

But little luck. Hunt was familiar with the tale. He didn't remember the man's name, only that he'd died of wounds taken in a duel over some debt. He'd already lost all the money and most of the lands. A cousin, Hunt's great-grandfather, had inherited what little remained, namely the title of Baron, a crumbling house and a small scrap of land. The Hunts had struggled ever since to hold onto the remnants. Lewis' marriage into a wealthy merchant family was doubtless seen as a Godsend by Great-Uncle Thomas.

"As such," Mother continued, "your great-uncle's view of those who indulge in such frivolities is tainted by family history. He has no desire to pass on what remains of the estate to one he feels will squander it in frivolous pursuits, and writes me his intention to pass everything to a distant cousin should you not see sense."

"I see." Hunt was fairly certain that the Laws of Succession would decide who inherited the title, not his uncle's prejudices, but it made little difference to him. He was willing to risk his claim to the Browning Shipping Company and fortune; an empty title and some scrubby land were small potatoes in comparison.

"Something for you to consider," Mother said, satisfied she had made her point. "Natural History is a fine hobby for a gentleman, but hardly a practical profession." He understood her thinking; Lord Wilton Hunt, 7th Baron of Ashwood, and Master of the Browning Shipping Company was a more desirable son than an impoverished scientist.

Two knocks rattled off the lounge door. One of the maids, Maggie, entered carrying a tray of sandwiches and sweetmeats. A second maid, unknown to Hunt, followed behind with a tray bearing two glasses and a jug of lemonade.

His mother looked up and nodded in approbation. "Luncheon, excellent." Her eyes fell on his slender frame. "Help yourself to the sandwiches, Wilton."

*

Hunt leaned back in his seat and toyed with his wine glass. His mother, uncle, aunt and cousins chattered incessantly while he maintained an expression of polite engagement. The waiter escorted his father to the table.

Everyone stood. "Hello, Father," Hunt said. "I trust you're in good health?"

Lewis Hunt looked over at his son, and Hunt was struck by the resemblance between them. Father's hair was brown to Hunt's red, and a moustache grew from his upper lip, but the similarity was undeniable. "I'm well, thank you. Happy Birthday, Wilton." He greeted his wife and the other guests, and they resumed their seats.

Hunt found the ensuing small-talk interminable and ignored most of it. He nodded and smiled appropriately as was his duty as guest of honour, and tolerated the toasts made by his father and uncle.

"Wilton," said his cousin Helen, "I understand you are studying Natural Science. That sounds interesting, have you found it so?"

Hunt noted Mother's faint scowl and Neil's speculative look. Neither reaction surprised him. If he was disowned, his cousin Neil was next in line to inherit ownership of the Browning Shipping Company. His mother and aunt's brother had preceded their father Joshua Browning in death, the family assets passing to Edith Hunt. "I've found it interesting. Difficult, but interesting. My parents have been most supportive."

Mother smiled tightly at the lie, reluctant to contradict him in public and unwilling to add weight to Neil's ambitions.

"We're pleased to support Wilton in his endeavours."

Liar. He acknowledged her with a smile.

"Lewis, how fares the company?" Aunt Mary asked, betraying that her thoughts also ran to its eventual disposition.

"Edith manages it," Father reminded her, sipping wine from his glass. "I'm led to believe it fares robustly."

"Indeed," Mother said, casting her sister a pointed look. "Most robustly."

Dessert and coffee followed the meal, after which the party returned to the Hunt home. Hunt had rather hoped they would decline the invitation, but no such luck. He, his father, uncle and cousin Neil retired to the parlour for cigars and whisky while the ladies decamped to the drawing room.

Hunt sat alone with his father while Uncle Richard and Neil freshened up. "How has London been treating you, sir?" Father stayed there a week or two every month on business.

Father exhaled a puff of smoke. "Much as it always has. Why, do you plan to revisit?"

"Not at this time, sir," Hunt said. "I was merely curious. You do spend a lot of time there."

"Yes," Father nodded. "My presence has been required more so of late. But I'll be home for the next month."

"We've seen so little of each other recently."

"Quite so, son. Uncle Thomas wrote after you."

"So Mother said." Hunt was well aware that the only person less impressed with his foray into the sciences than Mother was his great-uncle. "She also says that should you precede Uncle Thomas in death, he wishes to designate some cousin his heir rather than myself."

Father snorted. "Uncle Thomas has no say in the future Baron Ashwood. The Rule of Succession are clear."

Further discourse on the subject was ended by the arrival of Hunt's uncle and cousin.

"Richard and Neil, good of you both to attend," Father said.

Uncle Richard looked jovial, well-lubricated by the earlier wine and brandy. "We're grateful, Lewis, that you and Edith invited us to celebrate Wilton's birthday." Hunt had always liked Uncle Richard. Boring, but he meant well.

Cousin Neil was cut from a different cloth. The rumours of Hunt's disinheritance suggested Neil would inherit the Browning Shipping Company on Edith Hunt's retirement or death. He already held high position within the company but hungered for further advancement. Thus far, Hunt's mother had endeavoured to play down the estrangement.

Neil was clearly enjoying his cigar. "I don't know how you can bear to leave such lovely surroundings, Wilton."

"Your meaning escapes me." It was an effort to keep his tone civil.

Neil feigned a look of innocence. "My apologies, Cousin, I don't mean to imply anything. I know you're living elsewhere. I'm merely surprised you would choose to leave such a fine home."

Prick. "My father wished me to expand my experiences. Living away from home serves this purpose."

Father nodded. "Quite so. I do not wish for Wilton to be reliant upon inherited wealth."

Hunt concealed his surprise at the unexpected support from his father. The implication was that he had been sent out to learn independence. If such a thing was true, it put paid to Neil's hopes of inheriting the company. Hunt inhaled from his cigar to hide a smile.

Chapter Seven

Hunt awoke, disorientated to find himself in his old bed. Sunlight flared through the window. There was activity downstairs as the servants left for church. In deference to the Sabbath, few chores were carried out on a Sunday. He rolled out of bed, reluctant to leave its comforts. At least his extended family had declined to stay overnight.

He dressed after hastily bathing, putting on a cutaway morning coat. Suspecting his attendance at church would be required, he had packed it in his trunk before leaving Foley's flat.

Hunt joined his parents in the hallway downstairs, dusting off his top hat. Mother appraised him in a single look, finding no cause for complaint.

Father looked him over and nodded his approval. "Good. Let's be off." A cabriolet waited outside to convey them to Glasgow's High Street.

The journey was unremarkable, and from there they walked to St Mungo's Cathedral, his parents ahead. Hunt was struck by the familiarity of it. As far back as he could remember, the Hunts had gone to church on Sunday, and as a child, Hunt had enjoyed the intimacy of it. In those early days he had held his father's hand, suitably awed by the occasion. The family had kept up their devotions in London.

A church elder handed each of them a worn hymnbook, giving Hunt's parents a familiar nod.

Old wood creaked as they sat on the pews. Hunt recalled a childhood memory in which he had unthinkingly uttered a blasphemy; Father's wrath, so rarely unleashed, had been terrifying. Even Mother, never reluctant to play a role in correcting his faults, stepped well clear of father and son during that unpleasantness.

The venerable Reverend Mitchell held the service and opened with the familiar hymns that had served him well over the years. The hymns were followed by a sermon denouncing the ungodly practices of Catholicism. Practices, Reverend Mitchell warned his congregation, certain to lead the misguided papists straight to Lucifer's company in Hell. Good Calvinist values, the Reverend assured them, were the only sure path to salvation. He continued preaching at great length and even greater volume about the imperilment of their souls, sternly advising them on the necessary steps to avoid damnation. This very cathedral, he reminded them, had been wrested from the Catholics during the Reformation. St Mungo doubtless rested easier in his tomb below, he opined, free from Roman corruption. Ending the sermon with further reminders about the Papal menace and the evils of liquor, the Reverend directed them to the last hymn. *Thank God.*

Hunt and his parents left the cathedral at the conclusion of the service, pausing to speak with Reverend Mitchell as they passed him at the doors. Hunt trailed behind as they walked to the cabriolet waiting to return them home.

*

The Sunday luncheon had been prepared the previous day and left in the pantry. Hunt and his parents served themselves and ate in the dining room. Mother glanced between husband and son with a speculative eye.

Hunt finished his sandwich. "Delicious. Do thank Mrs McCrae for me, Mother. May I be excused?" He began to stand.

A gesture from his mother dropped him back to his seat. "I'll pass on your gratitude, Wilton, but before you hurry off your father wishes a word." She left the dining room.

Father appeared in no hurry to finish his luncheon, so Hunt took another chicken sandwich.

Father finished his food in his own good time and focused his grey eyes on Hunt. "So, son, are your studies progressing?"

"Yes, sir." Hunt almost choked on his sandwich, immediately hating his instinctual haste to answer. He was no longer a child to be browbeaten or cowed by a parent.

He braced himself for words on how foolish he was to abandon Law, but instead his father contented himself with a nod. “Good.”

“That’s it? I expected a lecture.” Hunt cleared his throat, surprised at his own bluntness and feeling no little trepidation at how his father might respond.

Father just smiled. “I’ve found that your mother is best employed in that regard.”

Hunt stirred, almost daring to believe that his father took his side. If so, then perhaps his days of body snatching were at an end. “I’m surprised to hear that. I thought you shared Mother’s disapproval at my change in direction.”

A chuckle rumbled in Father’s chest. “I’ve always expected you to do what suits you, regardless of my opinion or your mother’s. But,” he held up a cautionary finger, “don’t expect this to mean you are welcome to return home. I rather like the idea of you having to earn your own way. Defiance has its price.”

“I’m pleased my tumble from grace has amused you.”

“Having to earn your own bread and board is scarcely a fall from grace. If you encounter any *real* difficulties, Wilton, you know where to find me.”

“I’ll bear that in mind.” He wondered if misplacing a corpse counted as a real difficulty.

“I’m glad we had this chat. Let’s join your mother in the drawing room. Try to look suitably contrite; you’ve just been instructed to mend your ways.”

They stood, each mirroring the other’s grin.

Mother looked up as the pair entered the drawing room, her eyes flickering between father and son. Hunt tried to look both grave and thoughtful, hoping his mother didn’t mistake it for indigestion. Father sat to Mother’s left on the couch and directed Hunt to one of the armchairs.

“Thank you both for a pleasant birthday and an enjoyable visit.” To his surprise, he mostly meant it. His previous birthday had been too soon after their estrangement, the wounds raw and tempers frayed.

“It was our pleasure, Wilton,” Mother assured him. She likely believed the father-and-son discussion would hasten his return to sensibility.

"Our son's return to the roost is always a cause for celebration." Father looked at him. "Your mother and I have been invited to spend next Friday and Saturday at Dunclutha, Sir Arthur Williamson's estate. We would be pleased if you would accompany us."

Mother looked startled for perhaps a heartbeat before directing a look of pleased enquiry at Hunt. "I had forgotten about that. Your father's correct, we would be delighted."

Her smile was perhaps a little too forced; she wasn't delighted at all. Hunt suspected it was partly because her pariah son was best kept away from the family's social circle until he returned to his senses, and partly because she wasn't used to her husband making such invitations without discussing them first with her. Hunt cruelly assumed a thoughtful look, not deigning to rush his answer.

After perhaps five seconds of awkward silence he decided he had tortured his mother enough. "I would be happy to attend. Friday, you say? What time should I be here for?"

Evidently Hunt wasn't the only one to derive some small pleasure at tweaking Mother's nose; Father directed a questioning look at her. "What time would be suitable, dear?"

Having been outplayed by both husband and son, Mother did her best to appear gracious. "Eight o'clock in the morning. A carriage will convey us there." She sharpened her tone. "I expect you to be punctual and suitably attired."

"Of course, Mother." His amusement at discomforting his mother aside, he began to wonder at his decision to accept the invitation. His visit had done much to mend bridges with his parents, but if he caused embarrassment then he could find himself disowned altogether. Neil inheriting the company while Hunt spent the remainder of his days digging up bodies made for a displeasing thought.

Mother's train of thought evidently echoed Hunt's own. "Your Uncle Richard and Aunt Mary are attending, also. I do hope they bring Neil and Helen."

*

It was early evening by the time Hunt returned to the flat. He found Foley within the sitting room, a half-finished whisky on the table.

"Hunt," Foley greeted him. "How was the visit home?"

"Better than expected," Hunt said. "We went out for dinner last night. My cousin Neil was very curious about my studies and living arrangements."

"It's nice to know he cares."

"Not really. He was hoping to hear I'd been disowned, making him heir to the company." He poured himself a whisky and relaxed into an armchair.

"Sounds like a bastard. You should have punched him. What else did you get up to?"

"His parentage isn't in question but punching him does hold a certain appeal. I'll consider it for future encounters. What else? Oh, I went to church with my parents this morning."

Foley smirked, no doubt having spent his own Sunday morning recovering from Saturday night. "Are you feeling properly redeemed?"

"Oh yes, saved for another week. So long as I avoid Catholics and strong drink. Cheers." He toasted Foley, a Roman Catholic, and tossed back some of the whisky.

Foley crossed himself and emptied his own glass. "What about immoral women?"

"None attended, alas."

"I mean, did the good minister warn you of them?"

Hunt shrugged. "Reverend Mitchell made no mention of them. Perhaps he's saving them for next week?"

"He can save some for me. So, you had a fine dinner, saw off a greedy cousin and saved your soul. Anything else?"

He finished his whisky. "I've been cordially invited to stay at a family friend's estate on Friday and Saturday."

Foley smirked and mimicked Hunt's voice. "That sounds jolly. Am I invited?"

"Sadly not. My father issued the invitation without consulting my mother, and he made no mention of me bringing a guest." He smiled, remembering his mother's poorly hidden consternation at his own impromptu invite.

Foley smiled. "Your mother wasn't happy?"

"She harbours some odd notion that I might shame the family."

"Ah," Foley nodded in feigned understanding. "A fair concern."

"She certainly thinks so. She informed me of her hope that my cousins could attend, also."

"It must be a relief for your mother to have a respectable nephew to rely upon come the day her only son is revealed as a whisky-soaked rogue."

Hunt looked askance at Foley. "I keep meaning to introduce you to my mother. Then I recall that you both share similar, unfounded opinions of me."

"Well, what do I know? I'm just a liquor-loving papist drinking his way to Hell."

"At least you'll have company." They clinked glasses.

Chapter Eight

The cell was dark and damp, its walls stained with mildew. A metal pail sat in the corner, bent and tarnished. The squat wooden bed creaked under the prisoner's weight, his chest rattling with every breath. Not that it mattered; he had few enough remaining.

Richard Canning had been Her Majesty's guest at the Duke Street Prison for the past three weeks, and time had not improved his opinion of the place. He ate, slept and worked in the small cell, separating threads from tarred rope in exchange for coin to trade for food and other amenities. His blanket was one such amenity, threadbare and flea-ridden though it was.

A butcher by trade, he had spent his first week in the prison kitchens preparing food alongside a prisoner named McDermid. His temper, frayed by seven days of confinement and filthy conditions, was exacerbated by McDermid's coarse nature and uncleanly habits. The acquaintanceship ended badly.

Canning smiled, remembering the guards' expressions as they entered the kitchen in response to the screams and found *so much blood*. McDermid's first mistake had been to goad him. His second was to do so while Canning was peeling potatoes and not cutting meat. A butcher's knife would have seen McDermid to a quick end, whereas the potato knife proved crude, blunt and *slow*. Canning had been confined to his cell from that day on, left to reflect on his sins in solitude like a scolded child. Not that he minded; he preferred his own company.

Canning's demons had hidden behind a mask of quiet respectability all his life, watching as he worked hard and attended Mass every Sunday. But when he chose to indulge them – and it was his choice – his victims saw his true face, one last gift of honesty before he took everything from them. Their screams didn't trouble him; what did was the silence when all that remained was dead flesh and stagnant blood.

Canning didn't know where the darkness in his soul came from, nor did he care. He was as God made him.

It was pride that proved his undoing, pride and arrogance. He had been careless and caught. Gleeful newspaper editors printed what little they knew and invented whatever they didn't to fill their columns and sell their papers, selling him as Glasgow's Jack. His mask of normalcy had fallen off during the trial and hadn't fitted him since. But what was done was done; he would spend one last night in his cell and be hanged at dawn. And then *he* would be done.

The cell door viewer opened. Light glimmered.

"Prisoner, stand at the back of the cell." The wardens never lowered their guard around him, not since the kitchen. That wouldn't stop them from delivering a beating if he was slow to comply, so he rolled off the bed and stepped back a few paces.

He wondered who cared enough to visit. There was a rumour that the hangman would guarantee a quick death for a small payment. If the guards acted as agents on his behalf, they would be disappointed. Execution methods were a topic of interest to Canning given his activities, and he had read enough to know Marwood's long drop method ensured an instant broken neck. The door swung open with an iron howl.

Two guards stood at the entrance and another two men stood behind them. Canning wondered who they were, more irritated than curious. He was no freak to be gawked at, and any who thought otherwise would be bloodily corrected.

"Canning, your lawyer and a priest are here." The guard never took his eyes off him as he spoke, truncheon clenched in his right hand. The second guard held the lantern.

Dark joy blossomed in his heart at the mention of his lawyer, but the man who entered the cell wasn't William Cotter. He was twenty years too young and a stranger. Canning looked at the Catholic priest and found himself being studied in turn.

"We will require some time alone with the prisoner," the

fair-haired priest said. His black top hat was taller than the lawyer's, a remnant from an earlier fashion.

"That's not a good idea, Father," cautioned one of the guards. "This man–"

"I'm aware of his crimes." Calmly.

The alleged lawyer cleared his throat, perspiring despite the cool night. "The prisoner is represented by my company. He has the right to consult with his lawyer, and to meet with a priest to confess his sins and receive Last Rites."

Unwilling to argue, the guards allowed the pair to enter the cell. They left their lantern and closed the door over, waiting outside in the corridor.

Canning ignored the priest and focused instead on the lawyer. He spoke, his tone polite as always. "I don't know you, and I wasn't expecting any visitors. Why didn't Mr Cotter come himself? He defended me." *And what a defence it was. Rarely have I seen a man accept defeat with such relief.*

He had committed only four of the murders he'd been convicted of, but Cotter's indifferent efforts on his behalf ensured the jury found him guilty of all charges regardless. True, there were a further six victims whom he had *not* been connected with, but the injustice still rankled.

The lawyer kept his distance. "Mr Cotter is otherwise occupied. I'm Mr Stokes. You should know an appeal for a stay of execution was lodged as a matter of course, but ultimately–"

"Refused." The word lingered in the cell, the prisoner confirming his own execution in the morning.

"Quite so, Mr Canning." Stokes tugged at his shirt collar and cleared his throat.

Canning turned his back and stared out of the barred window into the night's darkness. "Thank you, Mr Stokes. Please give Mr Cotter my *very best*."

Stokes didn't move. "Father George wishes to speak with you, Mr Canning."

Richard Canning didn't bother looking at him. "Take the priest with you." He would not waste his last hours suffering the pious prattle of some collared fool.

"I want to save you," the priest said.

Canning laughed, still facing the window. Surely even God's mercy had its limits? "Are you aware of my crimes, Father?"

"I'm aware."

"And are you aware that if you take one step closer, I'll kill you?" He spoke calmly but quite sincerely. They couldn't hang him twice.

"I know you would make every effort to do so." Was that *amusement* in the priest's voice?

"You're not afraid." Canning regarded the blond-haired priest with interest. It wasn't a question; he was well-used to the fear of others and sensed its absence in the priest.

"No."

"Is your faith so strong?" He was genuinely curious. Did the priest expect a host of angels to descend on the prison? They hadn't troubled themselves to save his previous victims.

The priest kept his voice low. "Hear me out."

Canning's phlegm-wracked laugh rattled around the cell. "I'm busy tonight. Return in the morning." He spat a wad of bloody phlegm into the pail.

"You hang in the morning."

"Aye. Hanged until dead." He hesitated, feeling the man's gaze on him. "Can you stop it?"

"No. You *will* hang." The priest sounded certain.

Canning waited silently, but the priest's gaze was inscrutable, his eyes lost in the gloom.

"I'll explain our proposal to Mr Canning, Stokes, and take the appropriate steps. There is no need for you to remain."

Stokes rapped on the cell door with an alacrity that betrayed his relief. "Guards."

The door opened. "Mr Canning is confessing his sins and receiving Last Rites," Stokes explained as he exited the cell with the lantern. The door slammed shut. Darkness enveloped them as the priest stepped closer.

The priest spoke, and Canning listened.

*

Hunt stood next to Wilfred and fed the horse a piece of apple to placate him. Foley slouched in the front of his wagon, still befuddled from the previous night's whisky. They waited in the prison yard with a small crowd made up mostly of prison guards, journalists holding notebooks, and city officials present as a matter of form. Three men stood apart; the prison governor, the sheriff and a physician sent to confirm the bastard really was dead.

The governor was grey-haired, the sheriff white, but both faced the execution shed with the same grim-faced anticipation. The balding physician had a fleshy face and looked impatient for it to be over.

"Are you lads here to take the body away?" the sheriff asked Hunt.

Hunt nodded. "Yes, sir."

The sheriff shook his head. "You're early. He'll be left dangling for an hour. Did you not know that?"

"No, we did not." The grey-bricked execution shed was minimally built, its grim function being the only consideration. Loitering around for an hour in the prison's shadow held no appeal, but they had no choice. "No priest?"

"One attended him last night, and he wanted none to attend this morning. He did request a shave, so a barber attends to him now."

A razor was one of Canning's favoured weapons, Hunt remembered from the papers. He hoped guards were also present.

A hint of orange peeked over the eastern horizon, iron-grey clouds otherwise dominating the dawn sky. Several prison guards escorted a man across the yard. "Wake up, Foley. It's time."

"*About* bloody time."

Sure enough, the prisoner was led over to the execution shed. The guards escorting him were big men who took no chances with the infamous killer. Hunt had imagined Canning to be a brute, tall and menacing, but he was of average height. Prison life had left him gaunt and pale, with dark greasy hair clinging to the sides of his head.

Murder was no stranger to Glasgow, but Canning's brutality had elevated him above the common thugs and cut-throats who usually breathed their last on the gallows. He had agreed – doubtless in exchange for some privilege – for his body to go to the medical school for use in an anatomy lesson; the alternative was a lime-filled coffin in an unmarked grave on the prison grounds.

Hunt shivered, wishing to be gone from the place. Duke Street Prison was a grim edifice broken up by small barred windows, and it wasn't lost on Hunt that his own activities were less than legal. "If we're not careful, we might end up in here," he said quietly.

Foley shook his head. "Not likely."

"I'm heartened by your optimism."

He grinned. "You misunderstand. Some men are kept here, but it's mostly women now. Canning's here because the hangings are still done here. We'd probably be sent to Barlinnie Prison."

"Ah." Hunt doubted Barlinnie was an improvement. *Best not get caught then.*

This was Hunt's first execution, but it seemed to him that Canning looked entirely too pleased with himself for a man minutes from the noose. Canning looked up at the sky, and for the first time there was something akin to regret on the condemned man's face. "I had hoped for a red dawn and a blue sky," he announced as the execution shed door was opened. He took one last look at the sky and smiled.

Hunt and Foley were among the last to enter the building, finding it devoid of decoration. There was nothing but naked brickwork, a stone floor and the gallows at the far end. Canning stood on those gallows, still smiling at some private joke when the masked executioner placed a hood over his head and tightened the noose.

The command was given, and the trapdoor collapsed, Richard Canning dropping into the pit below. Hunt expected the drop to break his neck but was proven wrong when Canning's legs kicked out. A murmur passed over the small crowd. The executioner left the platform and tried to grab hold of a leg, but couldn't reach them down the pit.

The tortured sounds coming from the choking man were like nothing human, like nothing Hunt had heard before or ever wished to hear again. He looked around the crowded room, but no one moved to end Canning's suffering. Everyone just watched with grim expressions, waiting for it to end.

Canning's violent convulsions eventually ceased, and he hung limp from the gibbet. Hunt blew out a breath, repulsed by the whole experience. Three of the journalists looked ill, one ready to vomit.

"That was bloody awful," Foley said.

Hunt nodded, not trusting himself to speak.

The governor opened the door. "Let's wait outside." That suggestion was greeted with enthusiasm, everyone leaving save for two guards assigned to stay with the hanging body. No mention was made of the botched execution, though the hangman was given a hard look.

The governor gathered the journalists together. "An evil man has faced justice. While the sentence was not carried out as smoothly as intended, it has been carried out. Reporting the full circumstances might distract people from the relief that Canning is dead. I invite you all to consider the sensibilities of your readers and omit the full details of the execution."

The journalists seemed to be in agreement, perhaps more concerned with exclusion from future executions if their articles displeased the governor. Hunt had no doubt the official record would state that Canning died instantly of a broken neck, and no one would care enough to dispute it.

The hour dragged on, and at its passing the governor directed the guards to cut the body down from the gallows. They carried it out of the shed and laid it down on the ground. The physician pulled the hood from Canning's head and examined him for signs of life. Hunt looked down at the corpse, disconcerted by the bulging eyes and purple blotches on the face. He'd thought himself an old hand at death, but Canning hadn't felt the undertaker's prettying touch like the corpses he exhumed.

The physician looked up. "This man is dead. I can detect no breath and feel no pulse."

The sheriff nodded and looked at Foley. "Good, take him to the medical school. Perhaps the students can learn something from this devil."

Hunt and Foley stepped forward and wrapped the body in sackcloth. Two prison guards helped them load it onto the back of the wagon.

The wagon rolled across the city towards the university, Foley driving as always. The journey took longer than usual due to the morning congestion of trams, wagons and carriages.

"It's queer to be doing this in the daylight, Hunt."

Hunt laughed. "Yes, it is novel. Maybe we can prevail upon the professor for more jobs like this?"

"The only payment we got for this job was a dead girl's description, remember? And not the girl we're looking for."

Hunt conceded there to be truth in that. Their nocturnal jobs were more lucrative due to their illegality.

They arrived at the university where the sandstone medical school waited. Hunt hopped off the wagon and went in to announce their arrival while Foley remained with their cargo.

The professor who escorted them into the mortuary with Canning's corpse was a stranger, nodding genially to a group of students passing by. "I've not seen you here before," he said to Hunt and Foley. They carried the body on a stretcher.

"We owed Professor Miller a favour," Foley said as they passed a cleaner scrubbing the wooden floor, too engrossed in her work to look up.

"I didn't think you were the usual chaps," the professor said.

"Not so fast," Hunt cautioned Foley quietly as they carried the stretcher along a pale green corridor smelling strongly of bleach and formaldehyde. "We're meant to be strangers here, remember?"

Foley nodded his approval at Hunt's presence of mind. If they appeared too familiar with the layout of the mortuary, it might raise awkward questions.

The professor, a more amiable man than Miller, expressed his eagerness to view Canning's brain. "It could provide us with so much," he explained. "Think of it; with study, we could identify the part of the brain responsible for evil. How do sinners differ from saints? It has been too difficult to tell, as most of us are a mixture of both. But now we have the brain of a *truly* evil man. If I can compare it with the brain of an innocent, it could be the key to *everything*."

"So you'll be doing the necessaries, Professor?" Foley asked, amused by his enthusiasm.

The man sniffed. "No, Professor Miller will perform the

honours tomorrow morning. I still want the brain though. To *discover* evil."

Hunt wished evil weighed less. "A brave new world, Professor."

*

Something was wrong, Hunt realised on entering the university grounds the following morning. Groups of students stood on the grass talking. Not unusual, except that he was late, and they should be in the lecture halls, not gossiping outside. The mood was wrong, and the tone of the din was off, facial expressions ranging from shocked to excited; the wrong sort of excited. Something had happened.

He approached five students talking over each other. "Excuse me, what's going on?"

One of them turned to Hunt. "Haven't you heard?"

Obviously not, or I wouldn't be asking. "Heard what?"

They exchanged looks before their self-appointed spokesman answered. "There's been a murder. A professor was found dead this morning."

"How do you know it was murder?" challenged another student. "I just heard a man was found dead."

"Of course it's murder. I heard someone screaming about blood and a dead professor before the constables were summoned. All lectures have been cancelled."

Murder. Common in the wynds and slums of the city but unheard of in the university itself. It would be talked about for years. "It was definitely a professor?"

On that point they all agreed. "Aye, one of the medical assistants found him."

"In the mortuary, I heard," piped up one of the others.

A medical professor. Hunt felt his chest tighten. "Do you know his name?"

The students looked blankly at one another. "I can't remember," one of them confessed. "Someone did tell me."

"Was it a Professor Miller?"

The student's eyes widened in recognition. "Aye, that was the name. Angus Miller."

Hunt felt sick. He hadn't especially *liked* Miller, but the man didn't deserve to die. He wondered uneasily if Miller kept notes regarding his supplemental bodies and their supplier. If he had indeed been murdered, then all his journals and correspondence would come under scrutiny. *Shit…*

The other students didn't share his concerns. "The university will be shut for the next two days, and the medical college until the end of the week," one said.

"The polis will catch him," another predicted.

The student who had revealed the unexpected holiday snorted. "They never caught the Ripper."

"That was the London polis. *Our* polis caught Canning, the *Glasgow* Ripper."

Hunt left.

*

The shop bell jingled as Hunt entered. "You're back early." Foley dropped his newspaper onto the counter.

Hunt checked that the shop was empty of customers. "Miller's dead. Rumour suggests foul play."

Foley stared at him. "How?"

He shook his head. "I've no idea. He was found in the medical school mortuary this morning, and the police have closed the university. That's all I know."

"Do you think it's connected to us? Maybe someone found out Miller was stealing bodies and killed him for it."

Body snatchers had earned the ire of the city's populace decades prior, but there was nothing to suggest anyone knew they had resurrected the practice. "I don't think so, how would anyone know? Maybe there's a connection to Amy Newfield, Miller did do some snooping on our behalf."

"Don't forget that hanged killer we carted round to the college for him yesterday. Maybe giving us that job trod on some toes? I know a copper, we grew up together. I'll see if we can meet tomorrow for a few pints."

Hunt was taken aback by this show of initiative from Foley. "Good idea. You do realise that without Miller, our financial situation just turned to shit?"

"Oh, aye." Foley's tone was grim. "I realised."

Chapter Nine

Foley walked into the Old College Bar just after seven. The bar was small and confined to a single room with thick wooden beams supporting the low ceiling. Despite its size, the sparse lighting and heavy tobacco smoke gave the taproom a sense of privacy. It had been a few years since he'd last visited this particular public house, but he found it comfortably familiar. He sat on a stool at the bar and waited for his friend to arrive.

Not wanting to antagonise the bartender, Foley ordered an ale. That was half the reason, certainly. The other half was that he enjoyed a drink. Running a hand over an unshaven jaw, he permitted himself a rare moment of honest introspection; he didn't drink because he enjoyed it, he drank because he *needed* it. Couldn't stop, didn't want to. Melancholy had plagued him most of his life, and intoxication was the only cure.

A cure that exacted a heavy toll each morning, that made the struggle to rise from bed that much harder. He won every battle, but the victories were becoming increasingly hard-won and longer fought. His late father had once told him that drink was a good servant but a bad master; he knew now what he meant.

It had been different in the army. A hard life even for an officer, the discipline and duties had distracted him from his black moods and the poison inside that sapped his strength and snatched away dreams of hope and happiness. He had seen soldiers driven to drink by the horrors of battle, but what he remembered chiefly about his own such experiences was how *alive* he had felt with death all around.

Now there was no hiding from his melancholy. It was waiting for him each morning when he awoke, and it found him in his pharmacy shop from where there was no escape. It hid when he was busy serving customers but pulled the walls in around him when they left, until he could barely breathe.

He had been content in the army. Damn Seamus for dying, and damn himself for leaving the army to take his brother's place in that damned prison of a shop. A prison that offered escape in another form: laudanum. Alcohol mixed with opium for those bleakest of days when alcohol itself wasn't enough. His trade gave him easy access to the drug, and the knowledge of how much was safe to take.

Wil Hunt's arrival in his life had eased the loneliness and offered a welcome distraction. The money from Hunt's rent and body snatching for Miller had eased his money worries – though that latter income was now gone – but the risk of discovery had helped Foley, too. There was no time to feel sorry for yourself when you chanced having to explain to a police constable why there was a corpse in your wagon. Between the disappearing Newfield corpse and Miller's murder, his life had incident enough that his thoughts turned less often to the more final solution lying at the bottom of his old army trunk.

John Grant's arrival interrupted his self-contemplation. Foley finished his pint and ordered another two.

"Foley, how're you doing?" Grant asked as he joined him at the bar. His fair hair was cut short, he had grown a beard, and his face was more lined, but little else had changed about the man. Apart from the eyes; they were more guarded than Foley remembered.

He paid for the drinks and handed one to Grant, motioning for him to follow. "I can't complain, Grant. How's yourself and the missus?" He walked to a vacant table, his friend following.

"Grand, Foley, grand. She's pregnant with our second." He put his grey bowler hat on the table next to Foley's.

"Second? I didn't know you had a first." Foley sat across from Grant and tried to picture his friend as a father.

"You didn't? God, man, it *has* been a while. Wee John turns two in August. The babbie's due in September." The hardness in his eyes softened when he talked of his family.

Foley smiled and raised his glass in salutation, dismayed by how fast time seemed to pass. It raised uncomfortable questions about his own life. "Congratulations."

"Cheers. How's your shop? Are you stepping out with anyone?" he asked with a wink.

"The pharmacy's doing well." Foley didn't want to talk about it. "I was seeing a girl for a while, but nothing came of it." He shrugged. "How's life as a copper?"

Grant took another gulp of ale and wiped the foam from his mouth. "Busy. The hours are shite but the pay's not bad. I'm a sergeant now."

Foley leaned forward, lowering his voice. "To be honest, Grant, your job is why we're meeting, friendship aside."

Grant's smile lessened. "If I can help you, I will. But there are limits, even for an old friend."

Foley raised his hands in reassurance. "I know, I know. I won't get you into any bother. I'm just looking for some information."

"On what?"

"A Professor Angus Miller was found dead in the Glasgow University yesterday. I knew him, can you tell me anything about his death?"

"The professor?" Grant sipped from his beer thoughtfully. "I've heard about it, aye. Bit of a queer one. He was in the medical school mortuary two nights ago, preparing that bastard Canning for an autopsy demonstration in the morning. He was found dead instead."

"Aye, I know that much, I heard it was murder. It was me and a friend who took Canning's body from the prison to the college."

"You did? Odd job for a pharmacist. But aye, the case is a damned strange one. He was found yesterday morning by a mortuary assistant, lying on a table and covered with a bloody sheet."

"Sounds bad, but what was so strange about it?"

"Well, for one thing, the killer took their time with Miller."

"He was tortured?" Foley had thought Miller had maybe disturbed a thief and been killed in panic. That sounded unlikely now. *Poor bastard.*

"Oh aye, he had a right bad night." Grant gave him a look. "One more thing; we didn't find Canning's body anywhere in the college, and we searched every bloody inch."

Another murder and another missing body. Foley took a long draught from his pint and hunched his shoulders. "Was there anything else odd about it?"

"Aye. My inspector reckons it was an accomplice of Canning's who killed the professor and took Canning's body, but the doors were still locked, and the window was broken out, not in."

He mulled it over. "So, the killer was already inside?"

Grant finished his drink and nodded. "We're trying to keep that quiet. We don't want rumours of Canning being some sort of bogeyman."

Foley returned to the bar and brought back another two pints. "What about the girl murdered near the Southern Necropolis last week?"

Grant gave a derisive snort and leaned closer. His earlier reserve was gone. "Murder? More like murders. We've found four bodies over there in the past week, but there's something damned funny about that case, too. The first dead girl was in the newspapers, but the other three deaths were reported to the procurator fiscal as natural causes and kept quiet."

"Another *three?*" Foley almost choked on his ale. *What have we bloody gotten ourselves caught up in? Easy work and easier money, you said, Hunt.*

"Aye, another two lassies and a fella. The official story says they all died naturally, but I know Constable McIlroy, who was the first to see the second body, and Constable White, who saw the fourth. Both bodies had mangled throats, same as the first girl found. I'd wager my pay the third body suffered the same."

Another two dead girls. "Were they identified?"

"Aye; named, buried and forgotten."

"Either of them called Amy Newfield?"

Grant showed no recognition at the name. "No, who's she?"

Foley shook his head. "No one." The lack of journalistic interest piqued his interest. "Why haven't we heard anything about this?"

Grant sounded more weary than bitter. "You think this is the first time this has happened? Every now and then a body is found, sometimes mutilated, sometimes missing blood;

often both. And the procurator fiscal rules it accidental, natural or the work of a wild dog.

"But I've never heard of four such deaths all so soon or close to each other. Instead of telling the lads who walk that beat to spend more time there at night, they've been told to stay away from the Southern Necropolis after dark."

Where we dug up Amy Newfield, who's still missing. "Why would these murders be covered up? What's to gain?"

"Honestly? I've no idea. What I do know is that to question too closely can lead a man to a bad end. Two of my colleagues found a body three years ago. They didn't believe he died of the cold and made a nuisance of themselves about it. One was stabbed by a supposed footpad while off-duty, and the other apparently got drunk and fell in the Clyde. After that, we stopped looking too closely."

"Jesus," Foley muttered. It sounded like a conspiracy.

Grant looked him hard in the eye. "Why is this important to you? Miller you knew, fair enough. But what's he to do with the Southern Necropolis deaths?"

"Maybe nothing." Or maybe everything. "I won't know if I don't look."

Grant didn't look satisfied. "I hear Miller was maybe involved in something on the side. You wouldn't know anything about that, would you?"

Foley was tempted to confess the whole body snatching arrangement but decided against it. Miller might be dead, but it was Wil Hunt's secret too. "I did some business with him," he said after a moment. "Miller sent patients to me for medication, and I'd pay him for the custom."

Grant shook his head in amused acceptance of the explanation. "Enough of this shite, let's enjoy a few pints and speak of happier things. Cheers." He raised his pint.

Foley clinked his own glass against it, hating that he'd lied to one friend to protect another. "Cheers."

*

Hunt glanced at his pocket watch, more from habit than any real interest in the time. It was after eleven and the streets were empty.

Foley had returned home the previous night after meeting with his police friend, half-drunk and bearing disquieting news; there had been a further three suspicious deaths near the cemetery, and Miller's murder was not the result of a robbery gone bad. The bodies of Amy Newfield and Richard Canning were still missing, though Hunt clung to a faint hope that they'd discover Miss Newfield's fate. He hated mysteries. Ones he couldn't solve, at least.

With few other avenues of investigation available, Hunt had proposed that they visit the streets near to the Southern Necropolis the following night. Something was wrong there, and not knowing what happened to Amy Newfield's body was like an itch he couldn't scratch. Foley had grudgingly agreed to the plan on the condition that if they found nothing, they would drop their investigation and move on. With Miller dead, and motivated solely by curiosity and conscience, Hunt agreed it was almost time to admit defeat and direct their efforts to securing further employment.

Foley had suggested that they split up to cover more ground, each carrying a whistle to summon the other should trouble find them. A carriage passed Hunt at a stately canter, the curtain twitching aside to reveal the passenger's interest.

Hunt had thought it a fair plan at first, but with a further two hours of cold boredom looming ahead, his enthusiasm was waning. Mindful of the recent murders, he carried a baton for protection.

Movement in the distance caught his attention, and he spotted a ragged figure crossing the street. He would have blown his whistle and waited for Foley had it been a male, but the petite build suggested a female. Hunt broke into a run and followed her towards a derelict building. He held his whistle tightly, wondering if he should summon Foley anyway. If the female lived in the area, she might have seen something.

He slowed as he reached the building and freed his baton from his coat pocket. A wooden board hung loose from a window. The building's decayed condition suggested it had been derelict for a long time, an ideal haunt for the homeless and destitute. Hunt permitted himself a small smile as he fingered his whistle; she must be hiding inside. *Found you.* A soft scraping sounded to his right, and he turned.

A young woman stepped out from the shadows and moved towards him, a shapeless brown cloth falling from her shoulders. It was what lay beneath that he recognised first; Amy Newfield's funeral dress, bone-white cotton now stained and torn. The still serenity that had graced her features days earlier was gone, replaced by a feral hunger.

He stumbled backwards. Her hair was lank and tangled, dirt staining her pale, wasted face. But there was no doubt it was Amy Newfield. *Alive ... Miller was right.*

She lunged forwards and snatched at him. Both baton and whistle fell from his hands and clattered off the cobbles.

Caught off-guard and off-balance, Hunt struggled to break free from her grip but failed. He cried out, more from instinct than any conscious intent to alert Foley. She craned her neck up and her mouth snapped at his throat. Hunt swung his right elbow forward and cracked her on the side of the head. "Stop fighting, I'm here to help!"

She was momentarily stunned, but recovered before he could take the initiative, slamming him against the wall.

He fell winded to the ground and she pounced on him, her icy fingers clawing his throat. He tried to dislodge them, but was dismayed to find her strength a match for his. Shouting and footfalls could be heard in the distance. *Foley?* Fear and asphyxia numbed his limbs, making his resistance sluggish and ineffectual. His vision blurred…

The pressure left his throat and he gulped in air, relishing every burning breath. His vision cleared, and he saw Amy Newfield struggling in the grip of two rough-looking men wearing dirty, ill-mended clothes and dark bunnets. He struggled back to his feet and swallowed painfully.

Gathering up his tattered dignity, he nodded at his saviours. "Most timely, gentlemen, but don't hurt her. I think she's lost her wits."

One of the men turned to him, his scarred face flushed with excitement. "Your girl's a rough one, all right. If you can't handle her, maybe we should show you how?" He backhanded Miss Newfield, the blow driving her to her knees. His companion laughed.

Nausea soured Hunt's belly as he realised his troubles were

just beginning. He felt the urge to turn and run, to leave the girl to her fate; she had tried to kill him, after all, and even gallantry had its limits. If he was no match for one crazed girl, two footpads sharing a long familiarity with violence would make short, bloody work of him.

But he stood his ground, too scared to fight and too stubborn to run. "Leave her alone." His voice sounded feeble even to himself.

"Brewer, sort out Sir Galahad." The smaller man tightened his grip on Amy Newfield's arm. She knelt, oblivious, tendrils of filthy dark hair dangling across her bowed face.

The larger man advanced on Hunt and raised his fists, impatient to be done with him.

Fear and adrenalin clouded Hunt's ability to think. He just stood there, his thoughts fragmented. Where the hell was Foley?

The smaller man guarded Amy Newfield with an ugly look of anticipation on his pockmarked face while he waited for his friend to beat Hunt bloody.

Miss Newfield looked up, brushing the hair from her eyes. Despite her attack on him, Hunt felt a pang of pity; she was in for a bad night.

A single savage motion broke her free of the man's grip and she reared up at him. The man's attention was on the brewing fight, and he was knocked backwards. She ducked her head towards his throat, and his shriek echoed across the street as he tried and failed to push her off.

The larger footpad, Brewer, turned back to his friend. Both he and Hunt watched in disbelief as Amy Newfield savaged the downed man's throat and drank his spilling blood. The brute called Brewer ran at her. "Get off him, you mad bitch!" He aimed a brutal kick that sent her sprawling onto the road.

The smaller man lay on the ground and clutched his ravaged throat as blood streamed between his fingers and pooled between the cobbles.

Amy Newfield got back to her feet, her face smeared red. She licked off the blood around her mouth. Her fingers wiped off the blood her tongue couldn't reach, which in turn she licked clean. Brewer lunged at her and she met him head on. They struggled, and she briefly held her own against him, a footpad likely well-practiced in robbery and rapine.

Brewer's greater strength saw him gain the upper hand. Hunt was torn between aiding the girl who'd tried to kill him, or fleeing. A rapid tempo of horseshoes cracking against stone grew steadily louder, and he heard shouts coming from the opposite direction.

A carriage drew up and a door opened as it slowed. A woman swathed in a dark cloak jumped lithely out onto the road. The driver sat motionless in the front, studiously ignoring the confrontation.

Amy Newfield and the footpad separated to face the new arrival. The stranger grabbed hold of Brewer, her hands snaking towards his head and twisting savagely before he could react. He collapsed like a string-cut puppet.

The footpad dealt with, she turned to Miss Newfield who leapt at her, only to be fended off with insulting ease. A bone-deep chill washed over Hunt, a tidal wave of fear. Amy Newfield's expression revealed that she too had been struck by this inexplicable sensation, her defiance crumbling into cowed obedience.

The stranger escorted a passive Amy Newfield to the carriage and helped her inside. Hunt found his voice. "Miss Newfield!" he shouted, drawing the attention of both her and the stranger. He took a step back, wishing he'd kept his mouth shut for once. The woman stepped towards Hunt with the same predatory grace she'd exhibited in killing the footpad.

A gunshot rang out and she stopped. She gave Hunt a weighing look before returning to the carriage. The driver cracked his whip and the carriage rumbled off with Amy Newfield and her captor inside. A dark cloth covering the carriage's livery came loose to reveal the first few letters.

Hunt leaned over and threw up, conscious of someone running towards him. He looked up and recognised the newcomer as Foley. He didn't recognise the revolver he carried.

Foley was breathing heavily, his face flushed but eyes alert. "Did you just get beaten up by a girl?"

Hunt massaged his still-raw throat to hide the trembling of his hands. "It was Amy Newfield," he managed.

Foley's eyes widened, and he whistled at the name. "So you were beaten up by a *dead* girl?"

"Very funny." Hunt turned his attention to the footpads lying on the ground. One had a broken neck and the other bled heavily from his throat.

"I was at the far end of the road when I saw those two haul her off you. By the time I got here that carriage had arrived," Foley said.

"I saw that carriage earlier. Or one similar."

Foley nodded. "I saw it earlier tonight, too. We're not the only ones taking an interest in the deaths here."

"I don't know what that woman said to Miss Newfield, but she got into the carriage as meek as a lamb."

"So I saw." He shoved his revolver into a coat pocket.

Hunt envied his calm demeanour. Foley might have left the army, but the army hadn't left him. "Where did you get that gun?"

"It's my old service revolver." He grinned, or at least bared teeth. "I keep it in my trunk, but tonight I thought it might come in handy."

"You thought right. Newfield half-killed me, and the woman from the carriage looked set on finishing the job." Hunt remembered her gaze and shivered; she'd give Death pause.

Foley knelt by the two footpads. "This one's dead." He pointed to the other. "He's still alive but losing a lot of blood."

"Yes, she bit him." Hunt could still see Amy Newfield's pale face, blood dripping from her mouth.

"That's some bite. He'll die without help."

Hunt remembered the looks of bestial lust borne by the footpads. "Leave him, let's go."

Foley looked surprised at his callous disregard, but didn't argue. "Aye, you're right. The gunshots will bring trouble."

As they left, Foley glanced back. "Well, we found her. Alive, if not right in the head."

"Alive and feeding off blood. She drank his blood down like mother's milk."

"She *drank–?* Bloody hell. We've found the killer, then."

"Maybe. But if she's just a deranged madwoman killing

anyone she comes across, why'd the procurator fiscal write off three of her victims as natural deaths? How did a scrawny girl in her funeral dress manage to fight off two hardened bastards?" He thought back to the carriage that had arrived. "And why would anyone trouble themselves to collect her in a carriage?"

"I don't know. Did you see the carriage's livery?"

"It was mostly covered. All I saw was an *M*, a *c* and a *B* at the start. Christ!" He kicked at the kerb in frustration.

Foley looked thoughtful. "McBride Carriages, maybe. The family's got a bad name, but they own one of the larger carriage companies in the city. I'll visit them tomorrow and see if I can learn anything."

"Monday would be better," Hunt suggested. "Tomorrow's too soon, too obvious."

"Monday it is."

Hunt looked at him. "Or we could drop the matter." Not that he wanted to, but people were dying. He wanted to gauge Foley's resolve.

Foley didn't answer at first. "No. We dug her up, and now she's been taken. We owe it to her to find out who took her and why. Or it'll eat us up."

Hunt smiled. "My thoughts, too. Let's see where it leads."

Foley blew out a breath. "I need a drink."

Chapter Ten

Travelling from Glasgow to the west coast was a tedious affair, though the carriage was comfortable enough. The last stage of the journey passed mostly in silence as Mother read and Father rested his eyes. Hunt passed the time looking out of the window. The high moors were an untamed wilderness broken up by woodland and rugged hills. A herd of deer marked the carriage's passage with watchful suspicion while hardy sheep grazed placidly, their weaker kin culled by a hard winter. The land was beautiful to behold but slowed their progress.

Descending the steep Haylie Brae was fraught with danger, but the driver seemed up to the task and navigated the bend safely. The Isle of Cumbrae rose out of the Clyde Estuary to the west, blue waters turning iron-grey as dusk approached. The carriage reached the foot of the hill and passed through the seaside town of Largs.

Stone dykes carved up the eastern farmland and parcelled it into fields. The land might once have resembled the untamed moors passed through earlier, but it had long since been domesticated for agriculture. What had once been a mixed palette of wild greens and peaty browns had been distilled into patches of earthy-brown potato crops, grazing pastures of washed greens, and fields of golden barley.

Sir Arthur Williamson's Dunclutha estate lay to the north of Largs, much of it covered by woodland. The carriage passed a well-tended lawn decorated with several sculptures depicting figures in Greek or Roman-style dress, and two-foot high hedges arranged to form a mock maze. Dunclutha House was a large misshapen mansion standing four storeys tall, that had been extended twice, with a pillar standing on either side of the main entrance.

The carriage stopped in front of the house. Father opened his eyes. “Shall we?”

The driver opened the carriage doors and helped his passengers out. A footman waited to escort them inside while a further two unloaded their luggage. Hunt stretched his legs and filled his lungs with the evening air, marvelling at the unfamiliar smells. A resident of Glasgow, he was accustomed to less savoury odours.

It was good to be away from the city, if only for respite from recent events. Amy Newfield was alive, but there was more going on than a girl prematurely buried. Their errant ‘corpse’ had attracted the interest of an unknown party.

Hunt had spent a restless night reliving the encounter in his mind. He couldn’t put his finger on it but there had been something *wrong* about her, and not just her unnatural strength.

With Professor Miller dead, a more immediate problem had befallen him; money, and his forthcoming lack thereof. He had enough saved to see him through the summer, if he was frugal. But after that…

Enough. He would enjoy the weekend and work something out when he returned home. Perhaps Miller’s successor would be amenable to continuing the arrangement?

Sir Arthur Williamson waited in the foyer to greet them. Still trim despite entering his middle years, his once-black hair was mostly grey, and his face had gathered a few more lines.

“It was good of you to invite us, Sir Arthur,” Father said as they walked to the drawing room.

“Not at all, Hunt, your presence has been missed. I think it’s been eight months since we last met, in London?”

Father nodded. “I believe you’re right. Gareth Welworth’s soiree.”

Sir Arthur turned to Hunt. “It’s been longer since I last saw you, Wilton.”

“Yes, sir.” It had been a particularly hot summer, he remembered. “That was in London, too. Three years ago.”

“Indeed,” Mother said. “We spent the summer in London as a family. Mr and Mrs Dearing send their regrets, Sir Arthur. Mr Dearing’s mother isn’t keeping well, so he and the family have gone to visit her and will be unable to attend this weekend." Hunt had been sorry to learn Uncle Richard's mother was unwell, but not sorry that he would not have to suffer his cousins' company this weekend.

"I'm sorry to hear that, Mrs Hunt. Please give them my regards." Sir Arthur looked pained at the news and offered her a commiserating smile.

"The poor dear has never truly recovered from her last bout of pneumonia and sickens easily."

The other guests were in the drawing room, engaged in conversations of their own. Weekends at Sir Arthur's were well-regarded and well-attended affairs. A keen sportsman and resolute bachelor, hunting was one of his passions as evidenced by walls adorned with numerous trophy heads. By all accounts he had fended off several attempts to snare him in matrimony over the years. Whenever discussion turned to his status, he laughed it off and claimed to be too busy to give a wife the time and attention she deserved. It was whispered that his inclinations ran towards young men, but if so then he kept such assignations discreet. A cousin in Dumfries stood heir to the estate.

Sir Arthur led the Hunts over to the other guests, most of whom were unknown to Wilton. In a charming breach of etiquette, he insisted on introducing them himself, a task ordinarily performed by the butler. "Ladies and gentlemen, the last of our guests have arrived. It's my honour to introduce you all to Mr and Mrs Hunt, and their son Mr Wilton Hunt."

A series of polite bows and murmured courtesies followed.

Sir Arthur led the Hunts around the room and introduced them to the others, the first being a middle-aged couple. "…Mr and Mrs Singer. Mr Singer's involved in the tobacco trade. I hope you've brought some of your finer cigars with you, Singer."

Lord Smith was a retired High Court judge, already well-acquainted with the Hunt family. Hunt recognised Mr Archibald Stewart's name from the newspapers, noted for his small but growing industrial empire of mills and factories. Mr Henry Hollis was a noted architect, but aloof and appeared more interested in the house's architecture and aesthetics than in the other guests. Mr William Cotter was a respected lawyer, his wife looking uneasy at being a guest in such august surroundings.

Mr Cotter's name was familiar to Hunt, but he couldn't recall from where. Monsieur François Gerrard and his wife Madame Yvette Gerrard owned a Bordeaux vineyard. Their daughter Mademoiselle Amelie Gerrard captured Hunt's interest with her dusky skin, silky black hair and easy smile. His attention didn't go unnoticed by her sullen brother Monsieur Jacques Gerrard who crossed his arms and scowled.

The guests mingled while Sir Arthur's servants attended to their needs. A pair of maids brought in sandwiches and other light foods. Hunt sipped from his wine, conscious of his mother's pointed stare when he permitted his glass to be refilled.

Hunt was an admirer of Henry Hollis' architecture and sought to speak with him regarding his work but found him discomforted by the attention. Tall, gaunt and ungainly, Mr Hollis was ill-at-ease engaging in discourse.

Hunt approached William Cotter, having remembered why the name was familiar. "Sir, forgive my interest, but you defended Richard Canning, did you not?"

Cotter's face was red from the wine. His brooding silence made Hunt afraid that he'd overstepped his bounds. He was about to try and smooth it over with an apology when Cotter nodded ponderously. "Quite so." Eyes fogged by alcohol peered at Hunt. "I'm pleased to see a young man such as yourself take an interest in current affairs." Cotter turned away slightly.

Encouraged, Hunt decided to press on. "It must have been difficult to defend such an evil man."

Cotter nodded, refusing to look back at Hunt. "It was. Lord help me, it was. To know what that devil had done, to face the task of trying one's best to convince a jury otherwise…"

Cotter fell silent, and Hunt sensed he was done with that topic. He decided an admission of his own might coax a little more from the lawyer. "I was at the execution, sir."

His gaze flickered back to Hunt with renewed interest. "Then you saw him. You saw how deep the evil ran within him."

Hunt had seen no such thing. "Yes."

"In my long career I've defended many wicked men and women. Most were found guilty, some not guilty. Some of those found guilty I believe in my heart were innocent, just as some of those I freed were guilty. Whether driven by desperation or badness of character, I have always believed it my duty to provide each and every one I represent with the best defence possible."

Troubled eyes locked with Hunt's. "Until that man."

Hunt said nothing, embarrassed by Cotter's almost-confession. He decided not to tell him that Canning's body was missing; the man was haunted by demons enough. They parted and never spoke again.

He re-joined the others in time to witness Sir Arthur succeed in coaxing the Gerrards into trying a Spanish wine, having poured a little into each of their glasses. M. and Mme Gerrard diplomatically praised it but declined more. Mlle Gerrard gamely finished her glass and laughed as Sir Arthur poured a little more in. Jacques Gerrard sipped once and pointedly set his glass aside.

Ever the gracious host, Sir Arthur amiably conceded defeat and made amends with a fresh bottle of *Château Dephaun* 1885 from the Gerrards' own vineyards.

Mr Singer tapped insistently on an empty glass with a knife until the other guests fell silent. "Ladies and gentlemen, I would like to take this opportunity to thank Sir Arthur for his hospitality." He waited until the applause died. "As he has seen fit to honour us with a vintage from our French friends," he said, nodding to the Gerrards, "I feel I must reciprocate with a small token from my own industry." Obviously pre-arranged, a footman entered the room with an open box of Singer Cigars and handed them out. The rich tang of premium tobacco soon filled the room.

Hunt's father took him by the elbow and led him aside. "Well, Wilton, how have you fared this past week?" There had been little conversation in the carriage.

My employer died, and I was beaten up by a dead girl. It's been bloody marvellous. "I've few complaints, sir."

Father looked him in the eye. "I received a bill from the Albert Club for two meals I don't recall eating, wine and brandy I did not drink, and two cigars I certainly never smoked. Can you explain this?"

"…Yes." *Shit.*

Father nodded, still holding Hunt's penitent gaze. "Don't do it again, Wilton. Am I understood?"

Hunt nodded, suitably chastened. "Yes sir, I apologise. I'll repay it." With Miller dead, repaying such a debt would gut his savings, money he was relying on until he found another source of income.

Father shook his head. "Consider it a birthday gift."

He fought to keep the relief from his face. "Thank you, sir." His liberal consumption of wine emboldened him to ask, "On the subject of gifts, could I beg one further indulgence?"

Father gave him a doubting look, his tone reserved. "Perhaps. What is it?"

Hunt looked over at Amelie Gerrard by the fireplace. "Perhaps you could entertain Monsieur Gerrard?" He considered the girl's brother. "I think Monsieur Jacques Gerrard would also appreciate your company."

Father followed Hunt's gaze to the pretty French girl. She wore her hair high but disdained the tight curls that many women favoured. "Very well, Wilton," the suggestion of a smile tugging at his lips. "I'll see what I can do."

He smiled. "Thank you."

As Father distracted the two Frenchmen with conversation, Hunt slipped over to Mlle Gerrard's side. She wore a full-length blue skirt and a high-collared tight bodice that flattered her figure. The upper arms of the sleeves were puffed out; a new fashion coming in, or a French peculiarity? "*Bonsoir, Mademoiselle Gerrard.*"

Mlle Gerrard glanced at him. "*Bonsoir, Monsieur. Parlez-vous Français?*"

Hunt assumed an easy smile. "*Un peu.* I trust you're enjoying yourself?"

The young woman nodded, her brown eyes catching the light. "Very much so, Sir Arthur is most charming, *oui*?"

"*Oui*. What brought your family to Scotland?"

"*Maman*'s grandfather was Scottish. Papa promised this trip for her forty-fifth birthday."

"And how long will you be here for, if I may be so bold?"

“Four weeks. Papa is using the holiday to make new friends for his business.”

A surreptitious glance to his right confirmed that the two Gerrard men were still speaking with his father. He mustered his courage. “If you seek a guide to show you the hidden wonders of Glasgow, Mademoiselle Gerrard, it would be my honour.” He held his breath.

She sipped from her wine. After a long, torturous moment she nodded. “I would like that. There is a circus I wish to visit.”

Tension melted into happy turmoil. “Then I’m at your disposal, Mademoiselle. Feel free to call upon me at any time.”

She smiled. “I shall, Monsieur.”

Attrition depleted the guests as the night drew on, until only a few stalwarts remained within the drawing room. After Mlle Gerrard and her family retired to bed, Hunt felt disinclined to linger. A hunt was planned for the following day, and he’d need his wits about him. Drunk on wine, whisky and perhaps the early stirrings of love, he left for his room.

Chapter Eleven

Hunt awoke out of sorts and cursed his lack of temperance the night before. The hunt beckoned, and he was resolved to look his best in front of the other guests. One in particular. Knowing Sir Arthur often held hunts, he had packed a sturdy brown tweed Norfolk jacket, matching breeches, a flat cap, and dark brown leather shoes.

He attended downstairs and broke his fast with a generous helping of fried bacon, eggs and sausage. The other guests were all present, several also the worse for wear. Hatefully hale and hearty, Sir Arthur talked enthusiastically to M. Gerrard about the hunt he had planned. Hunt's father was as clear-eyed as ever. The man's tolerance for drink was ferocious, a trait he'd neglected to share with his son.

Sir Arthur tapped his spoon against a glass. "Good morning, ladies and gentlemen." His smile was predatory. "I've arranged a day of hunting for those of you with a sporting bent."

The announcement was met with approbation, muted in some cases.

Mlle Gerrard looked clear-eyed, and Hunt hoped she intended to accompany the hunt. She'd certainly dressed for the outdoors, wearing a cream blouse and tweed walking skirt. Her hair was tied back, hanging past her shoulders in a simple tail.

"I'm too old for such excitement," said Lord Smith. Henry Hollis mumbled a similar disclaimer. Given that the hunt was to be on foot with rifles rather than on horseback with hounds, most of the women elected to remain in the house. Mlle Gerrard proved the only exception.

The would-be hunters gathered outside after breakfast to await their munitions. Hunt entertained himself in the interim with fantasies of bagging a stag and basking in the mademoiselle's admiration. He was envisaging her sullen brother slogging back in failure when the rifles arrived. Hunt familiarised himself with the workings of the rifle, two years having passed since he had last hunted with one. He hoped the passage of time hadn't eroded his marksmanship much. *Cernunnos smile on me.*

The woodland was only a short distance from the house, a mix of conifers and deciduous trees that covered most of the estate to form Sir Arthur's private hunting grounds. Much of the woodland outside of the estate had been cleared for farmland, encouraging many of the native deer to migrate into Dunclutha. Many ended up in Sir Arthur's kitchen.

The party walked towards the woods and separated into small groups. Hunt found himself partnered with Mlle Gerrard and her brother, choosing to interpret it as a wink of divine favour. He led them through the woods with as much stealth as a city man was capable of, stepping on every dry branch and twig. Mlle Gerrard seemed untroubled by their slow progress, but Jacques Gerrard's dour presence proved problematic. *Maybe he'll trip and break a leg?* Hunt kicked aside a fallen branch. *But I mustn't get my hopes up.*

Movement in his periphery brought Hunt back to the moment.

He stopped and motioned for the others to follow suit. A stag grazed unsuspectingly a fair distance ahead. Jacques brightened on spying the animal, and Mlle Gerrard stared at it in wonder. Hunt knelt and studied the beast through the vegetation. It was a fully-grown buck crowned with ten point antlers. He made a decision and motioned for Jacques to take the shot; Mlle Gerrard's reaction to the stag led him to reconsider just how well-regarded the triumphant hunter would be in her eyes.

Jacques looked surprised but grudgingly grateful. He raised his rifle and took aim. A gunshot rang out in the distance and the stag looked up, tense and wary. Hunt covered his ears and motioned for Mlle Gerrard to follow suit. Jacques fired.

The stag didn't wait to see if he had been hit; he bolted into the undergrowth.

"*Merde*!" Jacques cursed as the three of them crashed

through the vegetation to where they had last seen the animal. "I would have had him was it not for that shot."

Hunt looked around, choosing to ignore the Frenchman's profanity. "I don't see any blood, Monsieur Gerrard. At least he's not wounded."

"*Bon*." Mlle Gerrard looked at him. "Good." Her enthusiasm for the hunt had waned.

"I thank you for letting me take the shot, Mr Hunt," Jacques Gerrard said grudgingly.

Hunt clapped him on the shoulder. "Let's get moving."

As the three continued their trek through the wood, he noted Mlle Gerrard's discomfort. "Mademoiselle, it is part of nature. There are no wolves here, so the deer roam with no predator but us. Without us they would breed and breed until there wasn't enough vegetation to sustain them, and then they would starve."

She didn't appear convinced. "He looked so regal."

"Yes, but such is nature. My father says that anyone who eats meat should kill an animal, skin it, dress it, and cook its meat at least once."

"Does he?" She glanced at him. "What an odd notion. Does he also grow his own crops?" she asked facetiously.

Hunt smiled at the thought. "Not to my knowledge. My mother's the gardener in our family, but flowers are her passion, not potatoes."

They continued on. He had started the day believing hunting to be an exciting pursuit; by day's end that notion had been thoroughly disabused. After four hours of mud, discomfort and failure, he was happy to concede defeat.

The three failed hunters returned to the house in time to see two slain deer being carried into the kitchen through the side door at Sir Arthur's direction. He spotted them and grinned. "Returning empty handed, eh? I bagged one, your father the other, Wilton. But don't worry, I've enough venison maturing from last week to feed us!"

Hunt dutifully smiled. "Congratulations, Sir Arthur. I'll pass the same to my father when I see him."

"See that you do. I hear it was a fine shot." Sir Arthur looked at the Gerrards. "Come, I'll show you my wine cellar." Hunt followed them through the kitchen door. The kitchen staff began to butcher the carcasses while Sir Arthur led Hunt and the Gerrard siblings down a winding staircase to the cellar.

The only light came from Sir Arthur's candle, but Hunt's eyes adjusted quickly. The cellar was wide and stone-floored, mostly empty aside from a large cask and sturdy wine-rack. He smelled old wood and stale beer. Sir Arthur led the brother and sister to the wine-rack and pulled out several of his rarer vintages for their inspection.

"This is *Château Pétrus*, from 1878," Sir Arthur said of one bottle he held reverently. Jacques Gerrard regarded it ambivalently, unsurprising as it came from a rival Bordeaux vineyard.

Not terribly interested in wine beyond its consumption, Hunt explored the cellar.

He noticed a door hidden in darkness at the end of the room. "Where does that lead to?"

"Nowhere," Sir Arthur answered, sounding unaccountably terse. "It's just an old storeroom. We should return upstairs."

Hunt gave the door one last look as he climbed back up to the kitchen. Sir Arthur's evasion only made him more curious, but he didn't begrudge any man his secrets.

*

Hunt undressed, his legs aching from the trek. Hot baths had been arranged for the hunt-weary guests, and Hunt spent thirty minutes relaxing in a copper tub before climbing out and drying himself. He shaved and dressed, feeling clean and refreshed. His reflection stared back from the shaving mirror, and he wondered whether he'd favour a moustache. A consideration for another day.

The guests sat at the long table in the dining room which was dimly lit for a more intimate atmosphere. Sir Arthur took his place at the end of the table, and two footmen waited to attend him and his guests. The only absence was Mr Hollis who had departed after breakfast.

Hunt sat next to his father and across from Amelie and Jacques Gerrard. He turned to his father. "I hear you shot a deer today, sir. Congratulations."

Father assumed a look of modest pleasure as the rest of the

table echoed Hunt's sentiment. "I was fortunate." He nodded to the elder Frenchman. "Truthfully, I'm indebted to Monsieur Gerrard for graciously permitting me the shot."

The table duly applauded M. Gerrard who reddened at the attention.

Sir Arthur cast a mischievous look at Wilton Hunt and Jacques Gerrard. "I think that your sons could learn from your example, gentlemen."

Jacques spoke first. "*Au contraire*, Sir Arthur. Mr Wilton Hunt permitted me to take his shot at the stag we spotted." He gave a shrug. "I missed."

Hunt was surprised at the normally sullen Jacques Gerrard speaking well of him, but he rose to the occasion. "Monsieur Gerrard is a guest in this country, and as such I thought it only hospitable that he be given the shot. The beast took flight through no fault of his; it was startled by another gunshot." He glanced at his father. "Perhaps yours, sir."

"Well spoken," said Sir Arthur.

"Regardless," Hunt said, standing up and feeling awkward as he did so, "I would like to propose a toast to our host who not only provided us with dinner, but who has also hosted us within his home." He raised his wine glass. "Sir Arthur."

The others repeated the toast.

Sir Arthur stood. "You are all most welcome. The pleasure of your fine company is thanks enough."

The soup course was served first, a thick broth hosting a heavy selection of vegetables and chunks of meat.

"That was well said," Father murmured.

"I'm not entirely graceless, sir."

"Not entirely, no. I am surprised at your generosity in allowing Jacques Gerrard to take your shot. Was it to placate him as part of your campaign to court his sister?"

Hunt shrugged. "I decided that letting him take the shot might raise me in his estimation. Besides, Mademoiselle Gerrard was rather taken with the stag. Shooting the beast was unlikely to win her favour."

Father gave him a shrewd look. "So, if your generosity towards Jacques failed to earn his regard, then he would have alienated his sister by killing the noble beast. Well played, Wilton."

He was surprised his father had discerned the motive behind his supposed generosity. "Thank you." *I think.*

"Though I'm still of the opinion that any man or woman who eats meat should at one time in their life hunt, kill–"

"–dress and cook an animal. I remember. Mademoiselle Gerrard asked if you also believe that those of us who eat vegetables should likewise sow and harvest."

"And deprive farmers of their livelihood? Perish the thought."

The soup plates were removed to make room for the venison, vegetables and gravy.

The meal was delicious, a far cry from the indifferent fare he cooked for himself in Foley's cramped kitchen. Hunt noticed his mother speaking with Mme Gerrard and hoped she was helping rather than hindering his chances with Mlle Gerrard. He held few illusions that his hoped-for friendship with the mademoiselle had any future but decided it worth pursuing regardless. Mother seemed fond of the Gerrard wine; perhaps that would encourage her to work on his behalf.

The group returned to the drawing room after dinner. More bottles of Gerrard wine awaited consumption, and the guests enthusiastically obliged.

Hunt approached Jacques Gerrard. "What you said at dinner was kind, thank you. You would have killed that stag had he not been startled."

The Frenchman gave a rare half-smile. "Thank you." He leaned closer. "But I still do not want you near my sister." He clapped Hunt hard on the back and walked off.

Damned French. Hunt joined his parents. "I'm glad you invited me."

"Not at all, son, you are most welcome." Father puffed contentedly from a cigar.

"Quite so, Wilton," Mother said. "Madame Gerrard and I have been discussing you."

She was deliberately holding him in suspense, he knew sourly.

"She has questions regarding your future, Wilton." She sipped from her wine and eyed him. "As do I."

Hunt cleared his throat, determined not to be manipulated.

"Perhaps you're both being presumptuous? I've offered to show the mademoiselle around Glasgow, nothing more."

But she knew him too well. "Oh, Wilton, you're clearly smitten with the girl."

"I'm studying science, not visiting opium dens." He tried not to sound petulant. *Is matricide really so terrible?*

"If you wish to request this girl's hand in marriage, you must have more to offer than animal drawings and quotes from Mr Charles Darwin. The Gerrards will only entertain your suit if you are in a respectable profession."

Quelle surprise. Hunt leaned against a wall and waited.

"If your heart is set *against* Law," her voice betrayed a lack of comprehension as to why this would be the case, "then you would do well to immerse yourself in our company and learn the trade."

Or I can dig up corpses when I'm not getting beaten up by them. For the first time he began to seriously doubt his course. Leaving home to be his own man was all good and well, but it didn't make him an attractive prospect for marriage. He hadn't considered that at the time. Living in comfort with a pretty wife and children scarcely compared to a life of ennui in a scabby flat above an ill-managed pharmacy run by an alcoholic laudanum-addict.

He barely noticed a footman refilling his glass.

*

Graham Andrews usually turned a blind eye to the antics of the other tenement residents, but even he noticed the rope lying outside his flat. One end was tied to the communal staircase bannister, the other end lying loose on the landing. He thought no more of it and put his key into the lock. It refused to turn, jammed stubbornly in the lock. He swore and pulled back on the door until the key relented. There was a rusty squeal of hinges as the door opened. *I need to get that damned thing oiled*. The flat was small and he lived, slept and ate in its single room. Food-smeared dishes sat piled up on the rough-finished table, and dirty clothes lay strewn on the floor.

Andrews ignored the clutter and placed a bottle of gin on

the table. The naked floorboards creaked under his weight as he struck a match to light a candle on the table.

"That's better," a voice said softly.

His flinch almost knocked the candle over. A closet door swung open and a man stepped out. His face was gaunt and wasted, but there was something familiar about him. He wore a dark grey suit.

"Careful, Mr Andrews, we don't want a fire."

Andrews looked around wildly and grabbed a knife from the table. "Who the hell are you?" A thought occurred to him. "How did you get in? That door was locked."

A heavy thud echoed off the wooden floor. He looked down and saw a large collection of keys all linked together by an iron ring.

"It took eight keys – or was it nine? – until I found one that matched your lock. You really need to get that door seen to, by the way. Maybe oil the hinges?"

Andrews tried to swallow down his fear. "Who are you?" he repeated. "What do you want – money?"

"No, not money. Don't you recognise me?" The stranger tilted his chin and looked left and right to give him a good look at his profile. "Or do you not even bother to look at the faces anymore?"

Confused, he said nothing.

"Still not familiar? Not even a little?" His smile turned cruel. "I know! Picture me with a black hood over my head and a noose around my neck. The newspapers said unkind things about me."

Andrews felt an ache in his chest. *No.* He knew the man now. "Canning," he whispered, raising the knife higher.

Richard Canning clapped his hands together slowly. "I knew you'd remember me eventually. We weren't formally introduced on Monday morning. Not even a handshake, hangman to hanged man."

"You died," Andrews told the dead man. *I sent you to Hell.*

"Oh, don't worry, you did your usual good work," came the mocking reassurance, followed by a pause. "Well, not quite your *usual* work, was it, Mr Andrews?" Canning took a step towards him, his eyes reflecting captured candlelight. His tone turned sharp and angry. "Was it?"

"Stay back," he pleaded.

Canning ignored him. "William Marwood devised a scientific method in 1872 that ensured my neck would be broken. Based on weight and height, I think." He crossed his arms. "Imagine my surprise when instead of a quick, clean drop, I suffered a slow, messy strangulation."

Andrews edged back. "How can you be here?"

Canning waved that off as unimportant.

"I was paid to do it." Andrews was desperate. "I was paid to make sure your neck didn't break."

Canning paused. "Who paid you?"

"Some priest. He said it was important!"

"A priest, interesting." Canning looked him in the eye. "A priest arranged my resurrection, if it can be called such. Perhaps my neck snapping would have prevented me from rising. Perhaps I owe you thanks after all?"

Andrews lowered his knife as Canning sounded reflective. *If I helped him cheat death, then maybe–*

"Unfortunately," Canning's tone turned jolly, "that same 'priest' sent me to kill you. 'Tie up the loose end,' he said. He's more Old Testament than New, I fear."

Andrews opened his mouth as Canning lunged. His knife fell to the floor, and a blow to his throat left him choking. He reeled in fresh agony as Canning's knee thumped into his groin. Canning grabbed him from under the shoulders and dragged him back towards the door and out into the close where the rope waited. He tried to cry out but failed, his throat still traumatised from the punch. Canning picked up the loose end of the rope from the landing and tied it round his neck. "Goodbye, Mr Andrews."

His fall over the bannister was short and brutal. The rope caught him and pulled tight around his neck. It burned his throat, and he tried to breathe, to scream. Only he couldn't.

Chapter Twelve

Tam Foley stood outside the McBride Carriages office and decided, not for the first time, that this was a bad idea. Hunt and he suspected that the carriage sent to catch Amy Newfield belonged to McBride Carriages, the McBrides being a family notorious for crime and violence. He was to visit this company and … what exactly? He couldn't bloody well ask them directly about it, and subtlety was not one of his strengths.

The McBride Carriages office and yard were located next to the Clyde, near Jamaica Street. Wagons were parked next to carriages, suggesting that they operated their haulage business from the same yard.

Foley took a breath. He'd fought amidst blood, shit and flies in the Sudan; he could do this. He gathered his nerve and entered the office.

The clerk at the front desk looked up from his ledger. "Can I help you?"

Foley tried for nonchalance. "I'm looking to hire a carriage for … Wednesday." *Idiot, I should have planned my story before coming in.*

"This Wednesday? Today's Monday, you're not giving us much notice. Wait here." The clerk disappeared into the back office.

Foley noted the room to be sparsely decorated, the floor rough unvarnished wood. He was still trying to decide just why he would need a carriage at such short notice when the clerk returned in the company of another man.

The new arrival looked stocky and tough, a real hard bastard with unkempt whiskers and a shaven head. Foley took him for a teamster at first. He wore a dark frock coat with a high starched collar, a thug dressed like a gentleman.

"I'm Roddy McBride. Donaldson tells me you're looking to hire a carriage?"

A McBride. Damn me. Foley's valiant struggle to piece together a story was not helped by the intimidating presence of the elder McBride brother. "Well, aye. I mean, I need a carriage to take a group of us to the Variety Theatre on Wednesday night, Mr McBride." He hoped they didn't ask what was playing; he had no idea.

McBride looked down at the clerk. "Wednesday, have we anything free?"

Donaldson opened a diary and leafed through it. "We've two carriages available, sir."

McBride nodded and gave Foley a weighing look. "Aye, we can help you. Donaldson will make the arrangements."

Foley forced a smile. "That's grand." He realised he was about to arrange a carriage he didn't need, while no closer to learning who hired the carriage that took the Newfield girl. "I saw one of your carriages last Thursday night and was impressed by how well the driver handled it. My mother will be riding with us, and she can't abide being jostled. If he's free, could we have that driver?" A few coins to him might reveal the identity of the lady passenger who broke a footpad's neck and took Amy Newfield away.

"What street did you see the carriage on, and what time?" Donaldson asked.

"Caledonia Road, late Thursday night." Foley prayed he wasn't sweating too much. The mood in the room changed, and he realised he'd managed to both strike gold and err badly with one comment.

McBride stared at him with narrowed eyes. "Caledonia Road, you say. You're mistaken. We had no carriages anywhere near there on Thursday."

Foley persevered. "I'm sure the carriage was one of yours. It was very late, after eleven."

"If it was after eleven, then it was dark. You made a mistake, it wasn't one of ours." McBride's tone discouraged further argument. "We've made a mistake, too; we've no carriages free on Wednesday. Be on your way."

Foley took the hint. "Sorry to bother you, I'll be leaving." He hurried out of the office, wondering why he kept letting

Hunt talk him into trouble. McBride's overreaction left him with little doubt that he'd found the right company and that they had something to hide. All that remained was to find a way to look at the company records and learn who hired the carriage. There was one sure way, but it carried risks. He smiled at Hunt's likely reaction.

*

The locomotive hauled its carriages across the iron bridge, smoke streaming from its funnel. It was already slowing as it approached the station, halting alongside the platform with a final hiss of steam.

The carriage doors swung open, and passengers spilled out onto a platform bustling with activity as commuters came and went. Piercing shrieks interrupted the general cacophony as guards blew their whistles and trains hooted in reply before departing. The air bore the smoky tang of burnt coal.

One disembarked passenger walked the platform with the straight-backed confidence of a military man. Wolfgang Steiner had never served in any nation's army, but war had consumed almost twenty of his forty-six years. It was a quiet and deadly war, without borders or battlefields, but with no end of casualties. Time would tell if Glasgow was another front in the conflict. Steiner pulled out his pocket watch and noted the time to be thirty-seven minutes past five.

He looked around the station and spotted a dark-haired, brawny, moustachioed man aged between twenty and thirty, standing near the entrance holding a newspaper in his left hand. Steiner approached him. "Hugues de Payens."

"Jacques de Molay," the man answered, his accent Scottish.

Steiner stared at him. The man tensed slightly, waiting. Steiner maintained his silence, hiding his amusement at the other's discomfort. Although the names of the first and last official grandmasters of the Knights Templar were reasonable passwords, they could conceivably be guessed by an enemy. He ended the impasse by revealing an enamelled red cross, satisfied at the man's diligence in not just accepting the code.

The younger man relaxed somewhat. "I'm Sergeant Jamie Burton. Welcome to Glasgow, sir."

"Knight-Inquisitor Wolfgang Steiner. How many men did you bring?" Steiner followed Burton out of the station. His cane tapped off the cobbles as they crossed the road.

"Ten of us were sent here from Edinburgh on Wednesday to prepare for your arrival."

"Arms and equipment?"

"We brought rifles, pistols, explosives and ammunition."

Steiner paid no mind to the reserve in Burton's tone. Inquisitors had that effect. The faithful chose their words carefully in his presence. The faithless were given no such choice; they told him everything in confessions born of pain and blood. "Good." That gave him eleven soldiers of Christ, himself included. God willing, they would be enough. "Are any of the men familiar with this city?"

"I grew up here, and three of the others know their way around."

Steiner nodded. For too long the enemy had held dominion over many towns and cities, but if God willed it, this one would be brought back into the light of Christ. "Have the men somewhere to stay?" His superior in London had assured him the Edinburgh chapterhouse would make the arrangements.

"Mr Stewart Munro, a friend of the Order living in Edinburgh, made his Glasgow house available to us. It won't take long to get there. Did you bring any men from London, sir?"

"None could be spared." He would have preferred to lead men he was familiar with on a mission such as this, but the demands of the Order dictated otherwise. *Deus Vult.*

"What of your luggage?"

"It will be delivered to the inn where I will be lodging."

"You won't be staying with the rest of us?" Burton's tone was careful; one did not lightly question an inquisitor about his business.

"Not for the most part. I will be meeting with the Order's agents and those of influence in this city. Not all I meet will be sympathetic to our cause, and I would not risk exposing us all." There was nothing to suggest any were corrupt, but caution was an old friend. A king's greed and a pope's treachery had seen the Templars disbanded, Grandmaster de Molay and many others burned for heresy. The remnant had gone to ground and spent the next five centuries waging a quiet war from the shadows, never gathering in one place.

"*You'll* be exposed, sir. A few of the men could lodge with you."

"I can attend to my own protection, Sergeant."

"Yes, sir." They walked on. "Are you from Germany originally?"

"Switzerland. What is this part of the city called?"

"Grahamston."

Munro's house was near the Merchant City, a townhouse left derelict since its owner moved to Edinburgh. They entered the building and Steiner was pleased to see the men had not been idle. The interior had been cleared of debris and scrubbed clean. Burton informed him that rooms had been converted into sleeping quarters, an armoury and training hall. They passed the dining room where several men ate.

The library was upstairs, and Steiner made a mental note to check it later for unsuitable texts. Heretical books poisoned the mind and soul, but made for such pleasing fires.

*

Flickers of orange danced across the darkening waters of the Clyde as the sun dipped below the western horizon. Lights glittered from boats moored along the river, and sailors staggered back to their berths.

Two dark-clothed figures took care to avoid being seen by anyone lurking near the river. They had their own business to attend to, best done unwitnessed.

Hunt crouched to allow Foley to use his back to climb the wall surrounding the McBride Carriages yard. Foley reached down and grabbed Hunt's hand. Using himself as a counterweight, he lowered himself down the other side while Hunt ascended the wall. Hunt dropped onto the ground, taking care not to land on Foley.

"Right," Foley whispered, "Let's get this over with."

Hunt concurred with that sentiment, conscious of the

consequences of being caught. He kept low and followed Foley towards the office. The yard was cloaked in darkness.

Foley reached the door and retrieved a tool from his bag. Hunt kept watch while Foley tried to force the door with the jemmy.

The lock broke. "Good work," Hunt breathed.

"Aye, now let's get inside." Foley shoved the door open.

Hunt followed him into the building, shutting the door and opening the lantern a little to give them just enough light to see. They searched the office quickly, aware of the risks. Glasgow's constabulary weren't their only concern; the McBrides dealt harshly with those who crossed them.

"Here," Foley said, pointing to several books sitting on a desk.

Hunt squinted down at them, having brought paper to record whatever they learned. "This one's an accounts book." He opened a second ledger, his heart quickening as he read. "A carriage was hired for every evening last week, no destination given. The Friday evening carriage booking was cancelled."

"Makes sense since Amy Newfield was found on Thursday night. Who hired it?"

"There's no name, just the initials B.H. But all bookings were billed to the Royal Princess's Theatre." Hunt frowned. "Why a theatre?"

"Maybe it's being used as a front for whoever we're looking for? They invest money in the theatre or a troupe hiring it, and the money coming out can't be connected to whoever paid it in." He peered at the ledger while Hunt copied the details onto parchment. "There's more."

Hunt pushed the book over. "It'll go quicker if you read and I write."

Foley obliged. "There's a carriage booked next week to take B.H from the theatre to the B.W.C, off Buchanan Street. No day given, it was written on the top of the page and circled." He frowned. "B.W.C?"

"The Black Wing Club," Hunt said in recognition. "It's a private club located in a lane between Buchanan and Queen Street."

"You sound sure."

"I'm a member." He smiled at Foley's expression.

"I might have known."

"Well, our course seems clear…" Hunt began.

"Let me guess," Foley interrupted. "It involves you lounging in your club sipping brandy nightly until B.H makes an appearance?"

"I'm sure it won't be as much fun as you're making it sound. In any case, we need to learn *when* our mysterious B.H plans to visit the club." He was conscious of how long they'd spent in the office. "We shouldn't linger."

"Aye, let's go." Foley pulled a large tin out from under a desk and smashed it open.

Hunt stared as he emptied it out. "What are you doing?"

"I'm taking the money, what does it look like I'm doing?"

"Why? We're not thieves."

"To make it look as though we are. We did break in, and it'll look suspicious if nothing's missing. I'd rather have Roddy McBride hunting for thieves than for us. Anyway, with Miller dead we need the money."

"Since you put it like that…"

The pair left the office and climbed back over the wall. Hunt landed lightly on his feet, feeling a thrill of danger as they made off down the street.

"Slow down," Foley cautioned. "We don't want to draw attention."

Hunt took a breath and forced himself to walk at a normal pace. "Right." His face felt flushed, but he knew the night air would soon cool him down.

"So, what now?" Foley asked.

An excellent question. Neither suggested ending the investigation; they were committed now, come what may. "Have you been to the theatre recently?"

"No, but I saw a play in Claggan's Tavern last year. There was damned near a riot, it was that bad."

Hunt remembered reading about it in the *Herald*. "Didn't a volley of vegetables bring the play to a premature end?"

"Not vegetables, no. Tables and chairs. The players took the hint and called it a night."

"Criticism requires a thick skin and quick reflexes. Participating behind the stage might be rewarding, though."

Foley gave him a knowing look. "At the Royal Princess's Theatre, maybe?"

"It's a thought. Even if we don't learn who B.H is, we'll at least earn some money."

Foley considered it. "Can't hurt, and we do need it."

Too right we do. "Speaking of money, just how much did you get from that tin?"

Chapter Thirteen

Steiner sat on a pew within St Andrew's Cathedral and waited. The cathedral had been completed only seventy-seven years previously, but despite the lack of steeple or bell tower, Steiner was reminded of medieval churches owing to it following the Gothic style. Supporting pillars curved inward at the top to form pointed arches, a design mirrored by the curving apse windows at the back. He studied the stained glass in the centre window depicting the Crucifixion, made all the more impressive illuminated by the afternoon sun.

Steiner had spent the previous night discussing plans with the sergeants Burton and Dumont. His first impression of Burton seemed accurate; tough and dependable. Pierre Dumont was almost fifty with a face carrying more scars than a butcher's block. Steiner liked the look of the hulking Frenchman, his sort the backbone of the Order.

The rest of his men ranged from untested recruits to veterans, two of whom had joined the Order when he himself was mending trousers in Geneva. Most of his band hailed from Britain and the rest of Europe, but one was an American of African origin. He had left the men under Burton's command while he visited those on his list. St Andrew's Cathedral was close to the temporary chapterhouse, so he began there.

A middle-aged woman left the confession box, and Steiner took her place. He was not Catholic but had no time for sectarian squabbles that served only the Enemy.

He shut the confessional box door. "*Non nobis Domine, non nobis*." The box was dark and cramped, smelling strongly of varnished wood. He slid his enamel red cross through the hatch.

For a time, he could hear only breathing from the adjoining box. "Mr Steiner?"

He said nothing. The answering half of the pass phrase would confirm the other man as Father Henry O'Keefe. Otherwise he would be answered with a blade in the throat; he knew Steiner's name.

"*Sed nomini Tuo da glorium*," said the priest with a tremor in his voice. He passed the cross back on a strip of white cotton.

"Father O'Keefe," Steiner acknowledged. This was their first meeting, but they had corresponded for three years.

"Did you have a good journey?"

"God saw me here safely."

"Aye, He did." There was a hesitance in the priest's voice. Father O'Keefe had written the Order with dire warnings for years, but it was one thing to request Templar aid and another to see it delivered. There would be consequences, bloody ones, and the priest had the wisdom to know that.

To business. "You wrote of evil infesting this city."

"Aye. I'll tell you what I can, which is little." Father O'Keefe took a moment to compose his thoughts. "There is a cabal at the heart of Glasgow ruling through fear, blackmail and murder. They own men from every walk of life, from footpads haunting the slums and taverns, to merchant princes in their townhouses and private clubs."

"Powerful men rule everywhere," Steiner said dismissively. "The meek shall inherit the earth, but not this week, I fear."

O'Keefe lowered his voice as if in fear of being overheard. "This cabal does not rule of its own volition, but on behalf of dark powers."

"Continue."

"Men whisper of the dead returning to prey on the living. Of treaties made with demons, and souls traded for power. Defiance is answered with death. But I may say no more."

"May you not?" Eleven Templars had travelled to Glasgow in part due to O'Keefe's warnings. If he thought he could withhold information, he would learn otherwise, priest or not.

"No." The silhouette straightened, his tone firm. "I will not break the sanctity of Confession, Mr Steiner."

That was a line Steiner expected no man to cross. "I

understand, Father, and will heed your words. Does this cabal have a name?"

"I've heard it called the Sooty Feather Society. Its leaders are tattooed with a symbol of some sort, I hear."

"What does this symbol look like?"

"I don't know," the priest admitted. "Only that it will be on an arm or the torso."

Perhaps another on his list could shed more light. "I plan to visit a Reverend John Redfort. Know you of him?" Redfort was unknown to the Order but reputed to be a man of rising influence in the Protestant Church of Scotland.

"Aye, I've heard of Redfort. Be on your guard with him. I warned you that this society has men from every station, and the clergy are alas no exception. This Redfort has risen quickly through the ranks of his church, owing more to power and wealth than humble devotion, I suspect."

O'Keefe's distaste for Redfort could be for good reason, or it could be a legacy of sectarian conflict. The rival Faiths bore one another little love. Steiner would heed the warning, but take it well-salted. "Do you claim your own Church to be free from such corruption?" If he did, he was a fool.

"I fear not," O'Keefe admitted with a heavy sigh. "With Catholicism's return to legitimacy being gradual and recent, we have escaped this society's interest for the most part. But the past century has seen many Catholics come to Glasgow, not least from Ireland. As our presence grows, so does their interest in us."

"Indeed, Father. I trust you will guard knowledge of my presence here with the same zeal you do your confessionals?"

"Of course."

"God go with you, Father." Steiner opened the box door.

"Go with God, my son. And mind what I said about this Redfort."

*

"Be seated, Inspector," Redfort said, comfortable in his study. Almost two weeks had passed since he had been tasked to investigate the killings in the Gorbals. The party responsible had been seized, but word had been passed down that Amy Newfield was a symptom of the problem, not the cause. If so, Redfort reasoned, it would be prudent to learn of any other significant killings and what connected them.

Inspector Kenmure sat. Tall and square-jawed, Kenmure looked every bit the seasoned policeman. He was keen-eyed and dogged in his investigations. And a Sooty Feather, body and soul.

"How fares your family?" Redfort asked with feigned interest.

"They're doing well, Reverend."

"I'm pleased to hear it." Redfort let his smile linger a moment before turning to business. "The Church is concerned about recent murders in the city. I pray daily that the miscreants are caught and hanged."

"Any help from the Church is appreciated, Reverend." He knew Redfort hadn't called this meeting on behalf of the Church. "The Southern Necropolis–"

"Is no longer of interest." Redfort clasped his hands. "That matter has been dealt with. But I fear the Devil's handiwork may have spread."

Redfort noted the look of surprise on Kenmure's face. Evidently the Council hadn't informed him of Amy Newfield's capture by Miss Guillam.

"Those murders–"

"Murder," Redfort stressed, irritated at Kenmure's lapse. The first killing had been reported as such, but the other deaths were officially accidental or natural. "My concern is with noteworthy deaths elsewhere."

The inspector took the hint. "A professor at the Glasgow University was murdered. An Angus Miller."

He remembered reading of it. "Appalling, Inspector."

"Aye. He was killed in the medical school mortuary while preparing a corpse."

Redfort leaned forward. "Really? Which corpse?"

"Richard Canning."

That name Redfort knew. "Canning," he said softly. A vicious killer, unmissed and unmourned.

Kenmure elaborated. "Miller was tortured first. The wounds reminded me of those found on most of Canning's victims."

He disliked the implication. “Canning’s dead.”

“Aye, but we didn’t find his body in the medical school.”

The world had an annoying habit of ignoring his likes and dislikes. “Troubling, Inspector. Is there anything else you can tell me?”

“The prison hangman, Andrews, was found hanging from a rope in his close on Monday morning.”

“A man taking his own life is always tragic.”

“Aye, Reverend. Tragic. Odd though that Andrews bought a bottle of gin and killed himself before drinking it.”

“Who can say what thoughts go through a troubled mind?”

Kenmure nodded, taking the hint; Andrews’ death was to be treated as suicide. “My report to the procurator fiscal will say as much.”

“Excellent, Inspector. I’m sure you’ll also find this murderer who broke into the mortuary to kill the professor and steal Canning’s body.” It was important Kenmure knew the approved narrative.

“We shall, Reverend.”

“Good. I would be grateful if you kept me abreast of any further deaths related to Canning, particularly any he wished harm.”

“Of course.”

Redfort stood. “A pleasure seeing you again, Inspector. Go with God.”

“Always, Reverend.” Kenmure left.

Redfort leaned back as the door closed. This Canning sounded a lead worthy of investigation. His people had enjoyed no success in finding any hint as to who might be responsible for upsetting the Council, but he had received no further visitors demanding answers either. And tonight, his cook was preparing lamb soaked in a mint sauce. His mouth watered in anticipation. He had a fine wine in mind, one sure to go well with the sauce.

Someone chapped on the door. Sighing, he put aside all thoughts of food. “Come.”

His secretary Henderson entered. “Reverend, there’s a foreigner demanding to speak with you.” Henderson sounded nervous. “Apologies, I forget his name. It sounded German.”

“He ‘demands’, does he?” Redfort was of a mind to see this

foreigner regret such insolence. *Does he not know who I am? By God, he'll learn!* Caution stayed him though. He'd rarely seen Henderson so agitated.

"He showed me a red cross," Henderson added.

The last remnants of his good mood died. *God be good, a Templar. Here.* "Show him in." Sweat pooled beneath his armpits and slid down his arms.

A tall, severe-looking man entered. His hair was tied back and speckled with grey, and he bore a goatee and moustache. He carried himself well, suggesting the cane to be an affectation.

Redfort stood and offered his hand. "I'm honoured to host a scion of the Templar Order beneath my roof. Pray sit."

Pale blue eyes pierced him as they exchanged a perfunctory handshake. "I am Wolfgang Steiner, Reverend." He sat, his back ramrod straight. "Knight-Inquisitor of the Templar Order." He had a shrewd look about him, a man who did not suffer fools. "I see you recognise the significance of the cross I showed your man."

"How should I address you?" Redfort rallied for calm, only to be routed by growing panic. He fell back into his own seat. *A foreigner, a relic of an Order too stubborn to know it's dead, and he might kill me on a whim.*

"Inquisitor will suffice, Reverend." Steiner addressed Redfort with the respect due his position, but with a reserve in his tone.

"Of course, Inquisitor. How might I be of aid?"

"You are familiar with the Order's continued existence. I am surprised; so few are."

I should have pretended ignorance. "I've heard rumours. My heart is gladdened they are true."

"Is it?"

Redfort cleared his throat. "How may I assist you?" he asked again.

Steiner leaned back in the chair. "I have been sent here to seek out the evil plaguing this city. Darkness lies at the heart of Glasgow. I intend to root it out, and I require whatever aid your Church can render."

"Of course, the Church is ever eager to help. We too are aware of the sin and vice that plague Glasgow, but alas, lack your martial skill to smite it." Redfort smiled deprecatingly.

If Redfort's declaration enthused Steiner, he did a fine job of hiding it. "You are aware, you say? What then can you tell me? Where should I and my fellows look? Where can we find the enemies of God?"

Sweat trickled down his brow. "I shall find out for you, Inquisitor. Leave me your address, and I will send a message-"

Chair legs squealed against the wooden floor as Steiner stood. "I think not. I find myself unconvinced. You seem well-fed and well-content with the privileges your position offers. You offend me. If I were to investigate, I suspect I would find that you have turned a blind eye to the evil here. I will return in three days, and you will have information for me, *Reverend,* or our next conversation will be less convivial. Am I understood?"

Redfort's sweat no longer trickled; it poured. "I won't disappoint you. God is my witness."

"He is, Reverend. Doubt it not."

"Wait," Redfort said as a thought occurred. "I may have something for you."

Steiner paused.

Redfort feigned a look of fearful reluctance. "If I tell you, I fear–"

"Your fears do not interest me," Steiner interrupted. "Speak."

Redfort decided then and there that however events unfolded, Steiner would not survive them. "I have heard of things happening, of demons haunting the night. I told Bishop Mann, and he assured me the Church would act. Nothing was done. I learned later that a secret society is in league with this evil, and that Bishop Mann sits on its council." Mann was not on the society's Council, but he did have another position Redfort coveted.

"Bishop Mann? Horace Mann?"

Redfort bobbed his head. "Yes." He assumed an expression of reluctance. "You must understand, it *pains* me to name a senior churchman apostate."

Steiner's tone was dry. "I suspect you will survive this discomfort. Where can I find him?"

"His Grace dines at the Carrick Club every Thursday evening."

"Where is this Carrick Club?"

"St Vincent Street near Buchanan Street."

"I will find it. God watch you, Reverend." Redfort couldn't tell if that was intended as a blessing or warning. Steiner strode out of the study before he could reply.

He stared at the door long after Steiner had left, unaccustomed to such humiliation. *That insolent, arrogant bastard! He dares to come into my city and order* me *around like a cur. I'll leave him dead in the gutter, I'll have dogs piss on his corpse and rats feed on his face. That bastard!*

He let his anger simmer for a while and then quashed it. He had turned peril into opportunity, and all that remained was to see what fruit it bore. Steiner's death could wait.

On reflection, perhaps he risked outsmarting himself by using the Templars to further his ecclesiastical ambitions; if Steiner took the Bishop alive for questioning he would soon realise that Redfort had lied. Worse, if he released Mann with the knowledge that Redfort had named him, the Council would learn of it and perhaps execute Redfort. Bishop Mann was not on the Council, but they did find him useful.

After giving the problem some thought, he composed a letter to the Bishop warning of a possible threat against his life. A second message was sent, summoning his man Jones.

Chapter Fourteen

"It's a background canvas, not the Mona bloody Lisa. Worry less about the detail and more about getting it done. The play opens on Monday."

The play opens on Monday seemed to be the stage manager's mantra, intoned with promises of dire consequence if the preparations were lacking. Hunt continued painting, his brushstrokes smooth and precise as he added the details that would tell the audience that the background canvas denoted a stable. "Yes, sir." Finding work at the Royal Princess's Theatre had been easier than he'd thought. He'd walked in yesterday afternoon two hours after the stage manager had dismissed three workers, and convinced Mr Francis to hire himself and Foley. Murray Francis was a man of mercurial moods, a characteristic that worsened as his troubled production of Marlowe's *Doctor Faustus* approached its opening. Demanding perfection one moment and alacrity the next, the production had suffered a high turnover of workers that only slowed progress.

Francis watched Hunt paint for a little longer. "Good work, though," he said grudgingly as he left.

Mrs Allen, one of the costume seamstresses, said. "You should be honoured."

Hunt smiled, keeping his eye on the work. "He'll probably be back in ten minutes to throw me out."

"Aye, like as not." She had been with the production for eight weeks, making her an old hand. There was a rough scraping sound as a carpenter sanded down a wooden prop. A modicum of sense had kept Fraser from offending the carpenters too much. "Your friend's here," Mrs Allen said.

Hunt looked round to see Foley approach. "Is that six o'clock already?"

Foley nodded. "Aye." He lowered his voice. "I don't know how I let you talk me into this. After all day in the shop, I can think of better ways to spend two hours of my evening."

Hunt was surprised at how fast the day had gone. He'd attended the theatre after his last lecture finished at two and had been painting since. He mimicked Murray Fraser. "That canvas won't paint itself, Foley." He smiled at Foley's suggestion at where he could put the canvas.

Foley picked up a paint brush and began layering dark blue paint onto a fresh canvas with broad strokes. It would be left to dry overnight, and Hunt would complete it tomorrow by adding stars and trees. That was how they worked; the less skilled coated the canvasses with background colours, and the artists later added the finer details.

Hunt enjoyed his time in the theatre, and he took pride in knowing that his work would be seen by hundreds. The only thing that dampened his enthusiasm was the real reason for him being there; learning what connected Amy Newfield, the McBrides, and the Royal Princess's Theatre.

He took a short break from painting and sat in the front stalls to watch the rehearsal. To his untrained eye it was going well, but the stage manager's raised voice suggested a differing opinion. After several minutes of berating the actors, one of them decided he'd had enough and explained to Francis in detailed terms exactly what he could do with the part before leaving.

Foley joined Hunt. "Who was that?"

The actor's name escaped him. "Lucifer."

"Preferred Hell to this shite, did he? Who was he playing?"

"Very amusing." The latest departure caused some consternation on stage.

"Well, that's another one gone," Christian Reed said. As the actor playing the lead role of Doctor Faustus, he was bolder than most in addressing the stage manager. "Anyone else you'd care to chase off, Mr Francis?"

"It's a small role," Murray Francis retorted. "I'll find someone."

"Small but pivotal. And the play opens on Monday," said Reed.

"I bloody know!" Francis' eyes rested on Hunt. "You there."

What have I done? "Me?"

"Aye, you. Come here."

Hunt climbed onto the stage, feeling every eye on him.

Francis looked him up and down. "Have you ever acted before?"

"No," Hunt said.

"Don't sell yourself short," Foley called out. "You can do a fine impression of a man forgetting whose round it is."

"You're our Lucifer," Francis decided.

"Me?"

"Him?" Foley laughed.

"I don't know the lines," Hunt objected. "And the play opens on Monday," he couldn't resist adding.

"You won't have many lines. You mostly just stand there and look diabolical. I'll double what I'm paying you now. I only need you for the first two days, I'll find someone else from Wednesday onwards." His desperation was obvious.

Hunt acquiesced. "Very well, but only two days."

"Good. I don't think we'll need to alter the costume much."

He nodded. *I'm to play the Devil. Oh joy.*

*

The Old Toll Bar was quiet even for a Wednesday night. Three regulars stood at the bar talking with the landlord.

"Your usual, gentlemen?" the landlord asked rhetorically on seeing Hunt and Foley. He had already started filling a pint glass with ale.

"My thanks, Mr McCoy, and one for yourself," Foley said.

"Very kind of you." His speech was low and measured, owing more to a Highland brogue than the Glaswegian drawl.

Foley reached into his pocket, but Hunt stopped him. "I'll get these, you find us a table."

"I'll try my best but no promises," Foley said with a wink. Aside from one bearded old boy sitting alone in a veil of pipe smoke, the other patrons all stood at the bar.

"Quiet night," Hunt remarked as McCoy poured the pints. The clock read thirty minutes past eight, giving them half an hour until the pub closed.

"Aye, as ye say." Eoin McCoy was a cordial man who

made his patrons feel welcome. Alcohol and short-fused tempers often proved an explosive mix, but those who sought to test the landlord's good nature saw another side to him. A club sat handily within reach to quell any trouble.

The interior had been recently remodelled at no small expense. Mahogany panels decorated the walls, and the long wooden bar stretched along the far side to curve in at both ends. Gas lighting had been installed, illuminating the decorative fittings. Palace bars such as the Old Toll were lavishly outfitted with expensive fittings to lure in patrons otherwise more inclined to drink at home. Hunt caught his reflection looking back from a gilded mirror decorating the gantry, four large casks resting on either side.

McCoy finished pouring the pints (drawing a third for himself) and pushed two over to Hunt. "Your good health."

"And yours." He paid for the drinks and joined Foley at a table in the far corner.

Foley raised his pint. "Cheers."

"Cheers." They clinked glasses. After studying from morning to lunch and working in the theatre the rest of the day, he'd earned his ale. It tasted rich and bitter, taking his empty stomach by surprise.

Foley took a long draught and wiped his mouth in satisfaction. "I needed that. So, what did you learn in the theatre?"

"That it's been a troubled production, with Murray Francis his own worst enemy," Hunt said with a straight face.

"I know that." Foley made an impatient sound. "Did you learn anything to tie the theatre or anyone there to the McBrides or B.H?"

"Not yet, but it's only our first day. No one I've spoken to has the initials B.H." He shrugged. "Maybe they've left?"

"Doubt it. Whoever paid for the carriage through the theatre has some clout. Forget the actors and stagehands; this B.H might not even have anything to do with the production itself."

That made sense. "The theatre accounts may have the answer, but I doubt a pair of lowly menials such as ourselves will get to see them."

"Nor even a grand thespian such as yourself. What the hell

possessed you to take the role?"

It seemed a good idea at the time. "Turning it down would've annoyed Murray Francis, and he might even have kicked us out."

"Fair point. But playing the Devil, Jesus Christ!" Foley crossed himself. "I hope you don't turn our luck."

"We're body snatchers with a dead employer and disappearing corpses. What luck?"

"It could be worse. We need to keep our wits about us, find this B.H, and see how things stand before going any further."

Hunt drank some ale. "If B.H is involved with the theatre, we can expect them to make an appearance sooner or later. After that, we'll see."

"Aye, we'll see." Foley finished his pint.

*

It was dark when Richard Canning arrived at the address, third in a row of townhouses in an affluent street. The night was his domain now, and he entered the rear garden unnoticed. He jemmied open the back door and entered the house with a thrill of anticipation. *I've been waiting for this.*

The ground floor rooms were cold and dark. Canning crept up the stairs, drawn to a light in the upper hallway.

The décor of the first bedroom suggested it to be the domain of an adolescent girl or young woman. He was disappointed by her absence, she would have been a real pleasure to kill. A child suffering for the sins of her father; it was pleasingly biblical. There was a light visible underneath the door of the furthest away room, but he ignored it for the time being. He entered the second room.

It was the master bedroom, evidenced by the large bed and furniture intended for both man and woman. It was empty too. He turned off the gas light in the hallway and approached the final door. Canning remembered promising its occupant a painful death, a vow made more from anger than any real expectation of success. He doubted its recipient had paid it much heed either; condemned men being dragged to prison to await the hangman's noose made poor assassins. He opened the door.

The occupant was sitting at a desk with his back to him. The room was illuminated by a gas light mounted on the wall, and the man continued his writing ignorant of Canning's presence. He was disinclined to rush matters, savouring the anticipation and remembering the echo of his words around the courtroom: "*I'll kill you, bastard. I'll hunt you and find you and send you screaming to Hell!*"

Perhaps it was a draft from the open door or perhaps it was some dulled remnant of instinct, but the writer ceased his scribbling and paused. "Who's there?"

Oh, this is too precious. "Who do you think, Mr Cotter? After all, I promised I'd find you."

Cotter's horror was sweet. "You … you're dead. They hanged you."

Canning affected a slouch against the doorway. "Not well enough, Mr Cotter." He chuckled in delight. This promised to be even more fun than killing the hangman.

Cotter raised a trembling hand. "Christ be good, it *is* you," he whispered.

"Yes, Mr Cotter. I'm here to express – express is the correct word, aye? – express my *dissatisfaction* with your efforts on my behalf during the trial." Canning assumed a look of disappointment. "Let's be honest, it wasn't your best work, was it? Your heart didn't seem to be *entirely* in it."

"Dear God, how can you be here?" Cotter cowered.

"Let's not trouble God. He's busy, I'm sure. All I want is for you to admit that you let the prosecution win."

"I … they had enough evidence, more than enough to convict you."

Canning conceded there to be truth in that. "Aye, Mr Cotter, I admit they had enough to convict me of some of the killings, but not all of them. I know, because I didn't commit all of them. I want you to admit that you did not defend me to the best of your ability."

He watched as Cotter found courage from within. Perhaps it was from the knowledge that he was dead regardless. "Aye, I admit it. I could have done better. I could have discredited some of the murders from your tally." Cotter looked Canning in the eye for the first time, defiant. "But you were *guilty*! I don't care if you didn't kill all of them. The jury didn't care.

You're a murderer, Canning, a *killer*. Who gives a damn who you killed and who you didn't?"

Canning nodded, calmed by Cotter's admission. "I give a damn. Thank you, Mr Cotter, for your honesty." He drew out his razor. "Now then, this *will* hurt." Cotter shrank back as he smiled. "I made you a promise, after all, and I'm a man of my word."

Chapter Fifteen

Professor Charles Sirk squinted over his spectacles at the geological timescale he'd scrawled on the blackboard. After a moment he wiped away some of the chalk and re-wrote part of it. Hunt scribbled furiously while Sirk summarised each period, his rapid speech hell for note-taking. Middle-aged with a shock of greying hair crowning his narrow face, he had an impatient manner with his students. Sometimes rude, usually condescending, he knew his subject; if caught in a rare mellow mood and asked the right questions, he was a wealth of knowledge.

The clock chimed as it struck four. "That is all for today, gentlemen. I suggest you familiarise yourself with the Triassic Period for next week." Sirk walked off without a further word.

Hunt stored his notes, ink and pens in his bag and left the university with a mixture of anticipation and trepidation. Sirk's Palaeontology class was Hunt's last for the day, leaving him free to meet Amelie Gerrard, albeit chaperoned by her mother. He intended to keep his promise to show her the Carpathian Circus.

A tram took him from the West End to the heart of the city in good time, dropping him off on the busy Argyle Street. He was to meet the Gerrards in the Arcade Café, a large coffee house next to the Argyll Arcade.

Finding himself in town a quarter-hour early, Hunt continued past the arch leading into the Arcade Café's courtyard, instead taking the next turn into the Argyll Arcade itself. It was unique in Glasgow thanks to a glass roof covering the entire mall, around the corner and through to Buchanan Street. Hosting jewellers, dressmakers and toy shops it was a popular destination for Hunt's mother and other gentlefolk who could imagine they were in a Parisian arcade.

Well-dressed couples enjoyed a leisurely stroll, some entering whatever shops took their fancy, others content to glance through the windows as they passed. It hadn't always been so tranquil. Hunt recalled reading about one Lieutenant Knox of the 15th Hussars Cavalry Regiment who had galloped through the arcade in full regalia as a wager over fifty years earlier, terrifying the unsuspecting patrons. The officer had got off with a small fine – until a newspaper campaign spurred a regimental enquiry resulting in Knox being posted to Madras in punishment.

The arcade was thankfully free of cavalrymen today, and so Hunt walked out onto Buchanan Street without incident. The Black Wing Club was nearby, situated in a side street just a little further up Buchanan Street. Thinking of the club recalled Hunt to his work at the theatre, an opportunity to discover who had taken Amy Newfield and why. All he knew of the one who hired the carriage that took her was their initials B.H, their connection to the theatre, and a meeting at the Black Wing Club at an unknown date and time.

None of which he need worry about today. Like the arcade itself, the Arcade Café was also accessible from Buchanan Street. Hunt turned into the lane towards the coffee house.

He found Madame and Mademoiselle Gerrard seated inside, greeting them with a kiss on each cheek. The French manner of greeting drew the attention of local patrons accustomed to more reserved British ways.

"How are you, Mr Hunt?" Mme Gerrard asked.

"I'm well, thank you, Madame Gerrard. And yourselves?" he enquired.

"I cannot complain."

Mlle Gerrard confirmed that she too was in good health.

"Will Monsieur Gerrard or your brother be joining us?" Hunt asked.

"No, Papa is meeting … local? … local wine merchants." Mlle Gerrard smiled. "And my brother has no interest in the circus."

"That's a shame," Hunt lied. *Probably afraid he might have fun and ruin his carefully cultivated scowl.*

Neither Gerrard looked particularly distressed at his absence. A waiter attended at the table to take their order. While the Gerrard women argued the merits of tea against coffee, Hunt looked around at their fellow patrons. Most appeared to be merchants discussing business over coffee, or shop proprietors enjoying a quiet drink before going home. A young couple sat oblivious to everyone else, the woman absently caressing her engagement ring. Hunt guessed the couple had bought the ring in the arcade that afternoon and visited the coffee house to celebrate their betrothal.

The waiter left with their order. "How are your parents, Mr Hunt?" Mme Gerrard asked.

"They were both well last I heard. We've not met since after Dunclutha," he admitted, "but their last letter reported no concerns."

"You do not meet often?" Mme Gerrard asked.

Something in her tone led Hunt to suspect she had caught wind of his parental estrangement, mending though it was. "Not as often as we'd like. Running the Browning Shipping Company keeps them busy, as do my studies," he offered as an explanation.

"Did you have many classes today?" Mlle Gerrard asked.

"Three," Hunt said, glad to be on safer ground. "Zoology, Botany, and Palaeontology."

She questioned him further regarding his studies, which he answered as best he could. Uncertain as to their religious fervour, he avoided any subject considered controversial. Many found it difficult to reconcile recent scientific theories that contradicted religious beliefs. Theologians had aged the earth in the region of 6,000 years; science put that number far higher.

Hunt also decided against disclosing his recent theatrical activities lest word get back to his parents. Playing on the stage would give them fits; playing *Lucifer* would be ill-received to say the least. To say nothing of how Mlle Gerrard and her parents might receive the revelation. Between that and his body snatching, it was disheartening to discover just how little of his life he was free to talk about.

The waiter returned with tea, coffee and scones. "Has Scotland kept you well-occupied?" Hunt asked, moving the conversation from himself.

"Yes, we have seen many places." Mlle Gerrard sipped coffee. "Last week we visited Edinburgh and St Andrews. Interesting places." She made a face. "But cold. *Maman*'s grandpapa was from Edinburgh."

Hunt smiled. "Spring's still young. Where else do you plan to visit?" He included Mme Gerrard in the question though she had left most of the talking to her daughter, content to chaperone. But listening to and considering every word, he had no doubt.

"We are travelling to Loch Lomond in two weeks," Mlle Gerrard said. "After that, I do not know." She glanced questioningly at her mother.

"We are undecided. Perhaps the remainder of our time here, perhaps elsewhere? We will have only days left before we return home." Mme Gerrard shrugged slightly. "I have seen where my Grandpapa was born, I am content."

Conscious that the Gerrards were due to return to France shortly after their trip to Loch Lomond, Hunt nearly articulated his wish that they spend their last days in Glasgow but feared being over-bold. He finished his tea instead.

"Do we have time to visit the circus?" Mlle Gerrard asked.

Hunt glanced at Mme Gerrard who signalled her permission with a slight nod. "It's in the Glasgow Green, which is nearby. I would be honoured to escort you both there."

*

Steiner stood with Burton near to the Carrick Club on St Vincent Street, squinting up at the building across the road from it. Several windows were open, but there was nothing to indicate which one Gray was stationed at. The dark-skinned American had a reputation for being a fearsome shot with a rifle and steady under pressure. That reputation might be tested.

A straw-filled wagon sat stationary nearby and Steiner made eye contact with the driver. Carter gave a small nod back. He was to wait in the wagon.

Steiner looked at his pocket watch and watched the steady

revolution of the second hand. Six o'clock. *Now we begin.* They walked openly towards the club entrance where two footmen stood. Burton affected a slouch, his hands tucked into his pockets in an effort to conceal his nerves. Steiner's cane tapped off the ground every three steps.

They passed the footmen unhindered and entered the foyer. Steiner continued to the reception desk while Burton loitered as if waiting for someone. The concierge at the reception desk assumed a well-practiced expression of welcome as Steiner approached. "Good evening, sir."

"Evening. I have a message for Bishop Mann. Might I impose upon you for assistance?" Steiner held up a folded slip of paper.

"Of course, sir." He rang a bell.

A footman attended the desk. "There's a message for Bishop Mann," the receptionist told him.

"I have been instructed to witness its delivery in person," Steiner said.

The concierge hesitated. "Club policy permits only members and guests within the dining room."

"This is a confidential Church matter and requires a response from his Grace. Your assistance would be appreciated." Two coins nestled between his fingers.

The concierge eyed them, and greed won out. "I think we can make an exception this once."

Steiner handed him and the footman a coin each. "His Grace will see you both rewarded further." He hoped his distraction gave Burton the opportunity to pass the desk unnoticed.

The footman led Steiner through the hall and into the dining room. The club was well appointed, its interior rooms long with high ceilings and bordered with plastered patterns. Those dining within were mostly middle-aged or older. Waiters threaded their way around the tables taking orders and conveying meals. Burton followed, keeping pace near the far wall.

Steiner did not know Bishop Mann by sight but trusted the footman did. His faith was not in vain, and he was escorted to a table two-thirds into the dining room. Two men aged between fifty and sixty sat at the table.

"Your Grace, there is a message for you," the footman said with formal deference.

The older of the men looked up, his hair more white than grey. There was a quick wariness about him that struck Steiner as odd, as if trouble was not entirely unexpected. "Yes, what is it?"

The footman lowered a small silver tray which bore Steiner's message, and the man revealed to be Bishop Horace Mann took it. He unfolded the note and frowned. "There's nothing written on this." He looked up at Steiner, his blue eyes suspicious. "Who–?"

Steiner shoved the footman aside and pulled out his derringer. He aimed it at Mann with the intention of ordering the Bishop to follow; a corpse was useless to him. Movement to his left, however, caused him to turn as three men at an adjacent table rose and drew revolvers from their jacket pockets. Steiner cursed his stupidity. Three men sitting at a table absent food or drink, with a watchful hardness about them? His failure to recognise them as guards was careless.

His derringer was small and designed for concealment, holding only a single bullet. The revolvers drawn by the three men before him held six bullets a-piece. His one against their eighteen; poor odds. Steiner threw himself to one side as they opened fire.

Murmurs of consternation became fearful cries as the diners realised what was happening. The dining room turned to chaos as tables and chairs were overturned, the fallen trampled in a panicked exodus. A waiter was the exception, keeping low but remaining otherwise calm. Steiner had no time to spare him further thought as the Bishop's guards fired again. Choosing the compact derringer over his revolver was not proving one of today's wiser decisions.

One of the gunmen closed the distance and Steiner saw no reason to waste the opportunity. He fired his single bullet and the man fell, his gun clattering off the floor. Dropping his now-empty derringer, Steiner looked in vain for the fallen revolver.

Mann's remaining two protectors spread out and closed in, braver now he had shot his bolt. Focused on Steiner, the leftmost failed to notice Burton approach and stiffened as he was dispatched by a knife to the back. The last guard standing turned to face Burton. Steiner drew a 17-inch blade from his cane and took advantage of the man's divided attention to close the distance.

The guard sensed Steiner's approach and swung the gun back. Steiner deflected it with his cane and stabbed the blade into the man's stomach. He looked around. "Where is the Bishop?"

Burton shrugged. "He made a run for it."

"Come," Steiner said. He cleaned blood from the blade and re-combined his sword-stick. The Bishop was old, not a nimble man, and perhaps still within reach. The one waiter who had taken cover rather than flee was nowhere to be seen, though several diners still cowered on the ground.

Steiner and Burton fought through the fleeing crowd only to be recognised by the footman who had led Steiner to the Bishop. "Him, he's behind this!"

That footman and one other tried to restrain Steiner, emboldened by him being apparently alone. The first grabbed at him only to gag as Steiner's fingers jabbed into his throat. The second swore and stepped forward even as Steiner's foot thundered into the first man's groin, doubling him over.

Burton intercepted the second, his fists snapping into the man's face in quick succession, and Steiner kicked his left leg out to send him sprawling to the ground. Burton kicked him hard to the head before he could rise again.

"Efficient," Steiner said in approval.

Burton answered him with a hard grin. "My pleasure, sir."

Steiner led Burton into the foyer and drew his sword once more. He grabbed the cowering concierge, the blade by his face stilling any scream. "Bishop Mann, did he pass here?"

A shaking hand pointed to a body on the floor.

Steiner released him and turned the body over. It was Mann, killed by a bullet to the chest. Curious and unfortunate. He re-sheathed his sword-stick and considered the body.

"Who shot him?" Burton asked, voicing Steiner's thoughts. "We sure as hell didn't."

"A good question, Sergeant, though one not requiring blasphemy."

"Sorry, sir. Do you think he caught a stray bullet?"

It would be ironic if the Bishop had been killed by one of his own men, but Steiner did not think that the case. Mann had been shot in the chest, yet had not faced his men while they fired at Steiner. Nor would he have been capable of leaving the dining room with such a wound. Someone else had shot him, and Steiner did not believe it a coincidence that his attempt to kidnap Mann happened at the same time another party chose to assassinate him.

Reverend Redfort claimed this man stood high in the society I hunt, and Father O'Keefe suggested such men were marked by a tattoo. He pulled out a knife and cut away at Mann's shirt. The Bishop's arms were unmarked. The only blemish to his chest was the bullet wound. Steiner turned the corpse over and found his back also unmarked.

"He had three armed men protecting him," Burton said. "Unusual, aye?"

Steiner stood. "Indeed, Sergeant. Somebody warned him about us." Steiner held a suspicion of who was responsible. Redfort was the one who named Mann to Steiner, telling when and where to find him. He only had Redfort's word that Mann even knew of the society, let alone held high position within it. And someone had conveniently killed the Bishop before he could be questioned. *Are you playing your own game, Redfort?*

"The police will be here soon, sir," Burton said.

"We will learn nothing else here." Nor from the city jail, so they hastened out onto the street where the wagon waited.

"About time," Carter grated, holding the reins tightly.

"There was a complication," Burton said. The sergeant had a fondness for understatement.

A gunshot echoed between the buildings. Steiner crouched and turned to see the guard he'd shot within the club standing at the entrance, wounded, but with a gun aimed in his direction. He looked at Steiner with a surprised expression – and fell. Steiner turned in time to see a window three storeys up and across from the club close; what he had started with his derringer, Gray had finished with a Winchester rifle.

Bells and whistles could be heard in the distance as Steiner and Burton climbed onto the wagon. It was time to leave.

"No prisoner?" Carter asked.

Steiner glanced at the straw in the wagon bed where he had planned to hide Mann on the trip back to the house. "No prisoner." Just unanswered questions.

*

Hunt escorted the Gerrard ladies down Argyle Street towards the Glasgow Green. It was a dry evening, at least, though the street was congested with wagons and carriages. A bell could be heard in the distance, ringing continuously and growing louder. Mademoiselle and Madame Gerrard gave him a quizzical look. There was no mistaking it for the slow, solemn toll of bells announcing the hour; its tempo spoke of alarm.

"It might be a fire wagon, or police," he said. Whatever it was, it was getting closer. Already he could see wagons, carriages and cabriolets grudgingly clear a gap for whatever approached.

The wagon causing the commotion squeezed between a tram and a cabriolet, the latter's truculent driver refusing to give more room. The wagon carried four police constables, Hunt saw, burly men who shouted insults at the cabriolet driver.

"What is happening?" Mlle Gerrard asked.

Hunt shook his head. "I've no idea." An incident of some significance, he'd wager, given the haste of the wagon and the grim expressions borne by the constables on board.

They crossed the street, avoiding horse dung where possible. It seemed to be everywhere, deposited in large piles and then spread over the cobbled streets by horse hooves and wheels. If nothing was done, one day would find the city buried under it.

They continued to the Glasgow Green by way of the promenade running alongside the River Clyde. Being the recipient of waste produced by decades of industrialisation (and the multitudes employed by it), the river smelled little better than the dung-smeared streets, but at least it was quieter.

Bridgeton workers who lived on the other side of the river

crossed the metallic St Andrew's Suspension Bridge. The Nelson Monument rose up from the Green, a brick pyramidal-shaped pillar over forty metres high. A woman stood at the Charlotte Street entrance to the park, handing out pamphlets. Mlle Gerrard accepted one and read it as they entered the park. A woman ahead of them folded her copy up and put it in her purse, but other copies had been less well received, littering the path ahead.

She frowned. "What does this word mean, Mr Hunt? Suffra…?" She showed him the pamphlet.

Hunt read it. "Suffrage. It's a movement campaigning for more rights for women, including the vote. They plan to meet in the park on Friday evening."

She shared a look with her mother. Their opaque expressions concealed whether they were for or against such rights.

Distant figures strolled through the park with no apparent destination in mind, but most visitors had come for the circus. Unlike others Hunt had seen, the Carpathian Circus had no main tent to contain its attractions. Instead many of its acts were performed in the open air or in smaller tents scattered around. Stalls sold food, drink and trinkets to those visitors with coin to spend. Caravans and wagons belonging to the circus-folk were clustered together, away from the acts. The years and miles had taken their toll, but they looked otherwise well maintained.

Hunt walked alongside the young Frenchwoman as they strolled amidst the revelry and eccentricity. Circus men and women manned stalls and strolled around with a theatrical swagger, explosions of vibrant colour amidst the more soberly dressed locals. The circus women wore long skirts and loose blouses, garments dyed bright blue or red mixed with earthier browns and greens. The men wore loose red or blue shirts that hung over dark trousers. Aside from some wearing wide-brimmed hats, most of the men were bare-headed, but embroidered headscarves were common among the women.

Some juggled while acrobats executed feats of gymnastic excellence. Fire breathers exhaled gouts of flame and fortune-tellers spun reassuring lies in incense-choked tents.

Trained horses performed tricks on command, and elephants paraded under the guidance of wary handlers. Once-regal lions languished in barred wagons, forever denied the plains of Africa.

"Are you enjoying yourself?" Hunt asked.

She smiled. "Yes. I have visited circuses before, but never one with such…"

"Mystery?"

"Yes, mystery. This circus has travelled all over Europe." She smiled. "Do you like mystery, Monsieur?"

"Of course." *Ones I can solve.* His investigation at the theatre was still to bear fruit.

"How far have you travelled?"

"I've been as far as London, but no further, I'm afraid."

She pointed at some of the circus children roaming around. "They have seen more of life than we may ever see."

"Oh, we may find ourselves surprised."

She laughed. Her mother gave them space as she followed, but she was never far behind.

One of the circus stalls offered an unfamiliarly scented herbal tea. Hunt assumed a gallant smile and offered to buy them both a cup, an offer accepted.

He paid for the tea and handed a cup each to Mme and Mlle Gerrard, foregoing one himself. They both drank and nodded their approval.

"I'm pleased you like it, Mademoiselle Gerrard."

"You may call me Amelie, if you wish, Mr Hunt.

He smiled, heart quickening. "It would be my very great pleasure, Amelie. And please, Wilton." There had been worse days.

Chapter Sixteen

The cabriolet stopped outside a row of elegant townhouses in the Woodside area of Glasgow's West End. It was a clean and prosperous street, night and day to the overcrowded slums housing most of the population. Steiner alighted and paid the fare exactly. He climbed the steps leading up to the black-painted front door of number fourteen and banged the silver knocker three times.

A maid answered the door and Steiner removed his hat. "Good afternoon. Inform Lady Delaney that Wolfgang Steiner wishes to speak with her." He had sent Lady Delaney a calling card yesterday and received an invitation to call upon her today.

The maid took his bowler hat and coat, and led him through the hall. Its walls were white, the floor checked with black and white tiles. She showed him into the sitting room and left to fetch her mistress. Floral maroon wallpaper covered the walls, and the varnished wooden floor was brightly polished. A large Persian rug was spread out across the middle of the room, its weaves worn and faded with age.

The white marble fireplace was clean and free of soot. An old framed picture, of a young Lady Caroline Delaney with her husband and two children, sat on the mantelpiece. Light caught the glass to reveal clusters of fingerprints around the edge, telling him it was often handled. Old portraits of the family hung on the wall. Steiner envied her them; memories faded even if the pain did not. He almost touched the locket hanging around his neck, its metal cool against his skin.

His hostess entered the room, a woman in her early forties with dark, greying hair pulled back in a bun.

Steiner turned, arms folded behind his back as he respectfully bowed from the neck. "Good afternoon, Lady

Delaney. Thank you for seeing me."

She glided forwards with her hand outstretched which he dutifully kissed. "Welcome, Mr Steiner." She studied him with shrewd grey eyes. "You've aged since we last met in London."

"You have not."

She laughed. "Liar." She motioned for him to sit on the couch and took her place on a chair facing it. Neither spoke as the maid entered with a teapot, cups and saucers. Lady Delaney smiled up at her. "Thank you, Ellison. That will be all." The maid left the room while Lady Delaney poured tea into both cups. "I'd ask if you take milk, but I suspect you take it black."

"A little honey."

She sat back and sipped her tea. "What brings you here?"

"The Order has received reports of troubling activity in this city." He leaned forwards. "We received no such reports from you."

She was unruffled by the gentle implication. "There's been little worthy of report. Do your orders go beyond investigation?"

"I am to investigate and take whatever action I decide necessary, in God's name."

"If you insist on bringing God into our conversation, I'll have to ask you to leave." She tried to sound light-hearted, but there was anger in her voice and a warning in her eyes.

His nod was an acknowledgment, not an apology.

She leaned back and clasped her hands. "There *were* some attacks in this part of town over the winter. Three men and four women were killed over two weeks, with no investigation by the police. I believe a dog was blamed."

"You did not think this worth reporting?"

"Rest assured, Mr Steiner, that I dealt with the matter."

"Dealt with, Lady Delaney?"

"Dealt with." She sipped her tea.

The glint in her eyes and hard satisfaction in her voice convinced him to leave it alone. "Do you still swear by a Remington derringer?"

"It fits handily in my purse." She put her cup down. "Is a Webley revolver still your preference?"

"It has yet to fail me." His own derringer had been lost a day earlier during the Bishop Mann fiasco. He picked up the teapot and refilled their cups.

"Thank you. For what do I owe the pleasure of your company?"

"What do you know of the group pulling this city's strings?"

"It started last century as a Hellfire Club, made up of the rich and bored indulging in all manner of debaucheries. They encouraged each other to greater excesses, even devil worship."

She sipped tea and continued. "They took part in vile rites and dabbled in the blackest of the mystical arts – and dark powers in the city eventually answered. From then on they were owned body and soul, becoming the Black Wing Club, more colloquially known as the Sooty Feathers. Earlier this century the club bought a building and presented itself as a respectable institution, courting the city's high society and growing its numbers."

"But it still serves evil, yes?"

"Publicly the Black Wing Club is among Glasgow's most exclusive private clubs, with an impeccable reputation. But hidden at its rotten heart lies the Sooty Feather Society, as vile as ever. It counts many of influence among its members. Politicians, police, bankers, clergy, lawyers, merchants, doctors, criminals, killers and newspaper men – money, threats and blackmail get them whatever they want, and those who resist are killed. Or worse." She looked over Steiner's shoulder at the family picture on the mantelpiece.

"Continue," he said softly.

"My husband, a member of the Black Wing Club for two years, was offered initiation into the Sooty Feather Society after he was knighted. He was flattered, I think, perhaps a little amused to be courted by such important people. We were ignorant of the truth in those days." She looked away. "And happy."

Steiner nodded slowly. Her family's fate was known to him. "Are those initiated into the society from the club aware of the nature of the ones they serve?"

Lady Delaney shook her head. "My husband, Sir Andrew,

certainly wasn't, not at first. The truth is kept from initiates, I believe, for a time. When they are judged ready, their true masters are revealed to them and they are fully inducted into the society. Sir Andrew was an initiate for months before he was fully inducted." She looked away. "A perpetual fear seemed to take him from then on."

"I have been told the leaders of this society control the city."

"You speak of the Council." Lady Delaney sipped her tea and made a face.

She had heard of it. Encouraging. "Yes. I was told that Bishop Mann sat on it."

"I wouldn't know." She added a little milk to her tea. "He was shot yesterday, I hear. Your work? You're not known for having a light touch, but the public assassination of clergy seems out of character."

"I was there," Steiner allowed. "My plan was to abduct and question him, but someone else wanted him dead. I believe I was misled regarding the Bishop's allegiance, or at least his significance."

Lady Delaney raised an eyebrow. "Deliberately misled?"

"I suspect so. I will discuss the matter with the one responsible in due course. But he can wait."

"Not a discussion he will enjoy, I wager." Her smile was grim.

He will not. "A great deal of money must be required to control a city. Do you know who manages the society's money?"

"I believe I do, as it happens. My husband opened an account with the Heron Crowe Bank on joining the society. On asking why, he told me all members were encouraged to invest with that bank, that it would take over all loans owed to other institutions. A measure to prevent rivals from compromising members, he said. As we had no loans and it managed our interests competently, I let the matter lie at the time."

"And after your husband's death?"

"I closed our account with them. They are involved with the society but whether they know of those pulling the strings, I cannot say."

Steiner exhaled. "I would prefer not to lose time chasing what may lead nowhere."

Lady Delaney nodded. "Since you've taken the time to visit, it would be a shame to let you leave empty-handed." She went over to a small writing bureau and gathered an inkwell, pen and paper. Her pen scratched across the paper as she spoke. "I know little of the society's workings but perhaps I can lead you to it. I've no proof, mind, but I may know of one who sits on the Council. Mr Benjamin Howard was a family friend who sponsored my husband's membership into the society and very likely betrayed him when Sir Andrew balked at their plans. Mr Howard has done very well in the two decades since."

A cynical part of him noted her personal bias against this man, but he had known Caroline Delaney for years and never been given cause to doubt her. He would trust her until she gave him reason not to. "Where can I find him?"

She scribbled onto the paper again. "I've attempted to settle my family's account with him several times over the years, but he travels a lot and keeps his movements private. He is the patron of a local theatre and attends some of the shows. If you can get one of your people inside the theatre, you may learn when he next plans to attend."

"That should not present much difficulty." He had someone in mind, if she was willing.

*

There was a knock on the door.

"Enter," Redfort said, putting his pen down. Sunday's sermon could wait.

Sid Jones entered the study. "Good afternoon, Reverend," he said breathlessly.

He really must learn to master his expressions. His face is like an open book. "Afternoon, Jones." He held up a newspaper. "This morning's paper tells the awful news of Bishop Mann's murder in the Carrick Club yesterday afternoon." He shook his head. "Shocking."

"Yes, Reverend, shocking."

"What manner of godless creature could murder a man of

God, a *bishop*, in cold blood?"

Jones' ears reddened. "I couldn't say, Reverend."

"No, Jones. And nor should you. Ever."

"Yes, Reverend – I mean, no."

"That said, tell me what happened before you forget it forever." He motioned to the seat.

Jones sat. "I obtained a waiter's uniform before Bishop Mann arrived and managed to stay near his table. He brought three guards with him."

"I see he took my warning to heart."

"He was there maybe thirty minutes before a man approached the table with a small pistol, and then it all went to hell. Mann fled while his men kept the attacker busy. I followed after and shot him in the chest." He spoke matter-of-fact, as if killing a bishop was an everyday occurrence. Jones was of mediocre intelligence but not without his uses.

"Excellent work, Jones." Redfort had a restless ambition, rarely satisfied for long no matter his successes. He had coveted the mantle of Bishop for many years, though Mann's death was just the first step in his elevation; other ministers would seek the position. The assassination offered an opportunity for both elevation and to repay Steiner's insult. In full and with interest. *Speaking of whom…* "Describe this man."

Jones leaned back, remembering. "Tall, in his forties I think, with a goatee and moustache. He carried a cane."

Redfort nodded in recognition. "Wolfgang Steiner. Spread the word; he is to be killed. I'll inform the Council that Bishop Mann was murdered by Templars."

Jones frowned. "The Bishop's three guards killed Steiner, didn't they?"

"No, Jones. They died, he lived."

There was an expression of grudging respect on Jones' face. "He's not an easy man to kill."

So it seems. He had hoped the guards would deal with him while Jones killed the Bishop, but alas they were as inept at killing Steiner as they were in protecting Mann. "Remember that." Steiner's continued survival left him ambivalent at his – in hindsight – reckless scheme. Mann's death positioned him for elevation to Bishop but until the Templar was dead,

Redfort was in danger. He passed over Jones' payment. "What have you learned about Richard Canning's execution?"

Jones took the money. "The records say he died of a broken neck, but the sheriff who oversaw the hanging admits it went wrong and he choked to death. The attending physician confirmed Canning's death."

A feeling of unease pressed on Redfort. *Care was taken not to break his neck, suggesting he was Made. But by whom?* He couldn't ask the executioner; he had conveniently hanged himself. "You checked the prison records, did Canning have any visitors the night before he died?"

"Aye, a lawyer and a priest."

"Have the lawyer brought to me."

"Can't."

"I beg your pardon?"

Jones paled slightly at his tone and straightened in the chair. "Sorry, Reverend, but he's in York. His clerk says he wasn't involved in Canning's trial and had no business visiting him. Canning's trial lawyer, William Cotter, was murdered in his home two nights ago."

Redfort closed his eyes. Someone was cutting off loose ends and a dead man was settling scores. "What of the priest?"

"A Father George Herald. The Catholic Church has no priests with that name in the diocese."

He needed to digest what he'd learned before proceeding. The wrong question to the wrong person might see him dead, too. "That will be all for now. When you place the bounty on Steiner, impress upon the gangs that he is not to be taken lightly." The sooner Steiner was dealt with, the better. By now he no doubt suspected Redfort had used him, and the Council would reach the same conclusion if they captured and tortured the Templar. Dead men told no tales. *Well, that's not always true.*

*

Steiner stirred, still half asleep as the morning sun broke through gaps in the curtains. He felt the warmth of the woman lying next to him and took comfort in their closeness.

He wrapped an arm around his wife, his eyes still shut. She stirred, her hair brushing against his face. Saturday; a day to be spent with his wife and sons. Something nagged at him, but he pushed it from his mind.

He felt his wife draw away from him and heard the floorboards creak under her weight as she left the bed. "Get the children up, Giselle, and I will heat the water."

There was a hesitation. "I don't understand."

Steiner's eyes opened. She had answered in English, not German, and with an Irish lilt. Awareness came crashing down. *Ah. Why do I torment myself so?* He sat up and looked at his 'wife'.

A young woman of about twenty with long chestnut hair looked back, her expression uncertain. She had done well enough the day before, but the spell was broken, and she knew better than to try and mend it.

He broke the silence. "Wash and dress. We will leave the room together, break our fast and then go our separate ways. You are clear on your task?"

She nodded, excited and apprehensive in equal parts. "Aye. I'm to go to the Royal Princess's Theatre where I'm to play a small part in the production of *Doctor ... Fostas*?"

"*Faustus*," he corrected. "But yes."

"What happened to the original player?"

"I paid her to withdraw from the production, and the play director to re-cast you in her place. He is under the impression you are my niece." *Or mistress, by his expression.* He gave her a doubting look. "I assured him you can act. You will not disappoint?"

Miss Knox bristled. "I'm a professional actress, thank you very much. I'll do my bit."

"Good. Do not forget your true purpose there. Leave a message with the baker in Wyman's Pie Shop if you learn when Benjamin Howard is to attend the theatre."

"I understand."

"I have instructed the innkeeper that we will be visiting friends until Tuesday. We will return here and resume this charade at six that evening. Be punctual. Yes?"

The girl nodded uncertainly. "Aye."

Shabby but not unclean, he had endured worse accommodation than the King's Head Inn, and it gave him distance from his men. A large enamel basin provided bathing water. Steiner paid the girl little heed as they dressed, taking no interest in her nakedness. She was ill at ease dressing in front of him, though her discomfort seemed heightened rather than eased by his lack of interest. Men leering at her was perhaps a familiar irritant; cold indifference was something new.

The stout innkeeper assumed an expression of forced cheer on seeing them enter the taproom. "Good morning, Mr and Mrs Taylor. I hope the room was comfortable?"

Steiner assumed a Scottish accent. "Aye, Mr Brown, we have no complaints." Miss Knox just smiled.

Breakfast was a silent affair. Steiner chastised himself over his weakness; he could not let his wife and children go. Often on his travels he hired a prostitute to play the part of his wife. He was not interested in anything sexual; he was not so far gone to depravity. He merely paid them to spend the night with him and play the part in the morning. But it always ended poorly. He had no doubt they could feign interest in him, pretend to find him attractive, but to play the part of the loving wife and mother eluded most of them. *Just fuck us and leave*, said eyes older than their years. All he asked was that they lie with him at night and play the part of his long-dead wife. *Is it too much to ask? Was it too much to ask that she lived? And my boys…*

This time he had left the prostitutes well alone, visiting inns and theatres of the city in search of an actress needing work and money. To play a part would be second nature, he reasoned.

The search had produced Kerry Knox, a young Irish actress of middling talent serving ale in the Scotia Bar. Booth theatres of wood and canvas – called penny geggies – operated in the Glasgow Green from the July Fair until September, where she would make a meagre living in the hopes of one day finding work in one of Glasgow's established theatres performing to the middle and upper classes.

From September until June she found work as a barmaid,

earning a few extra pennies reciting the poetry of Rabbie Burns in the taproom. Steiner had been in the Scotia Bar during one such recital, finding it a competent if unexceptional performance. But good enough to suit his needs.

She had been indignant when he had made his offer, telling him to fuck off and find a whore. His explanation that nothing lewd was required had still left her on guard. *"All I require is that you play my wife. In public you will be Mrs Karen Taylor, married to Francis Taylor from Dundee. In private you are to be Giselle Steiner, my late wife, when required. I give you my word I require nothing more from you than your acting skills. You will be well paid."*

She made a better show of it than the prostitutes but still regarded him with some suspicion. They finished their breakfast and went their separate ways, him to his men, and her to the theatre. She seemed excited by the opportunity to finally perform in a real theatre, doubtless hoping it would not be her last time performing there.

Chapter Seventeen

July 1459

Brother Seoras sweated profusely as the street led him up the hill towards the cathedral, not helped by the hot summer sun and his black friar's robe. His mendicant order's old monastery sat near the site where the town's new university was being built. Abbot Robert had a message he wished taken to Bishop Andrew, and as the newest arrival to this chapter of the Dominican Order, such tasks mostly fell to Seoras.

The annual Fair was underway, drawing merchants and tradesmen to Glasgow from all over. The land surrounding the cathedral was mobbed with crowds come to buy and sell, but many saw his distinctive black robe and made way, greeting him with a respectful nod. The Blackfriars were well-regarded in the town, tending to the sick in hospitals established by the Church.

The cathedral was a magnificent structure, its large steeple soaring overhead, pointing up to the heavens. Nearby sat the Bishop's Castle, its five-storey keep a recent addition. Unsure whether Bishop Andrew was in the cathedral or the castle, Seoras decided to check the former first. He walked across the cemetery towards the side door, passing old graves covered by flat markers worn smooth by time and weather.

The cathedral offered a welcome respite from the sun, and a priest in the nave told Seoras he could find Bishop Andrew in the chapter-house. Sure enough, he found the Bishop there with his secretary, Father Coll.

"Brother…?" Bishop Andrew asked. He was grey-haired but a man of importance in the realm, involved in the affairs of kings as well as the Church.

Seoras swallowed, his mouth dry. "Brother Seoras, your Grace."

The Bishop studied him. "I've not seen you before, and you certainly don't sound like a Glasgow man."

"I was a brother in the Edinburgh monastery, sent here by the abbot in April," Seoras explained. "I was raised near Rannoch Moor in Perthshire." His move from Edinburgh was something he preferred not to discuss. He had offered Abbot Michael nothing but loyalty for over ten years, and to learn the man had broken his Vow of Poverty by stealing offerings made to the monastery had crushed him. He hoped Abbot Robert and Bishop Andrew would be more deserving of his loyalty.

"With that blond hair and blue eyes? You've Sassenach blood, Brother," Father Coll observed.

Seoras nodded. "Aye, Father." From somewhere on his father's side.

Bishop Andrew patted the sealed scroll he had delivered. "Assure Abbot Robert I'll give this my fullest attention. Go with God, Brother."

Chapter Eighteen

Weekends used to mean a respite from work for Hunt; no lectures and no resurrection work (Professor Miller, God rest him, had cherished his weekends too). That he was maybe an hour from finishing the last canvas meant no relief; Sunday was a day of rest, so today was the last rehearsal before the play opened on Monday. Foley was at the pharmacy, his stage work finished. They were to meet at the theatre in the evening before going to the circus.

As he knelt in the theatre workshop applying the finishing touches to the last background – a room in the Vatican – he reflected that it was a far cry from the wining, dining and hunting he'd enjoyed at Dunclutha the previous week.

Still, others he'd met at Dunclutha had suffered a worse week; Hunt had learned that morning of Mr Cotter's murder. More than the death itself troubled him. First Professor Miller had been brutally killed while preparing Canning's body – which had vanished – and now Canning's lawyer had suffered a similar fate.

"Bloody Francis," Mrs Allan muttered while sewing a sleeve onto a robe.

"What's he done now?" Hunt asked. He finished painting in a blue vase and started to add in a crucifix, using the last of the gold paint. The outdoor scene at night had been tedious, requiring him to paint in star after bloody star. *I should have painted in a big cloud instead.*

"Have you not heard? Lily Evitt quit last night for no reason, and His Highness had some new girl hired within an hour." She sneered. "If it turns out he's dismissed Lily to make space for some bint he's poking, there'll be hell to pay."

A casting change two days before the play opened struck

Hunt as passing strange, new as he was to the theatrical trade. Mrs Allan's reaction confirmed it wasn't normal practice. "Maybe Miss Evitt took ill?"

Mrs Allan sniffed. "All I know is I've had to shorten this costume so it fits His Lordship's latest fancy. Bloody tart."

A chestnut-haired girl he hadn't seen before walked up to the seamstress, sparing Hunt the briefest of glances. "Mrs Allan, is it? Mr Francis says you've got my costume." She hailed from the Emerald Isle, judging by her accent, or her parents had.

"Aye, it'll be ready soon," Mrs Allan replied sharply. Hunt was thankful the costume he'd inherited had required no alterations.

"Hello, I'm Wilton Hunt," he said.

She gave him a cursory look. "Kerry Knox, nice to meet you."

"What brings you to our little company two days before opening, Miss Knox?" He recalled his own late addition to the cast and wondered if Mrs Allan was making too much of Kerry Knox replacing Lily Evitt.

"My uncle told me one of the cast had left, so I offered my services."

Mrs Allan sniffed as she stitched.

Hunt didn't believe her aspersion that Miss Knox had seduced Murray Francis to get the part, but something in her manner seemed almost furtive. Not that his own employment was motivated by theatrical inclinations. He was there to find B.H and thereafter Amy Newfield.

"Here, it's done," said Mrs Allan as she thrust the costume into Miss Knox's arms.

"Thank you," Miss Knox said, taken aback by Mrs Allan's rudeness. She left.

"You might be doing her a disservice," Hunt observed.

"You might be shutting your mouth." But the following silence suggested she maybe regretted her discourtesy. She left him to his painting.

Hunt applied the finishing touch almost an hour later and laid down his brush for the last time. It was almost enough to make him hate the smell of paint, but he couldn't deny the satisfaction he felt in seeing his work on such a scale.

"Is that you done?" Murray Francis asked, not for the first time.

He blew out a breath. "That's me done."

"Excellent, fine work." He spared the background picture the briefest glance. "Now get into your costume. This is our last rehearsal before we–"

"–open on Monday," Hunt finished.

Suitably costumed, Hunt joined the rest of the cast on stage as Francis prepared them for the last rehearsal.

"You're an actor, too?"

He turned to see Miss Knox regarding him with some surprise. "Not as such, this is my first role. Only a few lines, but a pivotal role." He winked.

"I assumed you were…" she paused.

"Just a stagehand?" he finished.

She coloured. "I meant no offence."

"To take any would assume shame in such a position, Miss Knox."

"You don't talk like a stagehand," she said.

So much for him blending in. "I'm a university student." Not to mention heir to a barony and shipping company. "I'm doing this for the money."

"Do you know Mr Howard? Mr Benjamin Howard?"

The name pricked his scalp. *Benjamin Howard. B.H.* "No, should I?"

"He's the theatre's patron. Thought you'd maybe met him. Never mind."

He saw the same tautness in her she'd shown earlier when explaining how she got the role, and wondered at her interest in Benjamin Howard. He felt a warm flush at finally learning B.H's identity. *We're one step closer to Amy Newfield.*

"Who're you playing?"

He smiled. "Lucifer." He bowed. "At your service."

"Jesus." She crossed herself.

You'd think I'd grown horns. "Wilton, actually."

Murray Francis cleared his throat. "If you two are *quite* finished, maybe we can begin? … Thank you."

*

It was early in the evening when Hunt and Foley arrived at the circus. The sun still shone and there was a large crowd in attendance. Foley had expressed an eagerness to see it for himself on hearing Hunt's description after his visit with Amelie Gerrard.

The circus was unchanged from Hunt's last visit. A trio of white-faced clowns fought a mock battle with pig bladders, running from tent to tent while a man walked a tightrope overhead. The crowd gasped as two strange horses paraded across the grass, their hides striped black and white.

"Zebra," Hunt pointed. He'd half-believed them a myth, like unicorns.

Foley nodded. "I saw them in South Africa."

"Did you ride one?" He could see himself cutting quite the figure on the back of such a creature.

"No, they can't be ridden."

"Why not? They're just striped horses."

"I don't know, ask an African."

Hunt resolved to do so, assuming he ever met one.

"How did the rehearsal go?" Foley asked. "Did you fall on your arse?"

"No, I did not. It went well." A relief, since his next performance would be in front of hundreds. He felt a chill at the thought. "I finally have a name for B.H; Benjamin Howard. He's the patron, apparently."

"Then he'll likely show at the opening. We should keep an eye out for him."

"That's my thinking, too."

Foley nodded. "Else the whole thing was a waste of our time."

He'd expected a little more enthusiasm. "Not entirely, we made some money."

"Some." Foley seemed more interested in the circus.

A brawny man hefted a massive block of weights to the approbation of the crowd. Others bearing freakish deformities exhibited themselves to the horrified delight of the gawping Glaswegians. Hunt attended within the faded tent of a fortune teller.

"I'm going to be rich and happy," he informed Foley afterwards.

"Well, that's a weight off my mind. I've been losing sleep with worry. Did she promise you'd live to a good old age?"

"Actually, she said I'd die in the embrace of a woman."

Foley arched an eyebrow. "Doing what?"

"Don't know, I didn't want to spoil the surprise."

"The only surprise is you wasting money on a charlatan."

Hunt didn't reply. Her words had said one thing, but her eyes something else at the end, heavy with sudden fearful knowledge. He decided it was part of the performance and put it out of his mind.

Hours passed, and the circus showed no sign of ending. Day faded to dusk and some of the performers left, hurrying to their caravans without a backwards glance.

A new group of performers appeared, haughtier than the folk before. One lifted weights that would have crippled the earlier strongman. Several women with low-cut tunics and swaying hips worked the crowd, beckoning young men to follow them away from the tents. They enthusiastically obliged.

Dark-eyed men appeared, colourfully dressed and arrogantly aloof. Impressionable young women from the crowd hesitatingly answered their call and followed after.

Hunt and Foley were among the chosen. They were led to a secluded spot behind the caravans where a small crowd encircled a large fire. Bottles of fiery liquor were passed around, and a trio of fiddlers stood to the side.

A flurry of music sprang up, enticing the revellers to dance. Many acquiesced, circling the fire with pagan enthusiasm.

Hunt sat on the grass and drank, watching. Several circus dancers pulled their partners away from the fire and led them into the darkness.

Foley tugged on Hunt's arm. "I know him from somewhere."

Hunt followed Foley's gaze and squinted at a circus-man standing near the fire. Something about the stance as well as the man's face tickled his memory. "He does look familiar." He looked back but the man had disappeared.

Many of the dancers sat back down on the grass as the music slowed, but not all. Hunt watched as a woman led off a youth who grinned in delighted disbelief. One raven-haired beauty placed her hand on a local girl's arm and gently coaxed her away out of sight.

"One visit here, Hunt, and your Reverend Mitchell would have sermons enough for the rest of the year," Foley whispered.

Hunt had no idea what was in the bottles being passed around, but it burned fiercely. Most of the others left the fire as time passed, leaving them in the company of a few inebriates and some circus-folk. The circus-folk chattered in their own tongue and shared knowing looks. Hunt had little doubt the revellers were the topic of conversation. He took one last swig from the foreign liquor and got unsteadily to his feet. "I think we should be leaving."

"Now?" Foley sighed and took the bottle from Hunt, hiding it under his jacket as they left the Green.

Chapter Nineteen

Canning exercised his habitual discretion in following his prey through the late-night Glasgow streets. He was uncertain if they had recognised him, but kept such doubts unspoken when asking Marko for leave to follow and kill them. The memory of Cotter's death still excited him; it was his first post-execution kill done of his own accord rather than assigned, and it had whet his appetite for more.

His quarry disappeared into a tenement, and he watched, waiting. Minutes later a light shone behind one of the upper windows, followed by a second. The flat soon returned to darkness, and he waited a further hour before entering the close.

Communal stairs led him up to the first floor where the flat's locked door waited. Undeterred, he pulled out his ring of keys and methodically tried them in the lock one at a time.

The fifth key proved a match, unlocking the door. He entered the flat and stepped softly through the hall. A floorboard creaked under his weight and he froze, before slowly placing his foot elsewhere. The door on his left stood closest, so he opened it carefully and found an empty parlour. He turned back and opened the door across from it to discover a single, sleeping occupant. *No challenge at all.* Canning consoled himself with a promise to take his time with the second resident.

He drew his razor and quietly approached the bed where a young man slept unaware. A swift kill would give little satisfaction; Canning had more mischief in mind, gently pulling the blankets back to expose the sleeper's torso. He clamped his left hand over the man's mouth and slashed down across his chest.

The sleeper flinched, and his eyes snapped open in

response to the pain, but Canning held him down. The torn nightshirt turned black with blood, and the man twisted his head, prompting Canning to shove a wrist into his mouth to prevent any screams.

The sight and smell of blood made him impatient; best to be done quickly and move onto his second victim. He reached out to place the razor against the man's throat but was interrupted by a sharp burning in his left hand. The bastard had bitten him. He yanked his hand free from reflex rather than pain, and felt flesh tear as he did so.

As Canning's left hand pulled back, the young man spat out skin and blood. "Foley!"

Angry now, Canning punched his victim to the face and ducked down hungrily towards the bleeding chest. Part of him knew he should just kill the man and move onto the second, but the spilled blood overcame reason. A hand forced his head back, denying him. By chance they made eye contact and Canning revelled in the shocked recognition he saw there. *Haul me away from my hanging like offal, will you?* He bit into the man's arm, his hunger sharpened by the warm blood filling his mouth. *More...*

Something struck his side and burned, the blow coinciding with a flash and thunder. He saw a man in the doorway with a gun. It roared a further two times, one shot missing, the second striking his lower chest. He backed away, dismayed by how badly he could still be hurt. Seeing the gunman take aim again and left with no choice, he threw himself against the window.

It smashed, and he fell towards the ground…

*

Hunt clutched his bleeding chest, grimacing as pain cut through the shock. Curtains swayed restlessly as a breeze blew through the broken window. A sharp, acrid tang of gunpowder lingered in the room, and the rank taste of Canning's blood turned his stomach. *Canning. The bastard's dead, I saw him hang.*

"Are you alright?" Foley asked, still brandishing his revolver.

Hunt held the blanket to his chest to slow the bleeding. "It was Canning."

Foley stared at Hunt, his mouth open. "*Richard* Canning? He's dead. The doctor confirmed it after the hanging." He crossed himself. "Well, he's dead now or wishes he was." He walked over to the window and looked out. "Shit."

Hunt stirred at Foley's disbelieving tone. "What?"

"Bastard's gone … wait, there he is!" Foley raised his gun and took aim through the broken pane. After a moment he lowered it. "He limped off."

"You shot him at least once, he dived out of a window one floor up, and he can still *walk*?"

"Aye." Foley stepped back from the window.

"How's that possible?"

Foley shook his head. "How's it possible for a hanged man to be here in the first place, or a dead girl to kill people?"

He had no answers. "How did he find us, and why?"

Foley put the gun down and rubbed his jaw. "Canning … it was him we saw at the circus! Though God knows why he was there. Or why they took him in. He must have recognised us from the hanging and followed." He took cognisance of Hunt's wounds. "We need to get you sewn up."

Hunt looked down at the blood seeping through his blanket and grimaced. "Who'll help us at this hour, no questions asked?"

"A doctor of sorts lives nearby. Charles Sirk."

His chest felt on fire. "Professor Sirk?"

"Aye. He attended a medical school years ago before turning to science."

"So long as he can still use a needle and thread." Hunt pulled off the remains of his nightshirt and dressed hastily, wearing an old coat over a vest.

It took them perhaps ten minutes to reach the professor's house. Hunt's vest was soaked with blood by the time they arrived, and nausea threatened to overcome him. Foley banged on the door.

A querulous voice eventually answered from the other side. "Go away, do you *hear* me? Go *away!*"

"I've got a man bleeding out here," Foley shouted. "Open the damned door and let us in."

"Is that you, Mr Foley?"

"Aye, now open the Christ-be-fucked door!"

"…Aye."

Several bolts were slammed back before the door finally creaked open. A day earlier Hunt would have thought such precautions excessive; no longer. Professor Charles Sirk answered the door, a man in his fifties with a mess of curly grey hair. He allowed them inside.

Sirk looked at Hunt reproachfully over a pair of spectacles and then down at the floor. "This is not good. Not good at all."

"What?" Foley sounded concerned.

"Mr Hunt is bleeding all over my carpet. I'll never get that stain out. Ruined. *Completely* ruined." He led them down to the basement. Hunt had studied under Sirk for almost two years, but this was his first time in the professor's home.

They reached the foot of the stairs. Sirk used his candle to light several others scattered around, illuminating the basement. A stained wooden table lay near the centre of the room.

"Put him on the table," he ordered Foley while he fetched medical instruments.

"Aye, Professor." Foley helped Hunt up onto it.

Hunt lay back, feeling increasingly faint as Sirk peered over and studied the chest wound. He felt a painful jab on his arm and drifted away into blissful oblivion.

*

Hunt drifted back to consciousness, distantly aware that he was lying on a table in a strange room but unsure how or why. His limbs still felt numb, but memory of the night's events slowly returned.

A voice sounded to his right. "He's awake, excellent. Mr Foley, come over."

Hunt tried to speak, but nothing exited his mouth but mumbled nonsense.

Foley appeared, looking down. "Hunt, are you okay?"

He nodded, his mouth struggling to form words. In truth he'd rarely felt better.

Foley swore. "He's awake but can't speak."

Sirk studied Hunt for a moment. "Give the drug time to wear off. We'll wait upstairs, and you can recount tonight's escapade." Hunt was aware of them leaving.

True to Sirk's word the numbness faded, and he felt strong enough to get up. His arm and chest throbbed beneath the bandages, suggesting that whatever he'd been injected with was wearing off. The basement was cluttered with a variety of medical and scientific equipment, much of it coated in dust. A shirt hung from the door, and he put it on.

A wave of dizziness warned him to take his time climbing the stairs if he wanted to avoid fainting and falling back down them. One brush with death was enough for tonight.

He found Foley and Sirk upstairs in a book-littered parlour where used plates and mugs lay forgotten on a rim-stained coffee table. They were sitting in two of the three mismatched armchairs that sat haphazard in the room. The chair occupied by Sirk had seen more use than the other two, suggesting he entertained guests rarely, if at all.

The furniture ranged from Georgian to contemporary in a clash of styles. Faded wallpaper covered the walls which were otherwise barren, aside from a few cheap paintings probably chosen at random than for any aesthetic value. The fire had burned low, reduced to a few hot embers. More coal and a few jabs with the poker would stir it back to life, but the professor seemed content to let it die.

Sirk noticed him first. "Mr Hunt, excellent, on your feet at last. No dizziness or bleeding?"

Hunt shook his head. "I'm well, Professor." Aside from the pain. "My thanks." He noticed a few old photographs in the room, one showing a much younger Sirk in the company of several men. There was a look of nervous bravado about them, as if undertaking some risky adventure.

Sirk clasped his hands. "Good, good, *excellent*." His brown tweed trousers were rumpled, and Hunt had a feeling that the professor slept in that chair as often as not.

He offered his hand. "I'm indebted to you, Professor."

Sirk shook it. "You're welcome. If the pain becomes too much, take some more laudanum. Mr Foley can oblige you, I'm sure."

"I'm sure he can." Hunt looked at Foley. "How much did you tell about what happened?"

"Everything I saw. Why don't you tell us what I missed?"

Waking up to find Glasgow's Ripper cutting at him with a razor wasn't something he was keen to re-live. "There's little else to add. He slashed my chest and bit my arm. You were there for the rest." Hunt paused, the memories tumbling around. "He seemed excited by the blood, like he wanted to gorge himself on it." He shivered, and not from the cold. "I could barely hold him back."

"This isn't the first time you've been attacked by a supposed corpse with a taste for blood," Foley observed.

Hunt looked Sirk. "Is there a medical condition to explain this?"

Sirk appeared unaccountably agitated. "All I know is that if I hadn't stitched your wounds, you'd have bled to death."

"What about the dead man who did this?" Foley demanded. "He's been hanged, shot, jumped out of a window, and is still damned lively! Can you explain *that*, Professor?"

Sirk chewed on a knuckle, trembling slightly. "I don't know what you mean. I don't know anything."

Hunt and Foley exchanged looks. His reaction seemed peculiar; they expected scepticism, surprise at least, but not fear.

"You've heard of this before, haven't you?" Foley guessed.

"Can I get either of you some tea?" Sirk asked, ignoring Foley's question.

"Professor," Hunt said gently, "Over the past couple of weeks we've experienced things that defy explanation. If you can explain how a man we saw hanged to death managed to break into our home and survive being shot and jumping out a window, then please, enlighten us."

"Are you *sure* I can't interest either of you in tea? It's Darjeeling." Sirk anxiously looked from Hunt to Foley, refusing to acknowledge their questions.

A brief silence reigned. "Tea sounds grand," Foley said. "Sugar, no milk."

Sirk sniffed. "Sugar, indeed. I'll sweeten it with some honey." He faltered. "Except that I don't believe I have any."

Hunt exhaled as Sirk disappeared into his kitchen. "Is he

truly a doctor? I'll grant you he did a good job with my stitches, but he's insane! He often comes across abstracted during his lectures, but this…"

Foley waved it off. "He's not insane, just eccentric. My father told me he was once well-regarded in Edinburgh, but something happened, and he moved back here a changed man, abandoning Medicine for Palaeontology and Zoology."

Hunt wasn't entirely convinced. "I hope he doesn't ruin my tea." *And I'm not leaving until he tells me what he knows.*

Sirk soon reappeared, the proud bearer of three steaming cups, his early anxiety forgotten. "Enjoy, gentlemen."

Foley took a sip and made a face; Hunt discreetly pushed his own aside when Sirk's attention was elsewhere.

"So how have you been keeping, Professor?" Foley asked.

"Oh, you know, my experiments keep me busy."

"You sound very talented," Hunt said. "A physician as well as a scientist and teacher. Surely a man with your abilities shouldn't be toiling in obscurity?"

Sirk's expression became guarded, sensing more to Hunt's words than simple flattery. "I'm content as I am."

"You were about to tell us about our intruder's unexplained vitality," Foley said, his tone suggesting the topic was one of only passing interest.

Sirk's hands trembled slightly. "I don't know what you mean," he whispered. "I know nothing. Go away!" His gaze fell on a photograph sitting on a small table beside him, before guiltily flitting away. The picture showed Sirk sitting beside another young man in a public house, neither looking at the other, yet both bearing the same confident grin. The picture was old and grainy but captured a shared purpose and companionship.

"Professor," Hunt said, "We're up to our necks in trouble. Every time I think we're close to getting answers, I end up getting beaten up or cut by people commonly believed dead. I'd be grateful if you would just tell us what you know."

"I don't know *anything!*" Sirk yelled. "Go. Please, go, I beg you." He hunched up, covering his mouth with trembling hands.

He's broken. Hunt felt pity for the man. "I'm sorry, Professor. We'll leave you be." They let themselves out.

"At least we know who killed Miller. Poor sod," Foley said as they walked home.

Miller had been tortured to death, Hunt remembered, and considered himself lucky for Foley's intervention. "Do we tell the police?"

"Tell them what? That a dead man killed Professor Miller and then tried to kill us?" Foley shook his head. "We'd be lucky if all they did was kick our arses for wasting their time. No, if Canning visits again we'll deal with him ourselves."

Hunt didn't share his confidence. "He's survived hanging, shooting, and a long fall. What do you plan to try next?"

"Fire. Maybe beheading."

The casual hardness in his tone gave Hunt pause, and the remainder of the walk home passed in silence.

Chapter Twenty

A large crowd attended the opening night of *Doctor Faustus*, men and women dressed in their finest queuing at the Royal Princess's Theatre. A discerning purveyor of the theatre, Redfort usually preferred to wait for reviews before attending, but he made an exception in this case owing to complimentary tickets (excellent seats, of course) courtesy of Benjamin Howard. Those with the best seats were privileged to wait in the foyer rather than outside with the rest.

"…was invited, of course, but if it doesn't involve riding or killing, Sir Arthur's not interested," Howard was saying as Redfort joined him. "Reverend, delighted you could join us. You know Mr Stewart and Mr Owen, of course?"

"Indeed, Mr Howard, very well. A pleasure to see you both." He nodded to the other two men before returning his attention to Howard. "My gratitude for the ticket tonight. I'm partial to Marlowe as you well know."

Howard laughed and waved it off. "Think nothing of it." Tall and still athletic despite being in his middle years, he wore success well.

"My condolences, Reverend. A terrible loss to the church." Archibald Stewart shook his head.

It took Redfort a moment to realise what Stewart was talking about. "Ah yes, Bishop Mann. Truly tragic." He bowed his head.

Howard nodded. "The times we live in, Reverend. I hear the streets tomorrow will be crowded for his funeral, a testament to the love his grace inspired."

"He would be humbled to know he touched so many lives." Redfort dabbed an eye. "The poor were ever close to his heart." Mann's funeral costs could feed those same poor for weeks, but spectacle had its place.

"Reverend Mitchell will do a fine service, I'm sure," Owen said.

"His words will be inspiring," Redfort agreed. Not that anyone would hear them; the shepherdless flock would be looking to the clergyman conducting the funeral service for comfort and direction, making such a man a strong candidate to replace Mann. And so the morning would see the Reverend Mitchell's bowels gripped by flux, leaving Redfort free to conduct the funeral and thus position himself for elevation as Bishop. Assuming Jones succeeded in infiltrating Mitchell's kitchen.

"Has the Church decided on a replacement?" Owen asked.

Redfort gave him a disapproving look. "It would be unseemly to address such a matter until his grace's soul has been commended into God's care, and his vessel conveyed to its resting place." He supposed he himself should be spending the night in prayer rather than attending the theatre, but who would dare comment?

Owen went red. "Apologies, Reverend. That was crass of me."

A wave of the hand smoothed it over. "God will guide us to the right man." *I will guide us to the right man; me. No need to trouble God with the matter.*

The inner doors opened to allow the foremost patrons to take their seats. Redfort made his way alone from the foyer as Howard went backstage to meet the players. Mann's funeral occupied his thoughts, so when an arm bumped against his, it barely registered. His arm was bumped again, and he muttered, "Excuse me," his thoughts still on tomorrow's speech.

A third bump to his arm flared his temper, and he turned to berate the clumsy fool. His angry words died on seeing the party responsible.

Wolfgang Steiner stared at him, and he quailed at the intensity in that fanatic's eyes. Had Steiner come for him or was their paths crossing an unfortunate happenstance? The Templar did not seem to be one for Marlowe, but a theatre was hardly the place for an assassination. *Abraham Lincoln might beg to differ.*

"I am surprised to see you here, particularly on the eve of

your bishop's funeral, Reverend," Steiner said.

"Ah, a surprise seeing you here also, *Herr* Steiner." Redfort realised the inquisitor was in the company of a middle-aged woman who kept her face concealed from him. Perhaps he had come just for the show? He lowered his voice. "Was it necessary to kill Bishop Mann? Surely your Order does not sanction the murder of clergy?"

"Holding a position in the Church is no protection from my Order's judgement, Reverend, be assured." The threat was clear. "And spare me your pretend innocence. We both know I did not kill Bishop Mann. You used me for your own ends; be glad I have more pressing matters to attend to than you at present. It was a good performance you gave, worthy of the stage, perhaps."

"I assure you, Inquisitor, I confided to you in good faith." Steiner suspected, which was almost the same as knowing. But that 'almost' might stay his hand long enough for Redfort's agents to find and kill him first.

Steiner nodded to the still-curtained stage at the far end of the theatre. "*Doctor Faustus*, the tale of a man who trades his soul to devils in exchange for privilege and respect. Does that sound familiar, Reverend?"

"You go too far! I serve God–"

His indignation made Steiner smile. "No, Reverend. 'The god thou serv'st is thine own appetite.' You serve Satan and would 'offer lukewarm blood of new-born babes.' When Redfort dies, men shall 'regard his hellish fall, whose fiendful fortune may exhort the wise only to wonder at unlawful things'."

A chill took root in Redfort as Steiner quoted the play, and for once words failed him. There was an angry certainty in Steiner's voice. "You missed your calling, Steiner. The Templars' gain is the theatre's loss," he said finally.

Steiner looked him in the eye before leaving for his seat. "'Is't not midnight? Come, Mephistopheles!'" were his parting words.

Redfort stood in the aisle, shaken by the Templar's words. Past deeds passed his mind's eye unbidden. *Lukewarm blood indeed*. But he had made his choice long ago and from this path there was no return. "'Cast no more doubts. Come,

Mephistopheles, and bring glad tiding from great Lucifer'," he murmured to himself.

Veni, veni, Mephistophele!

*

"Damn the man," vented Murray Francis. "Minutes before the curtain goes up, and he wants to introduce himself."

"I'm of a mind to give Mr Howard the rough side of my tongue," said Christian Reed. The cast were nervous before the opening, Reed most of all since he played the title character.

Francis gave Reed a worried look. He might be vexed at Benjamin Howard's sense of timing, but the man was patron and required courting. "Ah, no, Reed. Best you take your position – the chorus are about to start."

"I'll take care of Mr Howard, sir," Hunt said, seizing the opportunity to finally meet the mysterious B.H.

"Would you, Hunt?"

Hunt shrugged. "It'll only take a few minutes, he'll want to be seated for the beginning. I'm not on until Act 2 Scene 3, so I'll have ample time to return and prepare."

"I'll meet him too," Miss Knox offered. Dressed in a costume verging on the scandalous, Hunt wagered her company would be more appreciated than his own.

"You're a Godsend, both of you." Francis' gratitude was palpable. He had no wish to offend a patron, even one failing to consider that players fraught with nerves on their opening night would not be convivial company prior to the curtain rising. "Come with me. The rest of you to your places."

A tall, middle-aged man with grey hair and a trimmed moustache waited, his expression genial. Hunt felt himself perspire. His impending theatrical debut made him nervous, but this meeting was worse. Here was a man involved in Amy Newfield's abduction. Hunt's work in the play, his agreement to play Lucifer; all done with the goal of confronting Benjamin Howard.

"Mr Howard, I regret Christian Reed will be unable to meet you until after his performance," Francis said, his shoulders hunched in subservience. "It is my pleasure, however, to introduce you to Mr William Hunt and Miss Kerry Knox, two of our players. Lucifer and Lechery respectively."

"The pleasure is mine." His manner was pleasant, but Hunt felt a sense of proprietorship from him; an entitlement that extended beyond the theatre to its players, if his bold inspection of Miss Knox was any indication.

"An honour, sir," Hunt said. He didn't correct him regarding his name. Using his real name at the theatre was in hindsight a mistake, one he hoped would not come back to haunt him.

Miss Knox showed no discomfort at Howard's stare, offering instead a coquettish smile and curtsey. Murray Francis took advantage of the distraction to mumble an excuse and leave.

"Will you be coming backstage afterwards, sir? Mr Reed and the rest of the players look forward to meeting you." Hunt had his man; now he just needed privacy to confront him.

Howard shook his head. "I regret not. I have a meeting later."

"Somewhere nice?" A wrong word would make Howard suspicious, but Hunt hoped his flushed face would be attributed to performance nerves.

Howard's attention was focused on Miss Knox's figure. "Just my club."

His club. The Black Wing Club, according to the ledger found in the McBride office. Hunt savoured the taste of success and felt his blood afire with exhilaration. He had his man and knew where he'd be after the play, giving Hunt an opportunity to see who he met and challenge him regarding Amy Newfield.

"Do you have a good view?" Miss Knox asked.

Howard had the grace to colour slightly. "Miss Knox?"

"Of the play," she clarified. "As patron you must have the best seat. And call me Kerry. We're not so formal in the theatre."

"Yes, of course. I'm in the main box. A benefit of patronage, Miss Kerry." He smiled at her. "I could show it to you."

Hunt caught his breath at the suggestive offer and expected

a disapproving reception from Miss Knox.

"I might like that, sir, after my performance," she said with a smile and bat of her lashes.

Howard seemed to have forgotten Hunt's presence. "You're Lechery, yes? A role I'm sure you'll play splendidly."

"Very kind, sir, but it is only a *small* role."

He took her meaning. "Perhaps we can discuss future roles afterwards?"

"Could we?" she asked breathlessly. Hunt had dismissed the speculation that she'd seduced Murray Francis to get the role as malicious gossip, but now he wondered. He hoped Howard enjoyed his assignation with Kerry Knox; he would have a less pleasant one with Hunt at the Black Wing Club later.

*

Foley sat in the gods, a term he'd heard during his stint in the theatre to describe the upper balcony. The gods offered the poorest view but the cheapest price, a trade-off he was happy to make. *Doctor Faustus* wasn't really to his taste, but he did enjoy seeing his work out on display. He was no actor though; any performance from him would be as wooden as the props. *I just hope Hunt doesn't embarrass himself.*

Speak of the devil. Hunt walked onto the stage, attended by Mephistopheles and Beelzebub.

"O, who art thou that look'st so terrible?" Christian Reed might be a pompous ass, but he was giving his all as Faustus.

A silence fell as Hunt just stood there. Someone coughed.

"I am Lucifer." Foley felt a chill as Hunt spoke at last, coldly regal in his white linen robe. "And this is my companion prince in hell."

Hunt's performance was excellent; he *was* Lucifer. The Seven Deadly Sins entered on his command, each spoken to in turn by 'Faustus'.

"What are you, Mistress Minx, the seventh and last?" Reed demanded.

Kerry Knox raised her arms invitingly. "Who, I, sir? I am the one that loves an inch of raw mutton better than an ell of fried stockfish, and the first letter of my name begins with lechery." Foley had only met her once during a brief visit backstage to wish the players well.

"Away, to Hell, to Hell!" Lucifer commanded. And the Sins obeyed.

*

The play was far from the best production that Steiner had seen – he preferred Goethe's *Faust* to Marlowe's *Doctor Faustus* – but he had suffered worse. In any case, he had not come for the show.

"Gentlemen, farewell. If I live till morning, I'll visit you; if not, Faustus is gone to Hell."

"Faustus, farewell," the scholars replied. Steiner tapped Lady Delaney on the arm. *It is time.* They left their seats and separated, Steiner heading for the exit. Miss Knox had played her part well, both on stage and with Howard beforehand.

It was cold outside and unfortunately dry; people walked faster in the rain, with their heads down and witnessing little. Three carriages waited outside the theatre, and Steiner had Lady Delaney's assurance that one of them was for the man he wanted. Sure enough, the driver of a wagon marked 'McBride Carriages' gave him a nod and raised the cap concealing his face; it was Burton.

*

Howard sat in the box alone, fingering the note signed 'Lechery'. The girl had accepted his invitation to join him after her performance, and Stewart and Owen had amiably agreed to leave the box early. She would be a happy diversion before and after his meeting with Miss Guillam at the Black Wing Club.

There was a knock at the door. *That'll be her*. Smiling, he opened the door and found himself face-to-face with a stranger. His first reaction was one of irritation, that instead of the Knox girl he faced a woman at least two decades older. She stared at him and offered no apology for the interruption. He realised then that he knew her after all, going cold at the recognition. "Lady Delaney," he managed.

She smiled. "Mr Howard," she said in greeting, their first meeting in twenty years. "I'm afraid Miss Knox won't be joining you. You'll have to make do with my company instead."

"I can't stay, I've a meeting tonight at my club," he heard himself saying and bit his lip.

"The Black Wing Club?"

So, she did remember it, and perhaps knew of its connection to her husband's death. She couldn't blame *him*, surely? It was Sir Andrew Delaney's stubbornness that led to the society taking the action it had, and none could have foreseen the consequences.

"You'll be meeting someone else tonight." The gun she pointed at him made it clear he had no choice.

Lady Delaney escorted him out of the theatre and pointed to the waiting carriage. "A pleasure seeing you again, Mr Howard. We shan't meet again."

"You're letting me go?" He felt confused relief; why go through all this only to let him go – to scare him?

He bore her silent scrutiny for a moment and decided not to risk her changing her mind. He hurried to his carriage and climbed inside.

A silhouette waited inside, a stranger with a foreign accent. "Good evening, Mr Howard. Remain inside or Lady Delaney will be most vexed." He banged his cane against the roof of the carriage and it moved forwards with a jolt. "My own man is driving, yours will awaken in the gutter with a headache in due course. Burton is competent and will convey us safely. We have matters to discuss."

Chapter Twenty-One

The cool night air caressed Hunt's face as he walked up Buchanan Street and turned right into the lane. No boos or vegetables had followed him off stage which boded well for tomorrow's second and final performance, but he had other concerns tonight. He pulled out his membership card and walked into the foyer of the Black Wing Club. After a week of seeking out Benjamin Howard's identity, Hunt at last knew who he was, where he'd be, and when.

His footsteps echoed off the marbled floor as he passed the reception desk. The club restaurant was to his right, closed for the evening. Wall-mounted gaslights lit up the foyer and imbued the marble wall facings with a pale golden sheen. Stone pillars formed an inner circle to support the upper levels. Hunt climbed the main stairs up to the first floor where a set of double doors opened into the main lounge.

The lounge was spacious and elegantly decorated with walls panelled in dark wood, and the floor boasting a rich green carpet. Leather chairs surrounded low standing tables, and the well-stocked bar at the end of the room served whisky, gin, brandy and wine.

Well-dressed members sat reading or talking while others lingered at the bar. Club membership was exclusive and by invitation only. Hunt's had been offered during his first year at the university; being heir to both a title and profitable business made him an attractive prospect to a club that collected members of influence and wealth.

The club's origins were cloaked in mystery, there being no shortage of rumour and innuendo concerning its long-dead founding members. Some claimed that a secret society still lay at its heart and indulged in all manner of debauchery and devil worship, but no one Hunt knew admitted to first-hand knowledge of such outlandish tales.

He bought a brandy from the bar and waited for Howard to arrive. With luck, whomever Howard was meeting would lead Hunt to the woman he saw on Caledonia Street, the woman who took Amy Newfield into her carriage after breaking a man's neck. What he'd do – what he could do – when he found her wasn't something he cared to consider just yet.

"Hunt."

Hunt recognised the speaker. "Irvine," he said in greeting as he stood, the movement aggravating his chest wound. "It's been a while."

"Aye, it's been a year or two since I've seen you here." Jock Irvine was a few years Hunt's senior and a member in very good standing. "How have you been?"

It had been eighteen months, give or take, since Hunt's last visit to the club. He'd maintained his membership, but his familial estrangement and money woes left him reluctant to visit. "Busy. I see some new faces here."

Irvine nodded. "Aye, we've not been idle." Someone waved over to him. "We'll talk later."

"I look forward to it."

Hunt wandered the room, taking his time with the brandy. There were card games such as whist and poker being played in a backroom, and two roulette wheels in another. He watched the wins and losses of the roulette players for a while before stepping up to the table on a whim and placing down several notes.

After a few lucky spins he got reckless and his winnings disappeared. He exercised prudence with his stake from then on to regain Lady Luck's favour, and he won a respectable amount back. Resisting the temptation to play on, he cashed out and returned to the lounge. He bought himself a whisky and kept watch as the crowd thinned out. There was still no sign of Howard, and his recollection of the rest of the evening faded into an indistinct haze.

*

Foley woke with a start as the front door banged shut,

surprised to find himself in his parlour armchair. It was a point of pride that he always made it to his bed no matter how much he drank. The disorientation passed, and he remembered Hunt in the theatre excitedly telling him that Benjamin Howard would be at the Black Wing Club that evening after the show. Foley's offer to accompany Hunt had been refused, Hunt being too junior a member to sign in guests.

"If you can manage not to drink yourself into a stupor, I'll tell you how it went later," the cheeky bastard had said before hurrying out of the theatre. That settled, Foley had watched the rest of the play before returning home.

Having limited himself to only two whiskies, he was surprised at himself for dozing off. On the other hand, the candle had burned down to a stub, suggesting the hour was late. Foley watched the parlour door expectantly, but no one entered.

He waited for Hunt to come in with a report of how the night went but time passed, and he didn't show his face. Anticipation turned to unease. Foley went to Hunt's room and knocked on the door.

"Who is it?"

"It's me." *Who the hell else would it be?*

Silence.

"Can I come in?"

"Yes."

Foley entered to find the room in darkness and Hunt sitting on the bed, staring into space. Foley used his candle to light the one on Hunt's bedside table.

"So how did it go?" Foley asked, irritated at having to prompt him.

Hunt looked up, his eyes glassy and unfocused. "The play?"

"Not the damned play! I was there, remember? Did Howard show at the club? Did he meet anyone? Did you find out his connection to the woman who took away Amy Newfield?"

Hunt paused. "No, he wasn't there."

"So you just stayed there and got drunk?" Foley was incensed. "I've been sitting up all night waiting."

"Why? It wasn't important."

Hunt's indifference took him aback. "Not important? We've spent two weeks investigating this. We broke into a building owned by a family it's unwise to cross. We wasted days working in that theatre just to learn Howard's name. And having finally found out who he is, and where and when he would be, you suddenly decide we've been wasting our time?"

"Well, we have," Hunt said, irritation filling the vacant look on his face. "We've been damn fools chasing our tails over nonsense."

On the verge of saying something he might later regret, Foley decided to leave Hunt to sober up. "We'll talk tomorrow." *Bastard can't hold his drink.*

*

The Tuesday morning dawn found Steiner awake, dressed and prepared for the task awaiting him. One of the first lessons he'd learned was that one never approached a prisoner unprepared. A moment's pause or look of indecision could shatter the necessary illusion that the inquisitor was in complete control. A prisoner must at no time feel he had won a victory, no matter how minor.

The prisoner had been chained in the cellar all night and forbidden food, water and sleep.

His own fast broken, Steiner descended into the cellar and studied the shackled prisoner. Lady Delaney had named him a member of the Black Wing Club and part of the secret society behind it. Benjamin Howard had a black feather tattooed on his right shoulder, confirming he held high position within it.

Steiner removed the hood from Howard's head and looked him in the eyes. "Good morning. I have questions for you. Answering truthfully will spare you much pain and discomfort."

The man hung from the wall, his arms clearly in pain. "Go and fuck yourself, you German bastard."

Steiner had heard such defiance before. "Refrain from using such language in my presence." He began sharpening a blade. *And I am Swiss.*

Once the blade was whetted razor-sharp, he sheathed it and advanced on the prisoner. Steiner was satisfied he had sufficient tools to overcome any reticence.

"I wish to learn of the Sooty Feathers Society behind the Black Wing Club," he said to the prisoner, "Lady Delaney believes you a member of high standing. That feather tattooed on your shoulder tells me she is right. Answer me, and there will be no need for this unpleasantness."

The prisoner drew fearfully back but refused to speak. Steiner was unconcerned; they all spoke in the end. He left, curtly motioning for the two soldiers outside to enter.

Fifteen minutes passed. Carter and Murdo beat the prisoner, softening him up while inflicting no damage that would interfere with the questioning; a man said little through a broken jaw. Steiner studied the beaten man, now chained to a seat in the middle of the cellar. "I have questions. I do hope you have answers." He made himself sound patient, almost relaxed. A man with all the time in the world. Cause the prisoner pain and haunt him with the prospect of weeks more to come.

"I don't know anything about any society," the prisoner mumbled through bloody lips.

"I think you are doing yourself a disservice. I think you do know of it." He squatted in front of Howard and looked him in the eye. "Perhaps I can aid your memory?"

He rose to his feet and took a small hammer from the table, Howard's eyes following it in apprehension. His hands were tied to the chair's armrests and thus easy targets. Steiner swung the hammer down and shattered a finger on Howard's left hand. He paid no heed to the screams but continued to swing the hammer down and down, and down again until all five fingers were broken.

He looked at the prisoner. "That was unpleasant. I pray you will answer my questions before I turn my attention to your right hand. Do you know of the society?"

Howard nodded, his face sickly and his left-hand fingers red and broken. "I know of it."

With the first admission made, more would follow. "You are a member, correct?"

Howard's breathing was strained but he said nothing.

Steiner swung the hammer down again in five rapid motions, smashing all five fingers on Howard's right hand. He wiped his brow, indifferent to Howard's renewed screams.

"Aye! Aye, I'm a member! But I don't know anything. Jesus!"

Steiner knew it was fear, not loyalty that held the prisoner's tongue, but he was confident his skills were sufficient to loosen it. He motioned for one of his men to hold Howard's head. Carter prised open his mouth.

"Are you on the Council?"

"'uck 'ou," Howard managed.

"I have already spoken to you regarding your language." Steiner reached into Howard's mouth with a set of pliers and wrenched out two molars, ignoring the screams. Blood and saliva dribbled down the prisoner's front.

Howard's breathing was shallow, and he sat slumped, his defiance gone. A day earlier he had been a powerful man, wealthy and self-assured. "Yeth, I'm on the Counthil."

Steiner looked down at the snivelling wreckage in disgust. *Broken. He could have saved himself from this.* Now for the important questions.

Steiner asked, and Howard answered. Almost fifteen years on the Council meant he knew it and the society it controlled intimately, but Steiner's interest lay in those behind it. He could spend weeks attacking the Sooty Feathers and their assets, and they would simply be replaced. He would get to them in time but first he wanted to strike at the hands pulling the strings. Howard claimed to know little of them, and Steiner believed him. To an extent.

Torture was an often unreliable tool, causing its subjects, in order to simply stop the pain, to confess to anything; or in this case to perhaps invent whatever he thought Steiner wanted to hear.

"The Caledonia Enterprise Bank?" Steiner let Howard thread his own noose. "Interesting."

"They handle the soshiety'sh finanshes," Howard lied.

Steiner nodded slowly. "Caledonia Enterprise." Now to draw the noose tight and choke him on his lie. "Not the

Heron Crowe Bank?"

Howard's flinch told Steiner he had hit the mark.

Steiner cut off Howard's left little finger, inured to the screams. "Every lie from now on will cost you a finger. When I ask a question, assume I already know the answer," he told Howard when he was sufficiently recovered to listen. "We have many weeks to continue this conversation. How many fingers remain to you shall depend on your honesty."

There. Was that the hint of a smile on Howard's clammy face when he raised the spectre of this continuing indefinitely? Several hours of questioning had broken Howard, the prospect of weeks more should have provoked despair. Unless Howard had good reason to believe his imprisonment would not last so long. *He hopes to be found and rescued, and soon. No, not hopes. He expects to be found.*

Steiner could not think how a diviner could track Howard down, but he knew little of how such things worked. Perhaps the Council had some other means of finding him. *I must finish this quickly, but not before I get something from him.*

"My patience nears an end. Tell me something worth my time about your masters, or I will remove every finger. Right now. And Howard; assume I already know the answer."

Even if Howard expected a rescue, he surely had no wish to live maimed. "There is a Crypt hidden in the Under-Market."

Steiner kept his face still. "Tell me the location and anything else I ought to know. Anything to let my men verify you speak the truth." *A Crypt. Excellent. Finally I can hunt my true prey.*

Howard revealed the location and how to identify its denizens, who, he admitted, frequented the Under-Market incognito.

"Before I send two of my men to verify this, do you wish to reconsider your answer?" Steiner pointedly lifted his knife and eyed Howard's remaining fingers.

"No. They will find the Crypt. Thome of thothe you theek are there, drethed ath I thaid."

Steiner believed him. If Howard believed a rescue was forthcoming, he expected his masters to kill the Templars before they could act on his information, and he had no wish to return to society more maimed than he was already. "I have no further questions." Steiner nodded to Harkins who ceased his scribing and left the cellar with a record of Howard's confessions. With no further need for the prisoner, Steiner wrapped a rope around his throat and pulled it tight.

Carter and Murdo wrapped the body up in sacking, their orders clear; make the body disappear. If the Council had the means to find Howard through unholy means, best not lead them here. If not, let them wonder at his fate.

Howard's execution was twenty years late, but he hoped Lady Delaney would gain some satisfaction from it. Peace would be too much to hope for.

Chapter Twenty-Two

Redfort followed his instructions to the letter and alighted his carriage near High Street an hour before midnight. He pulled up his hood and followed the narrow vennels leading deeper into the rookery. Entering such a place alone at night would be folly under normal circumstances, but he was confident that Miss Guillam's people had chased off the local vermin. She held the position of *Sexta*, the Council's Sixth Seat. Redfort took the greatest care not to offer her the slightest disrespect, and not just because she sat on the Council.

A narrow arch led him down a set of steps and under the railway bridge. Meeting one of the Council usually meant either approbation or censure, and he'd accomplished nothing worthy of the former. *Am I to be the sacrificial lamb, a lesson to motivate the others?*

The uncertainty was galling, especially in light of his success that morning. Bishop Mann's funeral had proceeded as Redfort planned, with him replacing the suddenly indisposed Reverend Mitchell. His (supposedly) impromptu eulogy had been well-received by the congregation and regarded as evidence of natural leadership by the ministers due to vote on Mann's successor. Many who'd supported Mitchell to succeed Mann as bishop now wavered. He was an old man, and a sudden illness cast doubts on his robustness. Redfort was hopeful he would be bishop-elect by the end of the week.

Unless the Council had him killed, of course.

Margot Guillam appeared from the darkness. "Reverend Redfort, you reported Templars in the city and your belief that they killed Bishop Mann. What have you learned since?"

Tread carefully. He rubbed his cold hands together. "My agents have not reported anything definite. I *have* learned these Templars are led by a Knight-Inquisitor Wolfgang Steiner, but not their number or location. I put out word that this Steiner was to be found and killed." It galled that he still lived. "He has not yet been found."

If Miss Guillam was troubled by the cold she gave no sign. *Her kind never do*. "Unfortunate that he is still at large. Perhaps you've been distracted by Church politics?"

He perspired despite the cold.

"The next time you order an assassination, I expect progress. They require more effort than giving an old man diarrhoea."

"Yes, Miss Guillam." She knew that he'd indisposed Mitchell, did she also suspect his involvement in Mann's death? Steiner *had* to be silenced.

But she wasn't quite done. "I didn't just summon you to discuss Templar interference. Have you found the time to investigate who Made this Richard Canning, or has composing eulogies occupied *all* your attention?"

If his answer failed to satisfy her, Redfort feared someone would soon have the task of composing *his* eulogy. "I've made extensive enquiries. Canning was visited by a priest and a lawyer the night before his execution. The lawyer, Stokes, is in York, we await his return. The diocese has no record of the priest, I believe it is *he* whom you seek."

She gave him a considering look. "Visitors would have been escorted to the cell. What do the guards say?"

"They vaguely remembered Stokes, however neither can recall anything about the priest."

Margot Guillam nodded. "So he Mesmered them. I want this 'priest' identified and found. I suspect more is happening than a rogue element indiscriminately killing and Making for the sake of it."

"I will continue to look into it." He paused. "Forgive my presumption, but you did not meet me here simply for an account of my investigation. There is something else, yes?"

She studied him. "Perceptive. Yes, there is something else. I was to meet Benjamin Howard at Sooty Feathers last night, but he did not appear."

"I spoke to him last night at the Royal Princess's Theatre," Redfort said, taken aback by the news. So that was Steiner's purpose there. Bold, to abduct one of the Council in so public a venue. He decided not to mention seeing Steiner there.

"He was last seen alive at the play." Unblinking eyes fixed on him. "A carriage was to take him from the theatre to the club, but the driver was found unconscious nearby. You know who Howard is." It wasn't a question.

It was no secret. "Yes, he is *Quintus*." The fifth of eight on the Council. "Is there not a contingency in place for councillors?" Every councillor supplied a vial of their blood. Should they go missing, the Council would employ a diviner to use the blood to find its donor. It meant anyone on the Council could always be found, whether they wished it or not.

Miss Guillam nodded. "A diviner was given Howard's blood this evening when it was clear he had disappeared, and accompanied the searchers. They found Howard in the river, weighted down in a sack. His body bore signs of extensive torture."

She was watching his reactions, Redfort knew. Gauging the veracity of his surprise to each revelation. "The work of a Templar Inquisitor," he said.

"It appears to be so. Though that begs the question of what led this Steiner to Howard. Or who."

"I doubt I was the only one to be visited by him." He had manipulated the Templars into attacking Bishop Mann, not Benjamin Howard. Ironic if the Council judged him guilty for a betrayal of which he was innocent.

"No, others have also reported contact with this Templar. Learn what you can and make no presumptions; Howard sat on the Council for many years and made his share of enemies. Perhaps the culprit is one of our own."

"I will give this matter my fullest attention." Inwardly he brightened. Howard's murder meant a vacant seat on the Council, a fitting reward for the one finding his killer. Having seen Steiner and suffered his insults at the theatre on the night of Howard's abduction, Redfort need waste no time investigating other suspects. And he had his own reasons for wanting Steiner dealt with.

"We will leave it in your hands. Congratulations on your forthcoming elevation as bishop."

His heart quickened. “That matter is still in God’s hands.” Still in his fellow ministers’ hands, rather.

“Is it?” She walked into the darkness. “Good night, *Your Grace*. We will hear from you soon.”

Redfort bowed, not bothering to hide his smile. “As you say, Miss Guillam. And thank you.

*

The bell above the door rang, alerting Foley to the arrival of a customer. Half-pleased at the custom, half-irritated by the interruption, he looked up from his paper to see the gaunt frame of Professor Sirk approach the counter.

Surprise caught Foley’s tongue a moment. “Afternoon, Professor.” Sirk had treated Hunt’s wounds well enough, but the circumstances behind them had caused the professor agitation. He had not expected to see Sirk so soon given their strained parting, but the need in his eyes told the purpose of his visit. Foley recognised it; hell, he shared it.

Sirk nodded. “Well met, Mr Foley.” He was reluctant, as always, to say what he wanted, but Foley knew.

“Your usual?”

“Aye.” He sounded almost defensive, though his vices were his own business as far as Foley was concerned. “I injected the last of my supply into your friend.”

“I’ll knock a penny off the price.” Foley moved a large half-empty bottle of laudanum from a shelf onto the counter.

“How are Mr Hunt’s injuries?” Sirk asked while Foley poured some into a measuring beaker.

“They’re healing well enough.” It was Hunt’s mind that troubled him now, not the wounds inflicted by Canning. Foley had questioned him yesterday morning again about his visit to the Black Wing Club, but he still insisted Howard never showed, nothing had happened, and they should forget the whole matter. When Foley pressed him further he seemed both angry and unfocused.

“You don’t seem very sure.”

Foley blinked. “What? Oh, he’s healing fine. But since Monday night he’s not been himself.”

“How so?”

Sirk didn't sound especially interested, but Foley felt a need to talk. "He was out two nights ago looking into the matter we alluded too, but since then he's been different. Vague when I ask him what he found out, and hostile when I press him." He remembered Hunt acting on stage. "It's almost like he's reading from a play, only not very well." Foley filled a smaller bottle and put a stopper in it. "Here you go." He looked up to see Sirk staring at him. "What?"

"Would you say Hunt is acting out of character?" Sirk asked with a quiet intensity.

"Aye, something about him has changed."

There was recognition on Sirk's face, fear too. "I want to see him," he said firmly, but with a measure of dread.

"What about tonight? My flat's above the shop."

"Expect me at seven o'clock." Sirk took the laudanum and left some coins. "Good day to you, Mr Foley."

Chapter Twenty-Three

Hunt sat in the parlour and suffered Professor Sirk's inspection of his injuries. The pain was a constant nuisance but one that lessened as the days passed. His chief irritation now was Foley pestering him about Monday night. Nothing had happened, so why keep going on about it?

The theatre, too, was fading into irrelevancy. He'd given his second and final performance the previous night, his thespian days done.

He wondered irritably why he'd wasted so much time investigating a missing body; it was trivial, why did it matter? Something nagged at him like a shadow on his periphery. Whatever it was remained frustratingly elusive, and his head seemed clearer when he left it alone.

"Aye, healing well enough and free from infection," Sirk said. The professor seemed distracted. Foley stood nearby with his arms folded, ill at ease. Hunt had walked in on the two talking quietly, about what he didn't know. *Me, maybe?*

"Mr Foley tells me you played Lucifer on the stage on Monday night," Sirk said.

"Yes, and Tuesday," Hunt said. His head ached a little.

"Fascinating," Sirk said. "How did you celebrate after?"

"I didn't. I came home and slept. I had an early lecture today."

"I meant Monday," Sirk said.

"I had lectures on Monday, too. You gave one, remember?"

"No, how did you celebrate on Monday?" Sirk persisted.

The ache in Hunt's head intensified. "I had a drink or two."

"Where?"

"Where?" Hunt felt cornered.

"That's what I'm asking," Sirk said. Hunt caught him exchanging a look with Foley. They were trying to trap him.

"On Tuesday? Nowhere. I went to bed early."

"Not yesterday, Monday! Where did you go for a drink? It's not a difficult question."

"Nor an important one," Hunt snapped. He almost asked why they bloody cared so much, but curiosity only hurt his head more. Anyway, it didn't matter.

"Did you meet anyone?" Foley asked. "Did you see Benjamin Howard?"

His head felt aflame. "No, I didn't see Benjamin bloody Howard!" That much he was sure of.

"Just before you left the theatre, you told me Howard would be at the Black Wing Club." Foley's voice drifted around him. "Why wouldn't he show?"

"I don't know! She wanted to know, too." The last slipped out before he could stop it.

"She?" Sirk's tone turned sharp. He gave Foley a querying look, but Foley shook his head. "It is what I feared," Sirk said. "He'll not remember."

"He'll remember even if I have to beat the memories out of him," Foley said roughly. "Bloody think, Hunt. It's Monday night and you're in the Black Wing Club waiting for Howard..."

There was something wrapped around his mind that tried to fight the words, something cold, hard and brittle. But something deeper, something older, colder and harder rose up. The brittle thing in his head cracked...

Hunt bought another drink and sipped it slowly, alone with his thoughts in the Black Wing Club. There was no sign of Benjamin Howard, and he decided he was wasting his time. The opening night of Doctor Faustus *had wearied him, and he had a further performance tomorrow night.*

He was about to leave the club when he felt a tap on his shoulder. He turned, thinking it another acquaintance wishing to say hello. Instead he was confronted by the pale apparition of Amy Newfield.

They stared at each other for a long time, neither speaking.

Hunt forced a smile. "Can I help you, miss?" He willed his face to betray nothing even as his heart pounded in his chest. She looked different than before, pink tingeing her cheeks, and her filthy tangled hair now clean and arranged. The remains of her funeral dress had been replaced with attire more appropriate to the location.

"Good evening, sir."

He took a step back, but she made no move to attack him. The feral creature who had almost killed him had been tamed as well as groomed. "Evening," he said, at a loss for words. He'd come to the club to confront Benjamin Howard about Amy Newfield, only to find her instead.

She smiled and offered her hand. "My name is Miss South."

He swallowed and accepted her hand. It felt cold. "A pleasure." He almost accepted the lie, but he was done with games. "Miss Newfield."

Her unblinking stare left him discomforted, marble eyes flickering with recognition. She leaned her head in closer to his, almost resting on his shoulder. "It is you," she said quietly. "I wondered why Miss Guillam sent me to fetch you. I remember you and another man in the cemetery, and you again days later outside it."

Hunt tensed. "So, you are Amy Newfield." It was more statement than question. His senses screamed that she was wrong. "Who is Miss Guillam?"

"My mistress." She tilted her head. "You remember her? She broke the bad man."

He did indeed. He also remembered the epitaph on Miss Newfield's gravestone. "Why don't you go home? You have a family."

There was an echo of sadness in her voice, an emotion remembered rather than felt. "My family buried me. I was told I can't go back, not ever. They think I'm dead, dead and buried."

"But you're..."

"Alive?" Glassy eyes stared into his, eyes that hardly blinked. "My life feels like another's memories. I was reborn in a coffin in the dark, and you were the midwife who pulled me out into the world." Her giggle sent a cold spike down his spine. "Alive?"

She was quite mad. "There were people killed near the cemetery, that was you, wasn't it? Why?"

Her head ducked slightly. "Newborns need to feed."

He still saw the killer in her, ragged and wild, but now held together by a pretty dress and hair pins, with Miss Guillam's hands on her strings. "Is Miss Guillam a member here?" Women members were few but not unheard of. He remembered her twisting a man's neck like a chicken's.

"Aye," Miss Newfield replied. "She'll be down soon. She said I was to talk to you."

Meaning she was upstairs. Hunt had never visited the upper level, it hosted the club's committee. And its supposed secret society, if the more fanciful rumours were true. He had no desire to see Miss Guillam again. "I must be leaving, give her my regards. Good night, Miss ... South."

"But Miss Guillam wants to speak to you."

"Later maybe." It was time to leave.

"Now would be better," another woman's voice said behind him, her local accent very lightly seasoned with French.

Fear cleansed Hunt of his slight intoxication.

"Amy, I'd like to speak with your friend." An auburn-haired woman joined them with hair arranged much like Miss Newfield's. Hunt felt a jolt as they made eye contact. Those same eyes had weighed his life near the Southern Necropolis. He was unable to place her age, guessing somewhere between twenty-five and thirty.

"Follow," she commanded, and Hunt found himself doing just that. Amy Newfield trotted obediently behind. They were led to a quiet corner of the club, dark and secluded.

"I am Margot Guillam. You are...?"

"Wilton Hunt," he replied, too scared to chance a lie.

"Why are you here, Mr Hunt?" Miss Guillam asked. "I'll know if you're lying."

He thought better than to test her. "I'm waiting for Benjamin Howard."

"A coincidence; so am I. It was arranged some time ago, so I am quite vexed he hasn't shown." She didn't blink. "Why is he not here?"

"I don't know," Hunt said, praying she believed him. "I met him at the theatre, he said he would be here after the show." He felt no need to mention having also learned of it

while breaking into the McBride Carriages office.

"I believe you," she said. "How are you involved?"

"I exhumed her." Hunt pointed at Amy Newfield. "I heard of deaths at the Southern Necropolis after, and..." He shrugged.

It was a poor state of affairs when a murderess regarded him with distaste. "Is digging up corpses a habit of yours, Mr Hunt?"

"A profession," he admitted. "A medical professor paid me for them."

"You're a fool in the wrong place at the wrong time," Miss Guillam decided. "Few outside our control who learn as much as you have survive such knowledge. But too many have died or disappeared recently, so perhaps a lighter touch is called for tonight." Guillam's voice hardened, and her eyes bored into Hunt's. "You don't remember meeting Amy Newfield tonight. You met no one tonight. You feel tired and need to sleep. There's no need to continue investigating this matter."

"Is this how you hide?" Hunt's thoughts were assailed by the woman's will.

"Yes, mostly. The Mesmer is a useful ability."

He mumbled something, his head feeling stuffed with wool.

"Amy, it's time we were off," Miss Guillam said. "Mr Howard will not be coming, it seems." Miss Newfield returned to her side almost fearfully, and the pair left without looking back. Hunt stood a while before his legs carried him towards the exit, his muddled thoughts urging him home...

Hunt's eyes opened, and he felt sweat on his brow and running down his arms as his will battled Margot Guillam's hold on it. Then the binding shattered like glass and the pain subsided. *She made me forget.* He looked at Foley and Sirk. "Jesus Christ," he blasphemed hoarsely.

"What happened?" Foley asked.

"Pour me something strong, and I'll tell you."

*

"This is good tea, Foley." Sirk slurped noisily from the cup.

His nerves fortified by the whisky, Hunt had related his newly recovered memory of meeting Margot Guillam and Amy Newfield in the club. Sirk had pressed him on several points.

"So, Howard really did never show?" Foley asked.

Hunt shook his head. "Not while I was there. We know he was to meet Margot Guillam, who was surprised by his absence also. Not that it matters now."

"No?" Foley asked.

"We only sought him out regarding his connection to the woman and carriage who took Amy Newfield from Caledonia Road," Hunt reminded him. "I encountered both at the club." *An encounter I'm fortunate to have survived.*

"How did this Guillam woman affect your memory so thoroughly?" Foley looked at Sirk. "Hypnosis?"

Sirk shook his head, the teacup hovering beneath his chin. "Whatever was done to him goes beyond hypnosis." He looked at Hunt. "What did she call it?"

"'Mesmer' was the word she used."

"You suspected that, did you not, Professor?" Foley asked. "When I told you Hunt was acting out of character."

"I've encountered it before, though Mr Hunt is the first I've known to recover the suppressed memories." Sirk shrugged. "It was either that or something worse."

"Worse?" Hunt asked. What Miss Guillam had done to him was bad enough.

Sirk waved it off. "You say this Amy Newfield was dead." Brown eyes flickered between them from beneath thick, unkempt eyebrows. "Are you certain?"

"Aye," Foley said.

Hunt nodded in agreement. "Canning too, hanged and thereafter pronounced dead by a doctor. That didn't stop him trying to kill me, and he survived being shot and falling from a window in this very flat."

Foley watched Sirk. "This isn't the first time you've heard of this, is it?"

Sirk's right hand trembled. "Very well." He pulled out a pipe and filled it with tobacco. "I tried to dissuade you at our last meeting." He lit the pipe and handed his cup to Foley. "Fill that with something medicinal and keep the bottle to hand." He turned back to Hunt. "Start at the beginning."

Hunt traded a look with Foley who nodded.

Sirk proved a good listener, sharp and attentive. Hunt told him of Amy Newfield's disappearance, of the deaths she'd caused, and of Canning's disappearance following Miller's murder. With Foley's encouragement he spoke of his encounter with Miss Newfield at the Southern Necropolis and of Miss Guillam's intervention.

Sirk inhaled from his pipe and blew out smoke. "A troubling tale, gentlemen, but not one unfamiliar to me."

Foley and Hunt exchanged glances. "How so?" Hunt asked.

Sirk shook his head. "I'll get to that. But let me impress upon you, what I tell you will change your perception of the world. The states of life and death *converge,* and unnatural forces exist between them."

"How would you explain the disappearance of a recently dug-up corpse?" Foley snorted. "It's not fairies, is it?"

Sirk peered over his spectacles at Foley and frowned. "Don't be naive, Foley. Fairies aren't real." His eyes had a haunted look about them, weighed down by dreadful knowledge. "I believe your Miss Newfield and Mr Canning – Miss Guillam too, most like – are *un*dead."

"*Un*dead? I don't *un*derstand." Foley looked at Hunt, but he only shrugged.

"Dead, but restored to something *like* life, but *not* life. No heartbeat, no need for breath, but able to walk and talk and *think* … and needing blood for sustenance. Absent all moral constraints." Sirk emptied his cup and helped himself to more whisky.

He sat back down. "There are myths dating back to antiquity of such creatures all over the world, from Eastern Europe to Africa to Asia. Tales of the dead returning to haunt the living. The how and why is beyond my ken, but I've had a few first-hand experiences with these undead, and all ended bloody. Food and drink give no sustenance; their sole succour comes from blood, preferably human.

"Some haunt sewers and cemeteries, others have infiltrated society, employing fear, murder and money to control the living." Sirk looked at Hunt. "Some among them can manipulate memory as you can attest."

"These undead, how do we fight them?" Foley asked, ever practical.

"Well, fire can destroy them. Sunlight too. Decapitation, naturally. This Canning survived being shot, suggesting resilience to what would kill most men."

Hunt shifted. "Sunlight?" *The long summer days must be hell on them. Winter, on the other hand...*

"I cannot explain why, but it is anathema to them. You will only encounter them at night, and they take refuge in dark, secluded places during the day."

"Sounds like Foley most mornings," Hunt couldn't resist.

Foley gave him a sour look. "Do you want to listen to the professor or make clever remarks?"

"No reason I can't do both." Hunt decided to push his luck. "May I ask how you came by this knowledge?"

A brooding look fell over Sirk's face and he fell silent for a moment. "I will tell you. But not here."

"Then where?" Foley asked.

Sirk finished his whisky. "I suggest we decamp to a public house."

The Old Toll Bar was only a few doors along from Foley's flat and not unduly crowded. Hunt and Sirk sat at a secluded table in the corner. "What's your drink, Professor?" Foley asked.

Sirk rubbed his jaw. "Oh, I really don't know."

"Another whisky, or maybe an ale?"

"A pint of ale would be appreciated. One tires of whisky," Sirk confided.

"If you say so." Foley turned to the barmaid. "Miss, three pints of the usual, please."

Three pints duly arrived.

Confident they were in no danger of being overheard, Hunt looked at Sirk. "You promised to tell us of how you learned of the undead."

"I made no such promise," Sirk corrected pedantically, "but yes, I shall tell you." He sighed and took another sip from his ale, ignorant of the foam left on his upper lip. "Very well. My tale begins some years ago, in Edinburgh.

"I was a young man, the ink still wet on my doctorate. Confident and possessed of a keen mind – if I say so myself –

the world before me seemed full of promise. So I believed." He smiled, an echo of that young man shining through eyes weighted by more than years. "A fellow was brought to me sorely wounded, and I tended to him with exemplary skill. My curiosity was aroused, and like you, I kept *pushing* until I learned the *truth*. Better I had remained ignorant.

"After a time, I found myself helping a small group of citizens investigating mysterious deaths much like you two. Our persistence paid off and we discovered the killers were not mortal. We hunted them throughout the city and our initial forays met with success. My efforts played no small part."

Hunt smiled at his lack of modesty.

"What happened?" Foley asked quietly.

Sirk looked down. "Success proved to be our downfall. The undead recognised us as a threat and lured us into a trap using one we trusted." His face twisted. "It was terrible, only three of us escaped. We spoke of vengeance, of fighting back, but we knew we wouldn't. Our spirit was broken."

An awkward silence followed. Sirk took two shaky gulps from his pint, eyes gleaming wet in the candlelight.

"So that was that?" Foley asked.

Sirk's smile was melancholy. "Aye. That was that. I moved back to Glasgow, fled really. I learned later that another organisation sent men who succeeded in cleansing the city. Mostly."

Hunt opened his mouth to ask about the other group, but Foley spoke first. "Who betrayed you?"

"John Harris. A fine man, dedicated to our cause."

"Then why did he betray you?" Hunt wanted to know.

Sirk dabbed at his eye. "He didn't, precisely. I told you there was worse than being Mesmered? Harris was caught by the undead who put a demon inside him. We suspected nothing, had no idea our friend was gone the moment the demon possessed him. It lured us into an ambush and taunted the few of us who survived as we fled, leaving our dead and dying friends behind."

"Demon?" Hunt asked in alarm. *Better and better. What next, Auld Nick himself?*

Sirk looked at him. "Aye. Did I not mention them?"

"No, Professor." Hunt finished his pint.

"Demons, hmm. I know a little. They can be summoned from Hell. To summon one the following is needed: A living person to host the demon, a human sacrifice, and the name of the demon. Blood from an undead. And a demonist."

"Demonist?" Foley asked.

"Someone able to perform the ceremony. Whether such ability is learned or attained from birth, I cannot say," he said with a shrug.

Different worlds indeed, Hunt reflected.

"I have a need to urinate," Sirk declared, standing up.

Foley caught Hunt's eye as Sirk left. "What do you think?"

"Of what?"

"Of his story! Of these … undead and demons. Is it true, or is he one tale shy of Bedlam?"

Hunt considered it. "Last week I'd have been all for committing him. But after what we've seen, I'm inclined to give him the benefit of the doubt."

Foley sighed. "I thought you'd say that. I wish I could disagree."

"It *is* the first lecture he's given in months that hasn't threatened to put me to sleep."

Sirk returned. "Now that Mr Hunt is back to his old self, do you intend to continue your investigation?"

Hunt and Foley exchanged looks. "Maybe," Foley said. "Where do you suggest we look next? The trail ended at the Black Wing Club."

"I propose we visit the Carpathian Circus where you saw Richard Canning," Sirk said.

"'We'?" Foley asked.

"I thought I'd join you. I'd welcome another chance to capture and study one of these creatures." There was an energy in the professor Hunt hadn't seen before, a glimpse of the young man who had hunted undead across and under Edinburgh.

"Your company and experience will be welcome, Professor." Hunt kept a straight face. "A boon companion who can stay sober will be a welcome addition."

"By all means," Foley said. "Hunt's not much use; he gets beaten up by dead girls, and when he finds them again, he's forgotten by morning."

"If you two can stay serious long enough, we should visit the circus tomorrow evening and see what's what." Sirk finished his pint.

Hunt and Foley both nodded. "I think we should toast this new association," Foley said.

Sirk regarded his empty glass before sliding it towards them. "Another pint would be gratefully received."

Chapter Twenty-Four

There were fewer people at the circus than during their last visit, but still a respectable number for a Thursday night. Hunt was resolved to look past the theatrics and sleights of hand to learn the truth of the place. Richard Canning's presence might have been coincidence and the circus-folk entirely innocent, but he suspected otherwise. Canning had been dressed as one of them. What possible use could a circus have for a hanged murderer even Death washed his hands of?

Hunt caught up with Foley and Professor Sirk, the latter enjoying a toffee apple. Sirk held a cane in his right-hand, though showed no sign of a limp. If Canning was there, they didn't see him. *So long as he doesn't see us.*

Hunt looked through the bright costumes and false smiles, sensing a menace lurking beneath. He was glad Foley had brought his gun; then remembered what they hunted.

Only a week had passed since he had brought Amelie to the circus, though it felt longer. He must have made a good impression; he and his parents were to dine with the Gerrards on Saturday night. *So why the hell am I risking another encounter with Richard Canning?* He'd been a murderous bastard alive, and death hadn't sweetened his nature.

Sirk watched a vacant-eyed woman stumble out of a fortune teller's tent. "Let's tarry here a while, gentlemen." A ruddy-faced man entered next.

Foley folded his arms. "What are we looking for?"

"That fellow to come out."

"Why? You want to ask him his future?" Foley asked, his tone earning him an irritated look.

"His present concerns me more. I want to see his condition when he returns," Sirk answered, eyes returning to the tent as he finished his toffee apple.

The man re-appeared after ten minutes, a stagger in his step that he hadn't entered with. Sirk walked up to him. "Ho there, what did the teller predict for you?"

The man stared at Sirk through glazed eyes, his face chalk-white. "She promised me a long and happy life," he slurred.

"That took ten minutes?" Foley shook his head.

Sirk stepped aside. "That sounds grand, don't let us keep you from it." The man staggered off without another word.

Foley turned to Sirk. "What was that about?"

"What did you see?" Sirk countered.

"A man with coin to waste?" Foley shrugged, not one for games.

"He seemed fine going in the tent," Hunt said. "but looked drunk – or maybe drugged – coming out?"

The professor sighed, running a hand through his unruly grey hair. "I despair of you two, I really do. He went in with a red face and a sure step. He came out pale and dull-witted. And with spots of blood on his collar." He said the last quietly, almost to himself.

"What does blood have to do with anything?" Foley asked, but Sirk didn't answer.

"He was Mesmered," Hunt guessed. "Why?"

"Maybe he realised she was a charlatan and wanted his money back?" Foley said unhelpfully.

Hunt recalled the man's change in pallor and the blood spots on his collar. Maybe she'd wanted more than his coin, and Mesmered him to forget her taking blood from him.

"Let's see what else is going on here." Sirk cleared his throat. "Over there." He nodded in the direction of a black-coated man wearing a distinctively tall top-hat who entered a caravan, his lower face concealed by a scarf.

"He's not dressed like one of the circus," Foley said, "but he must be. They wouldn't tolerate a stranger entering uninvited."

"Agreed," Sirk said softly. "I suggest we remove ourselves to a more covert location."

They left the circus and settled a short distance away in a small, heavily vegetated copse of trees. It was cloaked in blackness, allowing them to spy on the circus without fear of being spotted in turn. Time passed, but the circus seemed in no hurry to finish. Most of the torches were extinguished, a few small fires left to burn.

Hunt shifted in a fruitless attempt to make himself comfortable, his heavy coat keeping out the worst of the cold. It was too dark to see the time on his pocket watch, but he estimated it closer to dawn than midnight. Movement could still be seen around the circus, and he wondered if it ever completely slept. There was no sign of Richard Canning.

Foley crept over and passed Hunt his army field-glasses. "Look at the caravan our black-hatted friend entered earlier."

Hunt peered through the lenses, careful not to point them at a fire and ruin his night sight. He found the caravan in time to see Black Hat exit and walk to the nearest fire. Three loutish circus-men stood around it, laughing loudly as they shared a bottle. Their demeanour changed when Black Hat reached them, as if they feared him. The relief in their postures when he left the fire was unmistakable.

"What's he doing?" Foley wanted to know.

"Making some circus lads foul their breeches by the look of it. He's leaving the Green, walking towards the city, I'd say."

Sirk joined them. "Where could he be going at this hour? Very suspicious."

Hunt refrained from pointing out that three men skulking in bushes all night were in no position to cast stones.

"Only one way to find out." Foley pocketed his field glasses. "Come on."

The trio followed him out of the park, seeing only a tall-hatted silhouette as he left the lights of the circus behind.

"He's at home in the circus – acts like he owns it – but dresses like a local gentleman." Foley talked as they walked. "And what can't wait until morning, why leave at this time?"

"And on his own, with no regard for footpads," Sirk said. Tall and gaunt, the older man had no trouble keeping up. His comment put Hunt in mind of Margot Guillam, who proved herself more than a match for Glasgow's footpads near the Southern Necropolis.

The empty streets proved both help and hindrance in their pursuit, making Black Hat easy to follow but also increasing the risk of being seen. He unknowingly led them into the Saltmarket, past illicit taverns and crumbling tenements.

Two rogues stepped out from a lane and blocked Black Hat's way. Foley stepped into a doorway and indicated Hunt and Sirk do likewise. Hunt wondered if they should go to Black Hat's aid. They had no proof he was involved with Canning or the circus, and Hunt was unwilling to watch an innocent fall victim to footpads. Foley seemed of a like-mind, his right hand resting in the coat-pocket where he kept his revolver. But for the moment he seemed content to see how the confrontation played out.

The footpads' demeanour made their intentions clear. Black Hat unwound his scarf in answer. What he said to them, Hunt was too far to hear, but they backed off and fled. Black Hat's face gleamed white under the gas street-light, but the distance was too great to discern his features. He pulled up his scarf and continued on his way.

"A remarkably persuasive fellow," Sirk breathed.

"Aye," Foley said. "And one we'll lose if we don't hurry."

Having seen him scare two robbers into flight, Hunt wasn't sure that would be altogether bad. He let Foley lead the pursuit and considered the man they followed in a new light, no longer doubting a connection to Newfield, Canning and Guillam. They were pieces in the same puzzle, but how did they fit together? A young woman and a hanged murderer, both recently returned from death to a semblance of life. Margot Guillam, another likely undead who associated with theatre patrons such as Benjamin Howard, and villains like the McBrides.

How a foreign circus sheltering Canning was involved still eluded Hunt's comprehension. It all seemed fantastical to him, unbelievable that such unnatural events eluded the public knowledge. But if Foley's police friend had spoken true about murders being covered up, then controlling the newspapers would be no problem for such people. He might not know how the pieces all fitted together, but the picture grew alarmingly in size and significance.

They crossed into High Street and passed the old Tollbooth's steeple.

"Pick up the pace," Foley said as Black Hat turned into a narrow vennel separating two tenements, "or we'll lose him in there."

They followed the tall-hatted man into the vennel and found themselves navigating a maze of wynds and lanes separating the tenements of a rookery that had somehow escaped demolition. It was Glasgow's shame that entire families – mostly dispossessed Highlanders and Irish immigrants – were crammed into single squalid rooms bereft of sanitation or modesty. They were, hard as Hunt found to believe his own eyes, not even the least fortunate in this pit of destitution. As he followed Foley through passages so narrow they endured perpetual shade, he saw people huddled against walls. The fortunate slept in patches free from the waste produced by so dense a population.

There was little provision to get rid of that waste, the stench of which threatened to empty Hunt's stomach. Gutters had been set in the ground to channel the waste away, but there was simply too much of it. The rain would merely wash the stagnant urine and shit downhill in a sluggish river of slurry, to be replaced with more of the same from further up the hill.

Hunt believed Black Hat lost to them in the patchwork maze, but they turned a corner and caught sight of him ahead, his silhouette made distinct by his tall hat. He seemed to be embracing someone, and Hunt's first thought was that they had caught the man – dressed entirely out of place for such impoverished surroundings – in a clandestine liaison. Until Black Hat relaxed his embrace and let the other fall limply to the ground.

"Hey!" Foley shouted as he pulled his revolver free from his coat pocket.

Black Hat turned and took a step towards them, undaunted by their three-to-one advantage. A sudden fear seized Hunt. "I'll shoot," Foley called out, his voice betraying a similar trepidation. Black Hat seemed to consider challenging them regardless, then thought better of it and left. That gnawing fear left with him.

Foley struck a match off a wall while Sirk knelt next to Black Hat's victim, a hollow-cheeked boy clad in soiled rags. His skin was white, not just sun-deprived pale but bloodless-white. Twin pricks of match-light shone in his glassy eyes.

Sirk pressed two fingers against the boy's throat. "Dead,"

he said to no one's surprise.

"He looks like he bled to death," Foley said. He examined the ground. "But I don't see any blood."

Sirk exposed the right side of the boy's neck to reveal a smudge of drying blood. "There are marks here," he said softly.

"Bite marks?" Hunt asked.

"These are no normal teeth marks. Some of the corpses I examined in Edinburgh had wounds caused by human hands and teeth. But others had puncture marks like these…"

"What are you thinking?" Hunt asked, but Sirk didn't answer.

"I'm going to catch that bastard before he kills again," Foley gave the wynd a sour look. "If we can find him."

Hunt looked up at the fragment of sky visible between the buildings, greying into dawn. "You said the undead can't tolerate sunlight? If the man we hunt is such a creature, he'll seek cover."

Sirk gave Hunt a grudging nod, one he reserved for students displaying a modicum of intelligence. "He'll be heading somewhere dark, with no risk of being disturbed."

"The railway line runs along here, with a tunnel and buildings giving relief from the sun." Foley said. "Let's head in that direction."

Sirk's knees creaked as he stood, but he showed no less resolve.

Their pursuit of the black-hatted killer drew them deeper into the slums. A wide, stone railway bridge sat within, propping up the leaning tenements that surrounded it. They passed through an arch and walked down steps leading under the bridge.

Hunt expected to find the underbelly of the bridge deserted save for vagrants, but instead found himself amidst a bustling collection of market stalls and tents. Old houses and ramshackle shops grew around and within the bridge, mossy cobbles running underneath. Well-heeled ladies and gentlemen mingled with rough-clad outcasts. Lepers swathed from head to foot in cloth haunted the market edges, shunned by the wealthy and poor alike. Several of the stalls offered tattoos while others sold herbs and trinkets whose purpose

Hunt couldn't guess at.

Foley nudged him. "Let's quicken the pace before we lose him."

There was something – several things – wrong about the market, not least so many people present prior to dawn. Of Black Hat there was no sign. They explored the darkened corners and lichen-stained nooks under the bridge before searching the nearby goods yard above. But he was gone.

It was dawn by the time they found themselves back in the narrow maze of wynds and vennels that separated the closely packed tenements and squalid gin shops. The rookery was among the most overcrowded in the city, its denizens drowning their misery in cheap alcohol. Gaunt children roamed the filthy sunless lanes, barefoot and feral.

An empty bottle lay on the ground. Foley picked it up and sniffed inside, making a face. "I like a wee drink," he said with vast understatement, "but I'll pass on that."

"I've never seen you drink gin," Hunt commented.

"Me and a pal once bought a bootleg bottle of gin as boys. It nearly killed us. My father tested what was left in the bottle and found traces of turpentine and sulphuric acid." He sounded grim. "I'll never touch it again."

"You were lucky." Risking bootleg spirits could lead to madness or death. Slurred shouts echoed between the close-packed tenements, followed by a scream. A ragged group of men and women leaned against a wall in a drunken stupor, two of them fornicating with no regard for privacy.

Hunt and his friends didn't pass unnoticed. "Ah'll do ye fer a penny," a woman offered, staggering up close to Hunt. Bruises old and recent marked a gaunt face consumed by need. She might have been twenty but looked twice that, already well on her way to the grave. Filthy hair hung loose and neglected, her torn skirt and ragged blouse stained with blood, vomit and shit. She forced a grotesque smile, the few teeth remaining to her black with rot. Stinking of gin and decay, her breath made Hunt shy back.

"Ah, no thank you," he stammered as he walked round her.

"Ah'll do the three of ye fer a penny," she called out in desperation.

"We've other business to attend to," he politely declined,

but handed her a penny. She snatched it and ran, too consumed by her craving to acknowledge his charity.

They continued in silence. Two men blocked their passage, pulling knives. Everything about Hunt, Foley and Sirk marked them as trespassers in the rookery, a world of hopeless misery making all within either predator or prey. The two men clearly believed Hunt and his friends the latter.

Fear stabbed Hunt as he saw murder written in the men's eyes. No anger or hate motivated them, only a base instinct driving them to take whatever they could from whoever they could.

Foley revealed his gun and stared calmly back. The would-be robbers re-evaluated the three before them and backed away. No one spoke.

"This hole should be razed to the ground," Hunt said, his heart still hammering in his chest.

"And send these poor bastards where?" Foley asked, a question which Hunt couldn't answer. "Our friend in the black hat hasn't been here, or those two would be either dead or shitting themselves."

"Let's go back under the bridge," Sirk suggested. "He may still be there. Besides, that market has piqued my interest."

Chapter Twenty-Five

"A curious sight," Sirk remarked. "I had no idea such a place existed."

Hunt was inclined to hang back and observe, but Sirk showed no such reticence. He strolled through the market under the bridge like he owned the place, examining stalls with open curiosity. Some were like those in any market, selling food such as potatoes, carrots, apples and sausages. But there was also a stall bearing the sign 'Familyers', crowded with caged birds – mostly pigeons and crows – and small dogs, cats and foxes. And rats. *Who the hell buys rats, and why?*

Another stall sold herbs and reagents Hunt couldn't identify, and bottled potions. Even Foley, a qualified pharmacist, shrugged in ignorance at what was for sale.

The services, too, defied convention. Artificers sold charms and trinkets made from wood and metal, and took commissions for anything absent from their wares. Mediums told fortunes and offered communion with the dead. A few men and women loitered with signs identifying themselves as diviners. Three tattoo stalls were deserted while people queued at a fourth, the only difference that Hunt could discern being a fresh sign advertising "Bear essence – limited supply!" Whatever that meant.

"I didn't know there was a leper hostel here," Foley said.

"Me neither." Hunt had seen lepers earlier, but he had been too busy trying to find Black Hat to wonder at their presence under the bridge. He saw two of them enter a dilapidated tenement leaning against the bridge, its windows boarded and entrance perpetually in shadow.

Foley snapped his pocket watch shut. "Are we staying here much longer? It's almost eight, and I've a shop to open."

The hour took Hunt by surprise, the underside of the bridge untouched by the dawn. A night without sleep was taking its toll, and he was tempted to give his lectures a miss. Four hard-looking men passed them, their faces grim and purposeful.

"This market isn't going anywhere," Foley said on seeing Sirk's reluctance to leave.

"You're right," Sirk decided. "We can return later."

Foley nodded. "Aye, we can–"

Shouts and screams echoed under the bridge as all hell broke loose. Two lepers were attacked by the four men who'd just walked by. Gunshots followed, echoing louder in the covered area.

Foley crouched. "Get down," he ordered Hunt and Sirk as he pulled out his gun. Perhaps five men forced their way into the tenement housing the lepers.

Chaos ruled as others attacked the lepers outside with clubs, long knives and guns. A leper was dragged out from under the bridge into the sunshine, struggling in vain as the wrapped cloth was cut off to expose his skin. He screamed and thrashed as if on fire, and Hunt watched in disbelief as the man's skin, pale but clearly untouched by disease, reddened and blistered as if on fire. He tried to crawl back to the bridge, but his assailants hacked at his limbs and left him to burn.

Another was held face down by two men while a third hacked his head off.

Not all the lepers were overcome so easily. Two tore off their hampering mantles and engaged their attackers at close quarters, forcing them back. One assailant was separated from his fellows and borne to the ground where two of his would-be victims clawed and bit at him.

Hunt watched aghast as they devoured the man's blood, heedless of his agonised howls. They kept feeding even as two of the man's companions fired pistols into them.

"Why the hell are these bastards attacking lepers?" Foley asked, keeping close to Hunt and Sirk. Thus far neither group had shown any interest in them. Several stalls had been overturned as stall-holders and customers fled in panic while others tried to hide.

"They're not lepers," Sirk said, confirming Hunt's suspicions.

"Then what are they?" Foley asked.

"What we're looking for," Hunt answered. "Undead." The two feeding off the fallen man finally succumbed to their wounds. Even riddled with bullets, the gunmen took no chances and stabbed each in the heart. Their fallen comrade looked beyond help.

"A clever disguise," Sirk said. "The rags give them a measure of protection from the sun, and who would dare get close to a leper?"

Hunt pointed to the group attacking the undead. "Who are they?"

"Well they're not friends of the undead, clearly," Sirk said.

"Now's not the best time to be asking them," Foley said. "Stay low and maybe we'll be left alone."

More gunshots could be heard inside the tenement housing the 'lepers'. The last of the undead outside fell, and their killers took up positions near the house. They were joined by a scarred, hulking brute who left the house. "Steiner says the rest are in the cellar, watch for any who make it out," he ordered, his accent French.

The tenement took fire, smoke escaping from boarded windows as the flames spread unchecked. A mob of undead fled from a cellar hatch. Two assailants stood ready, holding glass bottles with cloth stuffed down the necks. On seeing their enemy flee they lit the cloth and flung the bottles. Fire engulfed two undead as they shattered.

There was no cohesion to the undead. Some sought only to flee while others flung themselves at the guard of men waiting for them. Madness took the rest and they attacked anyone in sight.

A well-dressed woman thrashed in futile resistance as a pale-skinned girl savaged her throat. A man Hunt assumed to be her husband beat at the undead girl to no avail. A stray bullet struck him, and he fell. The gunman fired again, and this time aimed true, hitting the creature.

Two undead cornered the tattooist who proved so popular that morning. The tattooist tore off his left shirt sleeve and sliced a knife through the bear tattoo engraved on his arm.

The sight of his blood only inflamed the undead further and they dragged him down to the ground. Surrounded by horror, the tattooist's self-mutilation seemed an act of inexplicable stupidity.

Or perhaps not. He flung them back with a strength beyond his build, his blows driving one to the ground. He grabbed a few bottles from his smashed stall and ran off.

Foley grabbed Hunt's arm. "We need to move!"

"If we do, we'll draw their attention."

"If we don't, we'll be cornered," Foley said. "We'll be safe in the daylight if we get out from under this bridge."

"'If'," Hunt muttered as the three of them tried to pass unmolested through the fighting.

"Look," Foley said, pointing into the chaotic melee.

Hunt obliged but couldn't see what caught Foley's eye. "At what?"

"I saw that bastard with the big black hat come out of the leper house – but he's gone now."

Shouts of "*Deus Vult*!" could be heard as the rest of the group attacking the undead left the burning tenement to aid their hard-pressed comrades. 'God wills it,' if Hunt recalled his Latin correctly. The leader was tall and grim-faced, carrying a pistol in one hand and a bloodied sword-stick blade in the other. He was a rock of calm in a storm of chaos, issuing commands in a Germanic accent.

Foley fired at two undead, what should have been mortal wounds only slowing them. Canning had shown a similar resilience to bullet wounds.

An attacker fired at one of the undead, his shots proving unaccountably more effective than Foley's, and the undead fell. His gun empty, the man tried frantically to reload, but a second undead bore him down. Sirk twisted the handle of his cane to release a three-inch spike which he drove into its back.

A third undead joined the fray with twice the strength of its fellows. Foley fired twice, but it shrugged off the bullets with a grimace and snarled at them. This undead differed, Hunt saw with horror, as its canines lengthened into fangs.

"Shit," Foley breathed. Hunt felt tendrils of fear press around him.

The undead's posturing proved its undoing as the tall Germanic-sounding fighter with the sword-stick stabbed it in the back, the tip of his blade emerging from its chest. It fell, and he stabbed it again. The swordsman didn't wait for their thanks.

"My bloody gun's little damned use," Foley complained even as he reloaded it.

"Aim for the heart or head," Sirk advised. "Anywhere else hurts them but won't put them down."

The one Sirk had stabbed in the back was dead so far as Hunt could tell, its heart pierced. The one with the fangs was dead too, but the first undead Foley had shot still lived (relatively speaking), writhing on the ground. The fight moved past them.

"We're taking it," Sirk decided. He pulled the rags off the one he'd killed and used them to bind the weakened undead's limbs.

Foley stared at him. "Have you lost your mind?"

"I'm quite sane. If we're to fight this menace, we must understand it." His tone was chillingly calm. "And that requires study."

"And just how do we move it from here to your house?"

"We'll hide it and return later with your wagon," Sirk said.

"*My* wagon? And just where are we to hide him – it?"

Seeing they were both too stubborn to back down, Hunt stepped in. "We'll hide it in a crate in the goods yard above and come back later. Regardless, we've no time to argue!"

The three of them subdued the wounded undead and carried it up the steps to the derelict goods yard, closed for seven years. The fight below was almost over, Hunt saw, the attackers' organisation overcoming the stronger but disorganised undead.

They were almost out of sight of the bridge when explosives sent the burning tenement crumbling down to the ground, burying any undead still in the cellar. The German and his men moved among the fallen, showing no mercy.

Chapter Twenty-Six

Hunt blinked. “Sorry, what did you say? My mind wandered.”

His mother’s expression was a blend of irritation and concern. “I asked how you’ve been doing. You look tired and distracted. Too many late nights?”

“Not as such, I’ve just had trouble sleeping.” That was as much of the truth as he could tell his mother. Thursday night into Friday morning had been spent spying on the Carpathian Circus, discovering that odd market near High Street, and lastly surviving the carnage that followed. He’d spent Friday afternoon helping move the crate holding the captured undead to Sirk’s home, and then endured a second night without sleep, haunted by what he’d seen.

In the end he’d left his bed and crept into the parlour in search of liquor, instead finding Foley passed out in his armchair, the selfish bastard having downed the last of the whisky. His bid to drink himself into a stupor thwarted, Hunt had sat in the kitchen and waited for dawn. After noon he lay on his bed until exhaustion finally won him a few precious hours of sleep, enough to sustain him for tonight’s dinner at the Albert Club.

“A dram of whisky can help with that,” his father said unhelpfully.

Yes, unless some arsehole has finished the whole damned bottle. The arrival of the Gerrards saved Hunt from replying. On this occasion the whole clan had come, wearing their best.

“You look very nice, Amelie,” Hunt said as greetings were exchanged. She wore a purple satin evening dress, its edges trimmed with iridescent beads. Three-quarter length sleeves clung tightly around her arms, and her figure was emphasised by the dress' narrow waist and boned bodice. Her black hair was pinned up high and topped by a wide-brimmed fedora hat. But what drew him were her eyes, bright and merry.

"You also, Wilton," she replied, politely if inaccurately. The past week had taken its toll.

A waiter arrived at the table to take their drinks order. Hunt decided on an oak-darkened red wine, a fitting accompaniment for steak. He remembered well the beef he'd eaten in the club during his visit with Foley, fully confident the chef would do it equal justice tonight. Even unwelcome memories of ravaged flesh and spilled blood failed to kill his appetite.

"An acceptable wine," M. Gerrard grudgingly allowed on hearing Hunt's choice. "But I prefer a more balanced finish."

"They have nothing from your own vineyards, Monsieur. This is one of their cellar's better offerings." In truth Hunt doubted he could differentiate between the wine he'd ordered and one of Gerrard's, but he had better sense than to admit that to a master vintner, not if he wanted the man's good opinion. And perhaps one day, his blessing.

"My wine has been very missing from Scotland, I admit. But my son and I have visited your owners of public houses and restaurants with our wine, and its virtues have won over many. I am … confident? … confident … that you will soon see the Gerrard label in your finest places." Gerrard looked round the table, inviting their approval.

"Bravo," Hunt's father said. "I trust they didn't need their arms twisted too much?"

Gerrard laughed. "No. We left the persuading to our wine. After one glass?" He waggled his fingers. "They were convinced!"

Jacques Gerrard looked quite smug about their success but offered no comment.

The waiter brought their drinks and took their dinner order, Jacques proving difficult. He only allowed the waiter to leave once he was satisfied his exact specifications had been noted. Antagonising restaurant staff was unwise; Hunt wouldn't be surprised if someone spat in Jacques' food.

An awkward silence followed his boorish display, only dispelled by M. Gerrard toasting everyone's health. Hunt made eye contact with his mother, quirking an eyebrow. She should count herself lucky; there were worse sons in the world than him, one sitting close by. Her replying expression suggested she was not convinced. Hunt supposed Jacques Gerrard's dedication to his family's trade balanced his poor manners in Mother's eyes. Correcting bad habits came easy to her, but her campaign to convince Hunt to abandon his scientific studies and either study Law or join the family company had stalled.

Mother looked at Amelie and Mme Gerrard. "Did you both enjoy your visit to the circus with Wilton?"

Amelie smiled. "Yes, very much."

Mme Gerrard nodded in agreement. "A memorable experience."

Hunt noted his mother's pleased smile. Her direct approach to return him to the fold had failed, so now she pressed at his flanks. She evidently believed marrying him off would do the trick. Hunt had to admit she might not be wrong.

The conversation turned to places visited by the Gerrards, and their thoughts on them. Hunt half-listened, his own thoughts yet again dragged back to the situation he'd fallen into. It was difficult to fathom that looking into a corpse's disappearance had flung him into a world where the dead killed the living and sustained themselves on their blood. No, he hadn't been flung into it. He had fought to get there in blind ignorance; every step, every wrong turn and every revelation had been a struggle against the conspiracy fogging the truth behind the undead.

Friday morning had seen Glasgow littered with over a score of bodies and a building destroyed – to no reaction. The bodies had been disposed of and the destruction explained by poorly maintained gas pipes in a derelict building, the story itself buried in the middle of the few papers that bothered to report it. Or perhaps were permitted to report it.

Hunt wondered at the cost and effort to keep such events, such *truths*, opaque to the rest of the world, but the undead did have an advantage. Mesmerisation. That he had succeeded in finding Amy Newfield, only to have that memory suppressed, gave him pause. Was that the only time such a thing had happened to him?

Had he in fact uncovered the truth again and again, only for it to be stripped away each time? He was forced to admit that the undead ability to Mesmer was really a blessing of sorts; without it murder would be their only recourse to protect their secrets, one they already employed without compunction. Enough. Tonight was to give him respite from such things, a taste of a different life.

His courage topped up by half a glass of wine, he took a breath. “Amelie, Kelvingrove Park is hosting a musical concert on Friday, if you’re interested…?”

“I am interested, but we will be in Loch Lomond by then,” Amelie said with an apologetic smile.

“Yes, too bad,” Jacques didn’t bother to hide his pleasure at Hunt’s thwarted invitation.

Mme Gerrard gave her son a thin-lipped glare, one Hunt had endured from his own mother many a time, before turning her attention to him. “We are to stay at the Colquhoun Arms Hotel, Mr Hunt. Come visit us at the end of next week.”

“A good idea, *Maman*,” Amelie said with a smile. Her brother looked like he’d eaten something foul.

The invitation met with M. Gerrard’s approval. “Why do you all not come? Sir Arthur Williamson hopes to be there also.”

“A kind invitation,” Father said, “but I must regretfully decline.”

“Our company is caught up in a case of litigation that just will not go away,” Mother explained. “Lewis is helping to resolve it, but it demands both our attentions. Or we’d be delighted to accept.”

Monsieur and Madame Gerrard offered their commiserations. “You will resolve it soon?” M. Gerrard asked Father.

“I will have the matter concluded to our satisfaction within days.” There was a predatory look in his father’s eyes Hunt hadn’t seen before.

Gerrard nodded his approval. “And you, Mr Hunt?”

My plans for this coming week, let me think – not playing Lucifer on stage, not having my mind meddled with by an undead woman in my club, not spending a cold night spying on a circus, absolutely not watching men and undead hack each other to bloody bits ... oh, and not abducting one for my professor to experiment on. Hunt smiled. “I’d be delighted to visit.” He planned to live a quieter life from now on, and a few days in the country sounded idyllic.

Gerrard nodded once. “Good. I arranged an account with a carriage company on the suggestion of Sir Arthur. We will arrange for you to be met on Friday morning and taken to the hotel.”

“I look forward to it.”

Mother nodded in satisfaction. “That sounds splendid. Wilton, you must stay with us on Thursday night. Meeting the carriage at our house will let it avoid the busy city streets.”

“A good idea, Mother,” he said before realising he was trading a slightly longer carriage ride on Friday morning for a Thursday evening of instruction and admonishment from his mother. Sometimes she forgot he was a full-grown man.

A smile played at his father’s lips. “Are you sure you don’t want to accompany Wilton to keep an eye on him, Edith?”

“I’m sure our son will be the perfect gentleman, Lewis.” The look she gave her husband was one of mock exasperation; the one she gave her son told him he *would* be the perfect gentleman, or else.

The conversation paused when dinner arrived, everyone’s attention focused on the steaming plates of food. Hunt was served first, an act of cruelty since he could only stare at the medium-cooked steak and accompanying vegetables until everyone else was served. It had been several days since his last proper meal, and his fingers itched to grab the cutlery and tear into the food. He interlocked his fingers and waited for the meal to begin.

He forced himself to eat at a leisurely pace, keen to make a good impression. He had been raised on manners and etiquette, and now wasn’t the time to cast them aside. His knife cut easily through the tender meat, hot juices oozing out onto the plate. It tasted as good as he remembered, pink but not bloody.

God, that’s good. He washed down that first mouthful with a little wine, its black pepper overtones complementing the flavour of the meat. The wine tasted of red and black berries, softened with vanilla, a hint of leather beneath the surface.

The Gerrards were unanimous in their approbation of the food. Hunt expected Jacques to at best begrudge a few words, but when the waiter came by to ask if everything was in order, he was effusive with praise. The waiter promised to pass Jacques' compliments to the chef; if they had repaid the Frenchman's earlier behaviour by spitting in his food, they probably felt bad about it now.

After days of self-neglect, Hunt's palette was overwhelmed by an evening of exceptional food, excellent wine, a lightly peated single malt whisky, and a cigar rolled from premium tobacco. The Hunts and Gerrards left the Albert Club sated and in good spirits, ready to go their separate ways. Father and Mother said their farewells to the Gerrards and Hunt, intending to walk home. Hunt felt an uncommon concern for his parents' safety; they lived not far from the club and were unlikely to meet footpads in this prosperous part of the West End, but even these streets seemed more dangerous than they had scant weeks ago.

Hunt watched his parents vanish into the night and led the Gerrards to a street frequented by cabriolets.

He bid them a good night each, leaving Amelie for last. "I hope you enjoy your time at Loch Lomond, it has some beautiful sights."

"We will have a pleasant time, I am sure. I will see you next week."

"Until next week." He watched her enter the cabriolet, still feeling the kiss she had left on each cheek. A second cabriolet pulled in as he flagged it down. He begrudged the cost of the fare, but he lived on the other side of the city. Walking such distance in the dark was unsafe, and he had more to fear than gangs and footpads.

Chapter Twenty-Seven

Sirk answered the door. "Do come in, gentlemen."

Hunt followed Foley into the professor's house, his feelings ambivalent. The events from Friday morning, only four days previous, were still vivid in his mind's eye. Their pursuit of the black-hatted killer had led them to the market hidden under the bridge and to a slaughter that still gave him a troubled sleep.

That most of the victims were undead masquerading as lepers did little to ease his mind. Innocents had also perished in that ruthless assault, and Hunt wondered at the identity of its authors. 'God wills it,' they had cried in Latin, the centuries-old cry of the Knights Templar. Did these men fashion themselves on those fanatics of old?

At the time other concerns had taken precedence, notably survival, escape, and later the removal of Sirk's captured undead from the goods yard to his address. Hunt had seen a weary-eyed Sirk at the university in the days since, but all the professor would say on the matter was that his project continued satisfactorily, and that Hunt and Foley were welcome to attend his house on Tuesday evening. After an uneventful four days – blessedly so – Hunt had been of two minds whether to attend or to divorce himself from the matter entirely. He reminded himself of his forthcoming trip to Loch Lomond on Friday, the prospect a cheering one.

Sirk led them down into the cellar. There was a rustling in the darkness and a fluidity to the shadows that materialised into a man-shaped horror as Sirk lit the cellar's lanterns.

"Jesus," Foley grimaced. Hunt held a handkerchief to his nose. Death had a smell all its own.

The undead prisoner was naked and chained to the wall. It could have passed for a living man on Friday morning under the bridge, but time's passage had flayed it cruelly in the days since. Rotting skin stretched thinly over bones while patches of lank hair hung loose and wild. It snapped its jaws at them, bared teeth made larger by receding lips and gums that put Hunt in mind of that other undead, the fanged one.

There was no awareness in its eyes, only a feral madness that reminded Hunt of his encounter with Amy Newfield near the Southern Necropolis. But even she hadn't been as far gone as this … man.

Foley stared at the moving corpse. "What have you done to him – it?"

"Studied it, mostly," Sirk said. He watched his captive with a clinical curiosity.

"He deteriorated to this state in only several days? Amy Newfield was never this far gone, nor Richard Canning," Hunt said.

"Amy Newfield was drinking the blood of her victims," Sirk reminded him. "I suspect Canning did likewise."

"So only four days without blood left him like this?" Hunt asked.

"Essentially, yes. Though his wounds accelerated the deterioration. My experiments did little to help or hinder him."

"Experiments?" Foley asked.

"I've read up on lore regarding the undead and weapons to use against them. We know that daylight is anathema to them, but holy water has no effect, nor do religious insignia."

"Maybe your holy water wasn't holy enough, Professor." Foley teased.

"I used water blessed by three priests," Sirk pointed out. "Garlic, too, proved ineffective. Though what was left added flavour to my stew."

Foley regarded the creature. "You said his wounds made this happen quicker, but my shots only seemed to slow him."

"Yours, aye. I examined it thoroughly and removed the bullets." He showed them a small tray holding three mangled bullets and pointed to the darkest one. "That's one of yours."

Foley studied the other two bullets. "Silver?"

"Indeed. Used by those who precipitated the attack and more effective than regular ammunition." Sirk put the tray back down. "Our friend doesn't react well to silver. Observe." He picked up a small silver knife and cut at the undead, causing it to recoil in pain. It stared at Sirk with hate-filled eyes. Hunt wondered how the professor managed to sleep under the same roof as the creature, chained or not.

"Will it…" Hunt fumbled for the right word, "die eventually or continue indefinitely?"

"I'm unsure," Sirk admitted.

"Can animal blood sustain them, or must it be human?" Foley wanted to know.

"I wondered the same thing and fed it pigs blood. There was no improvement in its condition, but its deterioration did stop briefly. I believe that animal blood can sustain them in a fashion, but only by imbibing a significant quantity."

"Would human blood restore it, or is it too far gone?" Hunt asked.

Sirk smiled. "An excellent question. And one of the reasons why I asked you here."

After some persuasion, Hunt and Foley let Sirk bleed them. Their blood was gathered in a bowl and passed to the undead. Hunt watched with nausea as it licked every last drop. Sirk opened a bottle of whisky and they settled in for the night.

Four hours passed, and the change in the undead was remarkable. He still looked more dead than alive, but his flesh looked healthier. The creature's thirst somewhat abated, Sirk decreed it was time to attempt conversation. Foley's revolver sat on the table as a precaution.

"Paul Naismith," the undead said on being asked his name. His cooperation came at a price; eventual freedom and the daily provision of blood until then. That was the carrot. Foley's gun was the stick made manifest, a warning of what awaited should he not cooperate. He assured them he would answer fully, one death evidently enough for Naismith. The name tickled Hunt's memory.

"When did you die, Mr Naismith?" Sirk asked. He had given him a blanket for modesty's sake. Not that that Naismith seemed to care much. All he desired was blood. Even the prospect of days – perhaps weeks – in this cellar didn't trouble him so long as he was given blood each day. Undeath might be a poor bastard cousin of immortality, but the removal of death's inevitability engendered an inhuman patience.

"A year ago," Naismith said. "January 1892."

Sirk nodded. "You were – forgive me, what is the term?"

"Made. I was Made last year." His voice was like a quill scraping over rough parchment.

"Tell me about it," Sirk said.

"I drank blood from a *Nephilim*, after which he bled me dry."

"A *Nephilim*?" Sirk asked.

"The offspring of the 'Sons of God' and the 'Daughters of Man'," Hunt answered slowly as an old memory resurfaced. "According to the Bible. The result of fallen angels mating with women, some take it to mean." He recalled his father reading Genesis to him, distaste in his voice on speaking of these mythical half-breeds.

Naismith shrugged. "Some call them vampyres. I know of no connection with fallen angels. The only Fallen I've heard of walking the earth are those Summoned from Hell, and they're confined to the human vessel they possess."

Hunt wondered if vampyres were the inspiration for the *Nephilim* myth, or if they had just taken the name.

"Were you forced, or were you Made by choice?" Foley asked.

"By choice," Naismith admitted. "I was dying of a tumour and was granted this as a reward for past services."

"*Nephilim*? Is that what you are?" Sirk asked.

Naismith shook his head. "Not quite. Not yet. The newly Made are called ghouls. In time we either rot and die, or Transition into a *Nephilim* proper."

"*Nephilim* can manifest fangs?" Hunt asked, remembering the different undead they had encountered at the market. "But not ghouls?"

Naismith nodded. "I'm to a *Nephilim* what a caterpillar is to a butterfly. When I complete the Transition I'll have greater strength, resilience, and injuries will heal faster. The Thirst will have less of a hold on me, and I'll have the ability to Mesmer."

"How long does it take a ghoul to become a *Nephilim*?" Sirk asked.

“There is no fixed time. It can depend on the ghoul, on the pedigree of the *Nephilim* who Made him, and on the quality and quantity of the blood consumed.”

“Quality?” Sirk asked. “I assume a ghoul drinking too much diseased blood can cause it to rot?”

“Yes.”

Hunt thought of Amy Newfield buried in her coffin before being exhumed. “How long after death does the Making take?”

“Between one day and three in most cases. The more *Nephilim* blood consumed, the quicker it happens.” The ghoul talked freely, but then he probably wondered what exactly his captors could do with that information in a city ruled by these *Nephilim*. Hunt wondered the same thing. Was Sirk looking for a realistic means to free Glasgow from the undead or was he merely indulging his scientific curiosity?

“Why were so many of you under the bridge?” Foley asked. “Seems dangerous to have so many of you together.”

Naismith looked at him unblinkingly. “Practicality. We are kept in Crypts, overseen by *Nephilim* until we Transition.” He barked out a hoarse laugh. “Can’t be trusted to resist the Thirst.” He eyed the bowl he’d been fed from, a growing want in his eyes.

Hunt suspected the thing that had once been Paul Naismith had just about exhausted his blood-given lucidity. “Do you know Amy Newfield or Richard Canning?”

The ghoul shook his head. “No. But there are several Crypts throughout and near the city. I don’t know how the Templars found us.”

“Templars?” Sirk asked.

A pallor had returned to Naismith’s face. “The men who attacked us.” He stared up at Sirk. “More.”

Sirk raised a hand. “Tell me of the Templars.”

“An enemy. I don’t know any more,” the ghoul answered brusquely.

“You were a member of the Black Wing Club; I remember seeing you back when I attended regularly,” Hunt said. “What connects the club to the *Nephilim*? Do you know a Margot Guillam?”

“More,” Naismith insisted. His eyes didn’t blink.

Sirk exhaled. "I think we've learned all we can from Mr Naismith." He picked up Foley's revolver and checked it was loaded before cocking it.

A vestige of awareness stirred within Naismith. "You promised–"

"To release you." Sirk finished. He fired into the ghoul's skull.

Hunt's ears rang painfully, and he saw rather than heard Foley mouth an obscenity. Blood and brain stained the floor, pooling around skull fragments.

Foley snatched his revolver from Sirk. "Warn us next time, Professor." He looked at the mess in disgust. "And you can clean that up yourself."

"You did promise to release him," Hunt said in mild reproach, his ears still hurting from the close-quarters gunshot.

Sirk gestured at the corpse, a callousness in his tone. "And I did."

"Could we not have questioned him further?"

Sirk shook his head. "There's a limit to how much blood I can safely harvest from the three of us, insufficient to make him lucid for more than a few minutes, and certainly not enough to feed him every day. We'll catch the next one undamaged, meaning it will require less blood."

Foley eyed the remains. "If you say so, Professor." Sirk was being optimistic about their chances of catching another undead, especially if they must avoid shooting it several times.

The reserve in Foley's tone matched Hunt's feelings on the matter. *Next one?* He was of the growing opinion that perhaps he'd given enough of his time and blood to this matter. But he said nothing.

*

Redfort sat silently as the room rustled with whispered speculation. The Council had summoned the Society's senior members for an emergency meeting, and refusal had not been an option. It was taking place in the usual venue, the main chamber of the Black Wing Club's upper floor. The occasion was nothing too dire, he hoped.

The Council sat along the centre table at the end of the room, the subordinate Sooty Feather members seated along two tables that stretched down from either end. Aside from the surviving seven who sat on the Council, only the senior members were in attendance, the twelve men and women of the inner circle.

The chamber was long and high ceilinged, its dark red walls crowned with plaster mouldings that surrounded the room and spread out overhead. Aged statues of Greek and Roman deities stood regularly spaced beside the walls, trophies brought to Glasgow by the first *Nephilim* to make the city their home when it was a small town. In those days the *Nephilim* had spread throughout the towns and villages of the west coast, their numbers few. As Glasgow's population grew, the city swallowed up many surrounding settlements, and the *Nephilim* consolidated their position within a city now large enough to support them.

The tobacco trade with America established Glasgow's first merchant princes, the more debauched among them founding a Hellfire Club that the *Nephilim* turned into the Sooty Feather Society, later forming the respectable Black Wing Club around it.

He remembered the first time he'd been allowed into this room, marking his elevation from initiate to member. His ambition's thirst had been slaked for a time, but he wouldn't be satisfied now until he sat on the Council itself. Always he wanted more, and was resigned to the probability that his ceaseless grasping for power would prove his downfall. *But not yet.*

Awe no longer blinded him to the room's fading lustre. The red paper was peeling from the wall in places, and the plaster mouldings and ceiling needed repainting. The carpets were worn with age, faded and almost bare in patches. Gas lighting had been installed in the rest of the club rooms below, but such modernisation had yet to reach the upper floor and council chamber, still reliant on candles.

If – *when* – he ascended to the Council, renewing the room's aging décor would be among his first tasks. The fittings weren't the only things in the Council chamber past their prime; a few on the Council itself were in need of replacement. That task would prove more difficult that replacing the carpets, but Redfort felt up to the challenge. One drawback of serving masters unbound by time was their occasional blindness to its passing. Their wits and vigour were undiminished by the passage of years, and they sometimes failed to recognise the toll it took on valued mortal servants. It was rare for more than two or three *Nephilim* to sit on the Council at any one time; they were content to delegate the duties and difficulties of managing the city to a trusted few among the living.

The room quietened as a gavel banged. "Silence." The last of the whispers ceased. The spokesman, *Secundus*, stood and surveyed those present. He was foremost among those whose best years were behind them, but the Regent still seemed to see him as he once was, rather than the slow, white-haired old man with shaking hands he had become. Seated next to him was Regent Edwards himself, the Council's *Primus*, whose attendance alone marked this as no ordinary meeting. He left the talking to *Secundus*, his upper features hidden behind a gold-plated mask. The rest of the Council sat masked to his left and right, save for the deceased *Quintus*, Benjamin Howard. The porcelain, Venetian-style half-masks were worn out of tradition, the identities of the Council known to all in the inner circle of the Society.

"The past few weeks have seen our interests threatened on a scale unprecedented since the formation of this Council." *Secundus* looked around the room after that announcement and stared at Redfort.

His chest tightened. This evening might not bode well for his ambitions. Or survival.

"Reverend Redfort was recently visited by a Templar named Wolfgang Steiner. His efforts to find and kill this Steiner have to date failed.

"This failure has given the Templars time to strike at the Council itself. Mr Howard – *Quintus* – was abducted, tortured and killed. We believe Steiner was also responsible for the earlier murder of Bishop Horace Mann."

Redfort's gaze remained on *Secundus*, but he felt many eyes on him. It was an unpleasant experience, only mitigated by his relief that they didn't know of his role in Mann's death.

Secundus continued. "Howard was not tortured for pleasure, we can be certain they questioned him. It is surely no coincidence that the Templars soon after attacked our Crypt in the Under-Market on Friday morning, slaying every ghoul and two of the three *Nephilim* caretakers. We cannot know what other secrets they pulled from Howard." His gaze flickered to a blond man sitting on the table across from Redfort, a tall black hat sitting before him on the table. Redfort recognised him from previous meetings, one who was not on the Council despite being among the city's few Elder *Nephilim*. He stood low in the Regent's favour. The surviving *Nephilim* from the Templar raid?

The Regent deigned to address the gathering. "Every effort must be made to find these Templars. They are no longer an annoyance, they are now a threat to our control over this city." He regarded Redfort with dead eyes that had seen the passage of centuries. "Finding them is your responsibility, Reverend."

Octavia, the junior-most of the eight – now seven – councillors, cleared her throat. "Forgive the interruption, but with all this attention – well-deserved to be sure – on the Templars, what of the rogue element Making ghouls without sanction? They're–"

"–a matter to be dealt with later. The Templars are to be dealt with *now*." The Regent's decree silenced any further comment from *Octavia*.

Margot Guillam, the only *Nephilim* currently on the Council save the Regent, spoke up. "I met a Wilton Hunt within Sooty Feathers on the night Howard failed to attend. Hunt claimed to be waiting for him too, so I Mesmered him to forget the matter. But it was he and an associate who exhumed Amy Newfield, the ghoul Made by this unknown party. Hunt also transported Richard Canning's body from the prison to the medical school, another suspected ghoul Made without sanction."

"Exhumed?" someone asked. "Why Make a ghoul only to allow the body buried?"

"It's an old trick to avoid the attention that comes from

bodies disappearing," Miss Guillam said. "The *Nephilim* feeds the subject enough blood to Turn before killing them, but not enough to Turn quickly. Judged correctly, the Maker can ensure the Transition does not complete until after the burial. He or she then has the body quietly exhumed and no one knows differently. We cannot tell how many ghouls our unknown *Nephilim* has Made; had they exhumed Amy Newfield rather than Hunt, we would still be none the wiser."

That raised the spectre of just how many ghouls had been Made without the Council's knowledge. A few? A dozen? Not hundreds, surely; the blood required to feed so many would have long since attracted attention.

"Unless Hunt is in the employ of this rogue *Nephilim*," *Secundus* said, "sent to exhume Newfield, only she escaped?"

"I've known the Hunt family for many years," Redfort said. "The parents attend the cathedral for Sunday Service." *I even baptised the boy as a baby.* He thought better of disclosing that. "The Hunts have no association with either ourselves or the Templars, to my knowledge."

"No association with Sooty Feathers that we can find, but both Wilton Hunt and his father Lewis are members of the Black Wing Club," Miss Guillam said. "The night Howard was taken was the first visit the younger Hunt has made to the club in months. Lewis Hunt maintains his membership but rarely attends."

Redfort clasped his hands, having forgotten that Lewis Hunt was a club member. He was reminded of a proposition by *Septimus* to induct Hunt as a Sooty Feather initiate some years ago, a proposition accepted by the Council but later overturned for no reason he could remember. The society numbered roughly fifty full members including the mortal councillors, the inner circle and the confirmed members. There were also an approximate fifty initiates, perhaps a quarter ready for Confirmation as fully inducted members. Only then would they learn of the undead and the mysteries of the society. Most would accept it; those who failed to would be dealt with.

"Is there anything to suggest this Wilton Hunt has any connection to the Templars?" *Secundus* asked.

"Directly, no, but he was at the theatre on the night Howard was taken," Miss Guillam said, "and attended the club to confront him."

"He surely cannot be working with the Templars *and* this rogue *Nephilim*," Redfort said. That would be a dangerous game indeed.

"I agree," Miss Guillam said. "Hunt claimed to be a body snatcher for a medical professor."

"Bring him in and have him questioned," the Regent decreed. "We will learn if he works for the Templars, rogue *Nephilim*, or is unaffiliated."

"I'll deal with him, Regent," the blond *Nephilim* with the black hat volunteered. "Where does this Wilton Hunt live?"

Redfort watched him. *What is his name? It will come to me in time ... Rannoch ... Rannich?*

Another councillor, *Septimus*, spoke. "Where he lives doesn't matter…"

Chapter Twenty-Eight

December 1460

Seoras sat in a quiet, darkened corner of the tavern, drinking from his tankard of ale. A lively fire burned, chasing off the winter chill. Seoras had believed the town a prosperous one, blessed by God. But after eighteen months, he had come to believe a shadow lurked in the heart of Glasgow.

Two cowled figures sat down across from him, faces hidden. "Brother Seoras," one said quietly. The other placed down two tankards of ale.

"Father Coll," Seoras said ambivalently, recognising the Bishop's secretary's voice. He was relieved the priest had come, but perturbed he had seen fit to bring a stranger.

"This is Reynard Destain, a Templar Knight," Father Coll said quietly.

Seoras stared at Coll's companion, his features hidden. "I thought the Templars were gone."

"The Order was disbanded, many brothers executed, our banks and assets seized, but not all forsook the fight," Destain said, his accent odd. "Father Coll claims there is something wrong in this town?" He sounded sceptical.

Seoras gathered his thoughts. "I have spent the winter tending to the sick in the hospital, and many are dying."

"People always die, especially in the winter," Destain said, unimpressed.

"Not like this. Too many are dying," Seoras said. "Men and women who should be healing are being found dead in the morning."

"Did you find any wounds on the bodies?" Destain asked.

"Yes, small wounds, usually on the necks," Seoras said. "The bodies were pale, as if missing blood. Bodies bearing such wounds have been found all year, but never in such numbers. It's as if…"

"As if something thought more deaths would be dismissed as the winter sickness." Destain sat silently for a moment. "Perhaps there is something here."

"Something?" Seoras felt a weight leave his chest. For months he had felt alone, not knowing if he was going mad, or if there truly was an evil lurking in the town.

The Templar Knight spoke of the demons and witches hiding amongst Mankind, of the corrupted dead that came alive at night to prey on the unwary living. Seoras found himself looking at the tavern door, listening to the howling wind and battering rain with fear in his heart. *Is this the world you have given us, Lord? Was poverty and disease not enough, have you forsaken us to Hell, too?*

"Can we fight them?" he found himself asking.

"They are at their strongest when the nights are longest and the days short," Destain cautioned. "Bide a while; I shall return with my brothers, and we shall put an end to this evil."

"We shall wait," Father Coll promised.

"We should tell Bishop Andrew," Seoras said.

"No," Destain cautioned. "If evil is truly entrenched in this town, you know not who to trust. Even a bishop."

Seoras expected Father Coll to defend the Bishop.

But he remained silent.

Chapter Twenty-Nine

It was a sunny Friday morning despite dark clouds looming far to the west. Hunt stood on the pavement outside his parents' home and waited for the carriage booked to take him north. His decision to turn a blind eye to the macabre underbelly of Glasgow had not been an easy one, but one he believed for the best. He and Foley had only got involved to explain Amy Newfield's disappearance, and that mystery was now solved. He'd tell Foley and Professor Sirk of his decision when he returned.

The Gerrards' invitation to stay with them at Loch Lomond had been a welcome one, and a sign that his courtship of Amelie continued to meet with parental approval. The weekend promised to be a pleasant distraction. *No grave-robbing, no vanishing bodies, and best of all no damned undead.*

He heard the carriage before he saw it, and watched it stop in front of the house. It was thoughtful of the Gerrards to send one. The carriage's familiar livery, however, made him blanch; McBride Carriages. Why did Sir Arthur have to recommend *that* company to M. Gerrard? The two horses slowed to a halt and the driver jumped down, loading Hunt's trunk onto the rack. He opened the passenger door to let Hunt in.

The journey north was long and often uncomfortable, albeit blessed with a vista of beautiful countryside. Fields of bright green grass stretched out for miles, rising up into hills and distant, towering mountains. The best came hours later when they reached the loch, turning right. Cliffs and mountains formed a wall to the right while looking to the left treated Hunt to stunning views of Loch Lomond's bright blue waters and the islands rising there-from, boasting beaches of white sand.

Hunt leaned back and tried to enjoy the trip despite lingering doubts. He was ill-prepared to fight a war against entrenched undead and their mortal servants; the living alone would see him in the ground without undue exertion.

Enjoy life, he decided. Recent events had shown that it could be all too brief. If his friendship with Amelie grew into something stronger then he should seize the opportunity. He inhaled deeply, savouring a lungful of air absent the city-odours he was accustomed to. It smelled like freedom, a fresh start.

The carriage passed through a village of clean-looking houses and a small inn built beside the loch. It rattled on towards a larger hotel at the edge of the village.

They stopped outside the Colquhoun Arms Hotel, a converted manor house with extensive grounds. Hunt stepped out and stretched his cramped legs while a porter carried his trunk into the hotel.

A fussy-looking man sat at the front desk and looked up as Hunt approached. "Good afternoon, sir."

"Afternoon. I'm Mr Hunt, with the Gerrard party. I believe I have a reservation?"

"Ah, yes. Our French guests."

"Keenly observed. Where can I find them?"

"They're in the garden, Mr Hunt. Room Twelve is yours, and your trunk will be waiting there. If you follow the hall to the end, it will lead you out to the garden."

"Thank you." He followed the man's instructions and found himself in a well-maintained garden bustling with snowdrops, daffodils and hedges that separated it from the rest of the grounds. The Gerrards sat at a table near the centre of the garden.

"Good afternoon, Monsieur Gerrard, Madame Gerrard. It was kind of you to send the carriage." Pity it was one of McBride's. He turned to the younger Gerrards. "Jacques, Amelie; a pleasure to see you both." He shook hands with the Gerrard men, and kissed the ladies on the cheek.

"Hello, Mr Hunt," said M. Gerrard. "I am pleased you could join us. We arrived on Monday and have found this hotel very hospitable."

Mme Gerrard looked up, shielding her eyes from the sun

with one hand. "What have you been doing this week, Mr Hunt?"

Well, I questioned a dead man before my professor shot his head off. "Nothing of note, Madame Gerrard, attending university as usual."

Jacques spared him a grudging nod, but Amelie smiled. "This is a very nice place, Wilton." Her smile seemed a touch forced, absent clear cause. He was disquieted by the possibility that her affection towards him was cooling.

"There are others here you may recognise," M. Gerrard said. "Sir Arthur Williamson and his cousin arrived last night."

"*Maman*," interrupted Amelie, "I wish to show Mr Hunt the grounds."

"Certainly, but do not be long."

"*Oui*, *Maman*." Hunt felt a shocked thrill as she took his hand, and they ventured further into the garden. Her forwardness routed any doubts that she still liked him.

She silently led him past a small pond. Fish swam about, some feeding off algae staining the bottom while sunlight played off those lazing near the surface.

Directness seemed to be the best approach. "Amelie, what's troubling you?"

She didn't answer immediately. "There is something I do not like about this place."

Not me, I hope. He looked around and saw only peace and well-tended beauty. "It may not be Bordeaux, but it has its charms."

Amelie shook her head as they walked out of the hedged garden into the grounds and followed a gravel-strewn path. Hunt doubted her parents would approve of them leaving the garden unchaperoned, but he said nothing. "I do not mean the scenery. I mean the … the … I do not know the word. The air, but not the air. It feels wrong."

Hunt's good mood faded. He couldn't even visit the country without tripping over trouble. "What do you mean?"

She hesitated, following the path towards a small forest on the edge of the estate. "The first days were good, but yesterday morning some gypsies camped in a nearby field."

"You don't like gypsies?" he teased.

She shunted his arm with her elbow. "Not these ones. They visited the hotel's stable. To buy oats for their horses, they said."

"I doubt the locals are happy at them being here, but there must be more to your suspicions than that?"

"Yes. This morning the mother of Jill, one of the chambermaids, came to the hotel. Her daughter did not return home last night. She thought she stayed the night at the hotel, but Jill did not, and no one has seen her since last night."

"Maybe she eloped with a local boy?"

Amelie shook her head. "No. I talked with Jill on the day I arrived. She is engaged to a man in the village who is still here."

"You think the gypsies are responsible? They often get accused of theft, yes, but kidnapping?"

"Last night I saw movement in the grounds. It was too dark to see how many, but people were here." Her voice held an iron certainty.

"Just how many gypsies are in the camp?"

"I do not know, I saw four caravans."

"I'll keep my eyes open for anything strange," Hunt promised. Having resolved to stay clear of trouble, he hoped Amelie was the victim of nothing more than her imagination, coloured by prejudice.

"Thank you, Monsieur," she said. Despite his attempt to reassure her, she still seemed ill-at-ease. "But you must be careful."

The path led into the woods where crushed granite gave way to hardened earth. Birds chirruped softly and hopped from branch to branch. Sunbeams pierced the canopy overhead, and vegetation rustled as squirrels scurried through the undergrowth. Her hand felt warm in his.

The path forked left and right. Hunt thought to turn right, but Amelie looked left. "I want to show you somewhere. It is not far."

They followed the path as it wound its way through the woods into a small clearing. An old mausoleum bathed in the sun, its gothic white stonework turned to mossy beige.

"This was built by the family that once lived here," Amelie said. "They sold the estate many years ago and the house became a hotel. I find peace here."

"It's certainly quiet." The entrance was shrouded in shadow.

"Yes." She chewed her lip as a soft breeze whispered disquietly in the trees. "Let's go back."

*

Hunt joined the rest of the guests in the dining room after changing into his tails. The Gerrards sat with Sir Arthur Williamson and a younger man.

Sir Arthur gave him a cordial nod. "Mr Hunt, it's good to see you again. I hear you and Miss Gerrard are becoming close." There was a sly bite in his tone that Hunt disliked.

"I count Mademoiselle Gerrard as a friend, yes, as I do her family, Sir Arthur."

"I did not mean to imply anything improper," Sir Arthur said, his hands held up in a conciliatory manner.

"I took no such meaning," Hunt lied, in no mood for a confrontation.

Sir Arthur waved it off as if forgotten and gestured to the younger man sitting quietly beside him. "This is Mr Neil Williamson, my cousin and heir. Neil, this is Mr Wilton Hunt."

Williamson reddened at the attention but nodded amiably. "A pleasure." He had an open, freckled face crowned with auburn hair. Hunt took a liking to him from the start.

"I'm going fishing tomorrow," Sir Arthur said. "Gentlemen, if you wish to join me you are, of course, welcome."

M. Gerrard and Jacques voiced their assent.

Hunt concurred. "I'll be there, sir."

"Excellent. Neil's coming, of course. Maybe he'll push me into the loch and claim his inheritance?" Sir Arthur joked.

"Fish, eh? I hear there's salmon in the loch," said Mr Gilbert, one of the other guests.

"Aye, and rainbow trout," Sir Arthur assured him.

"Don't get my wife's hopes up," Gilbert said in a mock-whisper. "She's partial to trout."

After dinner they retired to the lounge. A fair-haired man,

well-dressed and aged maybe thirty sat alone, making no effort to socialise with the others. “Who is he?” Hunt asked Amelie’s father. The man had missed dinner.

“Mr Rannoch, he arrived last night, also.” There was disapproval in Gerrard’s tone.

“You don’t like him?” Hunt intuited.

“He was not present for breakfast, and this is the first I have seen of him since last night. I cannot abide men who sleep the day away.”

An old piano sat in the corner of the room and after some encouragement from the others, Hunt sat down to play. He familiarised himself with the piano, pleased to discover it was in tune, and played some popular parlour music. Polite applause accompanied the last few notes, and he looked up to see Rannoch clapping with the others.

Sir Arthur rose and stood next to Rannoch. From the way M. Gerrard had spoken, Hunt expected Rannoch to be a heavy drinker, but he hadn’t once seen the man with a glass. “Mr Hunt, I’m honoured to introduce you to Mr George Rannoch. Rannoch, meet Mr Wilton Hunt.”

Hunt approached Rannoch and shook his hand, finding it cold to the touch. “A pleasure to meet you, sir.” Knowing Amelie’s father was present and possessed of a low opinion of Rannoch, Hunt was courteous, but distantly so.

Rannoch’s smile fell short of his eyes. “You play well, Mr Hunt.”

“Too kind, Mr Rannoch,” Hunt said modestly. A fourth man joined them, a servant, he presumed. His tanned complexion marked him as foreign, his features not unlike the men of the Carpathian Circus.

“My valet, Micha,” Rannoch said on seeing Hunt watch the new arrival. “Hungarian and new to these shores, is that not so, Micha?”

“Yes, sir.” Micha looked awkward and out of place.

“I’m sure he’ll serve you well, Rannoch.” Sir Arthur’s tone suggested an impatience to move the conversation away from the valet.

There was something about Rannoch that put Hunt off, the way he looked at him. He finished his drink, bid a goodnight to the Gerrards, and retired for the night.

Hunt lay in his bed, still unnerved by Rannoch's cold blue eyes. He was halfway asleep when a sound outside his room returned him to wakefulness. Floorboards creaked, followed by hushed whispers, and finally footsteps that faded into silence.

He watched the bedroom door until sleep took him.

Chapter Thirty

The breakfast table was lively with conversation, the food almost forgotten. Hunt noted George Rannoch's absence. *Not a morning man, it seems.* He sat with the Gerrards and leaned close to Jacques. "What have I missed?"

"You have not heard?"

"Clearly not. Heard what?"

Jacques bit into his toast and slowly chewed. Hunt embraced patience and allowed him his little game. Jacques swallowed the food and washed it down with some milk. "Good toast," he said.

"Glad to hear it. How's the milk?"

"It is good, too. Fresh." He put the glass down. "Two guests left the hotel before dawn without paying their bill. The manager, Monsieur Granger, is an unhappy man."

"I can see why he might be upset. Which guests?" He looked around the room and realised who was missing. "The Gilberts?"

Jacques nodded. "A surprise, *non*?"

"Yes, a surprise." He recalled the amiable Mr Gilbert. The man had seemed enthusiastic about the fishing trip, saying nothing to suggest he intended to slip off in the night. "They haven't just gone for an early morning walk?"

Smirking, Jacques took another sip of milk. "With all of their … belongings?"

Hunt remained doubtful. Mr Gilbert owned a pair of textile mills in Lanarkshire. It would be no great hardship for the hotel to have him prosecuted, a public embarrassment for the couple. The more he thought about it, the more doubts he had. Leaving the hotel unnoticed meant slipping out long before dawn. Where would they go, lumbered with baggage? He looked over at Amelie who met his eyes but said nothing.

First a chambermaid goes missing, and now the Gilberts.

*

"Nothing, Jones?" That wasn't the answer Redfort wanted to hear. It was unfortunately the same answer Jones had given the day before, and the day before that. "I'm getting tired of hearing that, very tired." Worse, he suspected the Council's patience was almost exhausted. *And then they'll turn to other methods of motivation.* He rubbed his tired eyes.

Jones did a fair job of masking his trepidation, but Redfort knew him too well to be fooled. "I'm sorry, Reverend. The reward has been doubled but no one knows anything."

Redfort struggled to control his temper, feeling trapped in his own study. He was tempted to leave the city for a while, but if he left he could never return. As bishop-elect he was loathe to abandon all he had worked for.

"Maybe the Templars are lying low until their next attack?"

Perhaps. Redfort leaned back in his chair. "I think it's time to consider another method," he said slowly. *I never wanted it to come to this.* But he'd started the preparations in case.

"Reverend…?"

"Fetch me a child, Jones. A street orphan no one will miss."

Confusion passed over Jones' face before comprehension turned it to fear. "Sir, you can't–"

He fingered the cross hanging round his throat. "I have no other choice. Do I trust in you to find the Templars, or do I take matters into my own hands?"

"Reverend, I–"

Redfort raised his hand. "That was rhetorical. Find a child and bring it here." He rose wearily from his chair. "I'll make the necessary preparations."

Once Jones had left, Redfort retrieved a key from his desk and unlocked a cabinet. A jar containing a brain preserved in formaldehyde sat on the shelf. Not just any brain, but the brain removed from the Templar corpse recovered from the Under-Market. Next to it sat a small bottle holding some of the Templar's blood mixed with an anti-coagulant. He pocketed the bottle and pulled out the jar.

He removed another key from the cabinet and went down to his cellar, lighting the way with a candle. A lantern sat on an old table in the middle of the cellar, and a row of shelves ran across the furthest wall holding bottles of wine. Leaving the jar on the table, he lit the lantern and walked over to the shelves. *If the Council learns what I'm about, they'll burn me.* He put that cheerful thought aside and dragged back an old set of dust-covered shelves to expose a padlocked door. He unlocked the padlock, and the door swung open with a rusty squeal.

The candlelight illuminated the interior of a small storage cupboard built into the cellar, the back wall lined with shelves. An old tin box and a dozen or so bottles sat on those shelves. He opened the tin and removed a leather-bound book, its yellowed pages brittle with age. Holding the book in his left hand, he pulled out a medium-sized bottle half-filled with a liquid so dark it was almost black. *Nephilim* blood, worth its weight in gold. Or his life, if he was caught with it.

He sat in the chair and stared at the items on the table. A brain in a jar, a bottle of *Nephilim* blood, and his necromancy grimoire. Candlelight danced across the ancient leather binding of the tome, black with age. Old as it was, the grimoire was a compilation of spells and instructions copied from scrolls older still, going back millennia. This book charted the evolution of the necromantic art since its long-forgotten birth in what Man now called Egypt. If the grimoire's author had given it a title, time's passage had long since worn it from the cover.

Necromancy. Redfort had been drawn to it as a young man, thinking it a path to power. The manipulation of the dead through sorcery intrigued him, but he'd been disheartened to learn just how much preparation was needed for even the simplest acts. His mentor had claimed more adept practitioners could raise and control several corpses; Redfort struggled to contact a single spirit or manipulate a corpse, and was left exhausted every time.

The *Nephilim* abhorred such practices and had directed the Council to be vigilant for any signs of them. Consequently, necromancers were few in number and cautious in its use. His mentor had been a shade too careless, suffering execution as a result. Redfort had inherited the brittle-paged grimoire and his mentor's bottle of *Nephilim* blood, an essential component.

Two hours passed. The cellar door creaked open and Jones walked down the steps with a young street urchin, aged maybe seven years. Jones knew of Redfort's occasional use of necromancy, but there was little risk of him telling. After finishing the last of his mentor's precious *Nephilim* blood two years previously, Redfort had tasked Jones to replenish the supply. The Council would kill Redfort for using necromancy, but Jones would fare no better for killing a *Nephilim* for its blood.

The child was in rags and had a starved, flea-bitten look about him. Redfort examined the boy, pleased to see a dulled look in his eyes. "He'll suffice."

Jones looked uncomfortable. "I took him to the kitchen and put laudanum in his broth. Is this–"

"Necessary? Yes, I fear it is." He poured some of his precious *Nephilim* blood into two cups. Jones took one of the cups and encouraged the drugged child to drink it down. The child gagged but didn't vomit.

Not relishing what he must do, Redfort drank from the second cup, forcing down the vile substance. His belly protested, but he was able to keep it down. He opened the jar containing the preserved brain and poured in a little *Nephilim* blood. He reluctantly placed his right hand inside and touched the brain. "Bring him here."

The child was pushed forward and Redfort placed his left hand on the boy's head. "Can I do anything?" Jones asked.

"You can keep quiet and ensure the child doesn't fall." Redfort looked down at the open book and softly chanted. The language was unrecognisable; he had no idea what he was saying, but it aided him in piercing the veil between life and what lay after, in making contact with the dead man's soul.

The world shrank, reduced to himself, the brain and the child. *Flicker*. Redfort sensed something, an echo of the Templar. He concentrated on it and chased down the remnants of the man. There were no words, only feelings and sensations not his own. *Confusion.* He made contact with the shattered remnants of the Templar's mind and soul, and it took all of his will to maintain control. Completing the rite to compel the Templar's obedience, Redfort channelled the soul fragment into the mind of the boy. It was not overly difficult; the boy was already drugged, and being young meant he had far fewer memories and sense of self to fight off the Templar unwillingly possessing him. A name came to him. *Murdo.*

It was done. Redfort's left hand dropped and for a moment his control over the boy wavered, but held. His right hand remained on the brain. His vision blurred so he closed his eyes, knowing he saw flashes of what the boy was seeing. It was disconcerting to see himself and somewhat disheartening. Mirrors were too kind by far.

He fed images of Steiner into the conflicted stew of consciousness that remained of the child and dead Templar, manipulating them to seek out the Templar hideout. Satisfied he had done enough, he struggled to speak. "Jones, take the boy outside and follow him."

For an hour, perhaps two, Redfort sat slumped in his chair and felt brain, blood and preserving fluid against his flesh as he struggled to maintain control over the possessed boy. Images flashed across his inner eye, glimpses of what the boy was seeing. Experienced necromancers were able to maintain a more complete link, but his own talents were lacking.

The boy led Jones into the Merchant City where Redfort could see houses in the distance. He saw them again, closer. Then closer again. The boy was focused on one townhouse in particular. *This house is his destination.* Two men sat outside drinking, or made a poor job pretending to, looking more like soldiers than common drunkards. *Steiner's sentries.* Exultation was followed by alarm; if they saw the boy in his condition, they might suspect something was amiss and flee. He yanked his hand out of the jar to sever the link. Jones would deal with the boy.

Breaking the spell was never easy and always painful. Debilitated with exhaustion, he sat unable to move and forced to wait until Jones returned. It wouldn't be for a while yet as the boy had to be killed. Suffocation was best; then the body could be left in an alley and dismissed as a natural death. It was a mercy, really. The boy's mind was gone.

He passed the time planning how to proceed. It would be too dangerous to send Jones to the Council with the information. Necromancy made the man uneasy, and Redfort feared the Council might sense that unease and press him as to how the location was obtained. *No, better to send Henderson. I'll tell him an agent of mine tracked down the Templars, and that I'm too sick to attend in person.* Which would not be a lie. He would be fit for nothing for the next day or two.

*

The barmaid brought over drinks, and Hunt smiled his thanks on receipt of the pint of beer. He was with the Gerrards and the Williamson cousins within the village's Lochside Inn, renowned locally for its fish dishes. The low ceilings and subdued lighting gave it a cosy atmosphere.

The pub was busy with locals, though none seemed to resent the presence of strangers. Iron clan badges and old swords hung from the ceiling and from hooks in the walls. Wood burned in a nearby fireplace.

"How did the fishing go?" Amelie asked. There was a mischievous edge to her voice that led Hunt to suspect she had already heard.

"It went well," he said, not entirely truthful. "The trout we caught will be served to us tonight." *She doesn't know.*

Amelie looked at Hunt, a smile still tugging at her lips. "Well done. How many did you catch?"

Her tone was just a touch too innocent. *She* does *know.* He opened his mouth to speak when Sir Arthur interrupted. "Mr Hunt was very enthusiastic, Mademoiselle Gerrard. So dogged in his pursuit that he followed them into the loch."

Amelie clapped. "Bravo, bravo."

Hunt sighed. "I wasn't paying attention and fell off the pier."

"Fell? You walked off the pier," said Jacques, the memory giving him pleasure. "In France we bring the fish to us, we do not go to them."

The others laughed, Amelie most of all. "You *walked* off…?" she asked before resuming her laughter.

Hunt smiled tightly and sipped from his pint.

The pub lived up to its culinary reputation, the fried trout proving delicious.

"So, what do you do, Mr Williamson?" Hunt asked Sir Arthur's cousin after the dinner plates had been cleared away.

"I'm a lawyer," Williamson replied deprecatingly. "Lots of legal tedium."

"Don't be modest, Neil," Sir Arthur chided kindly before turning to Hunt. "He's just been offered an excellent position at an office in Glasgow."

"Which I'll decline," Williamson said. "I'm happy where I am."

M. Gerrard stood before Sir Arthur had the chance to reply. "Madame Gerrard and I thank you for your company and the pleasure of your fish, but we will be returning to the hotel by carriage. Do not stay out too late." The last was said to Jacques and Amelie.

*

Storm clouds gathered restlessly over the western horizon. Hunt, Amelie, Jacques, Sir Arthur and Neil Williamson walked along the road leading to the hotel. The hour was too late for them to get a carriage, leaving no alternative but to walk.

Hunt wasn't quite drunk, but the consumed beer fogged his thoughts. He walked next to Amelie, her brother prowling ahead. Sir Arthur seemed uncharacteristically quiet, perhaps drunk despite his head for alcohol. Neil Williamson had a visible stagger to his step.

Hunt turned on hearing the approach of horses from the rear. A wagon passed the group and slowed. One man held the reigns while another two lounged in the back sharing a bottle of liquor. They wore loose earthy-coloured shirts and trousers, likely gypsies from the campsite.

Hunt mustered his best smile. "Evening, gentlemen. I presume by your destination and clothing that you're headed to the camp near the hotel? My friends and I would be very grateful if you could help us on our way."

The gypsy holding the reins looked down at him. He shouted back to his friends in the back of the wagon in a Gaelic-sounding language, and they replied in the same.

The driver grinned. "Climb up."

Hunt reciprocated. "My thanks!" Williamson, Sir Arthur and Jacques clambered onto the wagon. Hunt offered to help Amelie up.

She looked apprehensive. "I am not happy about this. What if they are involved in the people disappearing?"

"I doubt that, gypsies always get the blame for everything. Anyway, I'll protect you."

Her expression suggested doubts in his martial efficacy. "You have trouble walking." But she relented and climbed onto the wagon, ignoring appreciative looks from the three gypsies. Hunt climbed up after her, and the wagon carried on.

The two gypsies in the back were openly curious about their passengers and spoke in their own tongue, the accent almost Irish. Amelie hunched self-consciously near the back of the wagon.

"So, what brought you to the village?" Hunt hoped to distract their attention from Amelie.

"Food," the driver called back. Sure enough, the back of the wagon was littered with bags of oats and sacks of vegetables.

Another passed back a bottle and invited the passengers to share. Williamson and Jacques drank gamely from it, but screwed their faces after one swallow. Hunt hesitantly took a mouthful and coughed as it burned its way down his throat.

The wagon slowed as it neared the hotel, and the five of them jumped off and waved at the departing wagon.

"They were a friendly bunch," Williamson said.

Hunt nodded, though Amelie looked sceptical.

Chapter Thirty-One

Steiner sat in his room in the King's Head Inn and disassembled his pistol, running a steel-wire brush through its empty chambers to scrape out any remaining residue. He blew through the six holes and peered down them, satisfied they were clean. A small candle sat on the desk, giving him enough light to work with.

Miss Knox lay in the bed, their marital charade resumed once again. She lay on her side facing away from Steiner, chestnut hair spread over the pillow, her slow breathing suggesting she slept.

The Templars' destruction of the Crypt and its resident undead had earned them the Sooty Feathers' wrath, and that of their masters. Steiner had little doubt the society had cast wide its web of agents and informants, his masquerade as a married visitor from Dundee the only reason he remained undiscovered.

The success at the Crypt a week past on Friday morning had buoyed morale among the men despite the loss of Murdo and McIlwraith. Steiner had spent most nights at the King's Head while he revisited the Order's agents, hoping his early victories would encourage greater cooperation.

A bell rang urgently in the distance, getting louder and louder. Steiner tugged the curtain aside to see a fire wagon race up the street. An orange glow was visible, the city silhouetted. He realised the location of the fire; the street where his men were staying.

His hands shook a little as he quickly reassembled his pistol and loaded all six chambers. He slammed the pistol shut and grabbed his sword-stick as he left the room, taking care not to awaken Miss Knox. He was probably being paranoid, it could be any building on fire. Perhaps. *God help us*.

The house lent to them by Stewart Munro was a fifteen minute walk; it took him less than that to get there. He pushed his way through the gawping crowd, his suspicions confirmed. Flames consumed the house hosting his remaining eight men, too fierce for the firemen to prevent spreading to the adjacent buildings. Rain pattered down but not enough to make a difference.

He looked for his men among the crowd but saw only unfamiliar faces. Fragments of overheard conversation confirmed the fire to be no accident. A woman shouted how she had seen a fight erupt in the street, a group of men attacking those fleeing the blaze. Gunshots had been heard. A man living across the street recounted seeing two figures flee the street, only escaping the waiting arsonists thanks to someone firing a rifle from the top floor of the burning house.

It sounded like Gray. Steiner wondered if he was still in the house, choked by smoke or consumed by fire. A brave man to sacrifice himself covering the escape of his fellows.

Not all had escaped, Steiner knew. He passed the bodies of Morris and Whyte, lying bloody in the street. Other bodies lay covered nearby, maybe his men or maybe some of their attackers. But he disliked the look of some standing nearby, men with the look of predators. Killers, waiting to see who showed an undue interest in the bodies.

Instinct warned him to leave. The question of how the society found his men would have to wait, as would vengeance. It was possible those who attacked his men had his description. He quickened his pace.

Too late. On passing through a lane he realised he was being followed by at least four men. Taking no chances, he turned and ran, hoping to lose them in the maze of lanes and narrow streets. He drew his gun, comforted by its weight. Shouts rang out behind him, either to summon others or panic him into rash action.

Hounded by the echoing footsteps of his pursuers, Steiner increased his pace. If forced to, he would confront his enemy and martyr himself, but he had no taste for a futile death. Better to live and avenge the fallen.

Steiner spied a darkened path split off from a wynd and ran

into it, hoping it would lead him to safety. A half-fallen wall blocked the exit, but he would not be undone by brick and mortar. Pocketing his gun, he jumped and used his free hand to pull himself over the wall.

He almost landed on two pursuers, both carrying revolvers. Steiner didn't know who was the more surprised, he or them, but he was the first to react. He yanked the blade from his cane and stabbed the nearest. On pulling free his sword-stick he was dismayed to find the thin blade had caught on the man's ribs and snapped. Refusing to panic, he shoved the body into the second man and lunged, thrusting the jagged remnant of his sword-stick into the man's throat and leaving it there.

Steiner ran down the street to the King's Head, aware of no further pursuit. He prayed some of his men had escaped, but first he had to ensure his own escape and Miss Knox's. It was tempting to lie low in the inn but too risky. On entering the room, he woke a startled Miss Knox and told her to dress. One look at his face stilled any argument.

"What do we do now?" Miss Knox asked breathlessly as she pulled up her stockings.

"We cannot stay here, we must leave." He checked his pistol, lamenting the loss of his sword-stick.

She gestured at her belongings. "What about–"

"Leave them," he said, looking out of the window. The street was deserted for the moment. "We go now."

"Where are we going?" she asked as they fled the inn.

He hurried her through alleys and side streets, more concerned with avoiding pursuit than the risks therein. Any footpads who sought to accost them would be dealt with.

"Where are we going?" Miss Knox persisted.

"To visit a friend," he answered.

*

They were wet, weary and footsore by the time they reached the Woodside area. Steiner banged the round, silver door knocker three times. The door was eventually answered by the maid, Ellison. "Good evening," he greeted. "Please inform Lady Delaney that Mr Steiner wishes to speak with her."

Ellison blinked away sleep and gave him a stern look. "Sir, do you know the–"

"–time, yes, I am aware the hour is late. It is important. My poor brother has died. Tell her that exactly."

Ellison started to give an irritated sniff but remembered herself. "I'll inform Lady Delaney." She showed them into the parlour. "I'm sorry about your brother."

A carriage clock on the mantelpiece revealed the time to be forty-three minutes past midnight. Lady Delaney didn't keep them waiting long. She entered the room dressed in a house-robe with her greying hair hanging loose.

Steiner rose and offered her a curt bow from the neck. He hid his amusement as Miss Knox hastily stood and started to bow herself before giving an awkward curtsey. "Lady Delaney, I apologise for disturbing you at this hour."

She looked at him intently. "Ellison tells me your poor brother has died." She knew the code as well as any other Templar ally.

"Yes."

"I am sorry. How many will be able to attend the funeral?" *How many survived?*

"I am unsure. Perhaps just myself."

She closed her eyes briefly. "I'm sorry. I had hoped … well, never mind that now."

Miss Knox looked back and forth at them, bewildered. "Brother? I don't understand."

Lady Delaney looked quizzically at Steiner. "Who is your companion?"

"Lady Delaney, meet Miss Kerry Knox. Miss Knox, meet Lady Caroline Delaney. You recall Miss Knox's assistance in finding Benjamin Howard?"

"I do indeed. You have my gratitude, Miss Knox." Lady Delaney looked the young woman up and down. "However did you get caught up with this fanatic?"

"I was to … pretend to be his wife." Miss Knox shuffled her feet. "I'm an actress."

"You look like a drowned rat. I'll have Ellison prepare you a bath and lay out some dry clothing."

Ellison ushered Miss Knox out of the room and Lady Delaney motioned for Steiner to sit. She poured them each a generous brandy and sat across from him with an amused expression. "She seems rather young for you."

He bristled at the implication. "There is nothing improper, Lady Delaney. My word."

She accepted that at face value. "Tell me what happened."

Steiner drank some brandy, tasting liquid flame. "The house my people were staying in was set on fire, with killers waiting outside to ambush them. I was elsewhere." His absence burned like acid; him being there might not have saved his men, but he could have died with them.

"You were attacked by the Sooty Feather Society, I assume?"

"It can be assumed the society was responsible." He tried to shake off his melancholy with more brandy.

Her eyes were hard but not devoid of sympathy. "I am sorry, Steiner. I had high hopes of what you might accomplish here. Did you conclude matters with Mr Howard?"

Steiner nodded. "We had a long and fruitful conversation."

She smiled. "I'm delighted to hear that. His last, I hope?"

"He'll be conducting any future ones in Hell."

"A reprisal on this scale seems excessive for the killing of one man," she observed.

"They did not do it just to avenge him. From Howard we learned the location of a Crypt. We killed many undead and destroyed the Crypt with dynamite."

Her eyes widened in appreciation, and she raised her glass in salute. "I'm impressed. Your reputation is well-earned. How did they find you?"

"I do not know." He did not bother to hide his bitter frustration. "Treachery, perhaps. But only those under my command knew our location, and most if not all are dead." He looked away. "It is likely we were betrayed by chance, nothing more."

"The Council could have used a diviner."

He had considered that possibility earlier but dismissed it. "We left nothing a diviner could use to find us."

"And your companion? She was involved in Howard's capture in the theatre."

"She knows nothing else. She was to pose as my wife in

the inn when I stayed there. I must ask a favour. We require somewhere to stay. I do not know if it would be safe for Miss Knox to return to her home."

"I will welcome the company."

He gave a short bow, embarrassed by her generosity. "I am in your debt."

"Killing Benjamin Howard erases any debt." Her eyes glittered in the candlelight. "Will you continue your crusade?"

"If God wills it." He finished his brandy. "Our protocol in such circumstances is to leave a note addressed to Mr Mark Luke or Mr John Mark at the High Street post office. If you could leave a message from myself instructing my men on how to contact us, I would be grateful."

Lady Delaney sipped from her glass, untroubled by the brandy's potency. "God's will remains a mystery to me," she said coolly, "but I'll visit the post office on Monday."

"My thanks. If any of my men precede you, they may have left their own message."

"I'll make full enquiries, rest assured."

Miss Knox re-joined them, bathed and wrapped in a spare house-robe. "Thank you, Lady Delaney," she said awkwardly.

"That robe suits you. Mr Steiner and I have been talking. It may not be safe for you to return home, so you will both stay here as my guests."

"I'm – I'm grateful, Lady Delaney," Miss Knox stammered. "But I don't know what's going on. I was hired to play his wife, and now I'm in danger?"

Lady Delaney smiled at the frustration in her voice. "I'll tell you everything. In the morning." Steiner noted that she did not bother to consult with him first.

Chapter Thirty-Two

Falling…

Hunt awoke with a start, his heart pounding and skin clammy. The dregs from a bedside table glass failed to soothe his parched throat, and he reached for the water jug, dismayed to find it empty. *Damn it.* He crawled out of bed, thirsty and with a pressing need to piss, knowing he would find no rest until he did so. There was a pot tucked under the bed, into which he relieved his bladder with a sigh.

One need taken care of, he pulled on his housecoat and walked out into the dark hallway with the empty jug in hand. Taking care to make no noise, he approached the staircase with the singular intention of finding the kitchen.

There was a noise below. A glance over the twisting bannister revealed three shadowed figures dragging someone downstairs towards the hall. Hunt stood on the staircase, unsure of what to make of it. There could be an innocent explanation; a caught thief or a drunken porter being truculent as his fellows brought him back.

Neither explanation satisfied him. The furore of a captured intruder would have awoken the entire hotel, and the hour was too late to account for men returning from the pub. His choices were either return to bed and pretend to have seen nothing, or follow and investigate. Once, he would have followed without question, but recent brushes with death had instilled caution.

He reluctantly decided to follow, creeping downstairs to the reception hall in cautious pursuit. *I never did know when to mind my own business.* He kept hold of the water jug, ready to wield it as a weapon if need be. The front door was still shut, but he remembered the corridor that led out to the garden and found the side door unlocked. Shivering despite his housecoat, he stumbled blindly around the hedged garden before finding his way out onto the grounds. There was a scrape of gravel as the captive was dragged along the path. Hunt pursued, treading barefoot on the grass.

His stomach tightened as he realised they were going into the woods Amelie had shown him when he arrived. Nevertheless, he followed and soon felt earth and twigs underfoot. Branches clawed at his face and tore his housecoat, but he'd come too far to quit.

The mausoleum waited ahead, moonlight shining off its white stonework. Caution prompted him to approach from the side, and he slowly crept along the front of the building towards the entrance. He half-expected to find the door locked, but it moved at his touch. He pushed it open and winced at the slight squeal coming from its hinges.

It was dark inside. He walked in blindly, drawn to a small light at the far end. Dirt and stone felt rough against the soles of his feet, and his skin crawled at the thought of the mouldering corpses entombed around him. On reaching the light he realised it came from beneath an open trapdoor leading underground. He followed the wooden steps down, praying it wasn't a trap. A faint flicker of light was visible from the crypt below.

Rapid, shallow breaths marked his progress, each step downward measured by a dozen heartbeats. Wood creaked in protest, and he immediately removed his weight from the offending step. Hunt exhaled and resumed his descent. He had no idea what was going on below but was resolved to find out.

His better judgement often surrendered to curiosity. The childhood memory of a strange cocoon nestling in the crook of a tree came to mind, a curiosity he'd indulged by poking it with a stick. He'd succeeded in outrunning the enraged wasps, most of them at least. The consequences of being caught tonight would be worse than half-a-dozen stings.

There were muffled voices ahead, but he couldn't discern what they were saying. He needed to get closer. *Shit. Shit. Damn!*

The flickering light grew a little brighter as he neared the bottom. The steps ended in a small room storing several wooden crates. A short passage connected it to the main crypt which was lit by wooden torches held in iron holders. Hunt reached the crypt floor and crept around, peering into the main chamber as he hid behind a dust-coated crate.

A small group had gathered, five excluding the prisoner. Most stood in the shadows, their faces obscured. Sarcophagi had been dragged from the centre of the room to make space for the hooded captive whose wrists and ankles had been bound together. The light was too dim and the distance too great, but the prisoner's build identified him as male.

A dark-haired man walked into the centre and chanted in a language like nothing Hunt had ever heard before, not Latin nor any of its bastard offspring. Something in Hunt felt a spark of recognition on hearing that alien tongue, like almost recalling an unremembered dream. Hairs on the back of his neck rose.

There was something familiar about the speaker. Another man stood next to him, his blond hair flashing gold in the torchlight. Hunt's stomach tightened in recognition. George Rannoch. *What horror are you about tonight?* He knew the dark-haired chanter now: Rannoch's valet, Micha.

Rannoch ripped off the captive's hood, but the shadows crowding the crypt's floor left him little more than a cowering silhouette, one Hunt couldn't make out. A chest at the edge of the room was opened and a second prisoner was hauled out, arms and legs twisted by cramp. The second captive was male, thin with dark hair, middle-aged and unknown to Hunt. A man and woman dragged him into the centre, their features briefly revealed by the candlelight. Again, Hunt recognised neither.

Rannoch, whom Hunt assumed to be in charge, cut into his wrist and held it over the first prisoner. Dark blood dripped over a shadowed face.

Micha chanted the same word over and over, a word Hunt struggled to discern. It sounded like "*Beliel*," but he couldn't be sure and was damned if he'd go any closer. Micha was echoed by the others. The dress and accents of Micha and two of the others reminded Hunt of the circus-folk on Glasgow Green.

A wet gargled choke escaped as Rannoch ran his knife

across the throat of the second captive. Hunt's stomach bucked as blood sprayed out, the victim's arms held tight by the man and woman as his head thrashed in agony. The others appeared unaffected by the dying man's plight, watching him bleed out unflinchingly. After the sacrificed captive lost his brief struggle with Death, he was dragged aside and thereafter ignored. Fear kept Hunt rooted to the crate he hid behind, but he knew the blackhearts he spied on would leave the crypt sooner or later, and there was only one way in or out. *Who are these people, so comfortable with murder?*

He watched with increasing disbelief. The prisoner bound in the centre convulsed violently, and the chanting faltered. Hunt felt a chill deep in his soul as the candles dimmed and then flickered back to life with renewed vigour – as if the world itself had held its breath for a moment. The victim went limp, head lolling to one side.

Rannoch tentatively approached the prisoner and crouched next to him.

The prisoner twitched. Rannoch cut his bonds and helped him sit up, face shrouded in shadow. Hunt wondered at the sudden change in behaviour towards him.

Rannoch supported the former captive and motioned curtly to the others as he helped the man to his feet. They bowed their heads in obeisance.

Knowing he was moments from seeing the captive's face but knowing also this was his chance to flee, Hunt quietly crept back to the ladder and climbed up to the mausoleum. He'd seen enough. He left the mausoleum and ran blindly though the woods, further ruining his housecoat and wounding his feet. He considered both of scant account.

Hunt reached the hotel and entered through the still-unlocked side door. The hall was deserted and cloaked in darkness. He returned upstairs to his room, his bare feet sore and bleeding. Only once safe in his room did he recall the glass jug he had armed himself with, a jug he last recalled seeing below the crypt. *Fool!* If Rannoch or one of his coven stumbled over it, they would know their villainy had not gone unwitnessed. *Maybe they won't see it.*

Maybe. None the less, he looked around the room for a

means of protection while considering the purpose behind the kidnapping and murder. His hands shook, and he yearned for whisky or brandy to settle his nerves. His throat was still parched but the prospect of meeting George Rannoch down below stayed him from leaving his room until dawn's comforting light.

Hunt had no idea who the prisoner was, but he uneasily remembered Sirk's talk of demon possession. That could explain the sudden change in treatment and suggested Rannoch to be working for the undead, or perhaps even undead himself. *Maybe that's why we never see the bastard during the day.*

He lay in bed, alert for anyone attempting to force his door. A chest of drawers was now pressed against it to prevent easy entry. Sleep eluded him, and he spent the remainder of the night staring at the window, watching as night slowly brightened to morning. Thirsty and afraid, he listened to birdsong herald the dawn.

*

Hunt sat at the breakfast table, tired and withdrawn. All the other guests were in attendance except for Rannoch and Sir Arthur, none showing any sign of mistreatment. Someone had been killed, another possibly possessed by a demon, and Hunt wanted to believe it was all some twisted theatre. But he knew differently; it had been real, and a man had died.

"No disappearances this morning?" he asked, trying to sound flippant. "No more missing staff or guests evading their bill?"

"No," Jacques said, his eyes bloodshot. "Mr Rannoch left last night, but he paid in full."

Good. Hunt had no desire to meet Rannoch ever again. "Where is Sir Arthur?" he asked, wanting to identify the man possessed, praying silently Sir Arthur would appear, hale and hearty.

"He is not feeling well, he will be down later," Williamson said, speaking slowly and looking unwell himself. They all seemed to be paying the price for last night's overindulgence.

He had been seen, at least. Hunt nodded. *That stranger*

might have been sacrificed to allow a demon to possess Sir Arthur. If Sir Arthur is involved at all. He picked at his food. Were the Gilberts involved?

Amelie cornered him afterwards in the garden. "You said little during breakfast, Wilton. Too much beer last night?"

He forced a smile. "I may have overindulged."

"We are leaving soon, I hope you will be well for the journey." Her smile took on a cruel edge. "It will be bumpy ride, *oui*?"

"Yes, but I'll be fine. Please excuse me, I must pack."

He walked back into the hotel and stopped. Sir Arthur was loitering in the reception hall. There was something about the way Sir Arthur looked at him that made him uneasy. *Does a demon stare out of those eyes at me?* He fought the urge to step back, repulsed by the notion that the family friend may have been possessed.

He tried to think of something to say but was saved the need by Sir Arthur turning abruptly away.

*

Hunt stood cautiously outside the mausoleum. It looked no different than it had two days earlier except now he knew what lurked beneath. He reluctantly walked towards the entrance, half-hoping it had been re-locked. It hadn't, and the door swung open.

He took a breath and entered the mausoleum. Old stone sarcophagi rested against the walls, no longer hidden by night. The trapdoor was where he remembered it, and he descended to the lower level. His glass jug lay next to the crate where he had left it, hopefully unnoticed by Rannoch and the others. Some melted wax stained the floor, recent by the feel of it, and there was a dark patch on the ground that might have been blood. But there were no bodies. *It happened. I didn't dream it.* He left the crypt and returned to the hotel.

*

Two McBride carriages waited as porters loaded them with

luggage. Hunt and the Gerrards had packed a luncheon, knowing it would be late at night before they reached Glasgow. The Williamson cousins were staying at the hotel for a further day.

Two whips cracked, and the carriages moved with a jolt. Hunt looked to his front, the village having lost its charm. The mausoleum lay buried in the woods and out of sight; if only the memory of what he'd witnessed within could be so easily removed from his thoughts.

Storm clouds reached the Loch, unleashing heavy rains and winds that slowed the carriages as they navigated the winding road south. Hunt, Amelie and Jacques shared the second carriage.

A sudden jolt woke Hunt from his reverie, and he sat up, looking quizzically at Amelie and Jacques. "What is it?"

Amelie shrugged. "We stopped." Jacques wiped condensation from the window but could do nothing about the gloom outside.

They waited for the journey to resume but the carriage remained stationary. Hunt looked at his pocket watch; just after seven. His impatience got the better of him and he opened the door to land ankle-deep in mud. He swore freely, the profanity snatched by the wind. He slogged to the front of the carriage, perturbed to find the driver absent. Shielding his eyes from the rain, he spotted the first carriage ahead.

Hunt forced his way forwards, fighting the wind with every step. The drivers were huddled in conversation as he joined them, both wearing heavy overcoats and clutching their top hats lest the wind snatch them. One took a swig from a hip flask and handed it back to the other.

"What's happening?" Hunt shouted.

One of the drivers shouted something back.

"What?"

"I said, we can't go any further, the road's blocked ahead." A tree blocked the road, its fall apparently recent.

"We can't stay here all night," Hunt argued, appalled at the prospect. The wind howled mournfully over his shoulder, shaking trees at him like bony claws.

The driver pointed to the left, the rain darkening his red beard. "Walker spotted a trail over there, we'll follow it and find some cover. It might lead to a farm. The poor beasties can't take much more of this, can you, lads?" The last was said to the first carriage's two horses.

Hunt returned to the second carriage, cold and drenched. "We won't be reaching Glasgow tonight," he told Amelie and Jacques.

The carriage slowly resumed its journey and followed the narrow trail. The three passengers endured a rough ride, branches clawing at the sides and roof.

The trail widened into a muddy road that led to a farmhouse. *A farmhouse with a welcoming fire, I hope.*

Hunt climbed out again, followed this time by Amelie and Jacques. A few lights shone from the farmhouse's windows, and the driver of the lead carriage hammered on the stout wooden door.

It opened, and a man stood in the doorway, his grizzled face guarded and suspicious. "What do you lot want?"

"We're looking for shelter. The main road's blocked and our horses are fit to drop," the red-bearded driver explained.

The farmer's weathered face softened, grey whiskers hanging off his cheeks. "You must be mad, travelling in this weather." He shook his head. "Put the horses in the barn. You'd better all stay the night."

Hunt and the Gerrards were ushered into the farmhouse and left to huddle by the fire while the farmer and two drivers saw to the horses and carriages. The farmhouse, it turned out, had more rooms than occupants. The farmer lived alone, his wife dead and both daughters long-married, explaining why the kitchen was cluttered and the cracked stone floor unswept. Not that Hunt judged; had he been breaking his back from dawn until dusk in the fields, he'd leave chores unfinished too.

The farmer hadn't dined yet, an enticing pot of broth soup cooking on the range. Hunt sat back and felt the fire warm his face. He let himself relax. There was nothing to do but wait for the storm to pass.

Chapter Thirty-Three

John Brown's hospitality was rusty but well-meant, and gratefully received. Thin grey hair crowned his creased face, left unkempt by the wind. His brown trousers were patched in places, held up by braces.

He remained standing, burly arms crossed as he hovered over his uninvited guests, not sitting until M. Gerrard produced a bottle of scotch from his bag and made clear his intention to share it. After getting over his surprise at seven strangers turning up at his door, the farmer seemed grateful for the company. The storm showed no signs of relenting, its ferocity undiminished.

It was after ten o'clock. Mme Gerrard had gone up to one of the spare bedrooms after saying something in French to her husband and son. Her pointed look at the half-empty whisky bottle meant Hunt needed no translation.

He jumped as something banged outside. It banged a second time, then a third. Mr Brown frowned. "Barn door. I thought I'd bolted it." He began to stand, but Whiting, the red-bearded the driver, stood first.

"I'll get it. I want to check on the horses."

The other driver, Gerry Walker, stood as well. A black widows peak sat atop his long, dour face. "I'll go with you."

Whiting nodded. "Come on, then." They left the house, the wind howling through the doorway until it was slammed shut.

Hunt sat quietly at the table and drank his whisky. Mr Brown and M. Gerrard discussed the comparative qualities of Scottish and French soil, with Jacques throwing in an occasional comment. Hunt looked at Amelie and caught her watching him before turning away.

He got up and knelt before the fire, soaking up the heat. A

chambermaid vanishing without a trace. A couple disappearing in the middle of the night, apparently to avoid a hotel bill. A satanic ritual and human sacrifice. *What is the common thread tying them all together? A man was sacrificed, and another possibly possessed by a demon called Beliel. Was the chambermaid involved? The Gilberts?*

Who was possessed? The amiable Norry Gilbert? Sir Arthur Williamson? Neil Williamson? Jacques or Monsieur Gerrard, perhaps? Or someone else. Sirk would have a theory, no doubt, perhaps even a clever means of determining who. Foley would be a stalwart presence despite his sarcastic humour, an experienced fighter. *I wish they were here.*

Amelie knelt beside him. "You have been quiet, is something wrong?"

"It's just the storm." There was no need to worry her.

"No, you have been quiet this day." She studied him, her dark eyes revealing concern for him.

Flames danced over charred wood and coal that crackled in the fireplace. "You were right about the hotel. I think the chambermaid–"

"Jill."

"–Jill. I think she was kidnapped, probably killed. I would be surprised if the Gilberts ran off, I think they're dead too."

It took her a moment to digest Hunt's revelation. "*Mon Dieu.*" Her eyes shone with horror. "Who? Why?"

Not your gypsies. The front door opening saved him from deciding whether or not to tell her more. Walker entered the room, soaked and looking out of sorts. Hunt moved to let him get to the fire.

"Thanks," muttered the shivering driver. He pulled out a small metal flask and took a long draught from it, his hands shaking.

"Where's the other lad?" Mr Brown asked from the table.

Walker swallowed down the liquor. "The horses are a wee bit skittish, so he said he'd stay in the barn with them."

"Will he be warm enough?" M. Gerrard asked. "We can take him some blankets."

"There's no need," Walker said quickly, "He'll kip in one of the carriages." He rubbed his head, shaking water onto the floor. "Do you have a spare towel, Mr Brown?"

"There's some upstairs in a linen closet at the end of the hall." Brown puffed away on his pipe as Walker climbed the stairs.

M. Gerrard emptied his glass. "Where is the outhouse, Monsieur?"

Brown pulled the pipe from his mouth. "It's round the side of the house." He laid out an old backgammon board and set up the pieces as Gerrard went outside.

Hunt watched as Amelie and Mr Brown played, the farmer proving the better player. Jacques and Hunt were to play next, a match Hunt looked forward to. Unless he lost.

Jacques frowned at the back door. "My father should be back." Amelie looked up from the game, her expression mirroring Jacques' concern.

Hunt held the opinion that a man's bowel movements were his own business, but even so, M. Gerrard *had* been gone a long time. "Perhaps he's speaking to Mr Whiting in the barn?" Or perhaps he'd slipped and was lying injured outside. "I'll go out and look for him." He pulled on his coat and buttoned it up, taking a lantern with him.

He was battered by the rain as soon as he stepped past the door and almost lost his feet. The wind howled around the farm, wrestling with the trees. Hunt braced himself and walked round the outside of the house, muck clutching at his feet. The wooden outhouse sat hunched against the farmhouse. He knocked on the door, but it was unlocked and swung open.

It was empty. The barn, maybe? Hunt turned and retraced his footsteps. He unbolted the barn door and paused. If Whiting and possibly Gerrard were inside, how was the door bolted from the outside? He entered the barn and raised the lantern up high. Shadows drew back from the light and a horse nickered in the darkness. There were no other sounds within the barn. He walked towards the nearest carriage and shone the light inside. It was empty.

The second carriage sat beside the first. Hunt held up the lantern and climbed inside, smelling alcohol and seeing Whiting the driver huddled against the far door. He tugged him on the shoulder and felt something wet. The light fell on his hand, revealing it to be red with blood. He recoiled and almost fell from the carriage. *Dead. He's bloody dead.*

Hunt spun round, raising the lantern up high and shining it from side to side. No one was there. He took several breaths and forced himself to examine Whiting more closely. He lifted the man's head, the lantern revealing the scarlet smear of a slit throat. There was a stab wound on his belly, too. Hunt checked the man's hands and found no cuts or bruises. *If I was attacked with a knife, my instinct would be to raise my hands in defence.* The top of Whiting's shirt was wet with liquor. *He took a drink and got a knife in the gut, spilling the alcohol over himself. His throat was then slit. He knew his killer; it's one of us.*

But who? Monsieur Gerrard? The thought of Amelie's father being a killer was not a pleasant one. He liked and respected the man, not to mention his feelings for the daughter. An unpleasant possibility occurred. What if Gerrard was the man dragged to the crypt and possessed by the demon?

The barn door slammed shut, causing him to flinch. He jumped down from the carriage and stared at it. The door opened and shut again. Just the wind. But that didn't mean the killer wasn't still hidden inside, watching him.

Hunt fled the barn, not caring about the mud soaking his feet or the rain drenching him to his skin. He shoved open the back door and almost fell into the kitchen. The others looked at him surprise.

"What is it?" Jacques asked. "Where is my father?"

He tried to gather his thoughts. "I couldn't find him. But Whiting's dead."

Amelie's hand covered her mouth. Mr Brown shook his head in denial. "What happened?" he asked.

"He was killed. Someone stabbed him and cut his throat."

"My father. Where is he? Has something happened to him?" Amelie grabbed Hunt's arm.

Walker was back downstairs, still tense and uneasy. He shakily drank from the flask. "Killed? Who could have done it? We're in the middle of nowhere."

Hunt stared at the flask. *You look but you don't see*, his father used to tell him. He remembered seeing the two drivers standing on the road, Whiting drinking from the flask before passing it back to Walker. *There was no cup in the wagon, nor flask or bottle.* "Let me dry off," he pleaded, moving to the fire and prodding at the coals with a poker. "Can you check I shut the door?"

Walker turned to the door, and as he did Hunt swung the poker and struck him to the head. Walker lay on the ground, stunned or unconscious.

Jacques stood between Hunt and Amelie. "Have you gone mad? What are you doing?"

Mr Brown and Amelie stared at Hunt. The farmer stood, his fists clenched.

"It was him." Hunt pointed at Walker. "He killed Whiting."

"How can you know?" Jacques demanded.

"Someone gave Whiting a drink just before he was killed. There was liquor spilt down his front, and it was still wet," Hunt explained. "But I saw no cup or bottle in the carriage, and earlier I saw the two of them sharing a flask." He pointed at the hip flask lying next to the unconscious driver. "That one." It occurred to him someone else could have taken Whiting out a drink, such as M. Gerrard, and that Hunt may just have struck an innocent man. He quickly searched Walker and found a folding knife in his pocket. The blade was clean but there was wet blood on the hinge. *Oh, thank God.*

Amelie slowly nodded. "It was Mr Walker who told us Mr Whiting had decided to stay in the barn."

"Yes," Hunt said.

"Why kill him?" Jacques asked, frowning.

Why indeed?

"And my father?" Amelie asked quietly.

"I couldn't find him," Hunt said. "He wasn't in the outhouse or in the barn. Mr Brown, do you have a rope we can use to tie him up?"

Brown still seemed to be coming to terms with murder in his once-quiet farm. "Aye, I've got a length of it in my barn."

"Is it safe to go alone?" Amelie asked.

"The killer's caught, and if he wakes up, best to have these two lads here to handle him," Brown said, rising. "I'll be right back with the rope. If he moves, hit him again." The back door banged shut behind him.

Jacques stared hard at Walker. "Do you think he harmed my father? Killed him?"

"It's a possibility," Hunt was forced to admit. "Once he's tied up, we can look outside again. When he wakes up we can ask him." Something nagged at Hunt, something that didn't fit.

"I will ask him," Jacques promised, murder in his eyes.

Several minutes later, Hunt frowned as a realisation struck him. "Damn," he muttered. "Walker might have killed Whiting, but he hasn't left the house since your father went outside. He couldn't have killed *him*."

Amelie and Jacques looked at each other, both looking hopeful. "Then he might still be unhurt?" Amelie asked.

Or there's someone else out there. Hunt looked at the door. "Mr Brown should have been back by now."

"Maybe he cannot find the rope?" Amelie suggested.

Hunt took a breath. "Or Walker is not acting alone. Your father is still missing."

Jacques shook his head. "*Non*. How could there be another killer? There is no one else left."

Hunt left unspoken his suspicion that M. Gerrard had been possessed by a demon. "It was Walker who led us up here," he said instead. "Perhaps an accomplice was waiting nearby before we arrived?" An accomplice who earlier blocked the road to force their diversion.

The barn door banged three times. Hunt listened, but he heard only the wind. The wind quietened, but the door banged a further three times. Fear rose up inside him.

Jacques stepped towards the door. "We must help Monsieur Brown."

"No!" Hunt blocked the door. "It's probably a trap. Amelie, go upstairs and bring your mother down."

Jacques armed himself with a kitchen knife while his sister ran up the stairs. "What of Brown?"

"I think he's already dead," Hunt admitted.

"And my father?"

"I fear so." *Or he's working with Walker.*

Someone screamed upstairs.

Both Hunt and Jacques moved to the stairs, but Hunt pointed to the motionless Walker. "Wait here and keep an eye on him." He ran up the stairs to the bedroom where Madame Gerrard had gone to sleep.

Amelie stared at the bed, a trembling hand covering her mouth. The blanket had been pulled back and the bed was red with blood. Her mother lay face up, her throat a mangled mess.

He gently took hold of Amelie and escorted her out of the room. They were being killed, one by one, and he still had no clue as to the identity of Walker's accomplice. *Monsieur Gerrard. No. Not Amelie's father.* He had almost reached the foot of the stairs when a shadow drew back. Hunt stopped. "Jacques?"

The wind howled mournfully outside. A floorboard creaked out of sight in the kitchen. But no one answered.

"Jacques!" *Not her brother, too.*

"Wilton?" Amelie called down to him.

"Stay there, don't come down." Hunt swallowed his fear and retreated backwards up the stairs. He held a finger to his lips on seeing Amelie's questioning look, her face wet with tears.

They ran into a bedroom and shut the door. Hunt dragged furniture across the room to block the door while Amelie tied blankets together. The door handle rattled. He stared at it, willing the furniture to hold the door shut long enough for them to escape.

The chest slowly scraped along the floor. Amelie opened the window and held onto the makeshift rope as Hunt lowered her outside. The wind blew into the room and killed the candle's frail light. The weight left the blankets. *She's on the ground.* He climbed out and prayed the drop wasn't too far. A broken ankle would be hell on their escape.

They ran blindly from the farmhouse, heedless of the branches that snatched and tore at them. Hunt had no clue where they were going, knowing only that they had to get far away, to lose themselves in the storm.

Amelie stumbled, hampered by her shoes and long skirts. Hunt kept her on her feet. Branches snapped behind them, and he knew their pursuer wasn't far behind. "We need to keep moving," he urged. A gunshot rang out and Amelie tripped again. *Damned shoes.* "Get up, we need to run!"

She didn't answer. He knelt and tried to help her up, but she just lay there. "Amelie, get up!" Her head lolled limply to one side. *No no no...*

He knelt in the mud and cradled her as the rain mingled with his tears. *Her laughter in Dunclutha. Candlelight shining off her dusky skin. A pretty face made more so by her smile. Her wonder on seeing the stag, and her compassion for the beast. Walking by her side in the circus. Our walk alone in the woods. Her teasing in the pub, mischievous but not unkindly meant*. He had glimpsed life through her pretty dark eyes, a *future*, and fallen in love with it.

Two men stood over him and opened a lantern. Glassy eyes that had once shone with vivacity now reflected only lantern light.

"A lucky shot, Walker. The Council want Hunt alive. If you had hit him instead of her…"

"He was the taller one, sir. And not wearing a skirt." Walker made murder sound an everyday occurrence. Maybe for him it was.

Hunt looked up at both men and recognised the other as George Rannoch. *Bastards*. The first stirrings of anger penetrated his grief.

"Hello, Mr Hunt," Rannoch said.

"Why?" *Madame Gerrard. Jacques Gerrard. Mr Brown. Whiting. Amelie. Oh God. Amelie.* "Where's Monsieur Gerrard?" *Killed like the rest.*

"Dead in some sacking back at the farm," Rannoch said carelessly.

It was grief and anger rather than courage that drove Hunt to look Rannoch in the eye. "Am I next?"

"Unfortunately for you, no. You're to be taken back alive."

"Why all this? Why not just take me at the hotel?" *Why kill everyone else?*

"There are no witnesses out here." Rannoch's furtive glance at Walker suggested that wasn't the entire answer. "The storm helped."

Walker raised the rifle and swung it hard. A sharp agony engulfed Hunt's skull, and the last he knew was a sense of falling and the taste of mud.

Falling...

Chapter Thirty-Four

The storm moved east, sparing Glasgow from further heavy rain and wind, leaving only a bleak, grey sky behind. *A perfect fit with my mood.* Steiner restlessly left the window and stood next to the teapot sitting on the parlour table. He looked down at it in disgust and left it alone. He had done little else but drink tea these past two days, trapped in Lady Delaney's home.

Oh, he had tried to occupy himself with chores and other household tasks, but they did not answer his questions. Had any of his men escaped? Where were they? And how had the Sooty Feather Society learned of their location?

That had been on Saturday night. It was now Monday, and there was still nothing he could do but wait for Lady Delaney to return with news. She was to check the Templars' message drop at the High Street Post Office; his men would leave a message there if they were able, and those attending after Lady Delaney's visit would find the means to contact her.

And if no message waited for Lady Delaney? Was he to hide in her house and wait each day for men who may all be dead to contact him? How many days must he wait before he accepted that none lived? That would leave him with two paths; return to the London chapterhouse and report that he had not only killed all his men but failed to die decently with them, or continue his mission alone.

He would choose the latter, futile though it would undoubtedly prove. The front door opened, heralding Lady Delaney's return. With news, God willing.

"Mr Steiner, there was a message at the post office today." Lady Delaney's tone was casual, as if retrieving and delivering secret messages were daily activities.

"My thanks." His dour mood lightened. At least one of his

men had survived.

"My pleasure." She handed the message to Steiner and smiled in approval as he poured her tea.

He read the paper, and his heart quickened as the contents registered. "This is from one of my men. He wishes to meet whoever reads this tonight within the Crowned Stag public house twenty minutes to nine." The note was unsigned, but it complied with the protocol.

Lady Delaney looked at him sceptically as she stirred milk into her tea. "Very convenient, if you don't mind me saying so."

"Only my men knew of the arrangement with the post office."

She gently blew at her tea to cool it. "As you say. I left your own message in its place. If any more of your men survived, they will be able to contact us directly."

Steiner nodded. "My thanks."

Ellison rang the dinner bell and Miss Knox joined them at the dining table. Steiner said little, his thoughts occupied with whom the survivor could be and whether they were alone. Retaliation would depend on his numbers, and he indulged himself on mulling over the different ways he could make the Sooty Feathers pay. He was dimly aware of Miss Knox questioning Lady Delaney with regards to determining whether someone had been Mesmered.

Lady Delaney had insisted that if Miss Knox shared the danger, she should know what she was in danger from and had told the girl everything. Vampyres, ghouls, demons, werewolves; the whole sordid tale.

Kerry Knox seemed both scared and awed by it. Steiner wished that she leaned more to the former and believed she would be less enthusiastic if she knew more of Lady Delaney's history.

He followed them into the parlour after dinner. "Miss Knox, I am to meet someone tonight, but you will be safe here."

Miss Knox nodded, unconcerned. "Lady Delaney's promised to teach me how to use a knife."

Steiner's patience ended. "Lady Delaney, did you tell Miss Knox of your first encounter with a demon?"

Lady Delaney looked at him balefully, her lips narrowed. "No," she said in a brittle tone. "That was remiss of me."

Miss Knox frowned, not blind to the sudden tension.

Steiner spoke heavily. "This is a world of demons and monsters, but the people can be every bit as monstrous. It brings no enlightenment, no window to God; only pain and loss. I would have her understand this."

"Perhaps you're correct." Lady Delaney turned to Miss Knox and spoke matter-of-factly. "I was twenty-four years old and married to Sir Andrew Delaney, a dear man. We had two young sons, Andrew and Christopher. Andrew was six and Christopher four."

She looked over at the family picture on the mantelpiece, and Steiner felt a pang of guilt. But he wanted Kerry Knox pushed away, not drawn further in.

"Sir Andrew owned a carriage company and two mills. He employed children, but saw to their education by building a school and hiring a teacher. He was successful, very much so. I remember him telling me that the Black Wing Club had approached him and offered membership." She smiled in remembrance. "He seemed amused by the whole thing, but flattered too."

"He turned them down?" Miss Knox guessed.

"No, he accepted. After a while he was inducted into the secret society at its heart, the Sooty Feathers. He became withdrawn and secretive. Finally, he told me he wanted nothing more to do with this club and would end his association with it.

"Then one day he came home changed. He seemed to be in a good mood, but his humour was cruel. He was cold to me and indifferent to our children. For three days he was like this, until the final night when he returned home drunk."

Steiner closed his eyes. The tale had a grim ending. He almost regretted making her reveal it.

But she carried on mercilessly. "He sent our servants away on some contrived errand or other, leaving the four of us alone. I was overpowered and tied up. He brought in our children and murdered them before my eyes. I was treated cruelly in front of their bodies, after which he told me he wasn't my husband, that he was a demon Possessing him."

She sipped some tea, her hand trembling slightly.

"After he had finished with me he passed out from the alcohol. I freed myself and cut his throat," she said matter-of-fact. "My only regret is that I did not wake him first."

Miss Knox stared at her. "A demon?"

"Yes, my dear. Evidently this society needed the services of my husband's businesses. He refused them, so they had a demon Possess him. The one they picked was insane, however, and ruined their plans that night. But that did not bring back my Drew or our poor dead children."

Miss Knox stared at her. The mantelpiece clock ticked in the background. "How did you explain it to the polis?"

"I told them he had lost his mind. Despite the wounds I bore, I think I was bound for the noose. But a man unknown to me visited, claiming to be my lawyer. I was given a choice; agree to sell – for less than their worth – several of my husband's business interests to certain people, or be charged, tried, convicted and executed for his murder. I agreed, and found the police suddenly more sympathetic to my story."

Kerry frowned. "Why give you the choice?"

"To get those businesses they desired; otherwise they would have passed to Sir Andrew's brother in America." Her face twisted. "And so my husband's good name and reputation died with him and our children."

Steiner remembered his own dead loved ones and cleared his throat. "I should be leaving. Lady Delaney, if I do not return send a message to London and let my superiors know what happened here. And look after Miss Knox."

"Just go."

It wasn't the words that surprised him, but that it was from Miss Knox's lips they passed.

*

Steiner sat in the taproom of the Crowned Stag and sipped mechanically from a glass of watery ale. It tasted off, more bitter than he expected. The tavern was squalid, its floor damp with spilled beer, and the sparse lighting failed to hide the peeling paint. The room was rank with stale sweat that even the tobacco smoke couldn't mask. A few prostitutes approached him, all turned away. Several men tried to divest him of coin through threat or guile. All left empty-handed.

A discussion became heated and Steiner discerned from the raised voices that it concerned football. A refereeing decision at a match earlier in the week had inflamed an already fierce local rivalry.

"You fenian bastard!" The row escalated from verbal sparring into fisticuffs, and blows were traded by those involved. Steiner watched as the brawlers were given space and cheered on by other patrons, some not shy about throwing in a kick or two themselves. Two bruisers working for the tavern broke up the fight with heavy-handed efficiency and threw out those involved. A typical night in Glasgow.

Steiner favoured quieter establishments, but he was not here for the raucous atmosphere or bad ale. It was almost twenty minutes to nine, his man was due soon.

He stood, intending to visit the outhouse, when he felt unaccountably lightheaded and nauseous. The ale must have been stronger than he thought. Another wave of dizziness struck him, and he fell back down onto the stool. He took a breath, his vision blurring. *The ale ... drugged...*

Three blurred men approached his table, waiting for something. Steiner opened his mouth to speak, but the room seemed to spin...

*

Kerry Knox watched helplessly as three men dragged Steiner out of the tavern and threw him into the back of a barred wagon. One of the men entered after him while another climbed onto the front. The third and meanest-looking of Steiner's captors slammed the barred door shut and discouraged shocked onlookers from interference with a look. He remained behind when the wagon rattled off down the street with Steiner inside.

Kerry lifted her skirts slightly and hurried onto another street. She felt guilty slipping out of Lady Delaney's house to follow Steiner but had the consolation of being able to let her know his fate.

A hand grabbed her shoulder from behind and spun her around roughly. Steiner's third assailant had a hungry look on his face. "Where do you think you're going?"

Kerry flushed, and she stammered out the first excuse that came to mind. The expression on the man's face told her whatever she said would make no difference.

Her assailant tightened his grip, but he turned as fresh footsteps echoed off the cobbles. "Mind your own business," he snarled at the newcomer.

"This young woman is my business," a woman said. Kerry felt a wild hope as she recognised Lady Delaney's voice.

"I won't tell you agai–" A bang interrupted his threat, and he fell to the ground.

Lady Delaney stood with a tiny gun in her hand. "No, you won't." She noticed Kerry staring at the gun. "A derringer, my dear. Easy to use and conveniently sized to fit in one's purse. A prudent accessory for any lady." She took a bullet from her purse and reloaded the pistol's single chamber. "Particularly ones who insist on poking their noses into dangerous affairs," she chided.

"Thank you," Kerry gasped. "You followed me?"

"I followed Steiner," Lady Delaney corrected. "But I saw you here and not in my house where you were to remain. Steiner entrusted me with your safety, and I take such responsibilities seriously."

"But he's been kidnapped!"

Lady Delaney nodded calmly. "So I saw."

"Do you know by who?"

"Whom. By whom, Miss Knox. By the Sooty Feathers, I presume."

"How can you know that?" Kerry challenged.

Lady Delaney removed the silver pin from her hair-bob and knelt by the body before her. "By the nature of this creature here. He's undead." She stabbed the four-inch spike into his chest.

Kerry stared down at the dead man. *How did she know he was...*

Lady Delaney guessed her thoughts. "You must open your eyes, Miss Knox. This man had just captured a Templar inquisitor, a formidable opponent, and one who has caused the society much trouble. And then he caught you. Excitement enough to get the heart pumping, yes?

Kerry mumbled her agreement.

"Yet he remained pale-faced and showed no signs of heavy breathing. Hence he was either undead or a very calm man indeed." She thoroughly wiped the blood from the pin and stuck it back into her hair. "Which means the Sooty Feather Society. Which means the wagon that took him is owned by Roderick McBride."

"How do you know that?"

"My husband owned a carriage company, one of several businesses the Council desired control of, and why they had him Possessed when he defied them. The carriage company was among those I was forced to sell, specifically to a Samuel McBride. He bought it for half its value and subsumed it into his own wagon business which the society uses for their transport needs. His elder son, Roderick, assumed control on McBride's early death, and he serves the society also."

There was something in Lady Delaney's voice that suggested a dark tale behind Samuel McBride's 'early death'. "Can we rescue Mr Steiner?"

Lady Delaney walked at a brisk pace. "Perhaps. But first, we'll see if any of his men make contact before we consider settling accounts."

Chapter Thirty-Five

Foley awoke with a sore head and sour stomach. *Tuesday morning. I think?* He forced himself out of bed and noted that the blankets needed washed. He would fetch fresh ones that evening from the cupboard. Assuming he didn't just pass out on his bed still clothed, and not for the first time.

He splashed some water onto his face and peered into a cracked shaving mirror. The face that squinted back through bloodshot eyes looked as bad as he felt. There were a few days of growth on his face, but he had neither the time nor inclination to shave.

Hunt's door was still shut. He knocked on it in case Hunt had returned late during the night but there was no answer. He opened the door, hating to violate the man's privacy, but wanting to know if he was back. Hunt had said he'd return on Sunday night, but the bed hadn't been slept in. He should have been back yesterday at the latest. Foley decided to worry about it later. He had a shop to open and still hadn't broken his fast.

Knowing the pharmacy should have opened a quarter of an hour ago, he took a bowl of porridge downstairs with him; he could eat while he opened up.

The day passed much as every other. By four o'clock there was still no sign of Hunt, and worry gnawed at Foley's gut. Their experiences over the past few weeks suggested that his disappearance might not have an innocent explanation. He shut the shop early and returned upstairs to the flat. After half an hour of searching he found a crumpled piece of paper with Hunt's parents' address written on it. Maybe they knew where he was.

Conscious of his unkempt appearance, he quickly shaved and put on clean trousers. With a city to cross, he didn't bother cleaning his shoes but did put on his bowler hat. He left the tenement building and boarded a tram bound for the West End.

Foley stood nervously outside the Hunt residence, slightly intimidated by the expensive townhouse. He knocked on the door and waited. *If the bastard's in there dining on venison or bloody pheasant, I'll damn well kill him.*

A grey-haired man answered the door, surely too old to be Hunt's father. Foley cleared his throat. "My name's Mr Foley. Is Mr Wilton Hunt within?"

"Master Wilton is not within the residence."

Damnit. "May I speak with Mr or Mrs Hunt?"

"I'll fetch Mr Hunt." Greyhair ponderously returned inside.

A middle-aged man appeared at the door, wearing dark grey trousers, white shirt and a pinstriped waistcoat. He had an air of authority about him that put Foley in mind of his old battalion's colonel. Foley saw Hunt in the man's features and knew him to be Hunt's father.

"Mr Foley, Smith tells me you wish to speak to Wilton?"

Foley straightened his jacket. "Sir, I'm your son's landlord. He was due to return on Sunday night. As this is Tuesday, I was wondering if he was staying here or you'd heard from him."

Mr Hunt seemed to appraise him in a single glance, and Foley felt somehow wanting. "Wilton is not staying here, and I'm afraid neither Mrs Hunt nor I have seen him since Friday morning. He was to spend the weekend with family friends at Loch Lomond. He has not returned?"

"He has not, sir."

"Perhaps they've been delayed," Mr Hunt suggested. He stepped outside. "Though McBride Carriages are said to be reliable."

McBride? Hunt, you damned fool. Foley made eye contact with Mr Hunt. "McBride, you say?"

"Yes, that's the company Mr Gerrard hired to convey Wilton to the hotel."

Foley nodded. "Thank you, sir. I'll let you know if I hear anything."

Mr Hunt offered his hand. "A pleasure meeting you, Mr Foley. If Wilton contacts us, I'll inform him you are looking for him."

They shook hands briefly. “Likewise, sir.” Dark suspicions crowded his mind. *McBride. Damn the bastard.* He would wait one more night; if Hunt still hadn’t returned, he would undertake more drastic actions.

*

Lady Caroline Delaney’s guests sat in silence around her dining table while Ellison served dinner. Kerry had never eaten so well until Lady Delaney had taken her in, but tonight she barely noticed the food before her. *Maybe I’m getting spoiled?*

Or maybe it was the company. Three of Wolfgang Steiner’s people had followed the instructions left by Lady Delaney in the post office before Steiner’s abduction, making contact that morning. They had been mistrustful at first, but Lady Delaney dispelled their suspicions. Somewhat. Enough to convince them to attend her house that night to discuss rescuing Steiner.

Kerry was no stranger to the company of dangerous people, Steiner and Lady Delaney not least among them, and she sensed that same familiarity with violence in Burton, Carter and Gray. Carter was suspicious of them and made no secret of it, hard lines running down his scarred, stubbled face towards a mouth that looked like it never smiled. Kerry normally cared little what others thought of her, but when a man steeped in violence like Carter weighed her life with bitter, distrustful eyes, she knew trepidation.

The rangy black American, Gray, spoke little, but Lady Delaney seemed to watch him the most, as if he were the most dangerous of the three. Aged maybe twenty, he was clean-shaven except for a moustache. Kerry had believed him an African until he spoke.

There was nothing soft about the brown-haired Burton, but she was relieved he was in charge of the other two. He was the shortest of the three but solidly built. His accent placed him as native to Glasgow, and he at least treated Kerry and Lady Delaney cordially.

Lady Delaney had allowed – insisted – that they clean themselves up, providing a razor. They had all washed off the dirt and soot, but Carter alone didn't made use of the razor. He looked the sort who'd rather turn it on others. All three wore dirty, rumpled clothes that smelled of smoke, their white shirts stained with soot.

"We appreciate your hospitality, Lady Delaney," Burton said once Ellison had left the room. "We've been sleeping rough since the attack." All three Templars tried to hide their discomfort at the opulent surroundings, but Kerry recognised in them what she herself to some degree still felt in Lady Delaney's townhouse.

"It's the least I can do, Mr Burton. I may not be one of your Order, but we share a common goal." She was a considerate host, doing her best to put everyone at ease. But more troubled them than trying to decide which spoon to use. "Gentlemen, this is Miss Kerry Knox, an agent of Steiner's he left in my care."

Kerry felt a glow of pride in being called an agent, even if it wasn't strictly true.

Burton looked a little sceptical. "Forgive me, Miss Knox, but Inquisitor Steiner made no mention of you."

"Miss Knox played an instrumental role in Steiner's capture of Benjamin Howard," Caroline said, saving Kerry from having to think of a reply. It certainly sounded more adventurous than her initial task of pretending to be both Steiner's dead Swiss wife and his fictional Dundee wife.

Burton bowed his head, a new respect in his eyes. "That was well done, Miss Knox. Howard was a bad fuc – fellow." He went red and coughed. Lady Delaney acted like she hadn't noticed the bitten-off profanity, and Gray's lips twitched in an almost-smile.

Raised by a working class family in an overcrowded Duke Street tenement, Kerry was no stranger to such language. The constant 'Miss Knox-ing' was beginning to get tiresome, though; the people she came from had little use for such rigid formality, and her thespian acquaintances certainly didn't. Lady Delaney, on the other hand, would only be called Caroline by very close female friends in private, and Kerry dared not presume.

"How did they catch Steiner?" Carter asked, easing his tone only when he saw the look Burton gave him. He didn't bother to hide his lingering suspicions of Kerry and Lady Delaney. Kerry prayed Burton could keep him leashed.

"Steiner sent me to check the post office for messages from yourselves and leave one from him. The message I found left instructions for him to meet a survivor at the Crowned Stag Tavern." Lady Delaney glanced at Kerry. "It was a trap. He was taken and thrown into a wagon."

Gray was alone of the three Templars to eat, though he watched Lady Delaney as he did so.

"By how many?" Burton asked.

"Three. One remained behind, so I killed him. He was undead, the other two I cannot say."

That casual disclosure raised Burton and Carter's estimation of her, Kerry saw. Gray just took another mouthful of potato.

"I'm curious how the Sooty Feathers came to know your message protocol," Lady Delaney said.

Carter and Burton exchanged looks. "They may have taken some of us alive on Saturday night and tortured it out of them," Burton admitted.

Lady Delaney considered that. "Then they may have seen my own message." She said it calmly. Kerry herself felt a spike of panic on realising the society might know their identity, might even now be preparing to attack the house.

"Maybe, but I took down your message after reading it," Gray said. "If they had read it, they'd already have followed your instructions, and you'd know about it."

Lady Delaney nodded. "A good point, Mr Gray. Tell me about Saturday night."

Burton took a moment to compose himself. "It didn't last long. One minute nothing was amiss, the next several windows were smashed, and the rooms were on fire. Bottles filled with oil or liquor were lit and thrown through the glass. We barely had time to get outside, never mind arm ourselves. I think six of us made it out the house: Carter, me and four others."

"And they were waiting for us," Carter said. His rage was barely suppressed. "With guns and knives and God knows what else."

"Aye, and started killing." Burton nodded at Gray. "The

only reason Carter and I got away was him. He stayed inside that burning hell and shot at them from an upper window with his rifle. Made the bug–" he coughed, "–beggars pay. I was sure the others were killed, but maybe one was taken alive."

Gray looked unaffected by the tale of his heroism. Lady Delaney looked at the American. "Impressive, Mr Gray. How did you get out?"

"The window. Managed to jump to the next building and shimmy my way down." His bland expression turned to one of regret. "Had to leave my rifle behind, though."

"I'll get you another," Lady Delaney promised.

"All well and good," said Carter, "but it won't be any bloody use without some bastards to shoot at."

"Watch your language," Burton warned. "There are ladies present. And our business starts and ends with finding Steiner."

Lady Delaney didn't look to be in any danger of swooning from the profanity. She dabbed her mouth with a napkin. "That business I believe I can help you with. Steiner was taken away by a wagon owned by a Mr Roderick McBride."

"So, all we need to do is have a word with this McBride, then?" Carter looked pleased at the prospect.

"Seeing that discussion would please me, but there may be a better way to learn where Steiner was taken." She looked at them in turn. "Can I count on your cooperation in this endeavour?"

Gray – and Carter too, for a wonder – looked at Burton. The Templar sergeant nodded. "Aye, Lady Delaney, you can."

She smiled. "Excellent. Don't let your food get cold, gentlemen."

Chapter Thirty-Six

Drip drip drip. He lay in the darkness and listened. *Drip drip drip*. It never ended, a steady trickle of water striking off the stone floor. If they stopped giving him water, at least it wouldn't be thirst that killed him.

The cell had no windows, leaving him clueless as to how long he had been a prisoner. A few days, he suspected. It felt like weeks. Torture had been his greatest fear but thus far his captors had been content to let him rot. He rested his head in his hands and saw Amelie lying dead in the mud. *Was it my fault? Was she – were they – killed because of me?*

Hunt had regained consciousness in a carriage, but a blindfold remained over his eyes for the duration of the journey until he'd been thrown into this cell. He had remained silent at first, hoping to be forgotten. Then as time passed he had hollered for attention, fearing to be left alone to starve. That at least wasn't a problem as his jailors gave him a small amount of food each day. Poor fare, but his mouth watered at the thought of it. *Stale Bread and cold broth. Hunger garnishes every dish to perfection.* Feasting on tender steak and red wine with his parents and the Gerrards seemed like another man's life.

The cell door swung open and George Rannoch strode in, holding a tall, black hat Hunt had seen once before. "Mr Hunt, good to see you."

So it was you we followed from the circus. "Why did you kill the others?" *Amelie.*

Rannoch squatted down. "I only killed the farmer and the two Gerrard men. It was Walker who killed Mrs Gerrard and Whiting. And the daughter, of course. We left their bodies in the farm which we fired, if you're wondering. Walker reported it as an accident which killed everyone except himself."

Hunt spat. "Bastards. I'll kill you."

Rannoch bared his teeth, the incisors lengthening into fangs. "I wish you luck with that."

Hunt shrank back fearfully. "Why kill them?" he asked again, this time in a milder tone.

"They were with you. The Council has suffered setbacks recently and your name kept coming up. I volunteered to bring you here, absent witnesses."

It was *because of me*. He felt hollow inside. "How will you explain the deaths and my disappearance?"

"The road was blocked, forcing Walker and Whiting to make a detour to the farmhouse. Sadly, a fire broke out, possibly started by lightning striking the farmhouse." Rannoch's shrug suggested he had several explanations to hand. "Regardless, the farmhouse tragically burned and only Walker survived, being out in the barn at the time."

"You're one body short."

"In a fire, who can say if a body was destroyed or not? I carried you back to my own carriage hidden nearby, and Walker waited a day before reporting the fire."

Hunt felt sick. "My parents think I'm dead?"

"No, the carriages were hired by the Gerrards, remember? Walker has reported you only as an unknown male passenger. If your family know you were with the Gerrards, they may believe you're dead when they hear of their deaths."

Hunt closed his eyes and imagined his parents mourning him while he rotted in this cell. "What of your valet, Micha? Gone back to the circus?"

Rannoch's face became still. "I don't know what you're talking about. I know nothing of any circus. Micha was no more than a valet, and a poor one at that. I dismissed him."

A good poker face, but you were a second too late in assuming it. I'm a prisoner, why lie? Something seemed off. Rannoch had been honest about arranging the deaths of the Gerrards, why deny knowing the circus? Micha was no mere valet, so why pretend otherwise now? Unless that relationship was something his Council didn't know. That could explain why he wasn't kidnapped at the hotel. It suddenly seemed wise not to mention witnessing the demon

Possession. If Rannoch was keeping it from his fellows, then Hunt's knowledge of it would see him dead. *Dead sooner*.

He decided to try a different tack. "Why did Walker kill Whiting? They both worked for McBride."

"Yes, but Whiting was a new driver and a necessary sacrifice. It would look suspicious if both drivers survived while the farmer and all the passengers died."

"And the Gilberts?"

Rannoch's surprise seemed genuine this time. "I know nothing about them. To my knowledge they left to avoid paying their bill."

Hunt couldn't decide if he was lying or not. "And Jill the chambermaid?"

"I required something to sustain me while at the hotel." Rannoch dismissed his killing of her. "She was convenient."

"She had a mother and a fiancée."

"What of them?"

Rannoch's disregard for life left Hunt speechless for a moment. "Just how old are you?" he asked finally.

"I was born in 1432. The subtraction should be simple enough."

He's over four hundred years old – he precedes the Union ... the discovery of America! The enormity of it left Hunt at a loss for words. After over four centuries of regarding people as little more than cattle, he could see how Rannoch and his kind had become so blasé about killing. He understood it, but he'd be damned before he let the deaths of Amelie and her family pass without retribution.

"I'm to take you to answer some questions." Rannoch leaned close to Hunt, so close he could smell the foulness expelled with every word. "I suggest you answer fully and truthfully. But first, about this circus..."

*

Steiner sat in the darkness, his body wracked with pain. Destroying that Crypt and its resident undead had not endeared him to the vampyres or their puppet society, and his captors had been enthusiastic in their disapproval. But no bones seemed to be broken.

Better I had died with my men than suffer this slow death by degrees. They would torture him, he knew, and it would be a battle not to surrender and reveal everything he knew. His best hope was to goad one of his captors into killing him, or find the means to attend to it himself.

The cell door opened, and he shielded his eyes from the lantern light. *They seek to test me with another beating.*

But no violence was forthcoming. "Inquisitor Steiner." The voice was familiar. "I've laboured hard to see you humbled, the fruits of which lie before me."

"Redfort." Steiner spoke through swollen lips, his throat cracked from lack of water.

"You recognise me." The clergyman seemed pleased.

"It took me a moment; the last time we spoke, *Faustus,* you were soiling yourself in fear."

"I'm not 'soiling' myself now, am I?" The anger in Redfort's voice gave Steiner some small satisfaction.

His eyes adjusted to the light and he studied his visitors. Another man stood beside Redfort. His stance and build suggested him to be a fighter of sorts. "Even trapped, you still fear me."

"Jones wished to see you also, a reward for his success in catching you. Your little crusade is over, 'Inquisitor'. Your men are dead and you're our prisoner. By the time our questioners have finished with you, whatever inconvenience you've caused will have been more than compensated for."

"Do what you will. When you are done I will be with my brothers in the Kingdom of Heaven; when you die, an eternity of torment awaits you in Hell."

Redfort ignored that. "Don't you want to know how we trapped you? How we arranged for you to be at the tavern to pass you drugged ale?"

He did, but remained silent, not wishing to give him the satisfaction.

"You'll find out soon. I'll leave you to your thoughts." The cell door slammed shut, leaving Steiner alone once more. He forced himself to his knees and prayed.

*

Hunt's blindfold was pulled off and he was thrown hard to the ground. He was lifted to his knees but allowed to rise no further. A lantern was held next to his face by the guard flanking him. He blinked away tears as the light burned eyes now accustomed to the dark.

The only other light in the room came from the U-shaped table around him. Six masked figures sat behind it. He wondered if this would be his end, and swallowed fearfully.

"Wilton Hunt, your involvement in recent activities has brought you to our attention. You are a member of the Black Wing Club, correct?" The questioner stood over Hunt while those seated watched silently.

Hunt's throat was dry. "Correct."

"But you don't have the feather."

Feather? "No. Sir."

"Explain your involvement with Amy Newfield…"

Hunt answered, leaving out his meeting with Amy Newfield and Margot Guillam. Prudence suggested he pretend Miss Guillam's Mesmer still held. If he played the fearful fool, perhaps they would dismiss him as nuisance; being stubborn might make them suspect he was a Templar, and then he *would* be in the shit.

"…involvement with Richard Canning…"

He answered, including how the post-execution Canning had tried to kill him in Foley's flat. He didn't mention the circus, and a small part of him wondered at the omission.

"And Benjamin Howard?"

He thought quickly. "I met him at a theatre I worked in."

"A position you left the night after Howard was kidnapped. How did you know of Howard's involvement in the search for Amy Newfield?"

Shit. His hesitation earned him a blow to the face.

"How did you know of Howard's involvement in the search for Amy Newfield?" The question was repeated exactly as before.

"I broke into the McBride Carriages office," Hunt admitted through bloodied lips. "I found his initials and the theatre mentioned in a ledger."

"Why did you seek out Mr Howard? For the Templars?"

"No, I don't know any Templars." He decided the truth

would best serve him. “I was trying to find Amy Newfield, she was taken by a McBride carriage.”

“Did those who Made Amy Newfield send you to recover her?”

Hunt shook his head. “I don’t know who they are.” He admitted being present at the market under the bridge during the Templar battle with the undead, but denied involvement. He sure as hell didn’t mention abducting the ghoul Naismith for Sirk to experiment on.

“How did you find the Under-Market? Why were you there at such an hour?” the questioner asked.

A memory of following Black Hat (George Rannoch, his mind whispered) from the circus flickered through his mind, but something stopped him from speaking of it.

The questioner perhaps sensed Hunt knew more than he was telling and had him beaten once more. Again, he was asked, and again he was beaten. But he couldn’t speak of it even though part of him wanted to. Glass grew around that memory, turning opaque.

“There is something wrong.” A different voice spoke. “He has been Mesmered not to speak of something.”

Hunt lay battered on the ground, dimly hearing the conversation.

“I Mesmered him at Sooty Feathers to forget meeting myself and Miss Newfield, but this preceded the attack on the Under-Market.” Hunt recognised Margot Guillam’s voice from the Black Wing Club. “Someone else has Mesmered him since then. Recently.”

Mesmered recently? By whom? ... Why? ... Part of him shrieked that he knew the answers, but the Mesmer held.

“Is there any point continuing this today?”

“No,” someone answered. “Return him to his cell. I came for Steiner, not this young fool.”

“He knows too much to set free. Too much to Mesmer him to forget.”

“Agreed. He can serve as our sacrifice at the Moot.”

*

Steiner knelt defiantly before the six figures shadowed before him. *The Council, damn them.* He had hoped to meet these councillors but under circumstances favourable to him. His mouth tasted of blood that was not his own. Vampyre blood had been forced down his throat to prevent him attempting suicide; they knew he lived to kill the undead, not become one.

The Council's questioner wasted no time. "How many men did you bring to Glasgow?"

"Hundreds. We are everywhere." He hated lies but was not above deceiving the enemy.

"We killed your men. We just require confirmation of the number."

"If you killed all my men then simple arithmetic should answer your question."

"All your men? Not quite."

Steiner dared to hope that was an admission that some had escaped. Instead, another man was dragged in and thrown to the floor beside him. "Harkins."

"Yes, sir." Harkins' face was swollen with bruises old and new and caked with blood. "They caught me as we fled the burning house, God forgive me."

"He will, Harkins."

"For that, maybe." He bowed his head. "But they made me tell them about the message drop at the post office."

That explained how the Black Wing Club trapped him at the Crowned Stag; they had planted the message luring him there. "Have you seen any others?" Steiner hoped his capture would sate the Council and give Lady Delaney time to find any other survivors.

Harkins shook his head. "Only you. Did any escape?"

Steiner was tempted to lie, but he had too much respect for the man. "I do not know. But our time in this city has seen the enemy pay a price in blood."

"God willed it," Harkins whispered through broken teeth.

Steiner looked Harkins in the eye, knowing how this reunion would end. "*Non nobis Domine, non nobis, sed Nomini Tuo da gloriam.*" The Templar motto of old. One of the guards reached down and broke Harkins' neck. *Not unto us, O Lord, not unto us, but unto Thy Name give glory.*

Chapter Thirty-Seven

It was said that the night hid a multitude of sins. Foley hoped fervently that it hid his as he once again prepared to sneak into the McBride Carriages property. He crouched next to the wall and waited for Sirk to join him. "Hurry, man!" he whispered. It was almost eleven and dark, but he had no intention of being caught.

Sirk arrived. "I fear I'm not as young as I used to be." He looked up at the wall. "Did you not think to bring steps? How will we climb that?"

No, I bloody did not. "With sweat, mostly mine," Foley said. He motioned Sirk forward. "I'll help you over." He crouched down and held his hands out, one under the other.

Sirk stood on Foley's hands and clung to the top of the wall but failed to pull himself up. "Help would be appreciated," he said, strained alarm in his voice.

Foley gritted his teeth and lifted. "Use your arms."

"I wish *I* had thought of that! What other *excellent* advice do you have to offer?"

Foley struggled, but he eventually stood high enough to shove Sirk up onto the wall. The professor reached the top and toppled over.

Foley looked up at the wall and wondered if he'd be able to reach the top without assistance. He'd counted on Sirk reaching down to help him up. It took him four attempts to jump and catch the edge, and all his strength to haul himself up. He lowered himself into the grounds where Sirk nursed a sprained ankle.

"I landed poorly," Sirk complained.

"My heart bloody bleeds, Professor." His arms burned, and he'd banged his right knee climbing up.

Foley walked and Sirk limped to the office, alert for guards or dogs patrolling the grounds. There were none. Foley shoved his crowbar into the crack between the door and the frame, and pulled hard. The door opened with no resistance.

Sirk peered over Foley's shoulder. "That was easier than I expected."

"It was already forced." Foley opened the door wider with his crowbar. It was dark, and there was no way of telling if anyone was inside.

"Can I assist in any way?"

Foley handed Sirk the lantern. "You can hold this. Don't let out any light until we're inside." He drew his revolver as a precaution.

Sirk un-shuttered the lantern slightly as they entered the back office, casting just enough light to allow them to search. Foley looked around, his gut tightening. The room had been ransacked. "Someone's already been here."

"An unlikely coincidence," Sirk observed, favouring his left leg. "Does this change how we proceed?"

"Aye, we're leaving."

"Now? But we haven't looked."

"Now. Shutter that damned lantern." Foley led Sirk outside and closed the door behind them. He had hoped to find something in the office that would lead them to Hunt, but someone had got there first. It didn't bode well for their chances of finding their friend, but Foley would worry about that once they were safely away.

Sirk halted.

"Worry about your damned leg later, keep moving," Foley said as he tucked the crowbar into his belt.

"These gentlemen would rather we didn't."

Foley looked up. A half-dozen men spread out in front of them, most holding knives or clubs. Some were old, others little more than boys, most bearded, but all wore cheaply tailored clothing made to imitate a gentleman's apparel. Thugs paid by the McBrides. Foley briefly considered making a fight of it, but two brandished shotguns. *They'd rip us apart.* He placed his revolver on the ground and held his hands up.

They were taken by carriage to Walker's Bar in the Gorbals and held in the beer cellar. It was long after closing time, but the bar was likely owned by an associate of the McBrides, and as such stayed open at their pleasure. The cellar was damp and stank of stale beer. Rats could be heard in the darkness.

"I wonder why they didn't blindfold us," Sirk said. "Rather remiss of them not to." Their hands had been tied, however.

Foley had a bleak notion why their captors hadn't bothered with blindfolds but said nothing. *I should have left Sirk at home, poor bastard doesn't deserve this.*

A light appeared as four men entered the cellar and roughly took them up to the taproom. Unlike the usual South Side shebeens – illegal drinking dens – infesting Gorbals, Walker's Bar looked almost respectable. Walker's lacked the ornately carved wood fittings and stained glass windows featured by 'palace bars' such as the Old Toll Bar in a bid to attract a better class of clientele than gin-soaked drunkards, but the floor had been swept and the empty glasses cleared away. A well-stocked bar ran down the left side of the long taproom, tables and stools spread along the right side.

"I don't know you," a broken-nosed, broad-faced man in his forties said to Sirk. Foley's dwindling hopes were dashed on recognising him as Roddy McBride, patriarch of the notorious family. The expensive cut of his grey trousers, jacket and top hat were at odds with his brutish appearance. "But you," he said, turning to Foley, "I remember. The prick asking questions about my carriages two or three weeks ago. Got any more questions?"

"Aye," Foley brazened. "Your carriages were sent to Loch Lomond to bring five people back to Glasgow, my friend Wilton Hunt among them. He's not been seen since. Where is he?"

McBride laughed. "Your friend annoyed the wrong people and they wanted words with him. He won't be long for this world."

"Where is he?" Foley had the sick feeling he was too late. They had taken Hunt on Sunday. It was now Wednesday.

"You should be more worried about where you're going. You broke into my property earlier tonight and had the gall to come back again later. Forget something?"

"We didn't break in earlier," Sirk corrected. "We found the

door damaged upon our arrival."

McBride wasn't in the mood to listen. "I had my suspicions about you when you came asking about the carriages I'd hired out to Sooty Feathers, but let you go anyway," he told Foley. "I won't make that mistake again. I've no doubt you broke into my building that night, too. I've got business to attend to, but my brother will deal with you." He turned to a younger man. "See it done, Eddie."

The younger McBride nodded, aping the elder in his manner of dress (scum dressed like gentlemen). "Aye, Roddy. Do you want me to dump them in the usual place?"

"Aye." Roddy McBride strode out of the bar, leaving Eddie and four others to deal with Foley and Sirk. Eddie McBride was about thirty, thinner and softer-faced than his brother. His command of the other four men had a brittle air about it, a result of blood rather than merit.

"Mulahay, there are sacks in the cellar, go get them." Eddie McBride turned his attention to Foley and Sirk. "If you two put up a fight, we'll kill you hard. Do what you're told, and we'll make it quick."

Foley wasn't dying without a fight, but sense suggested that he wait for the ideal moment. *Which isn't now.*

"You should count yourselves lucky," Eddie said. "The last bastard caught thieving from us twice was left in the street without his hands, feet or tongue."

"Lucky us," said Foley. One of Eddie's men punched him in the gut. He was still catching his breath when Eddie's eyes widened in shock.

"Evening," a man said. He had entered unnoticed in the company of an older woman. He was in his twenties and moved like a man who could handle himself, stocky but not fat. The woman was in her forties with greying hair, wearing a long maroon dress and bonnet more suited for a ballroom than a tavern.

"Who the hell are you?" Eddie demanded.

The couple paid no mind to the two thugs carrying shotguns. "Weary travellers looking for a drink," the man said. "I'll have a pint of ale. Lady Delaney?"

The woman looked around the taproom with an air of distaste. "I suppose tea is out of the question, Mr Burton?"

"Are you two daft?" Eddie asked in a belligerent tone.

The man seemed to notice the prisoners for the first time. "Is this a bad time?"

Eddie signalled one of his men, and the stranger found himself staring down both barrels of a shotgun. The second shotgunner, his skin red and angry from some skin disease, levelled his weapon at the woman. Eddie grinned viciously. "Aye, you could say that. Got anything else you want to say?"

The man called Burton didn't seem unduly troubled. "Aye. Those only fire if you cock them," he advised. "Otherwise there's no reason for me not to do this." He grabbed the shotgun and twisted it.

Foley watched a stunned Eddie freeze as the stranger fought with the first shotgunner for his weapon. Fortunately for the younger McBride, his second shotgunner reacted immediately by turning his weapon on Burton. Unfortunately for the second shotgunner, he was no longer covering the woman. Foley watched a derringer slip down her sleeve into her waiting hand. Her shot put him down before he could fire.

His hands tied behind his back, Foley could only watch as Burton and the first shotgunner wrestled for control of the weapon.

Eddie McBride finally found his tongue. "I'll take the woman, Harvey. You gut that bastard!"

Eddie's third man nodded and entered the fray, swinging a sharp-bladed butcher's knife at Burton. Forced to release the shotgun to evade the knife, Burton leapt back. The first shotgunner's possession of the weapon now uncontested, he aimed it at Burton and cocked a barrel. "Good advice, bastard."

Perhaps alerted by the derringer shot, a rough-faced man had entered the bar and picked up the dead man's shotgun. Foley prayed he was on the side of Burton and Lady Delaney.

"Drop!" the new arrival shouted, and Burton obeyed. The second shotgun roared, flaying the first shotgunner.

Burton's ally cocked the shotgun's second barrel, but he couldn't shoot Harvey without hitting Burton also. He watched, frustration writ on his face. Harvey made an upwards lunge at Burton which he blocked with his left forearm. Almost too quick for Foley to see, Burton's right hand grabbed hold of Harvey's and yanked upwards as his left hand joined the right. He then pushed Harvey's right arm hard to the side, causing the bigger man to cry out and fall to the ground.

Harvey lay on his back, his right elbow on the ground and his forearm pointing up with his wrist bent palm-down as Burton's left hand applied pressure. He slammed his right hand down and Harvey's wrist broke. The big man screamed and dropped the knife.

Burton snatched the knife and cut Harvey's throat in a single, smooth motion.

"Nicely done," Lady Delaney congratulated. She held a poniard against Eddie McBride's throat.

A movement caught Foley's eye and he cried out a warning as Mulahay emerged from the cellar with Foley's revolver in his hand. A gunshot echoed round the bar, and Mulahay fell to the ground, blood running down his ample gut. Foley turned to see a black man at the back door lowering a rifle with a look of detached satisfaction on his face.

"Good shot, Gray," Burton said.

"Sit down," Lady Delaney ordered Eddie. The younger McBride obeyed, staring at the bodies of his men. The one killed by the shotgun was a bloodied ruin.

Foley and Sirk were cut free. "Your arrival was most fortuitous," said Sirk.

"Don't mention it," Burton said. "Now who the hell are you two?"

"I'm Professor Charles Sirk, my companion is Mr Thomas Foley."

The lady walked over. "A pleasure, gentlemen. I am Lady Caroline Delaney. My dependable associates are Messers James Burton, Joshua Gray and Paul Carter. Would I be correct to infer that your captivity here was due to more than a petty dispute or unpaid bar bill?"

Foley exchanged a look with Sirk who nodded. "The McBrides took our friend. We're trying to find him."

Lady Delaney nodded. "I presume that was the purpose of

your visit to the McBride Carriages office earlier tonight?"

"How do you know about that?" Foley asked.

She smiled. "We visited the office earlier. Mr Gray kept observations on the yard and saw them take you both."

"It was you who broke into the office before us," Foley half-accused. "For what?"

"Information. A friend of ours, Wolfgang Steiner by name, was kidnapped and taken away by a McBride wagon. Our burglary proved unhelpful, but we knew it would draw attention. So, we waited and followed those who investigated. Your rescue is fortunate happenstance." She gave Eddie McBride a steely look. "I'm confident young Mr McBride can provide the location of our missing friends."

"I'm telling you nothing," Eddie McBride declared with hollow defiance.

"Really? I think you'll find Mr Carter can be most persuasive." Lady Delaney gave Carter a nod.

Carter cracked his knuckles with an anticipatory grin. It wasn't long before Eddie was screaming. The others stood at the far end of the bar and left him to his work. Foley had the feeling Eddie lived in the shadow and under the protection of his feared older brother. It wouldn't be long before he broke. In the meantime, it wouldn't hurt to make friends with Carter's associates.

Foley poured ale for himself, Burton and Gray. A pint was left aside for Carter. Sirk took a whisky and Lady Delaney a brandy.

"Thanks for the warning," Burton said, gesturing to the dead Mulahay.

"Least I could do. Bastard was going to shoot you with my gun, after all." Foley hoped Burton would take the hint and return his revolver.

Burton studied the pistol. "A Webley-Pryse."

"You know your guns. It was a gift from my father when I got my commission."

Burton broke the pistol open and emptied out the bullets before handing it to Foley. It didn't take Carter long to make Eddie McBride talkative.

"Delaney. I've heard your name before," Eddie said slowly.

"Yes, I sold your late father my late husband's carriage company about twenty years ago. Not by choice."

The mention of his notorious family seemed to put starch back in Eddie's spine. "Then you know who my family is. You wouldn't dare kill me."

"Your father expressed the same belief."

Eddie's eyes widened as he took her meaning. "My father was killed by falling masonry, you lying bitch."

"Struck, yes, but that's not what killed him. I pushed the bricks as he passed under the building in question. He was injured and at first thought himself the victim of an accident, telling me to fetch help when I went down to check on him." She smiled in remembrance. "When I revealed I was there to kill him and why, he too thought his name would stay my hand. It was clear he would survive his injuries, so I killed him." She held up her poniard. "With this. Then I pushed a nail into the wound to make it appear accidental."

Lady Delaney spoke with a calm detachment that made Foley wonder about her sanity. He feared the revelation would renew Eddie McBride's defiance but instead he looked scared and alone.

Lady Delaney returned the small poniard to her hair bun. "Enough reminiscing. Where can we find Wolfgang Steiner?"

"And my friend Hunt," Foley added.

Eddie swallowed fearfully. "I don't know where Steiner is. He was to be taken to the Council, so we were to provide a wagon only, no driver."

Burton didn't look happy. "And you've heard nothing since? Does your brother know more?"

Eddie shook his head. "No one but the Council knows where they're keeping him. One of his captors stayed behind at the Crowned Stag in case more Templars showed, but he was found dead in the street. He was…"

"Undead," Lady Delaney finished. "I know, I killed him." Her nonchalance heightened Eddie's fear.

Foley shared a look with Sirk. They weren't alone in their knowledge and opposition of the undead.

Lady Delaney conferred quietly with her three companions, and Foley used the opportunity to question Eddie McBride again about Wil Hunt.

"I don't know. I don't even know what he looks like."

"But you recognise the name." It wasn't a question.

"We were paid to send two carriages to a hotel near Loch Lomond on Sunday and pick up five passengers. The carriages were diverted to a farmhouse off the road where Hunt was captured, and the other passengers killed. He was brought back to the city by Gerry Walker, I don't know where." Eddie glanced at the bar, suggesting Gerry Walker either owned the tavern or was related to the Walker who did.

"That's not very helpful," Foley said, resting a hand on Eddie's shoulder. At least Hunt had been brought back to the city and not killed out of hand. But three days had passed since then.

"The Council's organised a gathering for Friday night, most of the Sooty Feathers will be there," Eddie said desperately.

"Sooty Feathers?" Sirk queried.

"A name of sorts for the secret society at the heart of the Black Wing Club." Lady Delaney had overheard. "The undead use this society to control the city."

Foley was sceptical. "Hunt's a member of this club and knew nothing of the undead until recently."

"Most members don't," Lady Delaney said. "The Sooty Feathers recruit from the club, directed in turn by the Council."

"And the Council is undead?" Sirk asked.

"Some, no doubt, but others are human," Delaney answered brusquely, her attention fixed on Eddie. "Where is this gathering to take place?"

"Somewhere called Dunclutha. Our carriages are taking many there, but Roddy took care of that. I don't know any more," Eddie admitted, "except that the Council wants one of our prison wagons."

"Where is Dunclutha?" Burton asked.

Eddie shook his head with a grimace. His ignorance looked honest.

"It's an estate near Largs," Foley said in recognition. "Hunt's family know the owner." That coincidence made him uneasy.

Lady Delaney digested the information. "The society is going to Dunclutha and taking a prisoner with them. Hunt or Steiner?"

Eddie shook his head again. "I don't know. Either, or maybe both."

Delaney looked thoughtful. "You've been quite helpful." She nodded at Carter who approached the bound Eddie McBride from behind and pulled out a knife. Foley watched Carter draw it across Eddie's throat, blood reddening his white shirt. He tried to scream but managed only a wet gurgle, rocking back and forth on the chair he was tied to.

Lady Delaney looked at Foley and Sirk. "Now, what shall we do with you two gentlemen?"

Chapter Thirty-Eight

Foley considered his words carefully. It hadn't escaped his notice that Burton and Carter stood ready for trouble, or that Gray sat on a bar stool holding his rifle. Carter made no effort to clean Eddie McBride's blood from his knife. *Maybe he expects to bloody it again soon.*

Sirk spoke first. "Like yourselves, we too seek a friend held captive by the undead. I suggest we align ourselves against this common foe."

Carter sneered. "We found you two about to be killed by that little shit." He gave Eddie McBride's corpse a contemptuous wave. "What use would you be against vampyres?"

Sirk gave him a cool look. "I recognise you from that bit of trouble under the railway bridge near High Street. A bloody piece of work."

"You were there? Then you saw us slaughter two vampyres and two dozen ghouls." There was a fierce pride in Carter's voice.

Sirk nodded, then looked him steadily in the eye. "Foley and I fought there too. Not every undead was slain by your hand."

"Professor Sirk's also a doctor," Foley pointed out. "That's reason enough to include him. And I was a soldier for years."

"A doctor's always useful, and another gun could make a difference." Gray spoke for the first time since the fight ended, his accent American.

Carter spat, but Burton raised his hand. "You've had your say, Carter."

"Whatever you say, Sarge."

"'Sarge?'" Foley queried. "Are you soldiers?"

"Of a sort," Burton said. "We're sworn to the Templar Order."

"Templars?" Sirk's eyebrows rose. "A ghoul we captured made mention of you. Forgive my ignorance, but I understood that Order was disbanded in the early 14th century, many of its members executed for heresy."

"That charge was horseshit. The King of France owed the Templars money and put pressure on the Pope to disband the Order, seeing many put to death for heresy. One way to weasel out of a debt." Gray said wryly.

"Vampyres were behind the downfall," Burton said. "The Order at that time had too much power and influence for their comfort. The survivors regrouped in time. We've chapters here and abroad."

Carter barked out a laugh. "The French king and the pope both died the same year they disbanded the Order."

Foley doubted that to be a coincidence, and the battle in the market showed the contemporary Templars to be as ruthlessly fanatical as their medieval forebears. Something to be borne in mind; they might share a common foe, but Foley had no doubt the Templars would sacrifice him and Sirk if it served their mission.

Burton looked at Sirk. "When did you first learn of the undead?"

"During an unpleasant period in Edinburgh some years ago," Sirk answered.

Burton looked at the professor with awakened respect. "You're *that* Sirk? Ben Jefferies sometimes talks about his ghoul hunts years ago. Your name comes up."

"Jefferies is still alive?" Sirk sounded pleased. "A good man, hopeless at cards. I lost touch with him after…" He looked down and grimaced.

Burton nodded in understanding. "Jefferies said only three of you survived that trap. Undead activity flourished in Edinburgh afterwards, but the Templars established a chapter to fight them. Jefferies joined, and your friends were avenged. He's an old man now, but well." He looked at Foley. "You were in the army, Mr Foley?"

"Aye, commissioned as a lieutenant. I saw action in South Africa in 1881 and the Sudan in 1885."

"Always good to fight alongside another veteran," Burton said, Gray nodding in agreement. "I hope we'll be enough to rescue Steiner and your friend."

"Enough?" Sirk barked a laugh. "Forgive me, Mr Burton, but your ambitions seem rather modest. I don't doubt this Sooty Feather Society will be protected at Dunclutha, but a dozen of us should be sufficient to not only rescue our comrades but see an end to this society and its Council."

An awkward silence fell. "There won't be a dozen of us," said Burton. "The society attacked us on Saturday night. You're looking at what's left."

Sirk's face darkened. "Oh marvellous. So there is in fact five of us?"

"Six of us, Professor," Lady Delaney corrected.

Carter eyed her sceptically. "Forgive my bluntness, but it will be no place for a lady. We'll have a bloody fight on our hands."

"You were still in short trousers when I killed my first vampyre, Mr Carter," she said coolly. "You lack funds, correct?"

Burton nodded reluctantly. "Aye."

Lady Delaney's tone brooked no argument. "Then not only will I be paying the boat fares, lodgings and other expenses, but will also be supplying the arms and silver ammunition. As such I believe that means I'm in charge. If anyone disagrees, it's a long walk to Largs, so I suggest you start now."

The Templars mumbled their acquiescence.

She looked at Foley and Sirk, daring them to protest.

It was her life to risk. "You lead, we'll follow, Lady Delaney," Foley said.

She nodded in satisfaction. "Since that's settled, I suggest we meet tomorrow to plan this endeavour."

*

Richard Canning shuffled across the circus grounds, ignoring the eyes that followed him in the darkness. The circus vampyres had finally released him from the trunk, his punishment for failing to kill the two men. Returning shot and broken had also failed to impress his masters. The bottle Marko threw into the trunk with him had provided just enough blood to sustain his 'life' and no more.

He looked down at his hands, the flesh wrinkled and yellowed, almost numb to feeling. *This is a mockery of life. I decay with each passing day.* His body was riddled with corruption, rotting skin clinging to bone and tendon. His eyesight and hearing had deteriorated.

A woman sat on the steps of a wagon, looking well-sated. She looked at Canning and curled her lip to reveal fangs. He found the *Nephilim* among the circus-folk foreign and uncouth; the contempt they felt for him was echoed in every look and gesture. They had crossed a continent to fulfil an oath given two centuries past and had little time for newly Made ghouls with unproven loyalties.

Two circus-folk lingered outside the caravan, ostensibly malingering but in truth guarding it. They let him enter.

Four waited within. Bresnik, Lucia and Marko were the oldest of the circus *Nephilim*, each a survivor from the fall of their master two hundred years earlier. Marko had thick, black curly hair and an angular face. Lucia's long black hair hung loose past her shoulders, its rich lustre a sign she fed well and often. She favoured red blouses and blue skirts. Bresnik had a round face, bearded and balding, a large nose jutting out. All three bore the customary pale faces of the undead.

The circus' remaining thirteen *Nephilim* had been Made after the exile, most drawn from the circus-folk themselves over generations. They numbered no ghouls among their undead, all being full vampyres. Since arriving in Glasgow, they had Made many ghouls from the unsuspecting citizenry, most hidden elsewhere in the city in preparation for war. Starved of blood to the point of madness, they were expendable fodder. Canning alone was to stay with the circus.

"–has provided appropriate disguises," he heard the fourth *Nephilim* say, a visitor to the circus and Canning's master. Even the circus *Nephilim* deferred to him.

He was George Rannoch, born in Glasgow centuries past. Aside from an ill-fated period in Bucharest, he had haunted the city's streets ever since. His black silver-buttoned coat was a far cry from the priestly disguise worn during his prison visit to Canning the night before his execution, but the tall top hat was the same. A reprieve from Hell, Rannoch had promised in that dark cell. Freedom from morality, freedom from *mortality*. Freedom to kill.

"What must I do?" Canning had whispered, cognisant of his dawn appointment with the noose.

"Serve me, and you may indulge all your little passions." A look of compassion had crossed Rannoch's face, at odds with the frozen light in his dead eyes.

Canning had nodded.

Rannoch had smiled. "Then let us seal our pact with blood."

Canning had faltered. "My blood?"

*"*My *blood."*

The memory of that foul liquid blackness still lingered, tasting of ancient decay as it slid down his throat. He had choked on the gibbet and been reborn in the university mortuary that night. The professor present had been Canning's first post-mortem victim, and he had looked forward to many more over centuries beyond count.

Then hubris struck, and he failed to kill a man asleep in bed. Painful though his injuries had been, the fall from favour had proven more damaging by far. Dreams of gaining strength and stature had given way to a desperate hope for survival, hope that his decaying body would not simply die in that locked box.

This audience gave him hope that Rannoch was willing to forgive that earlier failure. *Or perhaps he seeks to correct a failure of his own; me.*

"Canning." Rannoch looked him up and down.

He endured the scrutiny. "Master?"

Rannoch folded his hands. "The men you failed to kill, whose besting of you incurred you my displeasure? You might be interested to know one of them is called Wilton Hunt and is in Sooty Feather custody. But that is not why I released you. I require a number of people to be killed on Friday night. Bresnik and Lucia will give you the details."

The thought of killing and feeding again sent a thrill down his creaking spine. "I'll see it done," he promised.

Rannoch looked him in the eye. "You were freed from your

mortal shackles in the belief that you would be useful. Don't fail me again."

Marko said something in his damned foreign tongue, candlelight gleaming off his waxed black moustache and grey skin. The other two laughed.

"See that Canning is fed a little tonight, Bresnik," Rannoch said. "Enough to sustain him."

The circus *Nephilim* nodded grudgingly.

*

Foley watched the sky above Largs gradually darken and the blue sea burn gold as the sun sank beyond the western horizon. Thursday had been spent exhaustively planning and equipping tonight's escapade, ending with only a few hours rest. A full night's sleep wasn't all he missed; he'd abstained from whisky and laudanum too. Waking up clear-headed was a novel experience, he conceded, but not one he wanted to make a habit of.

He and Sirk had met Lady Delaney, Burton, Carter and Gray by the river that morning and boarded a paddle steamer to Largs. On another day he'd have enjoyed a trip to the seaside town and the hospitality of the hotel Lady Delaney booked them into, but the knowledge of what awaited them that night hung heavily over the group. It reminded him of his time in the army before a battle; the wait was unbearable, and he just wanted the damned thing over with.

Lady Delaney had hired a private parlour in the hotel where they waited restlessly for dusk to fall. Foley entered, feeling self-conscious in an expensive black tailcoat, waistcoat, trousers, top hat, white shirt and bow tie that had all once belonged to Sir Andrew Delaney. Sirk was engrossed reading *Great Expectations*. Burton and Carter played cards while Gray meticulously cleaned and reassembled his rifle. Lady Delaney had provided the weapons and silver ammunition that the night's work required.

She made several adjustments until Foley's appearance met with her approval.

"You almost look respectable," Sirk commented.

Lady Delaney opened a small wooden box and pulled out a

black feather. She handed it to Foley. "This will see us inside the house." She passed him a porcelain Venetian Columbino half-mask enamelled white and sculpted to cover the top half of his face. "My husband attended few of these gatherings. He wouldn't speak much of them, but he did say all the guests were masked. This was his. I had a copy made for myself."

Foley carefully pocketed the mask and the feather. "How do we know it hasn't changed over the years?"

"We don't. But these societies tend to be rooted in habit and tradition." She glanced at the clock, a shaky breath the only indication of her own nerves. "Gentlemen, our transportation awaits."

Chapter Thirty-Nine

The hired carriage stopped in front of Sir Arthur Williamson's manor in the Dunclutha estate north of Largs. Foley sat nervously in the rear as he waited for the door to open. The plan had sounded easy enough; dress well and play the gentleman. His time in the army had been marked by countless skirmishes and one small battle, and he felt now like he had then. *I need a drink.* "I'm worried I might give us away," he confessed.

Lady Delaney sat across from him, cool as ever. "Don't fret so much, Mr Foley. Most of those attending tonight will be nervous, and rightly so. Be distant and don't try too hard."

"I don't like going in unarmed."

"We might be searched, and a gentleman's evening attire does not include a revolver." She pulled out a mask identical to Foley's and put it on. He followed suit with his own.

The carriage door swung open and the pair exited. Carter played the part of driver. Foley gave the Templar a curt nod and couldn't resist handing him a penny. "For your trouble, my good man. Don't waste it on gin."

Carter pocketed the coin and offered a sullen bow. "Sir." Sirk and the other two Templars waited at the edge of the estate in a wagon.

Foley, Delaney and Carter approached the house entrance which was brightly lit by lanterns. Three burly men stood at the door, their own half-masks made of dark cotton. Foley took a breath and pulled out the black feather.

The foremost guard stepped aside on seeing it. "Is your driver staying, sir?"

Thank God, it worked. Foley kept his relief hidden. "Aye." He slipped the feather back into his inside jacket pocket. *God help us.*

"Take the carriage round to the side, you'll see the others," the guard instructed Carter. "The side door leads into the kitchen where you'll find food and beer. Neither you nor the other drivers may leave the kitchen until morning."

Foley and Lady Delaney entered the house arm-in-arm. *So far so good.* He glanced at the silver pocket-watch Sirk had lent him. It was nine o'clock and most of the guests should have arrived. Servants flitted from room to room with drink-trays, wearing the same cotton masks as the guards, only white instead of black.

Lady Delaney nudged him. "Is that champagne? It was a long journey and my throat is parched."

He took the hint and removed two glasses from a passing tray, handing one to Lady Delaney. "Apologies." Dunclutha House was sparsely lit and crowded with shadows. The entrance hall was stone-floored, furnished with three small tables, two of which held a marble bust each. The upper walls were lined with stag heads, crossed swords and old muskets. A staircase sat at the end of the hall, leading up to the upper floors, and a guard stood at a door Foley guessed led to the kitchen. It was Foley's first time in a house of such size and he found it intimidating. The cost to maintain the place alone…

The other guests were dressed much as they were, the men wearing formal black tails and white bow ties, the women corseted dresses. All wore porcelain half-masks. Some masks differed slightly to their own and he leaned close to Lady Delaney. "I see masks with green trim and one that's red all over. A difference in rank, aye?"

Lady Delaney replied with a slight nod. "Perhaps. If so, parts of the house may be restricted to higher ranks. Be mindful of who goes where."

"If Hunt and Steiner are here, they'll probably be held in the cellar," Foley said. Their own masks were enamelled plain white. As Lady Delaney's husband had only attended once, it was logical to assume he had been at the lower end of the hierarchy. Assuming he told her the truth.

"I suspect so, but it's early yet. We should mingle and explore."

That made sense. "Have you met Sir Arthur Williamson before?"

"I'm acquainted with Sir Arthur," she said, "but not well enough to identify him while incognito."

The parlour and drawing room seemed to be where most of the members congregated, either standing or making use of the several couches and chaise longues. Oak tables and sideboards sat against the floral-papered walls, chipped from years of use. A chaise longue sat unoccupied and Foley noted the red upholstery was worn and faded with age. The parquet floor was polished but with several pieces in need of replacement.

Snippets of overheard discussion suggested many used the gathering to discuss business, unhindered by the theatricality of the masquerade theme.

The green-trimmed members were the most nervous, drinking heavily to calm their nerves. Perhaps a quarter of the guests were women. He leaned in to Lady Delaney, but she spoke first.

"Yes, I see. The green trim marks one as an initiate, perhaps here to have their membership confirmed. Our unmarked masks suggest confirmed membership."

"And the red?"

She didn't answer.

Most of the guards patrolled the grounds but there were several inside. They weren't visibly armed, but if the gathering was as important as it seemed, he wouldn't bet against it. If Hunt and Steiner could be freed without raising hell, all the better.

Foley and Lady Delaney returned to the entrance hall. Any drivers, valets or maids staying over were confined to the kitchen area, the guard's presence suggesting it was out of bounds to the guests.

"The cellar entrance should be next to the kitchen," Foley said.

"Yes. I hope Mr Carter is able to add the professor's sleeping draught to the drivers' ale. He can handle one or two, but not a roomful." She looked around. "We should go upstairs."

"If you want."

She kept her voice low. "You should be prepared. What we see up there may not be pleasant."

"I was in the army. I saw unpleasant every day."

"Tonight may see you revise your definition."

Others with plain masks climbed the stairs freely so Foley and Lady Delaney followed suit. They reached the next floor up unchallenged. Muffled sounds and the sweet, pungent smell of hashish drew Foley's attention to a door standing ajar. He peeked inside the darkened room and wished he hadn't. Men and women fornicated indiscriminately within, veiled by a haze of heavy smoke.

Servants carried drinks on the upper floor, too, but they were more skittish than those below, at the mercy of members free to elicit their services however they wished. Foley fantasised about revisiting the house with his revolver and a surplus of bullets.

Lady Delaney's grip on his arm told him her disapproval was akin to his own. They waited near the stairs leading up to the uppermost floor. "If this is what goes on here, what the hell goes on up there?"

"Worse than you think," she said as guests descended the stairs. "I believe the ones in red masks to be undead. Human blood is their vice."

The few red-masked members present mingled with the others, coaxing some to follow them upstairs. One simply grabbed a servant and dragged him away. Lady Delaney stiffened.

"We're here to rescue Hunt and Steiner," Foley reminded her. "Afterwards, we'll see." If he survived this insanity, he was going to drown his memories of tonight in whisky and laudanum.

Several individuals in all-silver masks ascended to the next floor, everyone else making way for them. Foley nudged Lady Delaney. "I bet you a pound to a shilling those in silver are in charge."

"No bet, Mr Foley."

Three members in white masks trimmed with silver climbed the stairs, but none in the plain masks followed them. "I don't think we can go up there," he said.

"No. It's getting late, we should find our friends and take matters from there."

An inebriated guest took hold of Lady Delaney's left arm,

his slurred words and manner suggestive of a lewd act. She calmly reached over with her free arm and the man was on his knees a moment later, gasping in pain. He backed off and stammered an apology.

"That looked sore," Foley said.

"Less so than had he reached for somewhere intimate." A tall older man in a silver-trimmed mask nodded his approval.

They walked back down the stairs to the ground floor and headed for the kitchen.

*

Redfort watched the couple walk down the stairs, the woman unruffled by her unpleasant encounter. He was surprised to see grey in her hair; she looked perhaps fifteen years older than the man on her arm. They disappeared out of sight. Redfort turned and strolled down the hall, ignoring debaucheries fuelled by youthful vim or the flagging stamina of those old enough to know better. He preferred to indulge his own appetites in private.

He touched the edge of his mask and felt the silver trim that marked him as a senior member of the Society and only one step below the Council. He remembered the pride he'd felt eight years ago on being given the mask in exchange for his plain white one, but now he felt only resentment. His hopes of taking the vacant council seat had ended that morning; another was to be granted the honour. A consequence of Steiner's accusation that he was responsible for Bishop Mann's death?

He had protested, claiming that Steiner had spoken to him of Bishop Mann, not vice versa, and as such Redfort had sent the late Bishop a warning. His claim that Steiner was lying to protect an agent made most doubt the captured Templar's claims. But perhaps the allegation had been enough to convince the Council to award the vacant seat elsewhere.

He'd learned that Horace Bruce, a retired army major, was to be given a silver mask and become the Council's new *Octavius*. His reward for leading the attack on the Templar house.

A man in a mask of silver engraved with the Roman

numeral for seven approached and greeted Redfort with a nod.

Redfort returned the nod with little enthusiasm. “Sir Arthur,” he said. “A success, as always. Your estate is lovely as ever.”

“The Regent wants to address us before the official assembly,” Sir Arthur said.

Does he, indeed?

*

Rannoch stood on the uppermost floor and watched three ghouls in red masks trimmed with white feed off servants lethargic from blood-loss. A *Nephilim* in an all-red mask watched closely to ensure they didn’t kill those they fed from. One of the ghouls was a young woman, aged about sixteen. Rannoch recognised her despite the mask, having Made her himself though she didn’t know it. Amy Newfield. She would have been exhumed and mentored by his circus allies had it not been for Hunt and his associate.

Newfield sensed his gaze and looked up at him, blood staining her chin. He pretended indifference. Her face bore the customary ambivalence of the newly Made; hunger warring with fading guilt and self-loathing, the remnants of her humanity.

It would have been simpler to have taken her body with him until she Turned undead, but he had Made many undead these past several weeks, more than enough to arouse the Council’s suspicions if the bodies just disappeared. The solution had been to leave the bodies for burial and exhume them afterwards. The procurator fiscal was a Sooty Feather who routinely signed off undead victims as natural or animal-caused deaths. Rannoch had simply ensured the fiscal did the same with his own victims, and then Mesmered him to forget doing so.

It had worked until Hunt had exhumed Newfield the day before his own people intended to, and her killings drew the Council’s attention. As well Rannoch had Mesmered the fiscal, otherwise the Council would have learned Rannoch had ordered her – and a score more deaths – declared natural.

They weren't idiots; a *Nephilim* Making so many ghouls so quickly was preparing for war.

On returning to the first floor he noted that most still mingled below on the ground floor. Ten of the fifty-odd initiates present were to be fully inducted into the society, trading their green-trimmed masks for plain white ones. It was during the Confirmation that initiates learned of the undead. For now, they were still blissfully ignorant of whom they truly served. That would change tonight.

Rannoch entered the upper lounge to stand with the others. Aside from the Council, only those with silver-trimmed masks were permitted entry.

Regent Edwards stood at the far end of the room, distinguished by the golden mask that also marked him as the Council's *Primus*. Rannoch maintained a look of deferential respect, one he'd feigned for two centuries. Another five councillors had arrived along with the *Nephilim* and humans from the inner circle. *Sexta* – Margot Guillam – remained in Glasgow to oversee the city during the Regent's absence. Guillam was the only *Nephilim* equal in strength to Rannoch and the Regent. She knew where the present Master, Niall Fisher, hid and was the sole direct contact between him and the Council. Not even the Regent knew where Niall Fisher's Crypt was; the Master had no wish to invite betrayal as he himself had betrayed his predecessor Erik Keel.

Rannoch turned his concentration back to the Regent. The first duty of the night, it seemed, would be to confirm ten of the initiates present to full membership. This ceremony would take place on the second floor while the remaining initiates remained on the ground floor. Hashish, opium, alcohol and other distractions were in place to keep the remaining initiates entertained during the night.

"…at which time *Septimus* and *Octavia* will each ascend a rank before the Council's newest member takes his seat and the mask of *Octavius*. Our last order of business will be the sacrifice of Wilton Hunt."

That last announcement was greeted with applause. The Sooty Feathers loved spectacle and they would get it, just not the one they expected. It would be remiss to neglect the Sooty Feathers remaining in Glasgow; Lucia and Bresnik had a list of names Rannoch wanted crossed off before dawn.

"Everyone will gather here," the Regent decreed, "in one hour's time. Hunt will be sacrificed downstairs." In front of everyone, even the initiates the Regent expected to leave still ignorant of ghouls and *Nephilim*. The Council would mark their reactions to the murder, identifying those unsuitable for Confirmation. Accidents were typically arranged for initiates overburdened with conscience.

The room emptied aside from the Regent. Rannoch looked Sir Arthur in the eye as he passed, and nodded. *It's time.*

Chapter Forty

Foley felt a tap on his shoulder. "Come," said Lady Delaney as the three guests loitering near the kitchen door finally left. Foley and Lady Delaney walked to the door.

A guard blocked the door. "Guests can go no further."

Lady Delaney stopped inches in front of him. "I am sorry, my husband is drunk. Do come along, Thomas." The guard stiffened suddenly and opened his mouth to cry out. Foley lunged forward and clamped his hand over the man's mouth as he sank to the ground. Delaney's right hand held a short poniard wet with the guard's blood.

Foley looked behind to make sure there were no witnesses. Lady Delaney searched the guard and used his key to unlock the kitchen door.

"I hope Sirk's potion worked or we'll have some explaining to do," he said as they dragged the body into the narrow corridor.

"Bring the body in here," someone said from the kitchen. It sounded like Carter.

"Is that all the drivers, valets and maids?" Foley asked Carter on seeing the drugged figures. "There're a lot of guests."

"Most of the carriages left for town after bringing their passengers," Carter said. He pointed to two corpses. "Those two weren't interested in the beer I drugged. Their bad luck."

"There's no time to waste," Lady Delaney said as they dragged the guard's body into the kitchen. "Put on the guard's jacket and mask, Mr Carter, and stand outside the door before his absence is noted."

Carter obeyed. "Good luck," he said as he went out to take the dead guard's place.

Thirteen men and four women lay unconscious, tied and

gagged as a precaution. Two bodies lay nearby, blood staining their jackets. One wore a guard's black mask, suggesting his job had been to ensure that boredom and drink didn't lead the drivers to mischief. A key sat on the table.

"Mr Burton and Mr Gray should be outside by now," Lady Delaney said.

Foley opened the kitchen door leading out to the garden and froze. A guard stood outside holding a pistol, the squeal of the door attracting his attention. The guard stared at him for a moment and nodded. "Foley, it's Burton." He waved over to bushes nearby.

Foley blew out a breath as Burton entered the kitchen, a black cotton mask covering his upper features.

"We killed the outside guard earlier," Burton explained, "but they sometimes patrol the grounds, so we didn't want an empty post to raise suspicions." Gray entered with him and removed pistols and bullets from a leather bag onto the table. Sirk had remained with the wagon.

Lady Delaney looked at Burton. "Mr Burton, as you're already masked, return outside and resume the guard's place. Mr Foley, take that fellow's mask," she pointed at the dead guard in the kitchen, "and come with me. We'll see if our friends are in the cellar. Join Professor Sirk at the wagon, Mr Gray, and cover our escape with your rifle."

Gray nodded. "Yes, ma'am." He and Burton left the house.

Foley recognised his pistol on the table and took it. He felt a hollowness in his gut; they would soon know if their efforts had been for naught. He unlocked the cellar door and ventured down into the darkness.

*

Redfort walked out of the sitting room into the main hall in search of a servant. His wine glass was empty, and he wanted another. His foul mood at not being given the vacant Council seat had only worsened on spying that damned Major Bruce talking and laughing with no less than three councillors. Bruce wore his mask, but his walrus moustache was distinctive, and vanity ensured that he never dressed without his damned medals. There was nothing else for it; Redfort was going to get drunk tonight. Gloriously drunk, and damn everyone else to hell.

A door opened, and he looked over hoping to see a servant bringing more wine. To his disappointment it proved only to be a guard. He watched the man, his quest for wine forgotten. That door, if Redfort recalled correctly, led to the kitchen. Which led down to the cellar and as such was to be locked and guarded at all times. *So why was the guard inside and away from his post?* The man appeared furtive. A call of nature, or did his absence have a more sinister explanation?

"Sir?"

Redfort started, so intent on the guard that he hadn't noticed his tiresome secretary's approach. "Henderson, I have my concerns about that guard – don't look at him! Now, I want you to find whoever is in charge of the guards and bring him here."

Henderson nodded. "At once, sir."

*

Henderson was in a quandary. Less than a member but more than a servant, he wore the grey cotton mask of those assigned to watch the initiates while the real society business was conducted upstairs. The few guards all looked the same to him, their black half-masks giving no clue as to rank. He spotted one talking with a councillor and decided to pass on the Bishop-elect's concerns to them. He suspected Redfort was making trouble for trouble's sake; he never did react well to disappointment.

The councillor's silver mask was engraved with the Roman numeral for seven, identifying the man as *Septimus*. Henderson cleared his throat. "Excuse me, sirs, but my master wishes to report a guard's suspicious behaviour."

He half-expected to be scolded for his interruption but both men stared at him. "Of course," *Septimus* said after a moment. "Marko, speak with this good fellow somewhere private and address his master's concerns."

"Come with me," said the guard called Marko. He spoke with an accent Henderson couldn't place.

His relief was palpable. He was led into a small room and

was about to speak when something coiled around his neck and tightened.

*

Foley and Lady Delaney followed the winding steps down into the cellar. They had almost reached the bottom when she spoke. “There will very likely be a guard down here. As you’re wearing a guard’s mask, it will be your task to approach and deal with him.”

“And if he’s undead?” He was armed but a gunshot risked attention.

“I suggest you strike him in the heart or head,” was her less than helpful advice. She handed him a knife. “I took this from the kitchen. It may be of use.”

“What would I do without you?” He continued alone.

The candles and wall-mounted torches gave the cellar a little light. An open door beyond the wine racks revealed a second chamber. A lone guard looked at Foley in surprise. “I’m not to be relieved for another few hours.”

Foley walked towards him, his knife hidden against the back of his forearm. “I know. They just wanted another man down here.”

The guard accepted the explanation.

Foley realised he still didn’t know if the guard was living or undead. He watched carefully and observed him breathe. Not undead, then – they only breathed to speak. That made killing him easier – and harder.

*

The snap of the lock turning returned Hunt to wakefulness. He sat hunched against the far wall in the cramped cell and watched the door swing open with ambivalence. On one hand it meant freedom from the cell; on the other it likely meant death. Any hope he’d once harboured of release was gone.

He felt he should meet his fate standing, but cramp thwarted him of even that small dignity. A silhouette stood in the doorway.

“Christ,” a familiar voice said. “I’ll say this for you, Hunt, you can produce one *hell* of a stink."

Hunt felt nothing at first, he didn't dare to hope. It wasn't really Tam Foley's voice, it was one last cruel trick before his captors dragged him out and killed him. A sacrifice, according to one of the more talkative guards.

The silhouette crossed its arms. "Coming, or are you waiting for some other stupid bastards willing to risk their lives for you?"

"Foley?" Hunt's voice was rusty from thirst and disuse.

A strong pair of arms reached in and hauled him out. "Who else were you expecting?"

Hunt stretched protesting muscles and felt hope rekindle within. Foley handed him a mug of water from the jailer's table which he gulped down to soothe his parched throat. His eyes didn't take long to adjust to the sparse lighting, and he noticed Foley was accompanied by woman in a long red high-necked dress. He glanced at Foley and realised his friend was in formal tails. "One could almost mistake you for a gentleman. Going to a ball afterwards?"

"Not quite," the lady answered coolly. "Your captors are hosting the party, but they neglected to extend us an invitation. We attended anyway." That explained the body behind them.

Foley made the introductions. "Lady Delaney, meet Mr Hunt. Hunt, Lady Delaney."

Hunt made an ironic bow. "A pleasure, Lady Delaney."

"The pleasantries can wait until we're well way from this place."

"I'll say." Hunt faced Foley. "These bastards murdered Amelie Gerrard and her family."

Foley grimaced. "I'm sorry."

"Who else came with you?" Hunt asked.

"Professor Sirk and three Templar lads."

"Templars? That ghoul we questioned in Sirk's cellar mentioned them." His captors also held them in low regard.

"Aye," Foley said. "Remember that gang who attacked the undead in the market under the bridge? Carter, Burton and Gray are what's left of them after the undead struck back."

Mention of that bloody morning made Hunt's head hurt, a familiar pain. He concentrated on it, focusing first on the market and then trying to remember what came before, what led him to the market. A cage around his mind shattered. Memories of the circus on the Green and the demon possession under the crypt returned to him in a dizzying flood. He remembered Rannoch visiting him in his cell to take him before the Council. The bastard had Mesmered him to forget the circus! "Where are we?"

"Dunclutha House, near Largs. Your friend Sir Arthur is up to his neck in this society."

Hunt recalled what he witnessed under the crypt. "Sir Arthur might not be himself. Remember that undead in the black hat we followed from the circus? He's a *Nephilim* called George Rannoch, and he summoned a demon called something like *Beliel* in some hellish–"

Lady Delaney grabbed Hunt's arm. "Did you say *Beliel*?" There was hatred in her voice and an old fear awoken.

Hunt nodded. "Rannoch's working with the Carpathian Circus, and they possessed some poor bastard with this *Beliel* – Sir Arthur, maybe." Unless Sir Arthur was already in league with Rannoch. "Rannoch Mesmered me to forget about the circus. I don't think he wanted me telling the society about it."

"You know this *Beliel*?" Foley asked. Lady Delaney's lost composure seemed to concern him more than talk of demons.

Lady Delaney took a breath. "We have history." She stared at Hunt. "I've never heard of anyone overcoming Mesmerisation. It's how the vampyres make those victims they don't kill forget."

Hunt massaged life back into his legs. "That's twice I've managed to break through it. Hurts like the devil though."

"Scribes can tattoo wards, and artificers can craft totems that offer protection from Mesmerisation." She rolled her sleeve up to reveal an open eye tattooed on her lower bicep. "But I've never heard of anything that can break an *existing* Mesmer."

Hunt remembered the tattooists and trinket-sellers in the Under-Market and realised they offered more than decorations and junk.

"We can discuss all this later," Foley said. "Let's find Steiner and get out of here."

"Mr Foley," Lady Delaney pointed out, "this cell is also locked. Bring the key."

Foley obliged and unlocked the cell. Hunt helped him remove the prisoner from the cell and stared in confusion as his face came into the light. It was Neil Williamson.

"Thank you, Hunt," Williamson said. "I've been in there for days."

Lady Delaney frowned. "Mr Hunt, care to explain who this man is?"

"It's Neil Williamson, Sir Arthur's cousin." He looked Williamson up and down, but he showed no signs of mistreatment. "Why were you locked up? I thought you were going back home from Loch Lomond?"

"I intended to, but my cousin persuaded me to stay a few days here." He took hold of Hunt's shirt. "Arthur's not himself!"

"You're safe now," Foley reassured him. "Is there another prisoner here?"

Williamson didn't answer, staring at Lady Delaney. "Who is she?"

"She's Lady Delaney, he's Mr Foley, and I'm keen to leave," Hunt said impatiently. He was happy to save Williamson, but if this Steiner was here they needed to release him and escape. His heart pounded in his ears and he felt light-headed and sick. He needed to *leave*!

"I see," Williamson said softly, still staring at her. "No, no one else is here."

"Foley, return upstairs and tell Burton we've found your friend, but that Steiner is not here." Talk of the demon *Beliel* had left Lady Delaney out of sorts.

Foley nodded and ran back up to the kitchen. Hunt recognised the adjacent room as the wine cellar from his previous visit to Dunclutha. Evidently this was Sir Arthur's private dungeon.

"You're carrying your years well, Caroline," he heard Williamson say. "And rescuing men from *Nephilim*, who would have thought that snivelling young lady of twenty years ago capable? I *am* impressed."

The back of Hunt's head exploded in pain.

*

Redfort waited impatiently. *Just how long does it take that fool Henderson to find someone?* That suspicious guard was still outside the kitchen, a brutish-looking fellow. Redfort relaxed as three guards appeared. *Finally, some answers.* Three of them produced knives and billy-clubs. *This isn't right…*

The two with knives fell on a red-masked guest, a *Nephilim*, their knives finding his heart. Other guards – or men or undead dressed as guards – came in through the front door and attacked the guests without provocation. Some among the guests joined them.

A coup from within, a rival House making a grab for Lord Fisher's territory? Neither scenario boded well. The guests' shock turned to panic, inflamed by a *Nephilim* Unveiling, and many were trampled underfoot.

Screams could be heard elsewhere in the house. Redfort thought the suspicious guard he had been watching would join in the chaos, but he looked as startled as everyone else and disappeared into the kitchen, slamming the door behind him. Redfort backed off and hurried up the stairs, less concerned about the cause of this madness than surviving it.

*

Foley reached the top step of the winding cellar staircase and was surprised to see Burton had returned into the house. The Templar sergeant had pulled the table against the door which was being hammered from outside the house. Some of the drivers had regained consciousness but were bound and gagged.

Burton turned. "The game's up. Four of the bastards approached me outside armed with shotguns and wanting in to secure the kitchen. Then they realised they didn't know me. I barely got inside to lock the door."

Shit, there goes our escape. "Why aren't they shooting?" He pulled off his mask, seeing no further need for it.

"Shotguns won't do much against that oak and will only make a lot of noise. I think they're up to something."

Before Foley could reply, screams could be heard from elsewhere in the house, followed by muffled bangs. Gunshots, he realised, and drew his pistol. "You're right. We're not the only ones here minded to ruin this party."

With the attack underway, the enemy outside realised stealth was no longer necessary. They smashed the small kitchen windows and reached inside with their shotguns.

Foley and Burton dropped to the ground as they fired, praying the pellets would miss. The shotguns discharged their second barrels. There was a brief respite as the men outside reloaded, allowing Foley and Burton to retaliate with their pistols. They fired blindly out of the shattered windows into the darkness.

"Get down," Burton ordered. Foley complied just in time to avoid a third volley. He rolled under the table and prayed it thick enough to protect him. The drivers and servants had no such protection and their blood now stained the walls and floor.

Foley saw Carter enter the kitchen from the main hall and throw his mask to the ground. He had a pistol in his hand. "Some of the guards are attacking the guests, I don't – Jesus!" The sour-faced Templar overcame his shock and fired furiously at the window. He grinned viciously as someone outside screamed, a dropped shotgun falling through the window into the kitchen.

Foley rolled out from under the table and was aware of Burton by his side as they joined Carter in firing out of the windows. Their attackers had evidently been told to secure or kill the drivers, and stop guests escaping via the kitchen. One of their own had been killed or wounded, and they faced a locked door defended by armed foes.

"They're here to stop anyone escaping," Foley said. "We've bloodied them, so I reckon they'll decide that means waiting outside for us to open the door, or their friends inside the house finishing us off."

Burton nodded. "Aye, so stay away from the windows." He looked at Carter. "Your return was timely."

"Never mind that, what the hell's going on?" Carter squinted at Foley. "Where's Lady Delaney and Steiner?"

"Steiner's not here," Foley admitted. "Not in the cellar,

anyway. We found Hunt and another prisoner." He looked at the cellar stairs. "They should be up here by now."

*

"Together again, Caroline," Hunt heard as his wits returned despite the pain in the back of his head. He was lying on the ground.

"*Beliel.*" Lady Delaney's voice trembled with hate. Hunt realised a Williamson had indeed been Possessed, but it was Neil rather than Sir Arthur.

"Is that any way to greet one's husband?"

"You were never my husband, even if you possessed his body for a few days. Why were you locked up? Irritated your new friends so soon?"

"It seems I'm considered something of a loose cannon by Rannoch, especially with what's planned for tonight. I was locked up this morning to keep me out of the way."

"What of Sir Arthur, does he know what you are?"

"Of course he does. He and Rannoch are betraying the Council together. Sir Arthur traded his cousin in exchange for becoming *Nephilim* himself in due course. His plan is to drink Rannoch's blood and die, I inherit his estate and falsify some documents stating I've got a son called such-and-such, and after this body dies years from now, Sir Arthur returns as my so-called son, the heir."

"And what do you get out of this?" Lady Delaney asked.

"I get to enjoy the pleasures of this world and a respite from Hell. I've also been promised a perpetual role in Rannoch's new order. As each Vessel dies, I get summoned into a new one."

"The Council had you possess my husband to control his assets, a task ruined by your wanton cruelty. Hell must have demons less insane, so why bring you back?"

"My service to this faction pre-dates Fisher's assassination of the original lord, Erik Keel. I'm the only demon Rannoch knows who could tell him what he wanted to know; the true name of his dead, deposed master. Well, the only one with a reason to do so."

"He brought you back for a *name?*"

"He needs that name to bring *Arakiel* back. Tonight, as it happens."

"And you want this *Arakiel* back, too?"

"I care not who rules so long as they keep me free from Hell. I served Erik Keel – *Arakiel* – and I served Fisher until your killing me while I Possessed your beloved removed me from his favour. I'll willingly serve *Arakiel* again. Hunt will make a fine Vessel for him."

That unpleasant revelation explained why Sir Arthur's people had kept him more or less whole, but only increased his desperation to escape. Hunt heard the scrape of boot leather against stone.

Williamson's – no, *Beliel's* – taunting voice continued. "Did you ever re-marry or have any more offspring?"

"No."

"Probably for the best, aye? Children can be so fragile. Yours certainly were."

There was a sound of scuffling and Hunt craned his neck round to see that Williamson – *Beliel* – had Lady Delaney in his grasp.

"I underestimated you last time," the demon sneered.

"You're making a habit of that," she gasped. "Now, Hunt!"

What? He was too foggy-headed to do anything, much less anything *now*, but it distracted *Beliel*. There was a bang and the demon fell to the ground.

Lady Delaney helped Hunt to his feet, a derringer in her free hand. He didn't like the look in her grey eyes, like madness trapped in ice. Didn't like it but understood it.

Beliel clutched his bleeding gut and whimpered as Lady Delaney dragged him back into his cell. She threw something in after him and pulled a burning torch free from the wall. That too she threw into the cell and slammed the door shut. There was a muffled whoosh followed by an agonised scream and the sudden stench of burning flesh.

Hunt stared at her. Killing was one thing, but *that*…

"Lamp oil," she explained in satisfaction. "I poured it over him. We should join the others."

They left *Beliel* to his last, long minutes of earthly torment.

Chapter Forty-One

Redfort ducked low as the violence below escalated and spread up to the first floor. The insurrection had been masterfully executed. He doubted the attackers numbered more than thirty, some masquerading as guards, others as guests, but panic and chaos had kept the Sooty Feathers from forming a cohesive defence.

Most of the guards had been outside and no doubt quietly killed and replaced as the night passed. The guards inside were too few and scattered to effectively resist. The *Nephilim* and ghouls present should have quashed the insurrection, but the enemy had countered that advantage with undead of their own. Regent Edwards, an Elder *Nephilim*, *should* be enough to turn the tide, but Redfort knew better than to wait for his arrival.

"Reverend!"

Jones. Thank God. "It's time we were leaving."

"Aye, I think I can get us out. Where's Henderson?"

"If he's still alive, he can make his own way out." *Damned if I'll wait for him.*

"Aye, sir."

Redfort spotted Major Bruce loitering on his own. Those medals he wore so proudly evidently weren't awarded for decisiveness. *An opportunity beckons.* "Jones, go fetch Major Bruce and tell him you can get us out of here."

"Sir?" Jones knew Redfort's feelings towards the man.

"Are you deaf? Major Bruce is to sit on the Council, and as such it is our duty to ensure *no harm befalls him*. Am I understood."

"Aye, sir." Jones was competent, but he could be annoyingly thick-witted.

Redfort followed Jones and Bruce into a small, windowed

room and shut the door. He had reservations about the plan; he was too old to be climbing out of windows even with Jones using the curtain to lower him down. But trusting in the mercy of those killing their way through the house appealed even less. Redfort had spent the previous night in a Largs inn. It would be locked up by the time they arrived, but the stable should be accessible. If not, a cold miserable night outside awaited.

If they succeeded in escaping outside. The door banged open and two rough-hewn men with sallow skin entered brandishing knives.

Jones fought the first while the second stalked Redfort and Bruce. To Redfort's disappointment and alarm the man ignored Bruce and lunged at him instead. The assailant was no fool; kill the weaker foe first and fast. Redfort lifted his right arm and fired his hidden derringer into the man's chest. He was no fool either.

Jones killed his own man and thereafter stabbed both in the heart as a precaution.

Bruce didn't comment on Redfort's breach of the society rule banning members from being armed at formal gatherings. "That was a fine shot, my friend."

Redfort reloaded the derringer's single chamber. "You're welcome, friend." He shot Bruce in the chest. "Jones, see to our escape. I'm too old for all this excitement."

*

Days of confinement had sapped Hunt's strength and climbing the cellar steps left him breathless. Oil lamps sparsely lit the kitchen, but their light still stung his dark-attuned eyes. He blinked until his eyes adjusted and almost wished he hadn't. The room was a mess of blood and bodies.

Foley clapped Hunt on the back. "What took you so long? Couldn't bear to leave the wines?"

Hunt leaned on the table for support. "I couldn't decide between the *Château Margaux* 1856 or the *Domaine Curot* 1878." He looked inquisitively at the two strangers.

"Hunt, meet Burton and Carter. Gentlemen, my good friend Hunt."

Hunt quickly shook their hands. “My thanks for the rescue. I’m sorry Steiner isn’t here.”

Foley looked past Hunt and Lady Delaney. “Where’s your friend with the demon-possessed cousin?”

“Sir Arthur isn’t possessed by *Beliel*, Neil Williamson was.” Lady Delaney corrected.

Foley looked at her. “Was?”

Her mouth twisted. “Was. Now that we’ve rescued Mr Hunt and sent the demon back to Hell, perhaps we should be leaving?” She surveyed the carnage. “But first perhaps you can explain all this? I disapprove of wanton slaughter.”

“That wasn’t us,” Burton assured her. “The society’s turned on itself, catching us in the middle.”

“Sir Arthur and a *Nephilim* called George Rannoch have turned on the Council,” Hunt said. “Neil Williamson was Possessed by the demon *Beliel* to tell Rannoch the true name of his dead Master, so he can bring him back.”

“That makes no damned sense,” Burton said. “*Nephilim* can’t be brought back from the dead.” He crossed himself.

“*Beliel* called Rannoch’s master *Arakiel*. I believe he’s a demon,” Lady Delaney said.

“*Beliel* was the demon who Possessed your husband and killed your children?” Carter asked bluntly.

“Yes. You can’t imagine the pleasure I had in killing him again.”

Carter grunted. “Hope you made the bastard suffer.”

Hunt took a breath. “She gut-shot and burned him alive.”

Lady Delaney ignored the looks the others gave her. “Our business here is done, we should be leaving,” she said briskly.

Burton pointed at the door leading outside. “Not through that door. There’re three or four lads waiting with shotguns.”

“We saw several undead in the house and plenty of guards outside,” Foley said. “They should give Rannoch’s people a fight.”

Carter shook his head. “Some of the undead are Rannoch’s, and the guards I saw running in turned on the guests. It won’t be a long fight, and they’ll soon force the hall door leading here.”

“The corridor separating the hall and kitchen is narrow

enough for us to bottle-neck any who get through the door," Foley said.

"True," Lady Delaney agreed. "But I don't care to spend an evening in this kitchen trading bullets until attrition settles the issue."

"We'll slip out into the hall," Burton decided. "With luck Rannoch's people will be too busy quelling resistance to notice us, and we can find another way out."

Lady Delaney nodded. "That does sound our best strategy."

"And if we're seen?" Foley asked.

Carter held up the shotgun dropped through the window by the man he'd shot. "Then we fight."

The others tried to hide it, but Hunt knew they were as scared as he was.

"Are you up for this?" Foley asked Hunt quietly.

Hunt laughed bitterly. "When I last visited this house I drank wine, feasted on venison and fell in love. Three weeks later saw her dead and me a prisoner." He looked Foley in the eye. "I may not be 'up for this', but I'll die before I go back in that cell."

Foley looked him in the eye and whatever he saw there satisfied him.

Carter pointed at the four surviving drivers and maids. "What about them? Sirk's drug's worn off." Bound and gagged, they could only stare up at their captors.

"They can stay here," Lady Delaney decided.

One of the drivers bled from a leg wound, and Hunt's heart quickened in recognition.

*

Canning walked softly through the streets of Glasgow, the blood of Ronald Stokes restoring him to his full strength. And he would need it for his last task of the night. The lawyer had been pathetic, begging for mercy – *from me?* – and insisting he was loyal to Rannoch. Canning had assured Stokes that his loyalty wasn't in doubt. Just his usefulness. He was more liability than asset.

Stokes' *blood* had been useful, sating Canning's thirst for the first time in many days. The illusion of life slowly returned to his hands, the flesh becoming supple as he crossed the city. Stokes had lived well, his blood rich and healthy. Ghouls forced to subsist too long on the blood of the diseased and weak risked a poor existence as a *Nephilim*, forever rotting. Those that survived the Transition.

He moved from shadow to shadow, fast when hidden, deliberately slow when exposed. Haste would betray him, spooking his prey, and Rannoch would not forgive another failure.

He was no novice at stalking a victim, exercising patience and relishing the chase almost as much as the kill. But for once Canning stalked a predator, not prey, one more practiced in the hunt and kill than himself. Fergus Cooper was a *Nephilim*, and one George Rannoch wanted dead. A knife and the location of Cooper's Crypt were all Canning needed, choosing to follow the *Nephilim* after dusk rather than risk an immediate attack.

He had no choice but to pass under a gaslight, assuming the posture of a drunkard as he did so. He held no illusions about this task; Rannoch likely cared little if Canning succeeded or not. If he failed, it was a near certainty that Cooper would save Rannoch the chore of killing Canning. And Rannoch would send a *Nephilim* rather than a ghoul to try again. Bresnik and Lucia hunted the ones Rannoch really wanted dead; Canning had been left with the lesser targets.

But dwelling among the circus' undead had allowed Canning to tease out a few truths about his condition. Cooper's death could mean more than regaining Rannoch's favour.

It didn't take Canning long to realise what Cooper was about; a predator recognised its own. The *Nephilim* was on the hunt himself. Cooper hired the services of an unwary whore, and Canning watched them disappear down a lane. He walked to the entrance of the lane and started counting to thirty. He got bored at twenty-five and slipped off his shoes.

Richard Canning crept into the cobbled lane, treading barefoot through rotting waste. There were jerky movements ahead. The whore was providing a service, just not the one she intended.

He had to move quick. The copper-haired *Nephilim* was

distracted while he fed, but the blood would soon strengthen him. Being short and skinny had little bearing on an undead's unnatural strength. A knife thrust into his heart would kill Cooper, invigorated or not. Gorging himself on a brothel full of whores would not change that, but Canning intended a riskier assassination tonight.

Blood-loss had weakened the whore, but she was not done yet. Canning was behind Cooper now, and drew his knife. The whore's eyes registered dulled surprise on seeing Canning, a dying moan leaving her throat. Canning gave her a little wave and smile. She had unwittingly helped him, after all, and courtesy cost nothing.

Cooper jerked as Canning's knife found his lower spine. The whore fell to the ground, ignored by both undead. One of them would join her soon, the issue decided before her heart gave its final beat.

Canning yanked his knife out, relieved it had not caught on the bone. Cooper swung at him, but Canning had ducked, anticipating the blow. His knife spilled the *Nephilim*'s guts onto the ground, and Cooper fell.

Canning slashed again and again at the face and throat of the *Nephilim* beneath him until blood-loss took its toll and the mutilated creature's struggles lessened. He hacked his knife deep into the chest, careful to avoid the heart. Dark blood spilled onto the ground and ran between the cobbles, but Canning ignored it. Undead blood offered him no sustenance. Demons, on the other hand, were strengthened by it for short periods.

He pulled aside the shattered ribs and ripped out the heart. There were two paths for a ghoul to become a vampire proper, a *Nephilim*; a few years drinking human blood, or eating the heart of a *Nephilim*. But the unholy power giving 'life' to the undead faded fast upon its death, rendering the heart useless unless eaten within moments. A quick look to his left and right confirmed he was alone, and he began quickly chewing through the toughened muscle.

Every bite tasted worse than the last, increasingly like meat gone bad. But he relished every vile-tasting mouthful and the knowledge that the next sunset would see him a ghoul no longer, but a vampyre in truth. *Nephilim*. He swallowed the last bloody piece.

Canning pulled off his bloody coat and tossed it over the dead *Nephilim*. His work done for the night, he left the lane and thought about returning to the circus. *So soon? The night's still young, is it not?*

A nearby house looked suitable and Canning's frantic knocking soon brought a resident to the door. A woman answered, her weary eyes alive with suspicion. "What d'ye want?" she demanded. Children squabbled inside. He could force his way in, but being invited inside would avoid a commotion that might alert neighbours or passers-by.

Canning bobbed his head. "Forgive me, ma'am, but I've been in a dreadful accident. My wife's hurt, can you spare me rags and lend me a bowl of water?" His bloody trousers added credence to his story.

The woman's eyes softened, and she opened the door wider. "Come in, my man'll help ye with the water."

Canning followed her inside with a widening smile.

*

Foley watched Hunt's expression turn from surprise to something darker as he stood over the driver with the wounded leg. "Hello, Walker."

The driver stared up at Hunt with a look of fearful recognition. Whatever he tried to say was muffled by the gag.

"This is the man who killed Amelie," Hunt explained dispassionately. "Between him and Rannoch, six innocent people were murdered on that farm."

Foley's chest tightened. He had never met the French girl, but Hunt's eyes had brightened whenever he spoke of her. *What the hell happened up there?*

Hunt stretched out his hand. "Foley, your revolver."

He didn't like the look in Hunt's eyes. "Maybe–"

"Your revolver. Please."

He reluctantly handed it over. "Make it quick."

Hunt stood over the wounded driver and looked down with glacial eyes. "For Amelie." He shot the man's good leg and a moment later his chest. The driver twitched and went still.

Foley expected Hunt to be shaking but his hands were still.

"I'm glad you killed him quickly. For a moment there I feared you'd make him suffer."

Hunt's voice was calm, too calm, and his eyes barely blinked. "I was aiming for his belly, but the gun fired high."

"Oh." Foley was wary of this new Wilton Hunt, cold and deliberate.

"He's dead now, it doesn't matter." He exhaled raggedly. "She's dead."

"I'm sorry," Foley said awkwardly. Hunt dropped to his knees and vomited. Foley crouched down and took the gun from his resisting fingers.

Burton watched Hunt. "Frozen hatred."

"What?" Foley walked away a few steps to give Hunt some space.

"That's what I call it, when a man traps his hate deep inside him but keeps his temper. Steiner's like that."

"I knew men like that in the army." He loaded silver bullets into a spare gun. Hunt would need it.

*

Rannoch and Sir Arthur led Regent Edwards into the upper floor room Sir Arthur claimed held his gun collection. Edwards looked at Rannoch. "As Elders, we are the strongest two here. Once we're armed we'll answer this outrage."

Pompous fool. Rannoch nodded along, amused that Edwards chose now to address him with respect. "Aye." Four guards entered the room behind them, faces hidden behind black cloth masks.

Edwards looked around, seeing only two dusty bookcases. "Where are the guns?"

Rannoch nodded at two of the guards, in truth Marko and another circus *Nephilim* called Victor. They turned on the two genuine guards.

The Regent wasn't slow to discern how matters lay. "Rannoch, you treacherous bastard." He backed away as his last guard fell beneath Marko's knife.

"Treacherous, Edwards? An interesting accusation from one who betrayed his master. You do remember Erik Keel?"

"Keel is dead."

It felt good to finally cast off two centuries of feigned fealty. "I'm bringing him back."

Edwards shook his head. "That's not possible."

"But it is. Remember *Beliel*? I Summoned him and learned Lord Keel's true name: *Arakiel*. We're Summoning him tonight."

The Regent spat. "*Grigori* or not, his body's gone. You'll be left with a demon for a master. What will that gain you? Will you still bow to him when age withers his Vessel and fogs its mind? Margot Guillam will inform Lord Fisher of your betrayal."

"I'm counting on it," Rannoch said. He saw realisation dawn in the Regent's eyes; he knew now the ambition of Rannoch's plan.

Edwards raised his hands to defend himself. He didn't ask for mercy or offer to turn coat, earning a small measure of grudging respect. "He'll kill you, Rannoch. And you, Williamson."

"Victor, go downstairs and tell Micha to come up," Rannoch instructed. "Then bring up Hunt and one of the prisoners. Free *Beliel* too." Hunt would make an acceptable Vessel for *Arakiel*.

Victor paused. "Which prisoner?"

"Any," Rannoch answered carelessly. The Summoning required a sacrifice, but Edwards needed to be captured first. Rannoch grappled with the erstwhile Regent and found their strength to be roughly equal. Marko assisted, and together they subdued and bound him. For two hundred years Rannoch had fantasised of besting Edwards one-on-one, but care had to be taken to capture rather than kill him.

*

Rannoch's people herded their captives into the parlour while ghouls drank blood from the fallen. The bloody feast occupied their attention and they failed to notice the small group slipping out of the kitchen. Hunt had little sympathy for the dead; they were part of a society that murdered innocents and summoned demons to achieve their goals, growing rich and fat in the service of vampyres.

"When I move, follow. Run, shoot and stop for nothing until you reach Sirk and Gray at the wagon," Burton instructed.

The burly Templar sprinted from the kitchen doorway into the main hall. Hunt took a breath and followed.

They had crossed a third of the hall when they were seen by two men leaving the parlour. Outnumbered and facing undead as well as the living, escape depended on speed, surprise and aggression. Their Thirst made the ghouls reluctant to abandon the bloodied dead, a hesitation Foley and Burton took advantage of to end them for good.

One of the two men leaving the parlour pulled out a gun, so Hunt fired his own at him. He missed. The man took aim at Hunt who fired a further three shots off in growing panic. All three missed the target, but one struck the gunman's companion.

The gunman looked in dismay at the fallen man and shouted something in his own tongue at Hunt. He took a few steps forward and re-aimed at Hunt but took a bullet to the gut before he could fire. Hunt saw Lady Delaney re-cock her gun and impatiently gesture for him to follow. He looked first at the man he'd shot by accident and was pleased to recognise him as Micha, Rannoch's demon summoner and pretend valet. Shots echoed behind them from the stairs leading to the upper floors. *No time now, celebrate later!*

They were being fired on by three men bringing down Sooty Feathers caught upstairs. Carter raised his shotgun and discharged one barrel into the group, not discriminating between captor or captive. Insurgent and Sooty Feather alike were flayed by shot.

The front doors opened as those stationed outside entered to investigate. Carter's shotgun roared again as he emptied the second barrel into them. "*Deus* fucking *Vult*!"

"Run," Burton shouted. With the path now clear, he led the other four on a desperate sprint through the front doors and out into the night.

Hunt had hoped the darkness would cover their escape, but a full moon shone traitorously down, and lanterns scattered throughout Dunclutha's garden marked the fugitives out to Rannoch's people. Days of confinement and meagre rations had sapped Hunt's stamina, his legs screaming in protest. Fear spurred him on, and he was aware of the bullets snapping at his heels.

They reached the driveway that cut through the grounds and led out of the estate, and their desperate flight continued. As did pursuit by their enemies. A wagon waited at the entrance, two silhouettes standing tall upon it. A rifle fired, its sound distinct from the pistol-fire of their pursuers. Shouts of anger turned to consternation as the mystery rifleman made the swiftest pursuers pay for their boldness.

"Good shooting, Gray," Burton gasped as they reached the wagon. The man called Gray made no reply, he just kept reloading and firing. Dismayed by the cool, methodical marksmanship, Rannoch's men lost their enthusiasm for the chase and fell back.

Hunt was the last to reach the wagon, whereupon he fell exhausted to the ground. Foley and Burton had to lift him up onto the wagon while Carter took the reins, driving the horses away from the estate as Hunt lay back, utterly spent. Lady Delaney sat across from him and cleaned mud from her bare feet. "My shoes were expensive," she explained regretfully, "but quite unsuited for running."

"Is anyone injured?" a familiar voice said. No one was.

"Professor," Hunt said as Sirk examined him.

"Indeed, Mr Hunt, it's good to see you." He held a lantern over Hunt. "How are you, did they treat you well?"

"They treated me to several beatings, but they kept me more or less whole." *To put a demon in me.*

"I'll look you over once we get back to the hotel," Sirk said.

Hunt nodded. He forced himself to sit up. "My thanks to you all for rescuing me. I'm in your debt."

"We didn't come just for you, those bastards also have our leader, Wolfgang Steiner," Carter called back. "You can repay us by helping us find him."

"Anything I can do," Hunt promised. He leaned back and gazed at the stars overhead.

Chapter Forty-Two

Rannoch watched Marko finish the sigils, drawn in his own blood. Two hundred years of waiting. He knew of three demons whose alignment with the House preceded Lord Keel's betrayal: *Ifriel*, *Asmodiel* and *Beliel*. Rannoch was almost certain all three knew Erik Keel's demonic name, but he also knew they had no reason to pass him the name and risk Niall Fisher's disfavour. If Rannoch failed and Fisher learned from whom he had discovered Lord Keel's true name, that demon would find its respites from Hell at an end. Rannoch knew better than to risk asking them during their time on Earth, lest they betray him to Fisher.

Until recently. Never the most stable of demons, *Beliel's* loss of control while possessing Sir Andrew Delaney had led to Fisher ordering the Society's demonists to never Summon *Beliel* again.

Rannoch had waited twenty years before calling the circus to Glasgow, ensuring that when Micha Summoned *Beliel*, the demon would have had ample time in Hell to understand it was out of Fisher's favour. *Beliel* would then be desperate enough to make a deal with Rannoch; supply Lord Keel's true name or never again walk the Earth. *Beliel* had been amenable, telling Rannoch the secret that had eluded him for two centuries; the name he needed to bring Lord Keel back from Hell, even if forced to endure a human body rather than his own.

Rannoch had imagined the Summoning of *Arakiel* to be an occasion of grandeur set somewhere with suitable gravitas. Instead it was to be in a dusty room with the furniture shoved aside. Edwards was bound securely in the middle.

"The preparations will soon be finished, Edwards. Marko has done a fine job with the sigils." He pointed to the circus

Nephilim. "He is among the last of *Arakiel*'s loyalists, besides myself. And Lucia and Bresnik." Who remained in Glasgow. "Do you remember them?"

"I don't." Edwards kept looking at the door, doubtless hoping to be rescued. "Strays from Keel's little war in Romania?"

"Aye. You and your little cabal didn't even bother to hunt them down."

"That will be corrected," Edwards promised. He looked at Rannoch. "I'll have you dismembered and left out for the sun."

"Not tonight. We haven't been idle."

"Then why can I still hear fighting?" Edwards challenged.

Rannoch wondered the same. The gunfire had moved outside the house.

Victor staggered into the room with a pained grimace on his face. He clutched his stomach with a bloodied hand, and Rannoch felt the stirrings of dread.

"Templars were in the house," Victor managed through the pain. "They killed *Beliel*, freed Hunt and put a silver bullet through my guts. Anton is leading the hunt after them."

The news vexed Rannoch, but it just meant finding a Vessel for *Arakiel* other than Hunt. There were plenty to choose from the prisoners. "Where is Micha? I want him to check the sigils and prepare himself."

Victor shook his head. "Micha is dead, he was shot during the Templar escape."

Frustration cut through Rannoch like a hot blade. Without Micha he had no demonist. He had no means of Summoning *Arakiel*.

Edwards began to laugh.

A red mist of rage settled over Rannoch, and when it lifted he found himself holding Edwards' severed head. The bastard still had the ghost of a smile on his lips.

Despair hung like a chain around his neck, but Rannoch knew he wasn't done just yet. He had intended the night's uprising to be a challenge to Fisher, to leave Margot Guillam no choice but to fetch the reclusive *Dominus Nephilim* from his hole. But he couldn't risk it, not without Summoning *Arakiel* to verify the demon was indeed Erik Keel. He needed time, and that meant playing the hero.

Marko stared at Edwards' body in dismay. The heart was to have been his reward and means of ascending to Elder, worthless after its owner's death. Rannoch was cognisant that his moment of madness had robbed Marko of that. Amends would be made. But first Victor's failure to protect Micha needed addressing.

Rannoch killed Victor with a silver knife, Mark watching the brief struggle without comment. "Now what?" the circus *Nephilim* asked sullenly.

"Go below," Rannoch said, cleaning Victor's blood from his long knife. "Tell the others loudly that the Regent has been killed, but another still fights and is coming for them. Tell them to take this foe alive if possible, but say nothing to suggest it's me. Then leave this house quietly before I arrive downstairs and take a carriage to Glasgow. I'll attend the circus once I've found a replacement demonist. Until then I'll contend with Margot Guillam for the regency."

"I understand," Marko said.

Rannoch heard doubt in his ally's voice. "This is a delay, nothing more. I regret depriving you of Edwards' heart, but Margot Guillam's will do just as well." He noticed Sir Arthur standing pale-faced to the side. "Take Sir Arthur downstairs and treat him as another prisoner."

Marko looked mollified. "Of course. I will need to feed first."

Sir Arthur had been standing quietly, looking fearful of Rannoch's wrath. "You choked Redfort's secretary unconscious and locked him up," he reminded the eastern *Nephilim*. "No one will notice his absence."

"If I have time, I will pay him visit." Marko grinned. He left with Sir Arthur, the latter playing the role of captive.

Rannoch wiped away the sigils and anything else that pointed to a planned Summoning. He regretted having to kill his own people below, but Micha's death made it necessary to convince the captured Sooty Feathers that he was saviour, not villain. He would free them and spin a tale of Edwards' last stand. Sir Arthur would then propose to the surviving councillors that Rannoch succeed Edwards as Regent and *Primus*. That would keep Guillam at bay until another demonist was found.

Rannoch judged enough time had passed and put on his mask to prevent the circus-folk from recognising him. With Victor dead and Marko leaving, his remaining people within the house were ghouls culled from Glasgow, and several of Marko's circus-men. Every one expendable, and none a match for an Elder.

*

Sir Arthur sat quietly on the parlour floor with the other prisoners and likewise played the part. He enjoyed gambling, the higher the stakes the bigger the thrill, and joining George Rannoch's cabal against the established order was his biggest so far. He was outwardly successful – a grand house on a large estate, a coveted seat on the Council of a secret society pulling the strings of the Second City of the British Empire, and a knighthood to cap it all.

But few knew his lavish lifestyle had crippled him with debts his declining income couldn't hope to repay. The Heron Crowe Bank held most of these debts; they held most debts accrued by Sooty Feathers, one more string to tie members to the society. But he now owed sums of such size that the bank refused to extend him further credit.

Gambling had got him into these straits and he now staked his very life on the biggest gamble of all; that George Rannoch could overthrow the reclusive Lord Fisher. His reward would be relief from his debts to Heron Crowe, the gift of undeath, and a place by *Arakiel*'s side.

Hunt's escape and *Beliel*'s death were minor setbacks. The death of Rannoch's demonist, however, was a blow. But if Rannoch's mummery could win over the captured society members then the plan might still succeed.

Thinking of *Beliel* gave Sir Arthur a pang of guilt. He had not lightly handed his cousin Neil over to be Possessed by the demon, but the sacrifice of his closest kin satisfied Rannoch and his allies that he was committed.

Marko had left with one of his men, needed to drive the carriage while the *Nephilim* hid curtained from the morning sun. There was a commotion outside the parlour and Sir

Arthur felt a thrill of anticipation; he was about to witness something memorable.

An unholy ruckus broke out in the hall as Rannoch attacked his own. Silence fell soon after and the prisoners exchanged looks, fear tinged with hope of rescue. The door opened, and the blood-drenched Elder entered the parlour armed only with a long silver hunting knife. The ghouls and circus-men attacked the masked interloper, unaware they fought their master.

None were a match for him. He moved and struck with unhurried power, undead and living alike falling to his blade. It lasted less than a minute and when it was over, Rannoch revealed his face to the captive Sooty Feathers. He stood before them, bloody and terrible, and most either wept or stared dumbstruck. Particularly the initiates, many having fainted at this introduction to the undead.

Sir Arthur knew what was expected of him. "A cheer for Mr Rannoch. Cheer our saviour!"

Rannoch just smiled as they bubbled with gratitude.

*

Hunt strolled along the promenade with Foley and Sirk, watching the tide wash clean the stony beach. He loved the salt in the morning air, absent the perpetual city stenches of shit, smoke and rotting waste. In Glasgow the Clyde was iron-grey and filthy with pollution; here it widened into a bright-blue estuary that embraced the Atlantic and glittered cleanly in the sunlight. Gulls wheeled and shrieked overhead or squabbled for scraps on the ground. A steam-driven merry-go-round spun as laughing children hugged the painted wooden horses, rising and falling to the squeal and clatter of a mechanised organ and monkey grinder. He had thought to die in that squalid cell; never was he happier to be wrong.

They had arrived at the hotel in Largs several hours before dawn. Still haunted by days of confinement, Hunt had elected to sleep in the wagon outside. Given the stench that clung to him, no one protested. At dawn the hotel's bath was filled with gloriously hot water. He had sat back in the tub at first, letting the hot water caress him. Then he had scrubbed his body clean of the past week before changing into clean clothes Foley had packed for him. If there was a way of cleaning the past week from his memories, it eluded him.

Sirk pointed to the north. “Do you see that hill there?”

It was unmissable, a solitary round hill rising above the fields. “What of it?” Foley asked.

“It’s a volcanic vent,” Sirk revealed.

“A volcanic what?”

“You have to ask?” Hunt asked in mock-surprise.

“Well, what is it, *Professor* Hunt?”

“It’s the remnant of a partially formed volcano that never erupted. Volcanic forces pushed it up millions of years ago. Since then the continents have moved.”

Sirk looked at him in surprise. “I didn’t know you were so geographically inclined. You’re less stupid than you look.”

“I’m a veritable encyclopaedia,” Hunt boasted, ignoring the last comment. In truth, his father had explained it years ago. Fields lay to the east of the town, stretching upwards into a barrier of hills and the occasional cliff of exposed rock.

The Isle of Cumbrae rose from the sea to the west, its smaller sibling Little Cumbrae just south of it. Hunt revelled at the sight of the open fields and hills to the east, so different from the artificial parks of the city. He pictured Amelie standing beside him, and was sure she would have loved it.

They reached the end of the promenade and turned back to meet the others for luncheon. “This Sir Arthur was a family friend?” Sirk asked.

“Yes.” Hunt gazed out to sea. Cumbrae sat between the mainland and the Isle of Arran, but the latter’s mountains towered over the smaller island. Fishing boats harvested the sea with nets, plundering its seemingly endless bounty.

Sirk looked away in disgust. “Your family should cultivate better friends.”

“I’ll pass that on, Professor.” That raised the spectre of what exactly to tell his parents. Telling them that the genial Sir Arthur was really a cold-hearted bastard who’d given his cousin to a demon and intended the same for Hunt was out of the question. On the other hand, could he really say nothing and risk his parents returning to Dunclutha unaware? The Gerrards had counted Sir Arthur a friend, too, and look where that had got them. *Best to just kill him.*

Hunt stopped. That last thought had slipped into his mind unbidden. Sir Arthur was no undead, he was a living man. When had Hunt decided that murder was no longer taboo but an acceptable solution?

Gerald Walker. Shooting Amelie's killer in cold blood was when he had crossed that line. Hunt quickened his pace to catch up with Foley and Sirk. Sir Arthur was doubtless the one who'd told the Sooty Feathers of Hunt's trip to Loch Lomond. That made him culpable for what happened to the Gerrards, to Amelie. His crimes had earned him death.

Best to just kill him.

The Anchor Inn faced the sea, squat and white-walled on the corner of Gallowgate Square. Lady Delaney and the three Templars sat at a table inside, ignored by the locals.

"Did you have a pleasant walk?" Lady Delaney asked.

"Aye, we did. How's the beer?" Foley asked Burton on spying his pint.

"It's–"

"–the only one you'll be having, so savour it," Lady Delaney advised pointedly. "We're booked on the next paddle steamer to Glasgow."

They drank their ales and ate luncheon in silence. Hunt ordered fish and potatoes, and he'd never enjoyed a meal more. The ale left him light-headed as they walked to the nearby pier.

He breathed in deep, tasting the bitter tang of smoke as they waited to board the paddle steamer *Galatea*. "You know," he confided to Foley, "When I was a lad I wanted to be a sailor."

"That would have been a great loss to the body snatching profession," Foley said dryly.

"Well, quite." He studied the paddle steamer, a behemoth of engineering. The ale was making him giddy.

Lady Delaney and Professor Sirk joined them and handed the pair a ticket each. "I'll see that you're reimbursed," Hunt promised.

"There's no need, Mr Hunt," she assured him. "The Templar Order will pay back any expenses."

"Really? Why not travel first-class then?"

"I don't care to press my luck." Her sharp eyes danced around the pier. "Speaking of the Templars, where *have* Christ's Poor Knights got to?"

"Christ knows." He spotted them bullying through the crowd towards them. "Ah, here they are, the three musketeers made flesh."

They boarded the steamer and took their seats inside as the boat pulled away. The seats were little more than planks of wood, white paint peeling from the metal walls. Hunt felt a moment of panic as those walls seemed to close around him, but he took a breath and stared out of the window at the churning water. He was lucky to be alive. Any notions he'd once held of life unfolding for the best had died on a rain-battered farm up north.

"You fought well last night, Foley," Burton said. "A steady hand with a gun." Carter nodded in grudging agreement.

"I used to beat him at darts," Hunt said, not to be outdone.

"I used to let you win," Foley retorted. "You're a bad loser."

Lady Delaney smiled. "If he's a bad loser, why did you stop letting him win?"

"Because he's a worse winner."

"What about Steiner?" Carter asked, impatient with the banter.

"*Beliel*'s revelation makes me fear for him," Lady Delaney said. "Rannoch may retaliate by Possessing him with this *Arakiel*."

"Not immediately," Hunt assured her. "That man I shot as we left the house? I remember him from *Beliel*'s Summoning; he was the demoner. He masqueraded as Rannoch's valet."

"Demonist," Sirk corrected.

"Aye? That will buy us some time. Rannoch will need to find another," Burton said.

The group quietened as two men approached them, the elder wearing a clergyman's collar. His eyes widened on seeing Hunt. "On second thoughts, I'd rather sit out on the deck, Jones," the clergyman said. Both left.

Hunt looked at Foley in confusion. "I thought I'd washed off the smell."

Foley shrugged. "Most of it. Maybe your bruises scared him off? Or he sensed my papist taint."

Lady Delaney frowned. "That was the Reverend John Redfort, recently announced Bishop-elect of Glasgow."

Foley whistled. "Bishop-elect? Sounds important. Wasn't the last bishop murdered a few weeks ago?"

Lady Delaney gave Burton a long look. "He was indeed."

"Steiner mentioned a Redfort. Didn't trust him," Carter said.

"What could bring an important fella like that down here?" Gray asked rhetorically in his soft drawl. "Anythin' special been happening round here?"

"You think he was at Dunclutha?" Foley asked.

"It's possible," the American said. The prospect of a church bishop being in league with vampyres and demons shook Hunt's already battered faith.

"We'll bear it in mind," Lady Delaney said. She put her head back and closed her eyes.

Chapter Forty-Three

April 1461

Seoras awoke, a taste of wet iron in his mouth. Confusion briefly reigned until his fragmented memories came together and reformed. He lay naked on a stone floor. His eyes adjusted to the darkness, and he saw three bodies lying on the ground. Broken red memories haunted him, memories of the woman and two men dying … dying as he tore their flesh open and drank their blood.

"Dear God," he prayed.

"God will not answer."

The silhouette of a man entered the room. "You believe that God, a being of eternity, has time for you? Such presumption. Such arrogance."

"Where are the others?" Reynard Destain had returned to Glasgow in the company of five brother Templars, hardened killers whose forebears had put the Holy Land to the sword. They had come to cleanse Glasgow.

"Dead."

Seoras closed his eyes. "Why am I still alive?"

The man chuckled. "Are you? Except to talk, have you needed to draw breath? Does a heart beat within your chest?"

Seoras paused. He sat there, not breathing, waiting for his body to tell him to. Nothing. He pressed a cold hand to his chest. Nothing. "What have you done to me?"

"Remember."

A memory returned, of pale men and women lurking in the trees as Father Coll led Seoras and the Templars to the gathering. To a sacrifice, he said. They had found death waiting instead. Seoras remembered their leader, the chalk-faced tall man cutting a wrist and pouring dead black blood down his throat before bearing down with long white fangs…

"You made me one of you. One of the damned." Despair took Seoras. Despair and anger. "The Church will destroy you."

"The Church?" The man laughed again. "Who do you think betrayed you and your fanatical friends? Father Coll serves me well, as do others among your brethren. Abbot Robert gives us no trouble, and Bishop Andrew is more concerned with politics."

Even dead, those revelations cut deep. *Ever am I betrayed by those I put my faith in.* "What are you?"

The man stepped closer. "The truth? I was what you call an angel, exiled from Heaven along with prideful, cursed Lucifer. I am perhaps the last of my kind to still walk the earth. You may call me Erik Keel."

An angel. He had drunk an angel's blood, and now lived despite dying…

"I dwelled in Heaven for untold ages before being cast out by *Mikiel* and his followers. Forget the primitive nonsense declared Gospel by corrupt and venal men. They serve their passions and greed foremost." Dark eyes stared down at him, eyes that had seen the passage of eternity. "Serve me, and we will forge our own everlasting Kingdom on Earth. And one day, perhaps, God will reveal Himself to us, and lead us home."

Seoras stared into those eyes. The abbots and bishop he had humbly followed had been revealed as hypocrites. Peddlers of lies. This was an angel, divinity made flesh and blood, a son of Heaven. At last a master worthy of his loyalty, of his faith.

"You've drunk of my blood and have been cured of mortality. I Make few *Nephilim* myself," the angel confided. "But I see something in you. Will you serve me?"

Seoras jerked a nod. "Yes," he whispered. "Lord."

Two others entered the room. A woman with reddish hair regarded him briefly before turning her attention to the man. "Master, I've brought John." Her accent reminded him of the dead Reynard Destain's. French, perhaps.

"Thank you, Margot." He turned back to Seoras. "Soon, you will be able to control your Thirst sufficiently to leave this Crypt. But you cannot stay in Glasgow; Brother Seoras must die, and years must pass before you can return. Until then, you will go with John Bearing to my holdings in Yorkshire."

"He'll need a new name," the woman called Margot observed. Seoras remembered seeing her rip out Destain's throat.

"Yes. Where are you from, Seoras?"

"Perthshire. Rannoch Moor, Lord."

"Seoras … what is that name anglicised, Margot?"

She thought about it. "George, Master."

"Brother Seoras is dead." Erik Keel smiled. "Rise, George of Rannoch Moor."

Chapter Forty-Four

Hunt stared at his parents' front door. He wanted to use the knocker, but something stayed his hand. Lady Delaney and the Templars had engaged a cabriolet on disembarking the ferry. She had offered to drop him off at his parents, but the prospect of being confined in a dark carriage with several others left him feeling like an iron bar was tightening around his chest. He had thanked them again and told Foley he'd be back home tomorrow. The long walk to his parents' house on Windsor Terrace had left him out of breath, but it had given him time to concoct an explanation for his absence that didn't involve kidnapping, demons or the undead. One spell of confinement was enough; he had no desire to be committed to another.

He took a ragged breath and knocked on the door.

Smith answered it and almost keeled over from shock on seeing Hunt. His parents were similarly stunned by his apparent return from the dead, though they maintained some composure. The venerable butler was led to the kitchen for a medicinal whisky while Hunt joined his parents in the drawing room.

He sat next to his mother on the couch and gratefully accepted a brandy from his father, unshed tears stinging his eyes. Mother took one also; Hunt could count on the fingers of one hand the times he'd seen her drink strong liquor.

Father gave him a penetrating look. "Where have you been, Wilton? We learned last night that the Gerrards died in a farmhouse fire. The ruin is still being searched, but we feared you died with them."

Hunt knew better than to tell the truth. "I escaped the blaze but struck my head and wandered off in the storm. Travellers found and took care of me, but I was unconscious for several days. I remember little, truth be told." He wished that *was* the truth.

Father didn't look convinced. "Those bruises look extensive. Some recent."

Hunt shrugged. "I ran blindly through woods and tripped a lot." An all-too-vivid memory of kneeling in the rain holding Amelie's body came unbidden to mind. He had hoped for catharsis in killing her murderer but felt only a dull satisfaction. It was just fatigue, he told himself. He'd feel more in time.

Mother gripped his hand tightly. "We're just relieved beyond measure to see you again, Wilton."

His father mercifully let the matter rest. "The Gerrards' remains are being removed to France. If you wish to attend the funeral, that can be arranged."

Hunt shook his head. He had no right to be there. "No, Father, that won't be necessary. I'd rather stay."

"Mr Foley called on us on Tuesday, I'll have him informed of your return."

"That won't be necessary either, I had a message sent on returning to the city." He suspected Foley's whisky and laudanum would be much diminished by morning.

"You'll stay here," Father said. It wasn't a question. "As long as you wish."

"Thank you." He stared at the wall. "Tonight only, though. I've business that needs attending to." *We're not done, Rannoch.*

"Very well, but once this business has been dealt with we should have a long discussion."

"Yes, Father," Hunt said tonelessly. *If I survive.*

*

The veneer of superiority that once cloaked the Council Room in Glasgow was gone, stripped away by the carnage at Dunclutha a day earlier. The Sooty Feather Moot had been intended as a celebration of its power; instead not one but two enemies had infiltrated it and spilled blood, including the Regent's.

Redfort looked around the room and noted the depleted

numbers. Death and injury accounted for most absences, but those due to fear were of greater concern. Almost twenty-four hours had passed since the attack and little was known of those responsible save that they had killed perhaps a quarter of the guests, and that their ranks had included undead. His secretary Henderson was still missing. Had this enemy so wished, every guest could have been slain.

The initiates presented a further problem. Ten of them were to have been confirmed to full membership, but all thirty-seven initiate survivors were now prematurely aware of the undead. Between ghouls feeding from corpses, and George Rannoch's spectacular counter-attack, hiding the truth from them was impossible. The challenge now was to identify those initiates suitable for Confirmation. If possible, the Council would confirm them all to replace the dead, but they would need to be watched. Accidents had already been arranged for a few whose reactions marked them as unsuitable.

Who ordered the attack remained a mystery; George Rannoch had taken no prisoners when he retook the house. Redfort's escape meant he had missed Rannoch's heroics, but the surviving members had talked of little else. It was an irony that Rannoch's victory owed no small thanks to the Templar incursion that had also depleted the enemy ranks. That a few Templar fugitives had not only learned of and infiltrated the Moot but put up a better fight than the society's own only salted the wounds.

Redfort assumed the men and woman he saw with Hunt on the paddle steamer that afternoon were the surviving Templars. Hunt had no known ties to that Order and the accepted theory was that his freedom was an accident of their fruitless search for Steiner. Redfort gave fervent thanks that that fanatic had been kept in Glasgow. Had Steiner been at Dunclutha and freed, he would have recognised Redfort on the steamer and happily thrown him overboard.

He looked over to the head table where the masked Council sat, the five that remained of them. The Regent's death had emptied the First Seat, leaving the Council leaderless. Major Bruce's death left the Eighth Seat still vacant, and one further Councillor had died at Dunclutha.

Secundus banged his gavel on the table. His upper face was masked but he looked a broken man to Redfort's eye. He was competent at the day-to-day Council business but lacked the strength to rule in times of crisis. "I declare this meeting open. The death of Regent Edwards is a tragedy, and–"

Septimus – Sir Arthur Williamson – cleared his throat. "Forgive the interruption. A tragedy, no. An outrage. We are under attack and in need of strong leadership. A new Council *Primus* is needed."

Secundus' posture betrayed his displeasure at the interruption. "You have someone in mind?" Once, perhaps, *Secundus* would have fought for the First Seat himself, but Redfort suspected he had no stomach for what was needed, and knew it.

Sir Arthur nodded. "I propose Mr Rannoch join the Council and take the First Seat as *Primus*."

Whispers rustled through the room. For a non-councillor to become its leader was unprecedented. Doubly so since the Regent had kept Rannoch off the Council. For Rannoch to take over Edwards' Council seat less than a day after his assassination was suspicious. That it was proposed by the man whose house had been so thoroughly infiltrated by those assassins…

Margot Guillam stared at the man to her right. She was the obvious choice to succeed Edwards as Regent and *Prima*, being both on the Council and in Lord Fisher's favour. But then, she had been absent from the Moot whereas Rannoch had rescued the survivors in spectacular fashion. A smattering of applause broke out and grew in confidence. Miss Guillam swallowed whatever objections she had.

"Seconded," *Octavia* said. She clearly saw which way the wind was blowing. Redfort suspected the Council's flirtation with democracy would prove a short-lived affair if Lord Fisher disagreed with how the vote fell.

The Council voted four-to-one in favour, and Rannoch took his place as its *Primus* and leader. "We will fill the other vacant seats soon," he decreed. "But our first task is to learn who ordered the attack on the Moot and repay them in kind."

Redfort had a shrewd idea Rannoch knew all too well who was behind it. Others also likely suspected the new *Primus*, but few would dare oppose the Elder *Nephilim*.

At least Redfort now knew the reason for their enemy Making so many ghouls from the populace; he or she needed an army of expendable killers. If Rannoch *was* responsible, Redfort knew it might be prudent to secretly applaud the move and serve the *Nephilim* as he had served his predecessor, Edwards. Regardless, he needed to proceed with care.

"What of the Templars?" someone asked.

"They are to be found and killed," Rannoch decreed.

"And Wilton Hunt?" Redfort asked. "He is back in the city."

"Have him watched. See if he leads you to the Templars." Rannoch looked around. "Is there any other business?"

"I have an audience with Lord Fisher soon," Miss Guillam said. "I propose the Council next meets on Friday to receive Lord Fisher's instructions, particularly regarding his choice of regent."

There was another stir at that. Regent Edwards had on occasion relinquished his Council Seat to another for a period, but the Council always served him foremost, regardless if he were *Primus* at the time.

"I thought that when a *Nephilim* held the Council's First Seat, he was *Primus* and regent both?" Sir Arthur asked. Rannoch said nothing.

"Not always," Miss Guillam said. "But the decision rests with Lord Fisher. I will bring his sealed decrees on Friday. Or perhaps, Sir Arthur, you wish him to attend personally?"

"Not at all," Sir Arthur was quick to say. Rannoch supressed a smile. Miss Guillam was reminding everyone present that regardless of what the Council decided, Lord Fisher ruled them all. The *Dominus* might well confirm Rannoch as *Primus* but hobble his power by appointing Margot Guillam regent, and thus above Rannoch. Or he might emerge from seclusion to clean his House by more direct means.

He would continue his investigation, Redfort decided, and see how the land lay before committing his loyalty to either Rannoch or Guillam.

Chapter Forty-Five

Despite a strong suggestion that he stay for dinner, Hunt insisted on leaving his parents' house after a late luncheon. To stay longer risked travelling alone in the dark and Hunt knew better than to risk that. Not given the nature of what hunted him.

He left the house at a brisk pace, but his strength had not fully recovered, and he was breathing hard by the time he reached Jamaica Street. Being Sunday, the shops were all shut. The bars too, or he would have visited one for a rest. And a pint.

Staying overnight in the family home had been a welcome return to a more innocent time, even if it had meant attending the cathedral in the morning. The service had evoked mixed feelings; the Sooty Feathers had intended execution and Rannoch had intended for a demon to possess his body, so the Almighty deserved some gratitude for sparing him those fates. On the other hand, he wouldn't have faced them if God hadn't given Hell a back door. Or decided that what the world *really needed* was blood-drinking undead to keep things interesting.

At least the Reverend Mitchell had found virtue in brevity. An affliction of dysentery a couple of weeks prior had reduced the venerable firebrand to a frail old man, little more than skin and bone crowned with wispy white hair.

Hunt stared in the direction of the Glasgow Green and wondered if the Carpathian Circus still performed there. To enter the park was folly, reckless to the point of madness. The sun shining overhead meant he need fear no undead for several hours yet, but their living servants were unhindered by it.

The reassuring weight of the gun in his pocket decided

him. Even if anyone recognised him, surely they would make no move with so many people about?

He entered the park and saw the circus still there, some of its performers sitting on the grass while their children played. But its tents were closed and its stalls unmanned. No one performed, and none of the circus-folk Hunt could see showed any intention of doing so. They ignored the people walking through the park and paid Hunt no more attention.

Hunt looked over at the caravans sitting apart from the tents and stalls, and wondered. He knew Rannoch visited the circus at times, and he had seen Canning here once. Were Rannoch and his surviving followers still in Largs or had they returned to Glasgow during the night? Perhaps they slumbered within those caravans, waiting to emerge with the dusk to dazzle, to Mesmer, to feed from unwary visitors.

Hunt walked away and crossed the St Andrew's Suspension Bridge. Darkness was creeping up on the city and Foley's flat was still some distance away.

He passed the Old Toll Bar, closed to all outward appearances. It felt like an age since he had left Foley's flat, in truth only about ten days. He had left it to stay with the Gerrards in Loch Lomond, daring to dream it heralded a new life. A week of death, captivity and horror had killed those dreams. Now he dreamed of killing George Rannoch.

Hunt entered the close and climbed the stairs up to Foley's flat. He still had his key, having left it at his parents' address before travelling north.

"Foley? It's me," he called out. If he was mistaken for an intruder, his homecoming might not end well.

No one answered. "Foley?" He was probably passed out in a drunken stupor, Hunt told himself. He drew his gun as a precaution, thumb ready to pull back the hammer. Lady Delaney had been kind enough to let him keep it.

The parlour was empty. No Foley, but no sign of a disturbance either. Hunt checked Foley's bedroom, then his own. No sign of the bastard; would a note have killed him? The front door had been locked and the windows were all shut, so no entry had been forced.

Hunt found the keys to Foley's shop downstairs and let himself in. It too was deserted. From the looks of it, several days had passed since it had last been opened. Foley's time had been spent searching for and rescuing Hunt, and he felt guilty at the trade his friend had lost.

That still didn't answer where Foley was. Frustrated concern gnawed at Hunt. Now he had an idea what Foley had endured when Hunt disappeared. Sirk had remarked on it.

Sirk. Maybe Foley was visiting the professor? That possibility cheered him. He left the flat, conscious of the setting sun. Sirk lived nearby, and the small risk of meeting an undead was outweighed by confirming that Foley was safe. He also had no wish to be alone after dark, even indoors.

He again passed the Old Toll Bar but stopped, giving the closed public house a suspicious look. He'd heard what sounded like a raised voice within, abruptly hushed. He peered through the windows but to no avail. The stained glass was intended to offer privacy to the bar's patrons and was no less opaque now.

Hunt attended at the side door and knocked three times. After a moment the landlord, McCoy, opened it a crack. He opened the door fully on recognising Hunt. "Come on inside before you draw attention." The impatient look he gave Hunt was clear; get in or go away.

One can't argue with an invitation like that. Hunt entered the bar which was spartanly lit with candles and about a third full. McCoy locked the door behind him. The conversations paused long enough for everyone to satisfy themselves that Hunt wasn't there on behalf of the authorities. He was thereafter ignored by everyone. Mostly everyone.

"Hunt," a familiar voice called out. A weight left his chest and shoulders on seeing Foley and Sirk sitting at a table. *Thank God*. He waved over to them.

"What can I get you?" McCoy asked from behind the bar. Prohibited from trading on a Sunday, McCoy and other publicans sometimes opened on the quiet, keeping the doors locked to maintain the legal fiction they were hosting a private party.

"A pint of ale," Hunt said. "Make it four, one for yourself."

"Very kind of you, sir." McCoy's unsteadiness suggested the other patrons had likewise included him in their rounds.

"The local constabulary don't cause you any problems?" Hunt asked.

McCoy chuckled. "Constable McAndrew is one of my regulars." He nodded over to a tall, stocky man drinking and laughing with two other men. "Our families are from the same village in the north. But not all his colleagues are so accommodating, so better to be safe, eh?"

Hunt nodded and took the drinks over to the table.

"Thanks," Foley said. He studied Hunt. "How were your parents?"

"Relieved by the safe return of their favourite son." Hunt sat down and took a long, long drink of ale. When he put the now half-empty glass down, he saw Sirk watching him.

"The city didn't run out of ale in your absence, Hunt," the professor said. "Neither Foley or myself have any intention of carrying you home, so I suggest you drink at a more leisurely pace."

Hunt wiped the foam from his upper lip and suppressed a burp. "As you say, Professor." Carried home or not, he had no intention of ending the night sober. "A pity our new friends aren't here."

"Carter strikes me as a mean drunk, and I don't think this is Lady Delaney's sort of place," Foley said with a shrug.

"Indeed not," Sirk said.

"Oh, aye?" Foley teased. "Carrying a torch for the lady?"

Sirk scowled at him with furled eyebrows. "Courting wealthy widows may be how *some* gentlemen spend their time, but I have worthier demands on mine. And besides," he said softly, "my tastes run elsewhere."

Foley thankfully let it drop. Hunt remembered that old picture of Sirk and another man, a confederate of his undead-hunting days, and thought he understood.

"So, what now, gentlemen?" Sirk asked. "We have recovered Hunt, slain a demon and returned home safely."

Foley considered it. "Well, we promised the Templar lads we'd help find this Steiner."

"The undead and their secret society are still a threat," Sirk said.

"A diminished menace," said Foley. "Last we saw of them, they were dead or taken prisoner by Rannoch and his

Carpathian Circus allies."

Hunt was less optimistic. "Rannoch has every reason to want us dead. He's cleaning house. It might take him time to get it in order, but when he's finished he'll come after us." Unless Hunt got to him first. He still owed him for the Gerrards.

Sirk leaned on the table. "We can assume Lady Delaney will contact us if and when they locate Steiner. Until then, we should focus on preparing for Rannoch's counter-move."

"Counter-move? I'll checkmate the bastard," Hunt said softly. *Somehow*.

Sirk gave him a piercing look. "We've yet to discuss your ability to overcome Mesmerisation. Not once, but twice. I could dismiss once as a Mesmer poorly applied by a young *Nephilim* … but you said this Rannoch is centuries old."

Hunt shrugged. "I can't explain it."

"Experimentation is unfortunately out of the question, but I'll research the matter," Sirk said.

Foley hiccupped. "Godspeed, Professor."

"I'm getting tired of ale," Sirk announced. "I have a lightly peated bottle of Jura back home, perhaps you gentlemen would care to share it?"

"Grand idea," Foley approved. "We can drink your whisky and plot against our enemies. We'll have a plan by tomorrow," he said confidently.

*

Redfort studied Ronald Stokes, the lawyer who along with a 'priest' had visited Richard Canning the night before his hanging. The lawyer's extended visit to York had been the first impediment to Redfort questioning him regarding the identity of that supposed priest.

The second impediment had been Stokes' murder on Friday night shortly after his return to Glasgow. Unfortunately, despite no known connection to the Sooty Feather Society, he was one of Glasgow's Red Friday victims, as the series of murders in the city had been dubbed.

"He won't be answering no questions," Jones said.

Redfort studied the corpse, half-pleased, half-sorry the rot hadn't yet taken it. The procurator fiscal – the Sooty Feather responsible for recording inconvenient deaths as natural, accidental or animal-related – had given Redfort access to the mortuary holding those killed in Glasgow that bloody night. "He will if I ask him the right way," Redfort said softly.

"You can't be serious," Jones said, aghast.

"You forget yourself," Redfort scolded. He suspected Rannoch's involvement but daren't act without knowing.

"Apologies, Reverend." Jones looked down.

"Stand outside and ensure I'm not disturbed."

"Yes, Reverend." He made no effort to hide his relief.

Unlike the dead Templar Redfort had used to find the Templars' house, Stokes' brain was still within its body. The necromancy required was thus simpler and needed no other vessel to house Stokes' shade.

Redfort drank a little of his illicit *Nephilim* blood and inserted a sturdy hypodermic deep through Stokes' right eye. Through the needle he injected a larger volume of *Nephilim* blood into the brain. He placed his hand on the corpse's forehead, and began the ritual.

Redfort recited the forbidden, alien words that allowed him to pierce the veil separating life and death, calling back the soul of Ronald Stokes from whatever afterlife held him. With the man's corpse before him, he had no need for a proxy as he had with the Templar Murdo.

The last incantation was completed. Redfort knew he had succeeded when his strength fled, and he felt a presence in the corpse beneath his hand.

"Stokes?" Redfort asked. There was no answer, and he focused his will. "Ronald Stokes, I command you answer me!"

Whatever fragment of Stokes' soul Redfort had dragged back from Heaven or Hell into its flesh, stirred. Stokes' dead lips twitched and air moved in his lungs for the first time in days. Animating the corpse was the simpler part of necromancy; it was bringing back the soul that drained the practitioner's strength.

"I have questions. The sooner you answer, the sooner I'll release you." Redfort strained to maintain control and knew time was short.

"Ask," was the whispered reply.

"You visited condemned prisoner Richard Canning with a false priest. Name him."

"Swore … not to." Fluid in the lungs made his speech watery.

"This 'priest' had little faith in you, Stokes," Redfort pointed out. "He had you murdered. Name him and be avenged."

For a long moment Redfort feared the dead lawyer would remain steadfast in his misplaced loyalty, but the lips moved again. "George … Rannoch."

Redfort smiled. Now he knew. But Miss Guillam would require proof, and a dead man's words hardly counted. Besides, she would kill a necromancer as soon as a traitor. "The prison guards were Mesmered to forget him. Did anyone else see Rannoch at the prison?" *Someone he may have forgotten to Mesmer.*

"… Clerk …"

The magic expired, and Stokes spoke his last.

*

"Bishop-elect."

Redfort stopped.

"I am curious at the purpose of this meeting, and the unusual time and place." Miss Guillam stood against a pillar. Her curiosity was justified, Redfort knew. It was presumptuous for a Sooty Feather to summon a councillor, particularly a *Nephilim*, and for him to schedule the meeting with the sun up risked deadly insult.

It was noon on Wednesday, the best Redfort could do to ensure no interference from Rannoch or any undead loyal to him. Miss Guillam had entered St Mungo's Cathedral before dawn and hidden in the crypt, trapped inside until dusk. She risked a trap, and Redfort risked exhausting her patience.

"George Rannoch is responsible for the Regent's assassination and Red Friday," he said.

Any surprise she allowed to show seemed more at him voicing such allegations than the allegations themselves. "You have proof, of course, that the hero and *Primus* of the

Council is a traitor? And you presume to investigate an Elder *Nephilim* and *Primus* without writ?"

"I make no such presumption," he dared. "*You* tasked me to discover who was Making ghouls such as Amy Newfield and Richard Canning without the Regent's permission. My investigation led to Mr Rannoch."

"So I did. Continue."

"We believe Canning was Made by a *Nephilim* disguised as a priest calling himself Father George Herald, one who Mesmered the guards to forget his features. I found a prison clerk who signed them in who was not Mesmered. He described this priest, the features matching Rannoch."

Her expression betrayed nothing. "What else?"

Redfort continued. "The dead ghouls recovered at Dunclutha have been identified as local citizens thought dead and buried. The fiscal routinely signs off any significant dead as natural causes, and it seems he did so for many of these ghouls. But on being questioned why, he cannot remember them at all."

Miss Guillam nodded. "Mesmered to forget. But hardly damning proof. Although…"

"Yes?" Redfort dared to ask.

"Miss Newfield has proven exceptionally fast in her development and requires less blood than expected to satisfy her Thirst. She may well Transition from ghoul to *Nephilim* within a year."

"I don't understand."

She tilted her head. "The more 'efficient' a ghoul or *Nephilim* – meaning the faster they develop – is an indication how few generations exist between their Maker and a *Grigori* – an original undead. Amy Newfield certainly shows such signs, and Rannoch was Made by Lord Keel. Keel always claimed he was not actually a *Nephilim*, but *Grigori*."

Redfort was not entirely clear on the difference but had more immediate concerns. "Is that enough to voice suspicion to Lord Fisher?"

Her gaze pierced him. "Leave *Nephilim* business to *Nephilim*, Redfort, if you care to live long enough to be confirmed as bishop." Her expression softened. "Rannoch's power grab is a provocation. He must know *Dominus* Fisher will destroy him."

"So why lure him out?"

"Precisely. That is why I hesitate to inform him tonight. If I move on Rannoch myself without proof, I risk arousing Lord Fisher's suspicions myself." She tapped the pillar thoughtfully. "I need deniability. And proxies."

Redfort understood. "Pawns."

Chapter Forty-Six

"You call that a measure?" Sirk gave his glass a theatrical poke.

"You mean he's poured already? I just assumed the glasses were damp, Professor." Hunt said. Empty whisky bottles bred, it seemed. Surely they hadn't drunk their way through so many since Sunday?

Foley gave them each a look and poured a little more from the bottle. "You've done little else but drink since Dunclutha."

"Don't exaggerate," Hunt said, though his comment was rather too close to the truth for comfort. It was a bad day when *Tam Foley* had concerns about a man's drinking. But it helped him sleep at night.

Hunt and Foley had visited Sirk's house every night since Sunday to discuss their next move against the undead and the Sooty Feather Society. They'd tout a few ideas and argue the pros and cons before drinking themselves into a stupor, accomplishing precious little. Hunt and Foley had spent those nights passed out in Sirk's parlour, though in truth that owed as much to fear as whisky.

It was now Wednesday night, five days since Hunt's rescue, and thus far the Sooty Feathers had left them be. But they still slept at Sirk's and blamed it on the drink. They returned to Foley's flat each morning and found the windows unbroken and the door untouched.

There was a knock at the door.

"Who could that be?" Sirk asked in irritation and got to his feet, knees creaking.

Hunt's heart quickened. Foley pulled out his revolver and made to stand, but Sirk waved him back down.

"No one knows I was involved with you," the professor

said. "I'll see who it is and tell them to bugger off."

"Be a bit politer than that, maybe?" Hunt suggested as Sirk left the room.

"I'll say 'please'," he called back. Foley sat back down but kept his gun out.

Sirk returned to the parlour in the company of a woman. "Hunt, this–"

Hunt's blood ran cold in recognition; it was Margot Guillam. "Shoot her!" he gasped.

Foley hesitated.

Now *he becomes a fucking gentleman,* was Hunt's frantic thought. "She's undead. Bloody *shoot*!" That killed Foley's doubt, and he swung his gun up and aimed.

Guillam shoved Sirk aside as Foley fired. His first shot missed but he re-cocked and fired again. The second shot struck the *Nephilim* who grimaced but lunged at Foley. He pulled the hammer back, pulled the trigger, and Hunt saw the flicker of the third bullet exiting Margot Guillam's back.

She slapped the gun from Foley's hand before he could fire a fourth time, and a chill of fear fell over the room. Hunt saw Foley's gun lying nearby, but she noticed, and he quailed under her glare.

"Bullets?" she spat, terrible and majestic. "I am *Margot Guillam,* not some new-Made ghoul feeding off beggars in the gutter." She grimaced. "And bullets made from silver. I ought to kill you for that alone."

Sirk had pulled himself up but thought better of standing. Foley's eyes were wide and his face chalk-white.

The *Nephilim* calmed despite the pain caused by the silver bullets. "But I came here to talk, not kill you." The pain on her face turned to shocked realisation. "You remember me, Hunt. You remembered my name and what I am, despite my Mesmer. That is unheard of." Her intense regard reminded Hunt of Sirk when the ghoul Naismith fell into his hands.

That wasn't a comforting thought given the professor's treatment of Naismith.

"He wore a talisman that night to protect against Mesmerisation," Foley said quickly.

Margot Guillam seemed to accept the lie. "I see. That explains it." Hunt blessed Foley for his quick thinking. His ability to break Mesmerisation was still unexplained, a mystery best kept from the undead.

"How did you find us?" Sirk asked. A *Nephilim* in his parlour was an unwelcome surprise, but already the professor's curiosity was overcoming his fear.

Miss Guillam pointed at Hunt and Foley. "I followed them. I recognised Hunt from the club and his … questioning."

Foley remained silent, doubtless hoping to avoid further attention. He'd shot her twice – with silver – and succeeded only in irritating her. Then again, she had wasted no time in disarming him. Hunt wondered how many more bullets were needed to stop her, and he suspected a well-placed one in the brain or heart would do the job. Quite why the undead required a lifeless pump to exist was beyond him, but whatever worked.

One bullet had passed through Miss Guillam but the other's silver content caused sufficient discomfort that she insisted Sirk remove it. That bloody bit of surgery done, they waited for her to explain the purpose of her visit.

"I was not at Dunclutha, but you were," she began, perhaps not the best subject to begin with. "Witnesses say you fought those who seized the house, so I know you were not in league with them. I suspect a George Rannoch orchestrated the insurrection, assassinated the Council leader, and then turned on his minions to win support for his own power bid."

Hunt forced back memories of Amelie's murder and his imprisonment. "So, the Sooty Feathers survived?" He had wondered if the whole society was dead, explaining the lack of retaliation.

"Yes, most of them. But they are in disarray."

You said them, not we. Hunt noted she considered herself apart from the society. It lent credence to the belief that as powerful as it was, the Sooty Feather Society was just a tool used by the undead to maintain control.

"Continue, please," Sirk said softly.

"Many of those who seized Dunclutha House were ghouls, identified as having died or disappeared in this city over the past two months. We learned that someone was Making ghouls from the citizenry without the Regent's writ. Dunclutha revealed those ghouls were Made to disrupt the

Moot and seize the Council and society members present." She looked at Hunt. "Were it not for your body snatching, Amy Newfield would have been among the attackers."

"The murderer Richard Canning is one of Rannoch's ghouls," Foley said. "Did you find his body at Dunclutha?"

"No, he either escaped or was not present. I am in a quandary," she admitted. "I dare not move against Rannoch myself. I have insufficient proof to turn the others against him, and know not who his allies are. I meet Lord Fisher soon. He has never fully trusted Rannoch, despite him turning coat, and may regard what little proof I do have as excuse enough to deal with him personally. But then, I suspect Rannoch's provocations are to manipulate me into involving Lord Fisher." She shook her head. "A trap? Perhaps."

Hunt wondered who 'Lord Fisher' was, but Foley spoke first. "I'm guessing you're telling us this for a reason. What do you want?"

The look she directed at Foley made it clear she had neither forgotten nor forgiven him for shooting her. "First, I propose we share information. And then I want you and your Templar friends to kill George Rannoch."

"Oh aye? Anything else?" Foley shook his head in disbelief.

"Why do you believe us capable?" Sirk asked. "That you're sitting here despite Foley's best efforts would suggest you overestimate our ability to kill *Nephilim*. This Rannoch is also no 'new-made ghoul feeding off beggars in the gutter'."

She eyed him. "Mortals call us revenants, vampyres, striga, nosferatu and other such names. As a sign of good faith, I'll not ask how you learned the term *Nephilim*. You and the Templars acquitted yourself well at Dunclutha. Even if you perish, you'll draw out Rannoch's allies and perhaps weaken him."

"Why would the Templars help you kill a rival? Why should we?" Hunt asked, bristling at the casual dismissal of their likely deaths.

Her smile displayed canines that lengthened into fangs. "The Templars will help because killing an Elder *Nephilim* is too good an opportunity for them to ignore, and because that

Nephilim has removed Wolfgang Steiner from Council custody into his own. Attacking Rannoch is their only hope of rescuing their leader.

"And you'll help because if you don't, you are useless to me and know too much. With Rannoch gone, I will lead the Council and can keep the wolves from your door." She smiled at Foley and Sirk, her fangs receding. "Roderick McBride has offered a large reward for the men who killed his brother Edward. He doesn't know who you are, but the descriptions he's passed around the city's criminal element are quite accurate. I can stay his hand should he learn your names."

Hunt blinked at Foley. "You killed a McBride? You didn't mention that."

"It slipped my mind in all the excitement." Foley shrugged. "Anyway, it was Carter who killed him. Roddy McBride left Sirk and me tied up with his brother Eddie and instructions to kill us. Our new friends intervened. Eddie McBride told us about Dunclutha, after some persuasion."

"Mr McBride strikes me as the sort who suffers disappointment poorly," Sirk said. "I think we'd prefer to stay out of his hands."

Hate simmered in Hunt's gut as he remembered Amelie lying dead in the mud. Her killer, Walker, was dead, but Rannoch had ordered it. "I'm in. I've business with Rannoch, Elder *Nephilim* or not."

"You'll need me to hold your hand," Foley said. "You've a habit of getting beaten up when I'm not around."

"I get beaten up when you *are* around. But thank you."

Sirk took a considering breath. "You pair can't be trusted to unbutton your flies before taking a piss without supervision. I'll graciously lend my not-inconsiderable intellect and wisdom."

"Your presence will be a boon," Hunt said. "We can hide behind your swollen head if they shoot at us."

"So, you're all agreed," Miss Guillam noted. "Do you have anything to offer before I leave this…" she looked around the unkempt parlour, "house?"

"We have information," Sirk said, "that might shed light on Rannoch's motives. In return, I'd welcome some history."

"Very well, speak." Miss Guillam waited. Sirk gestured Hunt to begin.

"The night before he killed my friends up north and captured me, I witnessed Rannoch at the Summoning of a demon called *Beliel*." Hunt spoke of meeting *Beliel* at Dunclutha and the demon's revelation that Rannoch had Summoned him to learn the true name of his dead master, *Arakiel*. Rannoch had planned to Summon *Arakiel* that night in Dunclutha, but the plan had been thwarted by Hunt shooting his demonist.

Margot Guillam laughed. "*Arakiel* – Erik Keel. So that old dog Rannoch still pines for his dead master. It makes sense now. Your story also confirms a very old claim."

"Oh?" Sirk quirked an eyebrow.

"I suppose some *Nephilim* history will do no harm; I don't imagine you'll live very long. For you to understand, I must go back to the beginning. You recall, of course, Lucifer's Rebellion?"

"Not personally, as it was before my time," Sirk answered dryly, "but the Bible mentions it in passing." Hunt remembered it featuring in his mother's favourite book, *Paradise Lost*.

"Very little is known; the first vampyres found it painful to talk of. The story goes that Lucifer, First of the Archangels, refused God's order to bow down to Mankind. He led a third of all angels in a rebellion to overthrow God, but the Archangel Michael rallied the rest of the Heavenly Host and prevailed. Lucifer Himself was defeated by Michael, and all the rebel angels were cast out of Heaven.

"Some stories have the fallen angels banished to Earth, others to Hell. *Nephilim* lore partially agrees with both. Lucifer's Host numbered in the millions and all but two hundred of those were smote down. The 'dead' rebels – for one cannot truly die in Heaven or Hell – were exiled to Hell. We know these as demons. The two hundred or so survivors, Lucifer among them, were cast down to Earth.

"This all happened thousands of years ago when Man was in his infancy. The Fallen sent here manifested in a human-like body, randomly male or female in appearance, though angels have no gender. They were as gods to the primitives they encountered, enslaving many. The Fallen were ageless and strong, immortal. They drew no breath, drank blood for sustenance and perished in the sunlight. The sun destroyed many in their first days of exile, banishing them to Hell to become demons like the rest."

"You're speaking of the first *Nephilim*," Sirk said.

But Miss Guillam shook her head. "Not quite. The *Grigori* we call them. They took slaves and warred among themselves. Lucifer was blamed for the Fall, so they stripped Him of His true name, naming Him Lucifer – Light-Bringer – and sought to destroy Him.

"Lucifer hid in a cave one night to escape the dawn and came across an outcast from her tribe. He fed from her, and she bit Him in the struggle, swallowing some of his blood. He killed her and thought nothing of it, awaiting sunset. And so the first undead was Made, by accident. Her name was Lilith."

Hunt drank whisky and listened. Sirk was fascinated, ever surrendering to his curiosity.

"Lucifer realised his advantage and Made an army of ghouls, the origin of the *Nephilim* myth. This enabled him to hold his own against his fellow Fallen. The surviving ghouls Transitioned into the *Nephilim,* the first non-*Grigori* vampyres, and over time the other Fallen learned how to create their own undead. Biblical lore records the *Nephilim* as the offspring of fallen angels and mortal women, but in truth they are simply mortals Made undead. The term *Nephilim* originally encompassed all undead save for the *Grigori*, but after a while it was used to differentiate ghouls from those fully Transitioned."

"What of magic?" Foley asked.

Miss Guillam gathered her thoughts. "A very small minority of humans have Talents commonly called 'magic'. Necromancers can communicate with the dead and animate corpses. We consider necromancy an abomination and kill all who practice it. Diviners can find items or people with the right link, an inborn ability. Scribes can confer certain protections and abilities through tattoos. Artificers can create totems and trinkets imbued with abilities or wards.

"The magickers relevant to our discussion are demonists.

With the right ritual, words taken from the bastardised angelic language – and *Nephilim* blood – a demonist can Summon a demon into a human Vessel. If they know the demon's true name."

"There is no way to cast the demon out?" Sirk asked.

"None." Miss Guillam shook her head. "The demon displaces the human soul which goes on to whatever afterlife awaits. Killing the Vessel is the only way to return the demon to Hell."

Foley frowned. "Wait, if there are scores of immortal fallen angels raising armies of undead and human slaves – where the hell are they?"

She smiled tightly. "Hell is correct. Being caught in sunlight during their first vulnerable hours on earth, subsequent wars with rival *Grigori* – and other misadventures – all conspired to kill off most *Grigori*. Others were undone by a newer threat; their own progeny. A ghoul fed sufficient blood can expect to become a *Nephilim* after a few years. Centuries will see a *Nephilim* Transition into an Elder such as myself. But there is a faster means to Transition.

"Eating the whole heart of a *Nephilim* turns a ghoul into a *Nephilim*. A *Nephilim* who overcomes and eats an Elder's heart will in turn become an Elder. After many centuries the oldest surviving Elder *Nephilim* found themselves almost a match for the Fallen. As time passed – and I speak of millennia – more and more *Grigori* fell to Elder *Nephilim*, Lucifer among them. An Elder who ate the heart of a *Grigori* became a *Dominus*. Most of those have in turn been slain by other Elders who thereafter Transitioned into *Domini* themselves."

Sirk cleared his throat. "How long does it take an Elder to become a *Dominus* without eating the heart of a *Dominus* or *Grigori*?"

Guillam shook her head. "No *Nephilim* has ever become a *Dominus* without eating the heart of one. It is either not possible or requires an age beyond that yet attained by a *Nephilim*."

Foley gave her a shrewd look. "So there's not many of these … *Domini* left, is there?"

She gave him a grudgingly appreciative look. "No. Every *Grigori* or *Dominus* who dies without its heart being eaten by an Elder is one that can never be replaced. I estimate no more than a score still existing in the world. They often remain hidden and rule through proxies. As for the *Grigori*, there may be a few hibernating in ancient tombs, but I think them all gone."

Hunt took a breath. "Which brings us to Rannoch and *Arakiel*."

"Yes. The founder of my House was called Erik Keel, assumed a *Dominus* by most though he claimed to be *Grigori*. Glasgow fell under his domain, though he held territory in other parts of the world. Two other *Nephilim* Houses squabbled over Bucharest three centuries ago, and Keel thought to take it from them. He spent eighty years there with many of our House's *Nephilim*, Making ghouls from the population to replace losses. George Rannoch had travelled with him, a *Nephilim* Made in the 15th century by Keel personally, which Rannoch considered a mark of honour.

"The war dragged on to the consternation of those of us in Glasgow. An Elder called Niall Fisher was restless for power and used Keel's neglect of Glasgow to form a cabal. He took many of us to Bucharest under the pretence of reinforcing Keel but secretly allied us with the two rival Houses."

Her eyes looked deep into the past. Hunt wondered if she still remembered who she was talking to. "We struck from inside and out, slaying Keel's loyalists. Keel himself killed most of our House's Elders in a fight that lasted all night. Fisher alone survived to rip out Keel's heart and eat it to become *Dominus*, assuming leadership of Keel's House; the heart can only be eaten by one. Myself and Thomas Edwards were the only surviving Elders. An Elder loyalist called … Bearing … escaped the main hall with a severed arm and savaged leg. When we found him, George Rannoch had eaten Bearing's heart and pledged his loyalty to us."

"He was believed?"

"We were suspicious. Bearing must have known escape was impossible, did he sacrifice himself so Rannoch could pretend to turn coat, now an Elder awaiting his chance to avenge Keel?" She shrugged. "But our losses were so high we could scarce afford to lose another Elder, even one newly Transitioned."

"Why did you not just hold down this Rannoch and have a more trusted *Nephilim* cut out and eat his heart to become Elder in his place?" Sirk asked.

Foley barked a laugh. "Pragmatism. If you were this Fisher, what would you prefer? Three lieutenants getting cosy with one another and plotting against you, or three potential rivals too busy eyeing each other?"

Miss Guillam ignored Foley's comment. "A few of Keel's Romanian recruits escaped. Our agents later learned they took over a circus and corrupted its people. But not its name, and we lacked the will to scour Europe for them."

"The Carpathian Circus," Hunt revealed. "We know they're working with Rannoch and were among those who attacked Dunclutha. The demonist who summoned *Beliel* in Loch Lomond was one of theirs."

Miss Guillam considered this revelation. "The circus will be dealt with once Rannoch is dead." She continued. "Keel was ancient. The Fallen *Arakiel*'s name became Erik Keel, and he kept his true name secret. Even Rannoch must not have known it if he needed to consult *Beliel*."

"And Rannoch wants to bring this *Arakiel* back from Hell as a demon and serve him?" Foley asked.

Miss Guillam frowned, talking almost to herself. "There is more to it. A dead *Nephilim* is dead, even a *Dominus*. But a *Grigori* can be restored … if the heart of a *Dominus* or *Grigori* is placed into its remains and its essence is Summoned by a demonist. That's why Rannoch is keen to lure out Lord Fisher; he's not content to serve *Arakiel* in a human Vessel, he plans to capture Fisher and use his heart to bring his old master back as a *Grigori*."

A millennia-old fallen angel ruling Glasgow wasn't a reassuring prospect for Hunt. Foley and Sirk's sickened expressions revealed their own discontent at the idea. "But Keel's original body must be long gone," Hunt objected.

"Lord Fisher keeps his remains as a trophy. He has spent most of the last two centuries in seclusion; *Domini* are ever targets for Elders hungry for power. That's why he appointed

Edwards as regent and left him to rule the city through a council of mortals." She blinked, realising she had said more than intended. Hunt hoped her loose tongue hadn't marked them for death.

"I think we're all agreed the return of this *Arakiel* is a bad thing, whatever body it wears," Sirk said in wry understatement. "Where can we find Rannoch?"

Margot Guillam stood. "You said Sir Arthur Williamson was part of Rannoch's conspiracy. Sir Arthur's the councillor who proposed Rannoch as *Primus*, suggesting he is part of Rannoch's plan and may lead you to him."

"Wonderful, but where's Sir Arthur" Foley wanted to know.

"I will send a guide able to help you find him. Kill Rannoch, and I'll encourage the Council to forget you so long as you live quietly from now on."

"Any advice?" Foley asked sarcastically.

"Take a lot of silver and shoot true. And gird your loins; the stronger the *Nephilim* the more intense their Unveiling."

"'Unveiling'?" Sirk queried.

In response, a chill settled over the room and stirred up old fears in Hunt. "That," she said. "It is how demons and *Nephilim* identify themselves to each other. As I recall, it is an unpleasant sensation for the living." She turned to the door and waited for Sirk to show her out. "Good luck be with you. Pray our paths never cross again."

Chapter Forty-Seven

Lady Delaney let Hunt into her house. "Evening, Mr Hunt. We received your message this morning. I'm pleased to hear that Steiner is still alive. I didn't think we would hear from you again."

"I didn't think you would either," Hunt admitted, taking off his hat and coat. "No maid?" He had adopted the look of a working-class man, wearing a woollen flat cap instead of his bowler or top hat. His face was rough with stubble, and he wore an older frock coat, worn thin and intended for donation to a second-hand shop. God help him if his mother caught sight of him. God help him if an undead or Sooty Feather recognised him despite his disguise.

"I gave Ellison her liberty for the evening. The others are waiting for you."

She led Hunt into the parlour where he found Burton, Gray, Carter and a young woman waiting.

Hunt felt a jolt as he recognised her. "Miss Knox."

Lady Delaney looked between them. "You're acquainted?"

"He played Lucifer in that play." Kerry Knox looked at Hunt in apology. "I forget your name."

Lady Delaney studied him appraisingly. "Really? I attended your opening night."

"I clearly made little impression," he said wryly. "Wilton Hunt," he reminded Miss Knox.

"I was at the theatre to settle an old debt, not for the performances," Lady Delaney said.

Hunt considered Miss Knox and Lady Delaney, a few pieces tumbling into place. "You weren't there just to act. Benjamin Howard's disappearance, that was you two?"

"And Steiner. Howard was a member of the Council and abetted in *Beliel*'s Possession of Sir Andrew, my husband."

A cold satisfaction entered Lady Delaney's voice. "I was at the theatre to see him off on his final journey."

Miss Knox shrugged. "I just made him think it was his lucky night, so he'd lower his guard."

"I was there," Hunt reminded her wryly. "You were very convincing."

"Now we've all said hello, maybe we can discuss rescuing Steiner," Carter interrupted. He hadn't cheered noticeably since Saturday.

Lady Delaney sighed. "So you've discovered his location? Wonderful, we'll leave immediately." She dropped the sarcasm from her tone. "We'll find him, Mr Carter. Be patient."

"I can help with that," Hunt said, glad to repay them for his rescue. He told them about Margot Guillam's visit the previous night and her unexpected offer. Doing a vampyre's dirty work didn't go down well, but the prospect of freeing Steiner, preventing a demon's return, and killing Rannoch made it more palatable to Lady Delaney and the Templars.

The doorbell rang.

Burton tensed. "Expecting more company?"

Lady Delaney shook her head and looked at Hunt. "Were you followed?"

"No," Hunt assured her. *I think*. His record in this regard was not exemplary.

The Templars exchanged looks and drew their guns. Miss Knox looked undecided between fear and excitement.

"I'll see who it is," Lady Delaney said.

"Is that safe?" Burton asked.

She gave him a cool look. "I didn't survive this long by being careless. You may accompany me. If it's a neighbour, try not to shoot them."

The pair left the parlour. Hunt strained to listen but could hear nothing distinct. Carter drank brandy with feigned nonchalance, but his right hand was never far from his revolver.

Lady Delaney entered the drawing room with a guarded expression.

"A neighbour?" Hunt asked. "Some good soul collecting for charitable causes?"

"No," she said.

A young woman entered after her, followed closely by Burton. Hunt's blood ran cold; it was Amy Newfield. "Ghoul!"

After a startled moment Carter had her in his sights, but Lady Delaney raised her hand. "I'll decide if anyone is to be shot under my roof, thank you, Mr Carter." She regarded Newfield with distaste. "You said you came with a message. Is this true, or should I let him shoot you, my carpets be damned?"

"I followed him," Amy Newfield said with a nod at Hunt, who felt himself redden. "Miss Guillam says Rannoch has found a demonist. If she is right the demon will be Summoned tonight in the presence of all Rannoch's favourites, Sir Arthur Williamson included. You're to go to Jamaica Street where another will bring your friends. From there you'll be led to Sir Arthur."

"*We'll* be led," Lady Delaney corrected. "You're coming along."

*

Foley had brought his wagon, Hunt saw, a more discreet means of transporting weapons than the bulky packs the Templars carried. *And our dead and wounded afterwards.* Sirk sat in the back with a stranger, presumably the guide Margot Guillam promised.

"Mr Foley," Lady Delaney said, "A pleasure seeing you again."

"All mine, Lady Delaney," Foley assured her. He stared at Amy Newfield in surprise before introducing the stranger with him, a furtive-looking fellow whose best days were long behind him. "Meet Jimmy Keane, our guide."

"Miss Newfield advises that you know our destination," Lady Delaney said. "Time is short, be so good as to tell us where we're going."

"I don't know," Keane said. He held up a small glass vial of blood. "I'm to take you to the man this came from. Miss Guillam said he'll be with whoever you're after."

"Just bloody tell us," Carter said in menacing tone. "Or you can pour that out to make room for your own."

"I don't know yet," Keane insisted. He had trembling hands and a jaundiced look to him, a man who liked to drink.

"He's a diviner," Sirk said, forestalling further threats from the volatile Carter. He looked at Keane. "Am I correct?"

Keane nodded. "Aye. One of the best, else the … lady wouldn't have hired me." He thumbed his chest proudly. "Hired me to follow this blood."

"Sir Arthur's," Amy Newfield clarified. "Everyone – every mortal – on the Council provides blood so they can be found if taken. Miss Guillam was able to get Sir Arthur's sample."

"'twas me she hired to find that murdered Mr Howard's body," Keane said. The Templars exchanged opaque looks.

"Then let us be off," Lady Delaney said. "Which direction, Mr Keane?"

Keane rubbed some of the blood between grubby fingers while everyone boarded the wagon. "Down there," he pointed. "Towards High Street," he added after consideration.

Foley got the wagon underway.

*

The Summoning was to take place in the Necropolis, the ground already consecrated with the necessary sigils. Cornelius Josiah, one of only three local demonists, had been hired to conduct the two rituals. He was only too eager to aid the Council's new *Primus,* ignorant of his role in aiding the planned downfall of the usurper Niall Fisher. A few torches had been lit near the centre, but not enough to draw attention. The city's police had been instructed to send its constables elsewhere.

Rannoch had ordered his sentries to patrol the Necropolis to ensure the ritual was not interrupted; everyone else had gathered to watch. The sacrifice was a dark-haired girl culled from an East End slum. *Arakiel*'s intended Vessel was a man close to an influential Sooty Feather. Rannoch cared not at all about the sacrifice; their age and gender was irrelevant. So long as their death sent out a soul to unsettle the veil between life and death sufficiently to allow a demon through to the Vessel.

Rannoch breathed air into his dead lungs. “Begin.”

Lucia slid her knife across the sacrifice’s throat. Blood spurted over the sigils, and the dying girl’s feeble struggles soon ceased. Canning leaned forward with an interested expression on his face. *Drawn to the blood, no doubt.* Rannoch had not anticipated Canning would use Cooper’s heart to Transition from ghoul to *Nephilim*, underestimating his knowledge. *A loose tongue in the circus must have wagged.* He was no threat to Rannoch yet, but would bear watching in the decades to come. For now, he was a useful tool.

Rannoch shoved a funnel into the Vessel’s mouth, pouring his own blood down it while Josiah chanted.

“*Arakiel*,” Josiah said, careful to enunciate the name as Rannoch instructed. “*Arakiel*,” Rannoch and the others repeated it.

They continued chanting, the tension thick with anticipation. This day had been two hundred years coming. It would only be bettered when Niall Fisher’s heart was used to restore *Arakiel* to his true flesh.

“*Arakiel*.”

*

“The Glasgow Necropolis? Rannoch’s going to summon a demon on top of a hill with only gravestones and monuments for cover?” Foley shook his head.

The revelation that he had been hired to aid the assassination of the Council’s new *Primus* hadn’t sat well with the seedy diviner, but he also feared defying the formidable Miss Guillam. “I don’t know about *him*, but whoever gave this blood is there,” Keane insisted sullenly. “I’ve done my bit, I’m off.”

Carter took hold of Keane and gave Lady Delaney a questioning look.

She nodded her assent. “He can go. Good night, Mr Keane. I hope we never meet again.”

Keane wasted no time in leaving.

“Can I help?” Amy Newfield asked.

Lady Delaney appraised the ghoul. “Can you?”

She tilted her chin. "I'll do what I can. My life is in the past, but it was a good one before Rannoch made me into this."

"I should come, too," Miss Knox piped up.

Lady Delaney smiled fondly at her, mentor to pupil. "Bravely spoken, Kerry, but you lack the training and experience. To be blunt, you would be a liability. Stay with the wagon."

"The *next* time we attack a centuries-old vampyre and his demon worshippers, you can come along," Hunt promised facetiously.

"You all remember the plan?" Burton asked. "Good."

Lady Delaney handed Carter an expensive-looking cane, its wood mahogany, its handle made from stainless steel. "This is a gift for Steiner. Keep it safe until we find him."

Carter nodded. "I'll give it to him."

"A moment," Hunt said, removing a half-bottle of whisky from his coat pocket. He looked at each of them in turn, his face half-cast in shadow. A naval toast came to mind. "Ladies and gentlemen, a Bloody War or a Sickly Season."

"A Bloody War or a Sickly Season," they all echoed, each in turn taking a swig from the bottle save Amy Newfield.

Kerry Knox stayed with the wagon while the other eight left for the nearby cemetery. A flicker of light on top of the hill suggested Keane had led them true.

St Mungo's Cathedral tower rose above its neighbouring buildings, a gothic finger pointed at the heavens. Glasgow's Necropolis sat prominently behind it, a hill covered by a growing collection of gothic tombs, monuments and gravestones memorialising the city's wealthy and distinguished dead. It was a hell of a city that treated its dead better than its living. Unlike the Southern Necropolis near the Gorbals, the late Professor Miller had never sent Hunt and Foley to disturb this cemetery's residents. Oddly fitting since he was now interred among them.

Hunt and his seven companions entered the cemetery, using the gravestones and mausoleums to conceal their ascent. The hill wasn't unguarded but knives in the dark had silenced the two sentries encountered thus far.

Gray ghosted ahead and climbed up onto one of the tombs with his rifle.

The others separated into two groups to execute a pincer movement. Burton led Delaney, Sirk and Newfield to the left while Hunt followed Carter and Foley to the right. Sick with nerves, part of him half-hoped they found no trace of Rannoch. Carter betrayed no fear; he looked like he begrudged every heartbeat between now and battle.

*

Steiner's blindfold was removed, and he realised in he was in a graveyard. No act of desecration was beyond these abominations. Something evil had happened minutes before, he knew. Something that chilled him to his core. Why he still lived was a mystery, even the beatings had stopped days prior and his food improved. It was not from kindness, he knew; his captors were incapable of that. If they wanted him alive, it was for a reason.

A blond man approached and looked down at him. "You don't look too bad." Steiner recognised him as the tall-hatted vampyre who had escaped the Under-Market Crypt. "Better than Benjamin Howard looked after you were done with him," the vampyre added. "I'm George Rannoch."

Steiner said nothing. The vampyre looked happy, exuberant even, his dead eyes mimicking life in the torchlight.

"You should know several of your people caused some trouble recently. They freed a prisoner and killed some of my people, including one who had an important part to play that night. Also a demon. They intended to free you, but of course you weren't there."

Hearing that not only did some of his men still live, but that they continued the fight made Steiner proud. Wetness gathered around his eyes. *Deus Vult.*

"Don't be too happy," Rannoch cautioned. "They only delayed me. My master, *Arakiel*, adjusts to his new Vessel as we speak. Your men's continued defiance has convinced me the Templars are a threat needing to be ended. My demonist will soon have you Possessed by *Beliel*. He can then journey to London in your flesh and finish what Pope Clement V started."

Steiner fought back his despair at the thought of a demon

infiltrating the Order in his body. *I am not Possessed yet.*

"*Beliel* may be unhappy that this new Vessel doesn't offer the privileges his previous did, but then he should have taken better care of it."

"My brothers will stop you," Steiner said, not really believing it.

Rannoch smiled. "They don't even know where–"

He was interrupted by gunfire. Gunfire that Steiner's practiced ear identified as getting louder. *Meaning closer.* It was Steiner's turn to smile. "Do they not?"

Chapter Forty-Eight

"What is happening?" Rannoch demanded on his return to the others.

Marko stood with a long knife in his hand. "We have company coming up hill."

"Templars?" Rannoch asked.

Marko shrugged.

"Deal with them," Rannoch instructed.

Rannoch had brought perhaps thirty to *Arakiel*'s Summoning, weapons too as a precaution. Marko distributed all the guns and sent those armed down the hill to intercept the intruders.

Rannoch knelt by the newly embodied demon. "*Arakiel*, can you understand me?" The Vessel looked weak and confused. Then he Unveiled, revealing the demon within. He Veiled and Unveiled erratically, much like a *Nephilim* but with no self-control; it would take the demon at least a day to gain full mastery over himself. Until then he needed to be kept hidden if he was to remain undetected.

"Who … you?" *Arakiel* asked weakly, still struggling to assimilate his Vessel's abilities and memories.

"I'm George Rannoch, my Lord, don't you remember me?"

Arakiel stared at Rannoch and nodded.

"What do you remember?" Rannoch pressed.

"Fisher," *Arakiel* spat out. "Traitor."

"Aye, my Lord, he betrayed and killed you. He rules now as *Dominus*, but I remained loyal."

Marko stepped forward.

"As did Marko, Lucia and Bresnik," Rannoch added, giving him a look. Marko and Lucia were present, but Bresnik remained with the circus.

"How long?"

"Two hundred years," Rannoch admitted. "Lucia, Bresnik and Marko escaped into exile and seized control of a circus while I feigned allegiance to Fisher and returned to Glasgow."

"Does Fisher live?" *Arakiel* asked, his voice stronger and his command of the language more assured.

"He does, my Lord." Rannoch said. "Now that you've returned to us, we will lure him out. He still boasts of keeping your remains as a trophy. With that and his heart and blood, we can restore you truly." To an angel made flesh.

*

Burton had warned them they'd be outnumbered and that to get pinned down was to give the enemy time to reinforce and dig in. They had to employ speed and surprise to overrun the enemy. The latter was gone thanks to a particularly alert sentry who lived just long enough to raise the alarm. Hunt knew they had to kill or rout the foremost defenders before reinforcements arrived down the hill.

The distinctive *crack* of Gray's rifle could be heard as he targeted those near the torches and the silhouettes of those not. Hunt hoped the American could tell friend from foe. He took cover behind a gravestone and traded shots with the enemy.

Foley joined him. "That was a shitty choice of toast," he said with a grin. He sounded alive in a way Hunt had only observed before at Dunclutha during their escape.

"What?" Was this the best time to critique his rallying speeches?

"It's an old navy toast," Foley said between shots. "It's essentially a hope that their superiors will die in battle or from illness, so they can get promoted. Not very apt considering we're rescuing Burton, Gray and Carter's boss."

Hunt flinched as a near-miss showered him with stone fragments. "Your battalion can't have been sorry to see you go, if that's what goes through your head in battle."

Carter joined them only long enough to shout at them to follow, then he made a mad rush up the hill heedless of the enemy shooting back.

"You heard him," Foley said as he sprinted after the Templar. Hunt forced down his fear and followed them.

There was no coherence to the fight, just a lot of shouting and shooting in the dark. They somehow survived their bold charge and killed the two nearest defenders, both circus-men by their garb. Hunt doubted either had died by his gun. If Burton, Sirk, Delaney and Newfield were delayed in joining them, Hunt knew he would be returning to the Cathedral and Necropolis in several days, only this time in a coffin.

*

Canning itched to join the fight, to test his new strength. The fighting drew closer, he knew. Whoever they were, they were nearly at the hill top.

Rannoch realised that too. "I didn't wait 200 years just to lose *Arakiel* to a stray bullet. Marko, Canning and Sir Arthur; escort the master to safety."

Canning was unarmed aside from a knife, but knew better than to argue. He followed Marko down the hill.

A man stepped out from a behind a gravestone and shot Marko. Marko grunted in pain but stabbed his shooter, felling him. Canning retrieved the dead man's gun.

"Carter!" a woman shouted, presumably the name of Marko's victim. Canning grinned and waved before following Marko and the others.

He realised they were being pursued and told Marko.

Marko looked back up the hill and nodded, his injury troubling him sufficiently that Canning knew their attackers were using silver ammunition. "Yes. You stay here and fight them. Be easy work for you, yes?"

Canning realised he was being left behind to slow the pursuers while *Arakiel* was removed to safety. As Marko had never liked him, he bought time and rid himself of the uppity Canning. Not a bad plan, with one alteration. Canning shot Marko in the knee.

Marko collapsed screaming. Canning smiled. "Buy us time. Be easy work for you, yes?" He tossed Marko his gun and made off before he could turn it on him.

"Where's Marcus?" Sir Arthur Williamson asked fearfully.

"*Marcus* kindly offered to sacrifice himself to aid our escape," Canning lied cheerfully, not bothering to correct Sir Arthur. "Wasn't that grand of him?"

Two desperate shots echoed behind them and were followed soon after by a man's scream. Canning risked a look back to see the silhouette of a woman standing over an unmoving Marko. He led *Arakiel* and Sir Arthur out of the Necropolis and didn't look back.

*

With Carter dead and Lady Delaney chasing after his killer, Hunt found himself alone. She'd given him her spare derringer ("It shoots to the left so compensate,") and he'd taken the cane she'd brought for Steiner from Carter's body. Hunt hadn't liked the sour Carter much, but there was no doubting his bravery.

The fighting seemed to have moved past him for the moment, so he ducked from gravestone to gravestone to get closer to the fire in the hope of finding Steiner. The hill still echoed with gunfire, sparks marking out the shooters. A rifle fired on occasion, letting Hunt know Gray still lived. *God knows who else does.*

Hunt found a man tied up behind a large plinth. "Steiner?" he whispered. He recognised the prisoner as the leader of the Templar raid on the Under-Market undead.

"Yes. Who are you?"

"Wilton Hunt, I'm here with some friends of yours." He cut the Templar free and handed him the cane, derringer and three small bullets. "A gift from Lady Delaney. About the gun, she says it–" A jolt of panic went through Hunt as he realised there was someone behind him. His arm was grabbed before he could raise his gun.

"Don't shoot, it's me," Burton whispered.

"Sergeant?" Steiner asked.

Hunt heard the grin in Burton's voice. "Aye, sir. Good to see you again."

"My thanks for the rescue, I regret putting you to so much trouble. Who is with you?"

"Carter and Gray are all that's left of the lads. Lady

Delaney's here, too. You've met Hunt; he's here with two friends. A ghoul's helping us, and your agent, Miss Knox, is nearby."

"Carter's dead," Hunt said, knowing there was no easy way to tell him. "Lady Delaney's chasing his killer."

"Shit," Burton swore.

"Where's Foley and the others?" Hunt wanted to know. The fight was ebbing, the gunfire much diminished. He didn't know if that meant it was nearly won or almost lost.

"I got separated from Foley, Sirk and Newfield," Burton said. "I'm out of bullets so I decided to find Steiner."

Hunt checked his gun. "I've three left."

"Rannoch Summoned a demon named *Arakiel*," Steiner said. "We must stop him."

"You're too late, Templar. *Arakiel* is safely away," a new voice said. *Rannoch. Oh Jesus.*

Rannoch and a black-haired woman stepped into the torchlight. Steiner pulled a blade free from his new cane. Burton drew a knife. The five of them stood amidst a forest of grey-stoned memorials to the dead, haloed by burning torchlight. Hunt remembered Amelie, her outer beauty and the bright spark within. He remembered kneeling in the mud and cradling her body, that spark extinguished. The creature before him had been behind her death and the death of her family, and those deaths demanded answer.

Hate and fear burned in Hunt's gut. He held no delusions that he was a match for either undead, but he was reassured by the two Templars beside him. He would either see Amelie avenged, or join her.

"Lucia's always wanted to fight a Templar," Rannoch said. "Try and not die too soon, Steiner, she relishes a good fight." Both he and Lucia brandished long knives, Rannoch also holding a smaller knife in his left hand.

Rannoch attacked Hunt and Burton while Lucia went for Steiner.

Steiner met the female *Nephilim*, managing to shoot his borrowed derringer before using his sword-stick to parry the first blow. The bullet caused the vampyre to flinch, but she kept hold of her blade. Steiner dropped the now empty derringer into a pocket. Hunt realised he'd failed to pass on

Lady Delaney's warning that the derringer's aim was slightly off.

Hunt and Burton faced Rannoch who evaded Hunt's shot. Hunt twisted as the Elder *Nephilim* threw a small knife at him, its blade cutting his upper arm. He yelped and dropped his gun. Burton fought Rannoch knife to knife, the pair circling and stabbing.

Hunt crouched, fumbling for the gun as his stomach curdled. Fear made him clumsy and his boot sent the gun skittering away. He reached over and grabbed hold of it.

Judging by the fresh wounds on Burton's arms, Rannoch had skills with a knife beyond throwing them. His knife stabbed out and Burton side-stepped to answer with a heart-aimed lunge. A cheer died on Hunt's lips as Rannoch's left hand whipped up to reveal a second blade which he buried in Burton's gut.

The burly Templar fell bleeding to the grass. George Rannoch advanced on Hunt with a predatory smile, his left knife red with Burton's blood. Hunt stood and raised his gun.

The *Nephilim* closed the gap, his fangs bared and long knives raised. Their eyes locked.

Hunt's fear threatened to turn to panic. He faltered and felt the urge to run before realising that Rannoch had Unveiled to amplify his fear. Something stirred deep inside Hunt, raw and primal. He could *see* the Unveiled *Nephilim*, its long years and formidable strength. Time seemed to slow as a calm settled over him. Something cold and dark rose from within, feeling *contempt* for the undead upstart that presumed to kill him.

Rannoch was perhaps two metres away and faltered, his expression turning to shock. Hunt's gun reached shoulder height, and his arm straightened.

The *Nephilim* snarled and resumed his charge.

Hunt cocked the gun and aimed.

Rannoch was a metre away, his right arm drawing back.

Part of Hunt shrieked at him to fire, but the impulse went unheeded. Still cold, he steadied his aim, letting the gun barrel dip slightly. His finger rested on the trigger.

The *Nephilim*'s right arm lanced forward, blade flashing silver.

Now. Hunt squeezed the trigger and stepped aside.

Rannoch staggered past him and sprawled to the ground. Hunt re-cocked the gun and fired into the back of his head. George Rannoch lay truly dead.

That cold envelope of empty calm turned to nausea, and he felt lessened without it. He knelt next to the injured Templar. "Burton."

The wounded man stirred slightly, his hands wrapped round his mid-rift, wet with blood and gore. "You get the bastard?" he forced out between gritted teeth.

"Yes." *I got him*. Hunt looked at the growing pool of blood in apprehension. "I should look at your wound."

"No … point, he cut me deep." Burton grimaced, his face pale and clammy. "Help Steiner."

Hunt turned. Steiner was losing ground against his own opponent and fast running out of room to manoeuvre. No desperation showed on his face, only a fierce concentration. Hunt checked his gun and confirmed it was empty. He picked up Burton's knife and waited for an opportunity.

His help proved unnecessary. Steiner stepped back and drew the derringer left-handed, pointing it at the *Nephilim*'s face. She flinched and jerked back, but Steiner didn't fire, instead skewering Lucia in the heart with a precisely delivered lunge.

Hunt walked over as the Templar pocketed the derringer. "Empty," Steiner explained with a wry smile. Remembering Lady Delaney's warning that the gun fired to the left, Hunt opened his mouth to belatedly warn Steiner when the Templar spoke first. "Burton?"

Hunt shook his head. "He's … not good." *Dying*.

Steiner knelt next to Burton and spoke quietly, examining the wound. Hunt walked away a short distance.

Steiner joined him a minute later and Hunt realised what he'd done. "You killed him!"

Steiner's glare caused Hunt to step back. "He was beyond saving. Better a comrade's quick mercy than the slow agony of a stomach wound."

Hunt reluctantly nodded. "I'm sorry," he said, knowing it to be inadequate. "About him and Carter."

"God willed it." Steiner reloaded the derringer.

Foley, Delaney, Gray, Newfield and Sirk joined them on top of the hill. “The last of them fled,” Foley said as Gray and Lady Delaney greeted Steiner. Sadness crossed his face on seeing Burton’s body.

“Carter died, too.”

Foley nodded. “Lady Delaney told me. She caught his killer and finished him off.”

“You gentleman can stay,” Lady Delaney said. “But I intend to be away from here before the Sooty Feathers or police investigate the disturbance and find all these bodies.”

Hunt and his six remaining companions returned to the wagon where Kerry Knox anxiously waited. Burton and Carter were covered in cloth and loaded onto the wagon.

Foley drove the wagon to Lady Delaney’s house where the two wrapped bodies were carried inside. The survivors gathered round the wagon to say farewell.

“What about me?” Amy Newfield asked, still uneasy in their company.

“You helped us,” Steiner said, right hand resting in a pocket, “and for that, I am sorry.” He pulled out Lady Delaney’s spare derringer and fired into Amy Newfield’s chest.

Hunt stared in disbelief as she collapsed wordlessly to the ground. He pointed his own gun at Steiner. “Damn you, why? She was on our side!”

Gray made to turn his rifle on Hunt but found Foley’s gun trained on him.

Kerry Knox looked shocked, either because of Steiner’s cold-hearted murder of Amy Newfield, or because the group’s survivors now looked set on killing one other. Sirk uneasily cleared his throat. “Gentlemen, I do not think this is wise…”

Steiner looked calmly at Hunt. “She was not on our side. She was a ghoul, an abomination, *undead*. How many would she have slain to slake her thirst had we let her go?”

Hunt voice shook with anger. “We dug her up, she was our responsibility, *my* responsibility! It was because of her we got dragged into this *goddamned mess* to begin with! She was an innocent, and it was my fault.”

Foley touched his arm. “Amy Newfield wasn’t Amelie

Gerrard, and you didn't kill either of them," he said gently.

"I think there's been enough violence for one night, gentlemen," Lady Delaney observed.

Hunt took a breath and lowered his gun, eyes hot with unshed tears.

"I regret we are separating on bad terms, but it was an honour to fight alongside you." Steiner gave a sharp bow from the neck. "Go with God."

"Go to hell."

Steiner, Lady Delaney, Gray and Kerry Knox entered the house, leaving Hunt, Foley and Sirk with the wagon.

"What will we do with her?" Foley asked, looking down at Amy Newfield's corpse.

"We'll take her with us," Hunt said.

"And then what?" pressed Foley.

Hunt looked at him silently.

Realisation shone in Foley's eyes and he smiled sadly. "Why the hell not?"

They wrapped up the body in cloth used to hide the guns and lifted her into the wagon. Hunt and Sirk sat in the back with Amy Newfield's corpse while Foley took the reins. The sky burned gold as dawn broke and a new day began.

Chapter Forty-Nine

"I'd ask if your belongings were all loaded onto the train, Mr Steiner, but…" Lady Delaney spread her hands as they stood next to the train carriage in the Queen Street Station.

Steiner allowed himself a faint smile. "I seem to have misplaced my luggage." With his own clothing lost or ruined, he was forced to rely on Lady Delaney's charity once again. The grey jacket and trousers he wore came from her late husband's wardrobe, and they hung loose on his shrunken frame.

The deaths of Burton and Carter had soured their slaying of Rannoch, as did their contentious parting with Hunt, Foley and Sirk. Gray joined them with two tickets to Edinburgh.

"Again, we are in your debt, Lady Delaney," Steiner said. She had paid for the tickets.

"Your Order will be receiving the bill in due course," she said with mock-severity.

"You have my word it will be honoured."

She studied him. "What reception do you expect in Edinburgh?"

He had been considering that himself. "I do not know. Nine men under my command died. My men, my responsibility."

"And what of the results? Two Elder vampyres slain along with many of their lesser brethren. What's left of the Council is doubtless in disarray, their veneer of power shattered. Dozens of their human servants have died and the faith of the survivors shaken. They are vulnerable."

Steiner barked out a rare laugh. "A clergyman manipulated me into aiding his murder of a bishop, my people were killed, and I was captured. I had to be rescued, you killed one demon and the other escaped. Rannoch killed the undead Regent and was slain in turn by Hunt. This Fisher rules still.

My contribution is suspect at best."

"You *contributed* to the destruction of many undead. Had we not been there, Rannoch would be replacing a vampyre lord with a fallen angel. Instead, the circus has fled the city, *Arakiel* presumably with them."

The circus *had* left. Steiner and Gray had attended the Glasgow Green just before midnight on Friday with the intention of quietly reconnoitring the circus. If *Arakiel* had been there, he would have died, along with any remaining undead. Instead the last two Templars found the Green empty of tents and caravans. The constable manning the Toll told them that the circus had left the city after dusk.

"I will report to the Edinburgh Chapterhouse, it will be in their hands," Steiner said. God willing, they would send him back with more men to finish what had been started.

Lady Delaney touched his arm. "I will write of anything I learn. If the opportunity to further inconvenience the undead and the Sooty Feathers presents itself, be assured I'll do what I can."

"I am sure you will. What of Miss Knox?"

"I'm taking her under my wing for the foreseeable future."

"I did not intend for her to become part of this fight," Steiner remonstrated mildly.

"Your intentions are insufficient to keep her out of it. She knows too much and wishes to be able to defend herself. And others, if need be." There was a knowing sadness in her voice, but pride also.

"She could have no better teacher," Steiner conceded.

"I'll welcome the company." Her smile was tinged with acceptance. "The years march on, and I'm not getting younger."

The guard blew his whistle.

Steiner touched his borrowed hat. "My gratitude for your aid in trying times. Go with God."

"Travel safe."

Steiner accompanied Gray onto the train and found an empty compartment. Never one for conversation, Gray leaned back and closed his eyes. Steiner looked out of the window and wondered if he would see Glasgow again. A whistle shrieked, and the train pulled out of the station, leaving the city behind.

*

Redfort ran his hands down the robe, pleased by the material. It felt satisfyingly expensive. His silver-trimmed porcelain mask had been replaced by one wholly silver and bearing the Roman symbol for seven. *The Council's* Septimus, *an honour well-deserved.* But not an honour he was alone in receiving. Others were to be raised to the Council to fill the missing seats.

Margot Guillam had been appointed Regent and *Prima* of the Council. Redfort hoped his contributions to her investigation of Rannoch would not go unremembered. His own anointment as Bishop was forthcoming also.

The already-fragile society had been rocked further by Margot Guillam's revelations concerning the now-dead George Rannoch. Rannoch had briefly been the House's *Primus*, and his treachery left the society paralysed. No one knew whom to trust.

Sir Arthur Williamson had disappeared and had been declared complicit in the treachery. His assets were seized and word spread among the city's underbelly to find him. Most were outraged by his betrayal, but Redfort chose to be circumspect, mindful of new opportunities.

He sat in the small room, waiting to be summoned. There would be little time to celebrate; once the new councillors were sworn in, the surviving society initiates were to be inducted as full members. A new day dawned for the Sooty Feather Society.

The door opened and Redfort walked towards it, smoothing his robe and putting on his silver mask. An additional piece of good news had been the safe return of his secretary, Henderson. It seemed the fool had been knocked out in Dunclutha after speaking to a guard involved in the conspiracy. The blow had clearly addled the man's wits, unimpressive though they were to begin with; it had taken him a week to return home.

Redfort put his secretary out of mind as he approached the waiting Council, to sit among them. God truly helped those who helped themselves. *Yes indeed.*

*

Canning was disturbed from his reverie – undead didn't truly sleep, they returned to a state perhaps a hair's width from death – by two loud thuds on the side of his coffin. He pushed aside the lid and rose, unsurprised to see Sir Arthur as the author of the kicks. He looked scruffy and increasingly agitated. The man's plan to ride Rannoch's coattails to power and immortality had ended in exile with a price on his head.

"What do you want?" Canning asked. He could smell liquor on the man's breath.

"The Master's back." Sir Arthur shied from saying *Arakiel*'s name as if the name alone would damn him. From a man who'd betrayed his own cousin to demonic possession, that was amusing.

They had taken sanctuary in a small flat owned by Sir Arthur under another name. *Arakiel* had mastered most of his Vessel's memories and was thus far successful in passing himself off as that man.

They found *Arakiel* in the parlour. Canning bowed. "Master, how did you fare today?"

"I've no wish to relate the petty tedium of this Vessel's life. Why Rannoch picked this one…" When he wasn't assuming his Vessel's voice, he spoke with a lazy, arrogant drawl.

Sir Arthur coughed. "It was intended to be temporary until we defeated Niall Fisher and restored your own body."

"At least your Vessel lives alone, unmarried and without children," Canning added. He was given a look that discouraged further levity.

"So, the last of my 'loyal' servants have fled, leaving me with a *Nephilim* not yet a month old and a man with a price on his head." *Arakiel* shook his head.

Canning thought this unfair. The heart he'd eaten had Transitioned him from ghoul to *Nephilim* years ahead of time. His canines now lengthened into fangs when he willed it, and no longer would he fall to mindless savagery when deprived of blood. He could control himself and when he felt the urge to kill it was one he exercised, not one he surrendered to. Self-control was central to his being; he killed because he wanted to, not because base need drove him.

Of course, Bresnik and the circus fleeing the city hadn't improved *Arakiel*'s mood.

"What do you require of us?" Canning asked. He'd tolerated their company out of curiosity. If *Arakiel* had some bold stroke in mind, he would see where it led. If not, he'd kill Sir Arthur and turn the city into his own hunting ground, unburdened by centuries-old feuds and antiquated dreams of power.

His caution was also influenced by prudence. Even the undead could die, and better a demon as patron should he end up in Hell.

Arakiel spoke to Sir Arthur. "Did you get money?"

"I was only able to get a small sum, Master, selling whatever valuables I had stored here."

Arakiel didn't look pleased. "What of the Templars who killed Rannoch, Marko and Lucia?"

"I recognised one of the men, he's no Templar," Sir Arthur said. "Wilton Hunt is a local who fancies himself a bit of a rogue. He poked his nose into our affairs, and I arranged for him to be captured."

"It evidently failed," *Arakiel* observed. Canning thought better of mentioning his own failed attempt to kill Hunt.

"No, Master, he was caught but later rescued."

Arakiel drummed his fingers on the arm of the chair. "Does this Hunt have family?"

"Aye," Sir Arthur said, eager to please. "His parents live in the West End. I've known them for years."

The demon had an ugly look in his eyes. "I want this Hunt punished for his interference."

"You want him killed?" Canning was eager for a second chance to kill Hunt and his friend.

"No, his parents will serve as lesson enough."

*

The moon hung above the night sky, starlight piercing the blackened canopy. Hunt rammed his shovel into the earth and pushed it in deep. He dragged it up and tipped its contents onto the growing pile of soil beside the grave.

Foley kept watch while Hunt dug himself deeper into the

grave, his sweat mingling with the dirt.

Sirk had returned home, possibly to immerse himself in laudanum and whisky, possibly not. The professor had changed since their first meeting with him, still eccentric but with a newfound focus. Or perhaps one reawakened. His escapades in Edinburgh had left him well-regarded by the Templars, men not easily impressed.

Hunt and Foley had slept away the rest of the day, leaving Amy's body in the shop basement until Saturday night.

"Hunt, that's your bit done, I'll do the rest."

Hunt blinked, realising he was standing three feet down. He climbed out and let Foley finish the last few feet while he kept vigil. No one came. The earlier murders discouraged late night pedestrians, and no one in the society rescinded the order keeping the police away at night.

"Have you thought about what you're going to do now?" Foley asked as he shovelled.

"No," Hunt admitted. "I'll continue with my studies and try to not get disowned by my parents. But … no. I imagine we'll need to live a quiet life and hope the Council forgets about us." And hope Margot Guillam didn't regret revealing the origins of the undead.

Iron struck wood. "Found it," Foley said. Hunt watched as he cleared off the loose soil and lifted the coffin lid.

Hunt allowed a little light to shine on the gravestone.

Amy Margaret Newfield
Dearly Beloved Daughter and Sister
Born 29th August 1876
Departed 12th March 1893
Thou art good; and Goodness still
Delighteth to forgive

A cloth-wrapped Amy Newfield lay next to the wheelbarrow. Hunt looked away. This was the first time he had visited a cemetery to *bury* someone, and he was keenly aware that an observer might assume the worst on seeing two men burying a body at night. The only sound was the rustle of grass behind him.

He felt that it wasn't just Amy Newfield they were burying; it was every friend and acquaintance who'd died since her exhumation. *Angus Miller. Neil Williamson. Ronald Whiting. John Brown. François Gerrard. Yvette Gerrard. Jacques Gerrard. Paul Carter. Jamie Burton. Amy Newfield.* He exhaled. *Amelie.*

"Right," Foley said as he climbed out of the grave. "Let's get this over with."

"Let's." He remembered Steiner shooting Amy Newfield, aiming for her heart with the derringer Hunt had given to him. Something tickled his memory.

"Hunt," said Foley, his voice tight. "Where's the body?"

Hunt turned and shone the light where they'd left her. There was naught but crushed grass.

Epilogue

He didn't miss daylight, Canning decided. Not in the least. He was made for the night, a predator. Death's brief embrace had only excised the last of his human weakness. Some considered vampyrism a curse, but not he. A curse? It was a blessing. Humanity ill-suited him, so he'd cast it off like a too-tight coat.

Tonight, he didn't hunt; tonight, he waited for the prey to come to him. The earlier rain had left the cobbles damp and glistening. Soon, he fancied, to run wet with blood.

"Are you quite sure there's a club around here, Sir Arthur?" A woman said as footsteps echoed down the lane.

Sir Arthur was a plausible liar, Canning had to credit him with that. "Of course, Mrs Hunt. It's not been open long."

The footsteps grew louder. Three sets.

"I hate to question a gentleman's sense of direction, but I fear you've taken a wrong turn," a male voice said.

"Have faith, Hunt." The plan was simple enough; Sir Arthur was to invite the Hunts out for dinner and lure them into the lane. It formed an L-shape and a lantern had been hung over a door at the end to create the illusion of there actually being a club.

Canning hugged the shadows as Sir Arthur and the Hunts turned onto the last stretch of the lane. The prospect of murder excited him as always. The grief it would cause their son made it all the sweeter.

"See, there it is," Sir Arthur said.

"So I see." Lewis Hunt didn't sound entirely convinced. Canning caught a glimpse of him taking a swig from a small metal flask. His wife gave him a look but said nothing. They passed the doorway concealing Canning.

"If that's a club," Lewis Hunt said, "it appears to be closed."

Canning judged it time and stepped out behind the trio. *Arakiel* emerged from the shadows at the end of the alley.

"I believe you owe us an explanation," Hunt said coolly. His wife nodded in thin-lipped agreement as *Arakiel* approached.

"I'm sorry, Hunt," Sir Arthur said as he took a step back. The Hunts looked at him and noticed Canning closing behind them.

Arakiel stopped about two metres in front of the Hunts. "Your son has interfered in my business and cost me dearly. You two will be a message to him that he should pick his enemies with more care."

"You brought us here just to give us a message for Wilton?" Edith Hunt sounded scornful. Canning grinned.

"You will *be* the message. Canning." *Arakiel* nodded at him.

He needed no encouragement. Lewis Hunt looked impassive as Canning lunged at him, either brave or in denial of the situation. He swung his knife towards Hunt's stomach as Sir Arthur took hold of Edith Hunt. Canning was to kill the man, but no one said it had to be quick.

The knife gleamed silver, catching the lantern light as it arched up towards Hunt's belly. Canning grunted in surprise as Hunt's left forearm dropped and blocked his knife-arm. He Unveiled and bared his fangs, but Hunt grabbed his arm with both hands and twisted. Canning yanked his arm free, or tried to. His strength was superior to that of a mortal man, but Lewis Hunt seemed ignorant of this fact. Canning felt his arm break at the elbow and his knife fell from nerveless fingers.

His head cracked against stone as Hunt brutally slammed him against the wall. *It's not supposed to be like this*. He cried out as his gut burned in agony and he looked down to see his own knife sticking out. There was no danger of the wound killing him, but it hurt like hell. Pain was less fun on the receiving end. He sank to the ground and looked up at the man he was supposed to kill, seeing the son reflected in the father. Hunt pulled out the knife, ripping more pain through Canning.

"I had no choice," Sir Arthur pleaded as Hunt faced him. "We've been friends for years!"

"It did not escape my notice that you betrayed my son to the Sooty Feathers. That thanks in part to you the Gerrards are dead and Wilton was kidnapped." There was a brief scuffle followed by tearing flesh, a gasp of pain, and the sound of a body hitting the ground. Canning smelled blood, a lot of it. Sir Arthur's.

Canning tried to rise, but Edith Hunt stepped in front of him with hooded eyes and a small pistol pointed at his chest. He lay back and watched.

Arakiel confronted Lewis Hunt with a knife of his own, enraged and Unveiled. And stopped as Hunt Unveiled himself also. Canning realised the depth of his mistake in attacking the man. *A demon, a damn demon.*

Arakiel went white. "*Samiel.*"

Wilton Hunt's father nodded. "*Arakiel.* It's been some time. Twenty-six years, in fact, since I was Summoned from Hell."

"You knew this was a trap," *Arakiel* accused.

"I didn't *know* tonight was a trap, but my flask contained *Nephilim* blood as a precaution. I'm aware Wilton has come to the Council's attention, and that Sir Arthur is – *was* – associated with them."

Arakiel had drunk some of Canning's blood – a source of temporary strength for demons – but of the two Unveiled demons, Hunt – *Samiel*? – appeared the stronger.

Canning looked up at Edith Hunt as *Samiel* and *Arakiel* talked. "Your husband's a demon," he told her, "do you know?"

"Of course I know." Her voice dripped with scorn. "I was present at his Summoning."

He didn't reply. Any woman hard enough to live with a demon wouldn't hesitate to kill. He returned his attention to Hunt and *Arakiel*.

Neither demon showed any inclination to attack the other, though both maintained a wary caution. "Will you set yourself against me?" *Arakiel* asked bluntly.

"I've no interest in your activities, so long as they do not interfere with my own. But there will be no more attempts on my son."

"What do you care of some boy whelped by your Vessel?"

Arakiel challenged. But he frowned, something nagging at him. "Sir Arthur said he's in his early twenties. But you Possessed Lewis Hunt *twenty-six* years ago…"

Hunt smiled. "Yes. Wilton is *my* son."

Arakiel looked staggered. "That's impossible. We cannot conceive. Possession renders our Vessels infertile."

Hunt's eyes glittered. "Being me has its privileges."

"Is he … one of us?"

"To some extent. He may be immune from Mesmerisation, and I believe I felt him briefly Unveil on Thursday night."

Arakiel nodded slowly. "I see. You'll let me go?"

"You and your pet, so long as you keep him leashed. There are to be no further attempts on my family. Agreed?"

"Agreed."

Hunt turned to his wife. "Come, my dear. I think we've reached an understanding."

Edith Hunt returned the derringer to her handbag. "Deftly managed, Lewis. Shall we visit the Albert Club?"

"It would be a shame to waste the evening." They walked off arm in arm.

Canning struggled to his feet and stared after the couple he had thought to kill. Sir Arthur Williamson lay dead on the cobbles. His blood would enable Canning to heal, but it was someone else's blood he craved. "I can find them, Master."

Arakiel stared down the lane at the departing couple. "No. Leave them be. The same for Wilton Hunt."

Canning's pride was sorely stung. "I can kill this *Samiel*, when he does not–"

"I said no!" *Arakiel* glared at him. "You do not understand who we just faced, do you?"

"A demon called *Samiel*," Canning replied sullenly.

"*Samiel* was his true name. We stripped him of it after the Fall. You know his other names better…"

Canning felt an unfamiliar thrill of fear as *Arakiel* named them, childhood fears given teeth once more. *Lucifer ... Satan. I faced the Devil Himself.*

And He has a son.

THE END

Acknowledgements

This novel has been years in the writing, helped by a number of people along the way who have my thanks. In no particular order and by no means a complete list:

My wife Dana for her love and support.
My family and friends for their support and encouragement.

Dana Craig, Christine Thomas, Alan Graham, Zoë Sumra and Daniel Stride for reading early drafts and offering feedback that helped make this book publishable.

Alison and Peter of Elsewhen Press for taking a chance on a first-time writer, editing the text and creating the excellent cover.

Elsewhen Press

delivering outstanding new talents in speculative fiction

Other titles from Elsewhen Press that you might enjoy

A LIFE LESS ORDINARY BY CHRISTOPHER NUTTALL

There is magic in the world, hiding in plain sight. If you search for it, you will find it, or it will find you. Welcome to the magical world.

Having lived all her life in Edinburgh, the last thing 25-year old Dizzy expected was to see a man with a real (if tiny) dragon on his shoulder. Following him, she discovered that she had stumbled from her mundane world into a parallel magical world, an alternate reality where dragons flew through the sky and the Great Powers watched over the world. Convinced that she had nothing to lose, she became apprenticed to the man with the dragon. He turned out to be one of the most powerful magicians in all of reality.

But powerful dark forces had their eye on this young and inexperienced magician, intending to use her for the ultimate act of evil – the apocalyptic destruction of all reality. If Dizzy does not realise what is happening to her and the worlds around her, she won't be able to stop their plan. A plan that will ravage both the magical and mundane worlds, consuming everything and everyone in fire.

ISBN: 9781908168337 (epub, kindle) / ISBN: 9781908168238 (336pp, paperback)
Visit bit.ly/ALLO-Nuttall

THE GHOST IN YOU BY KATRINA MOUNTFORT

A first-hand account from beyond the grave

What do you do if you're dead but haven't 'moved on'? You keep finding yourself back where you died, with very little control over when; sometimes you can be away for days, weeks or even months, and then you're back. Between times, when you're 'away', where do you go, what do you do? You've seen some other ghosts asleep at their graves, but you don't even know where your own grave is.

The living shiver if they walk through you, but they can neither see nor hear you. With practice you can pass through walls and doors, but curiously you can sit on a park bench without falling through it, climb stairs, even lie on a bed. You're stuck in the clothes you were wearing when you died, at the age you died. Waiting.

Then, after years of this intermittent existence, you realise what you have been waiting for, what it is that you have to do in order to finally move on. Just as you have found the best reason to stay.

That's what happened to Rowena…

A ghost story told from the perspective of the ghost herself, *The Ghost in You* is a first-hand account, from beyond the grave, by an innocent girl who dies before her time and tries to make sense of what is happening to her, while helping her friends and discovering her purpose.

ISBN: 9781911409328 (epub, kindle) / ISBN: 9781911409229 (184pp paperback)
Visit bit.ly/GhostInYou

Other titles from Elsewhen Press that you might enjoy

THE RHYMER
an Heredyssey
DOUGLAS THOMPSON

The Rhymer, an Heredyssey defies classification in any one literary genre. A satire on contemporary society, particularly the art world, it is also a comic-poetic meditation on the nature of life, death and morality.

A mysterious tramp wanders from town to town, taking a new name and identity from whoever he encounters first. Apparently amnesiac or even brain-damaged, Nadith Learmot nonetheless has other means to access the past and perhaps even the future: upon his chest a dial, down his sleeves wires that he can connect to the walls of old buildings from which he believes he can read their ghosts like imprints on tape. Haunting him constantly is the resemblance he apparently bears to his supposed brother, a successful artist called Zenir. Setting out to pursue Zenir and denounce or blackmail him out of spite, in his travels around the satellite towns and suburbs surrounding a city called Urbis, Nadith finds he is always two steps behind a figure as enigmatic and polyfaceted as himself. But through second hand snippets of news he increasingly learns of how his brother's fortunes are waning, while his own, to his surprise, are on the rise. Along the way, he encounters unexpected clues to his own true identity, how he came to lose his memory and acquire his strange 'contraption'. When Nadith finally catches up with Zenir, what will they make of each other?

Told entirely in the first person in a rhythmic stream of lyricism, Nadith's story reads like Shakespeare on acid, leaving the reader to guess at the truth that lies behind his madness. Is Nadith a mental health patient or a conman? ... Or as he himself comes to believe, the reincarnation of the thirteenth century Scottish seer True Thomas The Rhymer, a man who never lied nor died but disappeared one day to return to the realm of the faeries who had first given him his clairvoyant gifts?

Douglas Thompson's short stories have appeared in a wide range of magazines and anthologies. He won the Grolsch/Herald Question of Style Award in 1989 and second prize in the Neil Gunn Writing Competition in 2007. His first book, *Ultrameta*, published in 2009, was nominated for the Edge Hill Prize, and shortlisted for the BFS Best Newcomer Award. Since then he has published more novels, including *Entanglement* published by Elsewhen Press. *The Rhymer* is his eighth novel.

ISBN: 9781908168511 (epub, kindle) / ISBN: 9781908168412 (192pp paperback)
Visit bit.ly/TheRhymer-Heredyssey

Other titles from Elsewhen Press that you might enjoy

CAN'T DREAM WITHOUT YOU

FROM THE DARK CHRONICLES

TANYA REIMER

Legends say that tens of thousands of years ago, Whisperers were banished from the heavens, torn in half, and dumped on a mortal realm they didn't understand. Longing for their other half, they went from being powerful immortals to lonely leeches relying on humans to survive. Over the years, they earnt magic from demons, they left themselves Notebooks with hints, and by pairing up with human souls, they eventually found their other halves. Humbled by their experiences, they discovered the true purpose of life and many were worthy of returning to the heavens. But many were not.

The Dark Chronicles are stories that share the heartache of select unworthy Whisperers on their journey to immortality after The War of 2019. *Can't Dream Without You* is one of those stories, in which we meet Steve and Julia, two such heroes.

Steve isn't a normal boy. He plays with demons, his soul travels to a dream realm at night using mystical butterflies, and soon he'll earn the power to raise the dead. Al thinks that destroying him would do the world a favour, yet he just can't kill his own son. Wanting to acquire the power that raises the dead before Steve does, Al performs a ritual on Steve's sixteenth birthday. He transfers Steve's dark magic to Julia, an innocent girl he plans to kill. But Steve is determined to save Julia and sucks her soul to Dreamland. From the dream world, he invokes the help of her brother to keep her safe.

Five years later, Steve can't tell what's real or what's a nightmare. Julia's brother wants to kill him, a strange bald eagle is erasing memories, and Steve's caught in some bizarre bullfight on another realm with a cop hot on his trail looking to be Julia's hero. All the while, Steve and Julia must fight the desperate need to make their steamy dreams a reality.

ISBN: 9781908168924 (epub, kindle) / ISBN: 9781908168825 (288pp paperback)
Visit bit.ly/CantDream

Other titles from Elsewhen Press that you might enjoy

THE EMPTY THRONE
by DAVID M ALLAN

Three thrones, one of metal, one of wood and one of stone, stand in the Citadel. Between them shimmers a gateway to a new world, created four hundred years ago by the three magicians who made the thrones. When hostile incorporeal creatures came through the gateway, the magicians attempted to close it but failed. Since that time the creatures have tried to come through the gateway at irregular intervals, but the throne room is guarded by the Company of Tectors, established to defend against them. To try to stop the creatures, expeditions have been sent through the gateway, but none has ever returned.

On each throne appears an image of one of the Custoda, heroes who have led the expeditions through the gateway. While the Custoda occupy the thrones the gateway remains quiet and there are no incursions. Today, Dhanay, the newest knight admitted to the Company, is guarding the throne room. Like all the Tectors, Dhanay looks to the images of the Custoda for guidance.

But the Throne of Stone is empty. The latest incursion has started; a creature escaping into the world, a kulun capable of possessing and controlling humans.

The provincial rulers, the oldest and most powerful families, ignore the gateway and the Tectors, concentrating on playing politics and pursuing their own petty aims. Some even question the need for the Company, as incursions have been successfully contained within the Citadel for years. Family feuds, border disputes, deep-rooted rivalries and bigotry make for a potentially unstable world, and are a perfect environment for a kulun looking to create havoc…

ISBN: 9781911409359 (epub, kindle) / ISBN: 9781911409250 (304pp paperback)
Visit bit.ly/TheEmptyThrone

Other titles from Elsewhen Press that you might enjoy

THE DEEP AND SHINING DARK

BOOK 1 OF THE MAREK SERIES

JULIET KEMP

You know something's wrong when the cityangel turns up at your door

Magic within the city-state of Marek works without the need for bloodletting, unlike elsewhere in Teren, thanks to an agreement three hundred years ago between an angel and the founding fathers. It also ensures that political stability is protected from magical influence. Now, though, most sophisticates no longer even believe in magic *or* the cityangel.

But magic has suddenly stopped working, discovers Reb, one of the two sorcerers who survived a plague that wiped out virtually all of the rest. Soon she is forced to acknowledge that someone has deposed the cityangel without being able to replace it. Marcia, Heir to House Fereno, and one of the few in high society who is well-aware that magic still exists, stumbles across that same truth. But it is just one part of a much more ambitious plan to seize control of Marek.

Meanwhile, city Council members connive and conspire, unaware that they are being manipulated in a dangerous political game. A game that threatens the peace and security not just of the city, but all the states around the Oval Sea, including the shipboard traders of Salina upon whom Marek relies.

To stop the impending disaster, Reb and Marcia, despite their difference in status, must work together alongside the deposed cityangel and Jonas, a messenger from Salina. But first they must discover who is behind the plot, and each of them must try to decide who they can really trust.

Book 1 of Juliet Kemp's gripping new series

With "absolutely gorgeous" cover artwork by renowned artist Tony Allcock

ISBN: 9781911409342 (epub, kindle) / ISBN: 9781911409243 (272pp paperback)
Visit bit.ly/DeepShiningDark

About the Author

Aside from three months living on an oil tanker sailing back and forth between America and Africa, and two years living in a pub, David Craig grew up on the west coast of Scotland. He studied Software Engineering at university, but lost interest in the subject after (and admittedly prior to) graduation. He currently works as a resourcing administrator for a public service contact centre, and lives near Glasgow with his wife and two rabbits.

Being a published writer has been a life-long dream, and one he is delighted to finally realise with this, his debut novel. *Resurrection Men* is the first book in the *Sooty Feathers* series.